T4-AJF-578

THE JINX

THE
JINX

LARRY KAHN

REDFIELD PUBLISHERS
Atlanta

Published by
REDFIELD PUBLISHERS
P.O. Box 888870, Atlanta, Georgia 30356

*Epigraph apposite Chapter One reprinted with permission of Scribner,
a Division of Simon & Schuster, Inc., from THE GREAT GATSBY
(Authorized Text) by F. Scott Fitzgerald. Copyright 1925 by Charles
Scribner's Sons. Copyright renewed 1953 by Frances Scott Fitzgerald
Lanahan. Copyright © 1991, 1992 by Eleanor Lanahan,
Matthew J. Bruccoli and Samuel J. Lanahan as Trustees u/a dated
7/3/75 created by Frances Scott Fitzgerald Smith.*

Book design by Rivanne, Brooklyn, NY

Library of Congress Catalog Card Number: 99-64171

Printed in the United States of America

To Ellie,
my fellow dreamer,
my best friend,
my true love

ACKNOWLEDGMENTS

One of my favorite characters in literature is Don Quixote, a man whose dreams were so fanciful that his name has become synonymous with fantasy. Writing fiction has been a dream since my college days, a dream that became more and more quixotic as my responsibilities as a lawyer and a family man consumed my life. As the 2000 presidential election approached and my story idea, formulated over the course of 20 years, was fast becoming obsolete, I realized that my dream was on the verge of being quashed. Rather than let the windmill beat me, I entered an agonizing period of mid-life crisis that has produced *The Jinx* and a list of many people who I would like to thank.

My wife, Ellie, has been an unfailing source of encouragement, inspiration, love and, of course, proof-reading. She gave me the courage to take time off from work to pursue my dream despite the financial risks involved and the imminent threat of having me hanging around the house for a year. It has been a special year, and she is a very special person.

My two boys, Matthew and Michael, have also been a source of inspiration in more subtle ways. The pride in their voices when they introduced me to their friends as a writer was something I had never experienced in fourteen years as a lawyer.

The Jinx is very much about emotional legacies handed down from parent to child, and the support of my own parents, Bill and Florette Kahn, and my in-laws, Milton and Lillian Brownstein, in this venture was important to me. That being said, the emotional baggage carried by my characters is solely a product of my imagination and is no reflection of them. Perhaps it was their open-mindedness that sparked my interest in racism in the first place.

Linda Klaitz provided a friendly ear during a critical period in my life. She helped me voice my dreams and reach the insight that no tombstone ever read: "He was a great worker."

Even with my family's encouragement, it would have been difficult to take the risk of leaving my job without the support of the BellSouth Legal Department. Associate General Counsel Mark Hallenbeck agreed to hold my job open during my one year leave of absence, and Dan Bradley and John O'Connor have shouldered the extra burden without complaint. Whether they will admit to it or not, these were as much acts of friendship as corporate responsibility for which I am grateful.

The production of a novel is not as easy as it looks. Writing is a craft, one that I have learned on the fly by studying the works of accomplished authors, reading literary magazines and guides and making my own painful mistakes. I have been fortunate to be blessed with several readers who have been willing to gently (for the most part) point out my mistakes.

My wife, Ellie, has been a vigilant reader throughout the process. My parents, Bill and Florette, my brother, Howard, Carol Grinnell and Marina and Mark Nonnenmacher have provided excellent comments on various drafts. Mark Houghton and Worth Weller have also offered helpful advice.

I owe a special debt of gratitude to Patricia Sarrafian Ward, an award-winning writer, who took time out from her busy schedule to review an advanced draft of *The Jinx*. Her comments were thought-provoking, and the final version is much better because of her.

Thanks also are due to my editor, Joanne Sherman, who helped me with the finishing touches. After ten drafts, I have to admit to being blind to some of the flaws her watchful eyes detected.

Due to the magic of the Internet, I was able to do most of my technical research on my own. However, I would be remiss if I did not thank Dr. David Bregman for certain medical insights and Tony Turner of the Atlanta law firm of Mazursky & Dunaway for help with the details of trusts and estates law.

Finally, I owe a special thanks to Amy and Suzanne Feigenbaum of Rivanne Advertising, whose extraordinary production and design efforts have made this book a work of art.

THE JINX

In my younger and more vulnerable years my father gave me some advice that I've been turning over in my mind ever since.

—F. Scott Fitzgerald (opening line from *The Great Gatsby*)

ONE

ADAMS THOMPSON could not shake thoughts of The Assassin from his mind. New York was on fire, a fire he had started, yet the impassioned words of the young woman coiled in his guest chair were losing the battle for his attention.

"We're at the epicenter of what could become the worst race riots in thirty years, and you're gonna let us get scooped," Christy Kirk said. "Dammit, Mr. T, this could be the story of the century."

Thompson's gaze connected with her blazing brown eyes, the only hint that this tiny elf of a woman had the hardened soul of a reporter. She was so slight that Thompson was tempted to blow out a breath and watch her float away. But Christy Kirk was not so easily dismissed. Not by her sources, not by her editor at the City Desk and not even by the publisher of the *Herald Times*. Beneath that pixyish face and tangle of auburn hair lay the heart of a tiger.

Thompson broke Christy's Svengali-like stare, turning to face the window behind his desk. "Sunday's editorial triggered this mess," he said absently. "We're too involved to be objective."

He ran his fingers through the wisp of sandy hair that circled the lower reaches of his scalp. The view of the Hudson River usually calmed him, but not now. He could ignore the angry mob milling about on the street ten stories below. He could even deal patiently with Christy Kirk. But the frightening riddle that had plagued him since Wednesday, when he received the cryptic e-mail from The Assassin—a man long thought dead—made his head throb. *What does this imposter want from me?*

"This story is bigger than your opinion on the Board of Education's proposal to create a metropolitan area school district," Christy said.

It would have been easy to mistake her for one of the college interns employed by the *New York Herald Times,* Thompson thought, dressed as she was in their habitual uniform of brown suede jacket and blue jeans, but her voice resonated with a confidence that comes with experiencing success for hire.

"Black and white paramilitary groups are arming themselves," Christy continued. "There's been an increase in racial violence all across the country. Two dozen incidents were reported in the Army alone in the past six months. This is not racism as usual."

Thompson sighed. *If she only knew.* Christy Kirk was right. This story had to be written. But in one year, not now; in his words, not hers. With some more fanning of the flames by the *Herald Times*, his cousins—seven descendants of a common ancestor now dead more than 160 years—would have the inferno of racial hatred for which they lusted. The Royal Order of the Millennium Knight, as they called their secret familial society, was a runaway train that he desperately wanted to get off, but setting Christy Kirk loose on them was not the ticket. Until Wednesday, when he was contacted by The Assassin, Thompson was sure that there was no way out. *Now there was hope.*

"The white supremacy groups are all bluster," Thompson said calmly, turning to face Christy. "They've been arming themselves for years. And the Army has always attracted a violent element. That crowd outside is hot about my editorial and nothing more. They'll cool off, and then we'll go back to reporting the news, not making it."

Christy sprang from her chair with an intensity that startled Thompson. She fumbled with the window locks. A blast of crisp November air ushered in the sounds of the street. At first the chants of the throng of angry black men, women and children were difficult to distinguish, but the message they repeated soon became clear: "Thompson lies, he must die! Thompson lies, he must die!"

"Look at the anger, the pain, on those faces," Christy said, thrusting her arm forward for emphasis. "Your last editorial may have been the trigger, but rage like that doesn't arise overnight. Each racial incident in the military, each editorial sanctioning segregationist practices, each promotion that goes to a white candidate over a black man or woman and—"

"I admire your passion, but there's nothing new about racism," Thompson interjected brusquely. "Maybe you were never exposed to it growing up in Minnesota, but—"

"Don't patronize me, Mr. T," she said. "I've been a New Yorker since I was eighteen. My background is not the issue. Racial hostilities have risen to a new level. We've *got* to cover this story. Dammit, we *are* the story."

Thompson glowered at her. "Good newspapermen report the news, young lady, they don't make it." *Despite everything else he had become, he was still a newspaperman.*

"I'm sorry. I was out of line," Christy said, chastised but not beaten. "The fuss over this editorial may blow over, but sooner or later something is going to set off this powder keg. That kind of passion you're seeing down there can inspire ordinary people to extraordinary action."

Thompson and Christy were distracted by a flurry of activity in the crowd on the street below. Two men had taken a rope and were hanging an unflattering likeness of Thompson in effigy over a lamppost. The mob roared as the bloated mannequin was lit afire. The police maintained their distance.

Thompson wrinkled his face and subconsciously ran his hand across his flabby midsection. "That crowd wants blood," he said.

"Maybe we can offer them Roger as a human sacrifice," Christy said, straight-faced. Ordinarily, Thompson would frown at a young reporter's disrespect for the City Editor, Roger Martin, but he knew that Roger was Christy's lover as well as her boss.

He snorted. "You think you're joking," Thompson said. "They want my blood, I wrote the editorial, but they might take whoever we offer them. Even you."

"All the best stories carry risk," Christy said, her eyes—those smoldering eyes—locking on Thompson's. "I'll never be a great reporter if you won't let me take risks. Why are you—"

A knock on the open door to Thompson's office interrupted her. A bespectacled young clerk with slicked back hair peeked in nervously. Christy's glare shot daggers at him. "Watcha got, Pete?" Thompson asked.

"Sorry to bother you, sir," the clerk said. "Three more death threats in the morning mail. Anderson in Security wants to call the cops, maybe hire a bodyguard."

"Just three?" Thompson asked. "You see, Christy, the situation is already cooling down."

Pete shook his head uncertainly. "'Fraid not, sir. We tossed out hundreds of hate letters. Security just asked for the ones that threatened violence," Pete said. "But don't feel too bad—there's lots of fan mail, too."

Thompson slumped into his executive chair and swiveled to face the window. He became aware, again, of the angry chants rising up from the street. Fan mail. Sometimes he disgusted himself.

"Mr. Thompson," Pete said awkwardly. "What should I tell Security?"

Thompson whirled abruptly to face the clerk. "No police. No bodyguards." He waved Pete off, then turned to Christy. "No story."

"Aren't you worried about the death threats?" Christy asked with genuine concern. "Like you said, that mob sounds like it's out for blood."

Thompson looked up in surprise. Concern and tenderness suited Christy Kirk as badly as a pink party dress. "I appreciate the thought, but I'll be fine as long as I don't try to mingle with them—a lesson you'd be wise to learn yourself."

Christy ignored the thinly veiled reproach. "You've exposed a raw nerve with that editorial," she said, gesturing towards the window. "There are a lot of angry black people in New York City, and their fury seems to be directed at you this week."

Thompson could almost visualize the tug-of-war between his mind and his heart, a contest fought every day for the last twenty-one months. His sworn obligation to The Royal Order of the Millennium Knight was to provoke racial rebellion, a task that was in grave conflict with his natural sentiments.

"My intention was not to belittle African-Americans," Thompson lied. "Integration seemed like a noble goal thirty years ago, but experience has shown that the experiment failed. Our cultures are like oil and water. I stand by my editorial. The Board of Ed's proposal to bus children between suburban and city schools is unnatural."

Christy filled her cheeks with air, then expelled it. "Mr. T, whatever your intentions, using the word 'unnatural' conjures up an image of animals in a zoo. You could have made the case against the proposal by arguing that it's too costly and burdensome. You've ticked off a lot of people unnecessarily."

Thompson stifled a smile. "Well, maybe I should ask all the cub reporters to review my word choices before I run my editorials," he said.

Christy blushed. "Oops, looks like I've crossed the line, again."

The corners of Thompson's mouth turned up weakly. "Maybe you should take that as your cue to give up the race story and take an assignment from Roger at the City Desk," he said softly.

"I'm not conceding that easily," she said. "There's an important story here, and I'm the one to write it. I've already—"

"You've already what?" Thompson said. "Already offended the Fire Department?"

"That wasn't my fault," Christy said. She fidgeted in her chair defensively. A small fire had been set in the basement of the Herald Times building shortly after she wrote an investigative piece about corruption in the New York City Fire Department. "Nobody ever proved who set that fire."

"Before that it was the Sanitation Department," Thompson said. "Garbage on our front steps every day for a week. And before that it was the longshoremen. Face it, Christy, you rankle people. The perfect person to do a piece on race relations."

"Look, I'm not out there to make friends," she said. "I'm out there to get the story—and I *always* get the story."

"Maybe now, but a good reporter cultivates contacts," Thompson said. "Some day you'll need the Fire Department, and they won't be there for you. You've got to work with people, respect their position and their personal space. You've got the political instincts of a buffalo. You stampede over everyone."

"Maybe that political crap works for a middle-aged, Ivy League, WASP," she said angrily. "But it sure as hell doesn't work for me. People see this little...little—"

"Leprechaun," Thompson offered.

Christy scowled. "People think they can walk all over me because I'm so small. I'm tough because I have to be tough. I bite and I don't let go until I've got my story. *That's* what rankles people."

"Maybe a pit bull would have been a better analogy."

"You pick the analogy. I just want the assignment."

Thompson looked at his watch. Six-fifteen. The Assassin had requested—no, commanded—a meeting tonight, but had yet to set the time and place. The mob outside showed no signs of breaking up. He needed a drink. "You're not going to let go of me until I give in or fire you, are you?" Thompson asked.

She grinned. "You'd never fire me. I've heard the stories. You were a pit bull once, too."

Her smile was infectious. And her words rang true. They had called him a bulldog back then, but, like Christy Kirk, he had learned politics the hard way. Thompson viewed her as his special project. "What have you got so far?" he asked.

"I'm ready to rock 'n roll as soon as you say the word," she said. "I've got contacts with most of the white and black groups. The Klan, the Skinheads, the Dark Nation, the NOMAADs—"

"I haven't heard of the NOMAADs," Thompson said. "And I think the politically correct term is African-Americans these days."

"You're hearing the NOMAADs chanting right now," Christy said. "The National Organization for Mutual *African-American* Defense. They organized the rally outside."

"Mmm-hmmm." Thompson was distracted by a beep from the computer on his desk, alerting him that a new e-mail message awaited. Christy continued talking while Thompson attended to the computer. He tapped a key on the keyboard. The new message popped up on screen:

Nine o'clock. Your apartment. Alone. No tricks.

The message was signed once again with the horrifying cyber-name: "The Assassin."

Christy stopped speaking in mid-sentence. "Bad news, Mr. T?" she asked. "You look like you've seen a ghost."

"It's nothing," Thompson said, regaining his composure. He glanced at his watch. "I almost forgot about an appointment. I've got to run."

"And the assignment?" Christy asked.

Thompson was weary of battling. He could kill the story later. "Be careful," he said. "The African-American groups may smell blood when they see the *Herald Times* coming. And white supremacists aren't over-grown Boy Scouts."

"I suppose it's more politically correct to call them *Anglo-American* supremacists," Christy said, smiling on the way out the door. "And they won't even know what bit 'em."

A MAN SAT IN THE BACK of an unmarked van behind the Herald Times Building, away from the chanting hordes. He was eating potato chips while monitoring the sophisticated surveillance equipment that surrounded him in the van's dimly lit cargo compartment. Empty soda cans and moldy cartons from a Chinese takeout joint down the street littered the cramped area.

The man stopped chewing when Thompson opened The Assassin's cryptic message. *Finally*. His boss had been waiting for this one. He wiped his greasy hands on his pants, punched a number into his cellular telephone, then said: "Let me speak to the Director."

SAUSOLITO'S WAS NOT ADAMS THOMPSON'S usual Friday night haunt. He preferred a cigar and a few single malt scotch whiskeys at one of the gentlemen's clubs on the Upper West Side to wind down after another hectic week at the *Herald Times*. But *Sausolito's* was in Greenwich Village, and he did not want to stray far from home before his meeting with the man who claimed to be The Assassin.

It was the day after Thanksgiving, and *Sausolito's* was quiet. Adams sipped a Dewars, watching the Knicks game on the television in the corner. A scrawny NYU student with bright orange hair sat at the other end of the bar. The basketball season was only a month under way, but Thompson could tell that the 1999-2000 season was to be a rebuilding year for his beloved Knicks.

God, "1999-2000." Even saying it to himself made his head swim. One of his earliest memories was his seventh birthday in 1960. He remembered his father bringing home a rubber stamp kit that the *Herald Times* had tried to market the previous Christmas. The kit included a date stamp that went up to 1972. He recalled thinking at the time that 1972 seemed like forever. He ordered another Dewars.

Adams saddened as he thought about his father. It was almost two years since George Thompson had died.

A tall, well-built young man entering *Sausolito's* caught Adams's attention, interesting only in his remarkable resemblance to the Marlboro Man. He had a weather-beaten face and wore a suede jacket, cowboy hat and work boots. Adams observed him for a moment, then looked away as Marlboro sauntered towards the bar. Marlboro placed his hat on the counter, claimed the stool two down from Adams, and ordered a beer.

"Cold night, huh pops," Marlboro said, looking in Adams's direction.

"Hmmph. November in New York," Adams said.

Marlboro looked up at the television. "You a Knicks fan?" he asked.
"Uh-huh," Adams said.

"How they doin'?" Marlboro asked.

"Celtics are up by five," Adams said, frowning. "It doesn't look like they're 'The Team for the Next Millennium.'"

Marlboro chuckled. He slid over one stool, next to Adams, and extended his hand. "I'm Stone. Van Stone," he said.

Adams shook his hand. *Firm grip.* "Adams," he said hesitantly, reluctant to identify himself to this outlandish stranger.

"Mighty pleased to meet you, Mr. Adams," Marlboro said. "What brings you out alone tonight? You seem a little down, if you don't mind my sayin'."

Adams hesitated, again weighing the risk of revealing much of himself against the horror of dwelling on his own nightmarish thoughts. "I was thinking about my father," Adams said. "He passed away almost two years ago."

"I'm sorry. Were you close?"

"Hmmph. Not really," Adams said. "Not until he got sick. Prostate cancer."

"Nasty stuff," Marlboro said. "My dad died recently, too."

"My condolences," Adams said. "I hope you had a better relationship with yours."

"He wasn't around much. I spent some quality time with him before he died, though," Marlboro said. He sipped his beer. "Tell me about your dad. What kept you apart?"

"To tell you the truth, I don't know," Adams said. "My mother was killed in an accident when I was three. He sort of withdrew after that. Put all his energy into his work."

"What did he do?"

Adams sipped his drink. It had been a long time since he had trusted anyone. But he was enjoying the attention from this attractive young man. "Same thing as me. He was the publisher of the *Herald Times.*"

Marlboro slapped the counter. "You're Adams Thompson?" he said. "Man, you are one unpopular son of a bitch tonight! No wonder you're drinkin' alone."

Adams lifted his glass in a mock toast. "Thank you for reminding me, young man."

"Aw, hell, I don't care about any of that shit," Marlboro said. "I leave politics to the politicians. So, things between you and your old man couldn't have been too hostile if you followed in his footsteps."

"I think I took up journalism to impress him," Adams said. "I finished at the top of my class at the Columbia School of Journalism—the goddam Columbia School of Journalism—but that bastard wanted to hire me as a copy boy, the same way he started out."

"Did you do it?"

"My pride got the better of me," Adams said. "I took a job as a beat reporter at the *Daily News*. He hired me a couple of years later after I made a name for myself."

"Geez-us, will you look at that!" the scrawny orange-haired student said in a piercing, nasal voice. Adams and Marlboro looked up at the television to see the Knicks fall prey to a series of dazzling three-point shots by a young Celtics guard that Adams had not noticed before. The Knicks were down by twelve.

"I've got to ask you this," Marlboro said. "You seem like such a nice guy. Do you really believe the shit you write in those editorials? I mean, come on, it's been almost fifty years since Little Rock."

Adams glanced at the clock on the wall. Eight-thirty. "As much as I'd love to debate my politics, I've got an appointment," he said. "Son, it's been a pleasure."

Adams opened his wallet and pulled out a twenty. The slip of paper that his father had given him the night before he died caught his eye. It was a list. He kept it as a frightening reminder of the magnitude of what his family had achieved. These powerful men, his cousins, had made their ancestors' unlikely plan work. "The Heir Apparent. The Speaker. The Senator. The General. The Spy. The Publisher. The Doctor. The Caretaker. The Assassin." Adams returned the list to his wallet.

"I've enjoyed talkin' to you, too," Marlboro said. "Are ya lookin' for company tonight?"

Adams looked Marlboro straight in the eyes for a fleeting moment. A rush of thoughts filled his head. Could he trust this man? Did he have AIDS? What would George Thompson think about his 46-year old son cavorting with the Marlboro Man wearing nothing but his cowboy hat? It had been a long time since he had been intimate with anybody, but The Assassin awaited.

"No thank you, son," Adams replied. He dropped the twenty on the bar, slid off his stool and grabbed his tweed sports coat from the back of the chair. He caught a glimpse of his flabby countenance and balding head in the mirror behind the bar and scowled. "Have a good evening."

Adams walked out into the chilly November air. He glanced southwards, the brightly lit twin towers of the World Trade Center rising in the distance above the colorful, low-rise buildings of Greenwich Village, then strolled north on MacDougal Street, towards his Fifth Avenue apartment just beyond Washington Square. There was nobody else on the street.

Vivid memories flashed through Adams's mind as he marched towards his date with The Assassin. His eyes moistened as he recalled that solemn night two years earlier when he had finally gained his father's trust, and maybe even his love.

At first Adams had listened in disbelief as the story unfurled that evening over a bottle of Scotch whiskey, probably not unlike the evening when his ancestors hatched the conspiracy of all conspiracies to avenge the murder of their brother 160 years before. Adams was so horrified by the plot that his first impulse was to disclose it to the authorities if he could not persuade his father that the scheme was insane.

Surely, Adams had argued, reason must have intervened at some point during the past 160 years? But, no, the elder Thompson had convinced the younger that, indeed, the family had taken its vengeance like clockwork for a century and a half and was prepared to complete its mission as the millennium turned.

As he had listened to the tale and felt the passion of his father, seven generations removed from the grievous event, it had slowly dawned on him how this conspiracy had survived. The hate had been emblazoned in the hearts of each generation, each father to one son. Fathers share so few passionate moments with their sons. Until that night, Adams had experienced none. He could understand how such a moment at a tender age could shape a lifetime.

Even at his advanced age, Adams had caught some of the spirit of his infuriated clansmen from his own father that night. His yearning for George Thompson's love had been so great that it had overcome reason. With the eloquence that only a pint of fine Scotch can muster, he had sworn his eternal allegiance to The Royal Order of the Millennium Knight. It was a moment that he had come to regret.

As Adams replayed that night in his mind's eye, he did not observe the young man who had so eagerly engaged him in conversation emerge from *Sausolito's*. The man stopped and turned to light a cigarette with his back to the wind. He waited until Adams reached the corner of West Third Street, then followed, a half block behind.

The street lamps near the southwest entrance to Washington Square, at West Fourth Street, were broken. Adams shook his head. In the heart of New York University, the Square was once the soul of Greenwich Village. It had been alive at all hours. Now, at night, the Square had become a macabre haven for drug dealers and the homeless. Barren oaks danced in the dim light like monstrous skeletons in a graveyard.

Adams continued north, around the perimeter of the Square, rather than risk the shorter walk through it. His heart pounded.

Adams had fallen into the role of The Publisher almost by happenstance. His father had never encouraged him to choose a career in journalism. George Thompson had always assumed that he would be alive when the millennium turned, and he had not seen the need to involve his son. But Adams's contemporaries had been brought into the fold at an early age. Miraculously, they had positioned themselves even better than their ancestors could have imagined in their wildest, drunken dreams.

The group had never actually met, but they had assembled under the direction of The Caretaker via the Internet. For the past four years The Royal Order had refined their clandestine plot in weekly on-line chat sessions. All but The Assassin.

The Assassin had proven to be a weak link in the conspiracy. It had never been intended that he join the others; his task was to be completed in grim isolation. But as the details of the conspiracy were engineered, the role of The Assassin changed, and his participation had been required. Unfortunately, he was a reluctant accomplice. He had joined their Internet meetings only under duress. Eventually, after three years, he renounced The Royal Order.

The Assassin's punishment was swift. The Spy, whom Adams had identified as a malevolent force among the Knights, had eagerly undertaken the execution of The Assassin as his personal project. The murder was made to appear accidental. There was no investigation. The

Assassin had been long divorced, and his estranged family had not questioned that his death was anything but an alcohol-related mishap. All evidence of his involvement with The Royal Order had been erased. There
were no male heirs who could have assumed The Assassin's role upon his
death. The Spy had assured the others that all loose ends had been tied.

Until Wednesday, Adams had no reason to doubt The Spy's claims.
After the initial shock had subsided, Adams had debated with himself
whether to tell the other Knights about his contact with The Assassin.
Concealing information from The Spy was dangerous, but it was worth
the risk.

Perhaps he was not as dedicated to fulfilling his ancestors' vengeful
dream because he had learned of the plot later in life than his cousins.
For whatever reason, the inspiration that had come to him on that fateful night with his father had faded. He hoped that The Assassin might
prove an ally who could offer a graceful exit from this insanity.

In a few minutes he would have the answer. If The Assassin was of
like mind, together they would reveal the plot to all the world. If not,
he was too cowardly to face his cousins' wrath alone. The Presidency of
the United States would fall. The nation would be plunged into civil
war. The grand Final Vengeance for his ancestor's death—the vanquishment of the Negro race in America—would become a hideous
reality. It was in the hands of the gods. It was in the hands of this man
who called himself The Assassin.

Adams strolled alongside Washington Square, lost in thought. He
did not see the figure lurking in the shadows of the apartment building
on the corner of Washington Place, across the street to his left.
Marlboro, still a half block behind, near the entrance to the Square, saw
the trenchcoat-clad wraith leap out from the darkness, but it was too
late to shout a warning.

Adams turned with a start at the sound of rapidly approaching footsteps. He felt the blood drain from his face as he recognized the attacker barreling towards him not ten feet away. He stood paralyzed,
resigned to his fate. He closed his eyes a moment before a long, thin
blade plunged into his belly.

Adams gasped, and his eyes jerked open as the gut-wrenching pain
cut through him. He looked into his executioner's eyes. *Had the message from The Assassin been only a ruse?* The eyes of the devil yielded no
answers as the knife was yanked upwards into his heart.

The assailant raced away, west on Washington Place, as Adams fell limp to the sidewalk. He felt the warm trickle flowing from his wound. He knew that his would not be the last blood to spill. *There would be war.*

Then Adams heard more footsteps. It took a Herculean effort to open his eyes. He saw Marlboro hovering over him, but his vision was already fading to gray. *One last chance.*

Adams summoned all of his remaining strength. Breathing was difficult. "President," he gasped. "Assassination."

Marlboro knelt by the dying man's side. "Who?" he asked urgently.

"Knight," Adams whispered.

"You can't go to sleep on me yet, Pops," Marlboro said. "Give me a name."

Adams opened his mouth, but the words would not come. Then his world went blank.

Marlboro cursed, closed Adams's eyes, then looked around. No other witnesses. He carefully reached into Adams's slacks, prying out his wallet. He slipped it into his suede jacket, cautiously scanned the scene one more time, then walked briskly away, turning east on Washington Square North.

TWO

BEN KRAVNER strolled into the law offices of Kramer, Fox, Levy, Johnson & Blum in his navy blue jogging suit at the stroke of ten o'clock on Monday morning. His scraggly black hair was moist with sweat.

"Fritz wants to see you," Carol, Ben's secretary, said without looking up from her breakfast.

"What does *he* want?" Ben asked mockingly, as if, of course, Fritz Fox, the Grand Old Man of the firm, would have confided this to Carol. He and Harry Kramer formed the firm in the 1930s. Kramer died more than twenty years ago, but Fritz was still going strong. He was no longer the captain of the ship, that job now belonged to Leo Goldman, the head of the Corporate Department, but Fritz still maintained his stable of rich Trusts & Estates clients.

"He probably wants you to carry his briefcase to a client meeting," Carol wisecracked.

"Ouch." Ben winced, clasped his hands over his heart, and recoiled his sturdy six-foot frame, as if mortally wounded. "The truth hurts. I need a shower. Tell Agnes I'll be up to see Fritz in a few minutes."

Fifteen minutes later, Ben bounded up the internal stairwell, his long, wet hair parted on the left and combed back behind his ears. Kramer, Fox, as the firm was known in the trade, leased four floors at One Water Street, a 56-floor office tower at the foot of Manhattan. The Trusts & Estates Department was located on the 28th floor, but Ben's office would remain on the 25th floor until he accepted a permanent assignment.

Fritz was sitting with his back to the doorway, his feet resting on a credenza, enjoying his panoramic view of New York Harbor. Ben adjusted a brightly colored tie that would have made Picasso proud, then knocked on the open door.

"Well, well, well, look what the cat dragged in," Fritz chortled. With his thick Yiddish accent, it sounded like: "Vell, vell, vell." His voice was weak; he looked pale. "So, how is our Marathon Man?"

"Mornin', Mr. Fox," Ben said cheerfully. "Six and a half miles in forty minutes today."

"This is good, this is very good," Fritz said, his nearly bald head bobbing knowingly. A few stray tufts of white hair flew off in the direction the wind happened to be blowing that morning. "Now, your hair, if we could get you to cut it, we would make a mensch out of you yet."

Ben flashed his trademark crooked grin. "Every six months, whether it needs a trim or not."

Fritz chuckled, as he searched among the stacks of paper piled high on his mahogany desk for an item that eluded his shaky hands. Finally, he found a copy of the *Herald Times* and tossed it across the desk. "You have seen Saturday's newspaper?" he asked.

A glaring banner headline screamed of Adams Thompson's demise. "I saw the headlines on the newsstand when I was running this weekend," Ben said, as he sat in one of the two Queen Anne chairs opposite Fritz's desk. "Is Thompson your client?"

"The firm represents the *Herald Times* in corporate and litigation matters," Fritz said. "I handled George Thompson's personal matters until he died two years ago. Young Adams, he seemed to view me as part of his inheritance."

Ben tugged gently at his neatly trimmed, black mustache. He had been lobbying Fritz for weeks to let him handle an estate on his own. This one would surely raise his standing within the firm. Ever since he had rotated into the Trusts & Estates Department eight months ago, he had toiled in relative anonymity, drafting wills and trusts, while his colleagues in the Corporate and Litigation Departments worked on high profile mergers and acquisitions, the firm's bread and butter. He was falling behind in the game.

"Is Thompson's estate complex?" Ben asked.

"A will, a charitable trust. Interesting, maybe, complex, no," Fritz said, staring directly at Ben with his piercing blue eyes. His large aquiline nose gave him a proud, eagle-like appearance. "This is an important estate, though. I will be taking the lead."

Ben's jaw dropped. Fritz had read his mind. At ninety, he had not lost even a step mentally.

"I've been watching you for eight months now, Mr. Fox. I'm ready to do one on my own."

"Soon enough, Mr. Ben, soon enough," Fritz said. "You are still—"

He was interrupted by a brief coughing fit. "Excuse me. You are still on rotation. Most of the work, you will do. The clients, I'll make sure they see your face."

"You convinced me that I'd learn more lawyer skills here than in Corporate," Ben said. "I'm still doing research and drafting."

"Patience, Mr. Ben, patience," Fritz said. "Your friends, they are not getting the training you get from me. You want to revise merger agreements and review contracts, you can join the Corporate Department with my blessings. So be it."

Ben knew Fritz was right. His experience in the Corporate Department had been a disaster. Six months wasted reviewing contracts for a merger that was scuttled at the eleventh hour. No useful skills learned.

"I know, I know," Ben said impatiently. "But I want to be a lawyer, not a bag carrier."

"Soon enough," Fritz said. "But—"

"When?" Ben interrupted. An estate like this would not come around again any time soon. "What do I need to do to let you know I'm ready?"

Fritz straightened himself in his chair, then leaned forward. "Look, Ben, the tools, you have them all. But the edges, they are still a little rough," Fritz said evenly. He coughed, again. "My job is to round off those edges before I send you out to meet clients."

Ben blushed. Until now, he had not heard any criticism from the Old Man. "What do you mean?" he asked defensively. "You told me I was doing well."

"You soak up the law like a sponge. Like a sponge!" Fritz said. "And your drafting, flawless."

"Then what?"

Fritz stroked his chin with his thumb and forefinger as he contemplated his next words. "An example, maybe it will help," he said. "Clyde von Oster, you drew up those trust agreements for him last week. Rush job. Very complex. Excellent work."

"Yeah. And then the bastard left us sitting in his office for an hour while he took a personal call."

"Exactly! This is my point, you've proven it," Fritz said.

Ben frowned. "How?"

"Attitude. Von Oster, yes, he was rude. But he is *the client*," Fritz said. "Your face betrayed your anger."

"So? Our time is valuable, too," Ben said. "You're an important man, and he was flaunting his power over you."

"We are in a service business, young Ben," Fritz said. "We save this indignation for the courtroom."

"Von Oster—"

Fritz cut him off. "There are many von Osters on our client list. Your temper, control it. Always strive to appear unruffled no matter how rude the client, no matter how big the ego."

Fritz Fox was the last of a dying breed, the gentleman lawyer. It had been that quality that attracted Ben to him. Ben had tired quickly of the child-like fits of the spoiled, young partners in the Corporate Department. The law was all business to them. Clients were bank accounts to be sucked dry. Associates were workhorses to be worn to the point of exhaustion, then sent to pasture. Ben did not care for these people. He feared becoming one of them. He wanted to be like Fritz Fox.

"Okay, Mr. Fox," Ben said. He forced a smile. "You win. I'm ready for the next lesson."

"Good!" Fritz said. "Then shall we piece together the puzzle that was Adams George Thompson, Jr.?"

Ben took a pen out of his shirt pocket and opened his notebook. In stark contrast to corporate law, T&E practice was about people. You were admitted to the inner sanctum of your clients' lives. You saw their achievements and their failures, their happiness and their pain, their pride and their prejudice. They were forced to share their existence without inhibition. Fritz Fox had drawn Ben to T&E practice; it was Ben's voyeuristic tendency that kept him there for a second rotation. He was curious about what went on in people's minds. A complete picture of the client slowly emerged as the executor uncovered the pieces of his life one by one.

"Did Thompson have a large family?" Ben asked.

"No living relatives," Fritz said. "Specific monetary bequests to various charities, a few former servants, none more than $10,000. The balance, it all goes to the charitable trust for Calhoun College, a small university near Atlanta."

"What was his connection to Calhoun?" Ben asked.

Fritz shrugged. "One of the puzzle pieces, I suppose," he said.

"Is there someone I should call?" Ben asked.

"Tompkins James Frederick, Jr.," Fritz said, reading from a legal pad. "He is the dean. Tomorrow, we'll call him together. This morning, I'm feeling a little under the weather."

"What should I do to get up to speed?" Ben asked.

"Debby will—" Fritz closed his eyes and grimaced. "Oy vey."

"Are you okay, Mr. Fox?" Ben asked. "Do you need a drink of water?"

"No, no. I just need to rest," he said. He paused to catch his breath. "Debby, she will show you all the files you need and do all the things that paralegals do."

Fritz shifted his weight in his chair. He looked uncomfortable. "Tomorrow, I will be in if you have any questions," he said.

Ben saluted the elderly lawyer fondly and took his leave. He slid down the hall to the paralegal's office, stopping briefly to ask Fritz's secretary, Agnes, an elderly woman who had been with Fritz for about forty years, to keep an eye on the Old Man.

Debby's office was a glorified cubicle, really, enhanced only by a faux leather chair and a rectangular marker with brass letters spelling out "Deborah Colleen Barnett" pinned on the outside wall near the entrance. Ben figured Debby was about his age, 26, give or take a year. She had only joined the firm this past summer, but he found her to be pleasant looking, with a ready smile, long, frizzy, brown hair and a quiet confidence that had made her the present object of his infatuation.

"Hey, Debby C.," Ben said as he fake knocked on an invisible door. Debby was sitting at her desk reviewing a will.

"Hi, Ben," she responded in a neutral tone. "What can I do for you?"

"Fritz wants me to help him with the Thompson estate. Can you show me the files?"

"Sure. That's a pretty big estate. Are you handling it on your own?" she asked, now sounding slightly impressed.

"Yeah," Ben replied. "Mostly." *That's it, dazzle her with your brilliance.*

"Cool. Let me pull some things together from the file room and the vault, and I'll get you a package in an hour or two."

"Thanks, Debby."

"Sure thing," she said, smiling.

I wish, Ben thought to himself as he exited her workspace. It had been too long since he had been with a woman. *Four months.* He envisioned Debby's petite body snuggled next to his for a fleeting moment, then wondered how much time was spent at this firm and law firms all across the land thinking about sex instead of matters legal. And how much of that time was billed to clients. Way too much on both counts, he concluded.

"Help!" A woman's scream jolted Ben from his daydream. It was Agnes. Ben raced down the hallway.

Agnes was kneeling over Fritz's body beside his desk. She looked up, her eyes wide, the color drained from her face. "He's not breathing," she said.

"Call 911!" Ben shouted.

Agnes scrambled to the telephone. Ben checked Fritz's pulse. Nothing. No respiration. *Shit!* Ben's heart pounded. He was trained in CPR, but he had never been called upon to administer it. A small crowd was gathering inside the office, pressing forward for a glimpse of their fallen leader. Ben scanned their eyes. Panic everywhere.

"Everybody stand back!" Ben shouted. There was no time to wait for the paramedics. He knelt beside his dying friend and mentor. He loosened Fritz's bow tie and shirt collar, then tilted his head back to clear the airways.

Ben placed his mouth over Fritz's blue lips, then breathed five slow breaths. Then he clasped his hands above Fritz's heart, locked his elbows and pressed down slowly, repeating for fifteen compressions, about one per second, then two more breaths. *Still no pulse.*

"Dammit, Fritz, breathe!" he said.

Ben repeated the procedure. He started to compress his chest. Fritz belched up a mouthful of bile. *No pulse.* Ben cleared Fritz's mouth of the foul-smelling fluid. He took in a deep breath, then breathed the life-preserving air into Fritz's lungs. Ben gagged from the odor of Fritz's vomit, but continued.

Ben repeated the procedure, again. *Nothing.* He felt hope slipping away. He looked behind him. A dozen lawyers and staff looked on in horror. *One more time.*

Ben said a silent prayer to a God in whom he did not believe. "C'mon, Fritz," he said softly. *It's not your time, Old Man.* He began to compress the frail lawyer's chest. One... two... three... four... five... six...

"I've got a pulse!" Ben shouted.

Murmurs of relief filled the room. But Fritz still was not breathing. Ben continued to provide mouth-to-mouth resuscitation until the paramedics rushed in three minutes later. Ben sat with his back against the paneled wall, watching the paramedics work. They administered oxygen on the scene, then strapped Fritz to a stretcher and wheeled him out.

Ben was in a daze. He saw and heard the people around him, but it was as if they were actors in a play that he was watching from afar. Someone slapped him on the shoulder. "You did your best," another said. It was all a blur. He did not know whether Fritz was dead or alive. He fought back tears.

Ben hid in the men's room for awhile, rinsing out the acidic aftertaste of Fritz Fox's digestive tract. He looked in the mirror. His shirt was untucked on one side. His Picasso tie was askew. His mop of black hair was tossed about wildly. He straightened himself out a little, but he could not bring himself to care about anything so trivial as his appearance.

Ben wandered aimlessly through the halls in this semi-catatonic state until he found himself outside the closed door of his friend, Buzz Herzog, a second-year associate in the Corporate Department. He knocked.

"Enter!"

A thick-necked, soft-bellied young man with a crew cut was busily marking up a large document with a red pen. He did not look up.

"Hey, Buzz," Ben said. "Got a minute?"

"Tender offer, big guy. No time," Buzz said, his head still lowered. Buzz was not a risk-taker, and he was determined to make partner at Kramer, Fox. He figured the only sure-fire way to fulfill that ambition—only one out of fifteen new associates made partner—was to make the existing partners at Kramer, Fox rich. He billed more hours than any other associate—over three thousand in his first year. He achieved that dubious distinction by making Kramer, Fox his home and by billing almost every minute he was there to clients' accounts. He even took work with him to the men's room.

"I need to talk, Buzz," Ben pleaded. "Fritz had a heart attack."

Buzz looked up. "Serious?" he asked.

Ben nodded. "Yeah. I feel like shit."

"You look like shit, big guy," Buzz said. "Is the Old Man dead?"

"I don't know," Ben said. "I'm in a daze, man. I was talking to him one minute, then five minutes later I'm pumping his chest and giving him mouth-to-mouth. The paramedics took him away."

"What happens to you if he croaks?" Buzz asked.

Ben was stunned. *Did corporate lawyers even have hearts?* "Geez, I don't know," Ben said. "He's been like a grandfather to me. I haven't thought about how it affects my career."

"Think about it, big guy," Buzz said. "The only reason Leo tolerates the T&E Department is out of respect for the Old Man. It's not a money-maker. If he's dead, you may have wasted the last eight months."

Ben closed his eyes. *Was it only eight months he had wasted?* It was not even five years since he had entered Harvard Law School with grand ideas and a naïve dream of changing the world. He had cared about people and the issues that affected their daily lives. Now, he was drowning in a heartless money pit, pursuing an intense desire to win a game he cared little about. Fritz Fox had somehow made the place feel human. Now he might be gone.

"Do you see yourself doing this your whole life?" Ben asked.

"This is what I do," Buzz said. "You're not gonna get all sentimental on me now, are you?"

"I dunno," Ben said. *This is what I do.* An hour ago he had been focused on taking his career to the next level, desperately trying to wrangle another chip in the game from Fritz Fox. What would happen if he won, made partner, and discovered that his life was an empty shell? "I mean, does all this make you happy?"

Buzz scrunched his face. "Happy?" he said. "Ask me again in six years. If I'm alive, still married, and a partner here, I'll be happy. Maybe even two out of three. Right now I'm paying my dues. Nobody really gives a shit if I'm happy."

Buzz allowed Ben to vent his sorrows for another minute, then ejected him before another six-minute billing interval was lost. Ben returned to his office.

"Ben!" Carol said. "I heard about Fritz. Is he okay?"

Ben shrugged. "I don't know," he said. "The paramedics took him away about an hour ago."

"Well, Leo wants to see you in his office right away," Carol said. "Maybe he has news."

Ben's heart sank. Leo Goldman did not appear to be wasting any time in disbanding the Trusts & Estates Department. *Fritz was dead.*

The door to Leo Goldman's office was closed. Ben timidly approached Leo's secretary, a pretty Latin woman with a round face. Leo made Ben anxious. He made everybody anxious. He was one of the foremost experts on hostile takeover defenses in the industry, cleared five million dollars a year and ran Kramer, Fox like his personal fiefdom. "I'm Ben Kravner. Mr. Goldman left a message for me to see him."

"He's expecting you, Mr. Kravner," the secretary said. "Go right in."

Ben knocked and entered. Leo was sitting on a sofa, his six-foot, five-inch frame stretched out in front of him. Myra Rosenberg, a dumpy young partner in the Corporate Department, looked unhappy sitting caddy corner from Leo on the couch.

"Ben!" Leo boomed. "We just got good news. Fritz Fox is going to make it."

Ben felt his body relax some, but his heart still pounded in the presence of the great man himself. "That's terrific news," Ben said. "He had me worried for a few minutes."

"He's a tough old bird," Leo said. "An asset to the firm."

"He's been a great teacher," Ben said.

"That's good, that's good," Leo said. "Because Fritz *is* the Trusts & Estates Department. He's going to be out-of-pocket for a few weeks, and we're going to need you to take on some extra responsibility. The other associates in the department are all part-timers, and, frankly, they're going nowhere."

"I can do that," Ben said eagerly. He felt guilty that his breakthrough was coming at Fritz's expense, but the prospect began to lift him out of his post-trauma funk. "Anything for Fritz."

"Excellent," Leo said. "Myra will be the partner in charge of the T&E group in Fritz's absence. She'll handle assignments and will run client meetings. Bring her up to speed on the issues in all pending matters. We need to convince the clients that Kramer, Fox is still providing top notch legal service. It'll mean extra work for you, but I think you can handle it."

Myra rolled her eyes. Ben grimaced. Myra Rosenberg had a reputation among the young associates as a first class bitch. She had made partner by working Buzz Herzog-like hours, then began delegating and leaving the office at six o'clock every night after she grabbed the prize. That did not seem to discourage her from claiming credit for her team's hard work.

Ben trudged dejectedly towards the stairwell after the meeting. Despite Leo's words, the arrangement with Myra sounded like more work, but *less* responsibility. Myra probably would not even let him near a client. Thankfully, it was only a temporary arrangement. The important thing was that Fritz was alive.

"Hang on, Ben." It was Myra. "My office. Now."

Ben followed. Her office was only two doors down the hall. *Here it comes.*

Myra closed the door. She clenched her teeth. "I don't know what the fuck Leo thinks he's doing," she said in a screaming whisper. "But I can't handle a tender offer and baby-sit you at the same time."

"B-but—"

She stomped behind her desk. "You're on your own," she said. "Call me if you have an emergency."

"Do you want me to call you for client meetings?" Ben asked, wide-eyed.

"On. Your. Own," she said. "What part didn't you understand? You can waste your life in T&E, but there's no money and no glory. Just don't fuck anything up."

Debby hustled down to the 25th floor within moments after Ben called. A large red folder was tucked under her arm. She gave his small, spare office the once over. "Nice digs," she said, her frizzy hair bobbing slightly out of synch with her head.

Ben found her smile infectious despite his fragile mood. "If you like early-American prison," he said.

The furnishings, a contemporary wooden desk and matching credenza, were a notch or two below first rate. Sundry folders and books were scattered across the credenza. His desktop was a sea of paper. The walls were bare. Ben's framed diplomas leaned against the base of the back wall waiting to be hung.

Ben motioned for Debby to sit in one of two matching green upholstered chairs opposite his desk. He caught a whiff of her perfume floating across the room. *Stick to business.*

"You were great up there," Debby said. Ben sensed a new respect in her voice. "You saved Fritz's life."

"I was running on instinct," Ben said sheepishly. "I don't even remember most of what happened." He hesitated, subconsciously tugging on his mustache. "Listen, Leo put Myra Rosenberg in charge of T&E while Fritz is out, but she doesn't want anything to do with us. She said I'm on my own."

"Wow," Debby said. "Can you handle that?"

"Well, you know most of the administrative rules and procedures," Ben said. "And I've been watching Fritz. We should be able to bluff our way through an estate or two before the Old Man gets back."

"Cool. I'm game," Debby said. She handed him the thick red folder. There were several manila subfolders inside. "Here's the file I promised you. I rushed to finish when you called, but the documents should be in order. The will and charitable trust are in the first subfolder. Then general correspondence, personal documents, old drafts and that fat one at the end is full of memos from the tax lawyers."

"Gotta love those tax lawyers," Ben said.

She smiled. "They do tend to get long-winded," she said. "So, what else can I do to help?"

Ben glanced down at the list he had quickly scribbled. At the moment, it was short. That would change after he had some time to think. "There's no next-of-kin. Can you handle funeral arrangements?" Ben asked.

"The *Herald Times* called Mr. Fox this morning and said they'd arrange a memorial service," Debby said. "Thompson left instructions for his body to be cremated."

"Okay. Maybe call the crematorium, then, and find out what we need to do," Ben said.

"Sure thing," Debby said.

"I'll check in with the police and Calhoun College to introduce myself," Ben said. "We should both review the will and the charitable trust, then we can work up a plan to marshal the estate's assets."

"Thompson had a safe deposit box at Chase," Debby said. "I'll file the paperwork to get you access."

"Great," Ben said, then paused reflectively. Fritz Fox had been Ben's safety net. They only spent a small part of each day together, if any, but just knowing that Fritz was there gave him a confidence that he suddenly felt lacking. He wanted Debby to stay a bit longer to help fill the void, but truth be told, the practice of law was a solitary sport.

Before long had passed, Ben said: "That should keep us busy for a day or two while I get my bearings. Can you think of anything else that needs to be done right away?"

"Nope. You seem to be on top of things," Debby said, as she stood to leave. "But I'm here to help. Let me know if you need anything."

Ben called the Sixth Precinct in Greenwich Village first. Detective Johnson, the officer assigned to the Thompson case, informed Ben that there were no leads. Arrangements were made to pick up Thompson's personal effects. His wallet was still missing.

Ben was not familiar with Calhoun College. A quick Internet search on his desktop computer revealed that it was a small, private university just outside of Atlanta. The school's web site provided Dean Frederick's telephone number.

"Buddy Frederick," a man's voice answered after the first ring.

The nickname caught Ben off guard. "Um...Dean Frederick?" he asked.

"Yes. Who's this?"

"This is Ben Kravner. I'm a lawyer with Kramer, Fox in New York. We're administering an estate that has named Calhoun College as its primary beneficiary. I was wondering if I could make an appointment to speak with you about it."

Dean Frederick's drawl became more pronounced as he spoke at length. "Of course," he said. "We've been trying to develop our estate giving program without much success, I'm afraid. Was it one of our alumni?"

"No, the donor is Adams Thompson, the publisher of the *New York Herald Times*," Ben said. "He was killed on Friday night."

Dean Frederick paused momentarily. "Adams was a close friend," he said. "I read about his passing in the local paper and was deeply saddened."

"I'm sorry," Ben said. "What was his connection to Calhoun College?"

"Nothing really," the Dean replied. "I'm surprised. We shared a love of history and the north Georgia mountains. He spoke to me about donating some historical documents he had collected and some personal essays, but we hadn't talked about money."

"It'll take some time before the College actually sees the money," Ben said. "But I need to visit Atlanta to examine Mr. Thompson's vaca-

tion home, and I'd like to go over the details of the estate administration with you on the same trip. Do you have any time available next
week?"

After they agreed on an appointment for the following Monday,
Ben swung his chair toward the window behind his desk. He looked
out over the grays and browns of Brooklyn.

His world had changed today.

The man he most admired and respected had almost left his life and
a ghost he knew nothing about had entered it. He reflected on the puz-
zles that were Fritz Fox and Adams Thompson. Both men were driven
by a passion that had lifted them to the top of their professions. But
Fritz Fox was much beloved—by family, friends, colleagues and clients;
at first blush, Thompson appeared to be one of the most hated men in
New York, his life an empty shell.

Ben hoped that this life, so abruptly ended, would take shape as he
reviewed every aspect of its existence. He might be the only person on
the planet to ever *really* know Adams George Thompson, Jr.

But, for Ben, there was more to this odyssey than plumbing the
depths of Thompson's soul. There was an element of self-discovery. Ben
believed that he was motivated by the same passion that had driven
Fritz Fox to greatness and Adams Thompson to notoriety. It was time
to piece together the puzzle that was Benjamin Franklin Kravner. It was
time to be great.

THREE

THE NEWSROOM at the *Herald Times* was still a somber place on Tuesday afternoon. Christy Kirk sat slumped at her workstation, one of fifty identical plain metal desks that lined the newsroom like an oversized classroom, sad about the loss of her mentor, resentful that she was alone in her knowledge of their special relationship.

Almost alone. She peered across the sea of desks and computers to the City Editor's office. Roger knew, and he was fuming. As the City Editor, Roger Martin expected reporters assigned to the City Desk to report to him and only to him. As Christy's lover, he expected an even higher degree of loyalty. He claimed that *he* wanted to be the experienced hand that guided her career, but Christy thought it more likely that he envied her special access to Thompson.

The issue would have been mooted by Thompson's death, except that Roger was in a snit about the story she had wrangled from Thompson on Friday, and he had been avoiding her all weekend. Roger professed to be upset because he was losing a reporter off the City Desk for several weeks. But Christy knew it was more than that. She had flaunted her relationship with Thompson to nail a story she did not deserve. The story belonged to a more senior reporter. Roger thought the story belonged to him.

Christy caught Roger's eye through the glass window in his office that allowed him to look out over the newsroom. She waved. He gestured solemnly for her to join him. She sighed. Maybe this was the big breakup.

Christy entered Roger's office without knocking, closing the door behind her. Roger was editing a piece, his shirtsleeves rolled up around the elbows, his tie loosened around his neck. He was a handsome man—tall, wavy brown hair, full beard masking a freckled face, and, at 35, ten years older than Christy.

Roger put down his pencil. "Sit," he said sternly.

The snit continued. "I know you're ticked off," Christy said, flopping into an armchair. "But let's talk about it over a drink after work, not here."

He rolled his eyeballs. It was an annoying habit. Christy suspected that it was not a conscious act, but the contempt it revealed, whether directed at her or womankind generally, infuriated her.

"This is about work," he said. "I'm taking you off the race story."

"I'll drop it right now if you tell me you'll write it yourself," Christy said.

"Look, I showed you my clippings file because I wanted to share my ideas with you," Roger said. "I'll bet you were scheming to pitch the story to Thompson yourself the whole time."

"I knew that you'd never go back to reporting," Christy said. "And that story has to be written now. There are a zillion small organizations arming themselves."

"So why not come to me and ask for the file?" Roger asked. "Why sneak around behind my back?"

"Because you're a thinker, not a doer," she said. "You'd think and think and think until somebody else grabbed the glory. I kinda hoped that you'd be happy that I took the initiative."

"Oh, bullshit. You'll say anything to get what you want," he said angrily. "Enough talk. Thompson's dead. So is the story."

"You can't do that. It's not a City Desk assignment. Only the new publisher can kill it."

"You're still assigned to the City Desk," Roger said. Then his expression changed, as if he suddenly realized the hopelessness of trying to overpower her. His voice softened. "It's too dangerous. I don't want you to do it."

She glared at him. "Now who's full of B.S.?" she asked. "You thought of the idea, and you want to coddle it. Dare to do it or get off my back."

"Thompson was probably killed over that editorial," Roger said. "What kind of reaction do you think you'll get when you show up at NOMAAD headquarters with a *Herald Times* press card? It's too risky. I care—"

Christy stood abruptly. "Dammit, you just don't get it!" she said. "No great story is without risk. This is *the* story of the year—maybe of the century—and I'm going to write it, either for the *Herald Times* or for some other rag. Unless I get a pink slip in the mail, I'll assume I'm still on the job."

Roger sputtered a response, but Christy was already out the door. She stopped at her desk only to collect her purse, then made a beeline for Roger's apartment. She had lied to Adams Thompson. She had no contacts, no research—only the items in Roger's folder. Her folder.

Christy left the key to Roger's apartment on his kitchen table. She did not leave a note.

FOUR

IT WAS A RISKY APPROACH, but one that had produced surprisingly good results in recent weeks. He decided to take the plunge.

"Strip for me," Master Ben commanded.

Betsy paused for a moment before responding. "That sounds like an interesting proposition, darlin'," she teased, with a hint of a Southern accent. "Play a sexy song on the stereo."

"I'll put on something by Clapton. How 'bout Layla?" he asked.

"Perfect." Betsy began to sway from side to side, in time to the music, giving Ben her sexiest look. She was a goddess—tall and slender, with long, blonde hair and blue eyes. He tensed with anticipation.

Betsy ran her hands down her silky, white blouse, then along her short, black skirt. She began to undress slowly, her hips swinging in time to the music, in a routine of strutting and preening that had doubtlessly entertained many men before Ben.

"Click." Ben felt the blood rush to points south as Betsy unclasped her bra, and it fell to the floor. She turned her back to him, raised herself up on her toes, arched her back, and slid her white lace panties over her hips.

"I can feel you leaning forward to get that first glimpse of my backside, darlin'," she said, smiling. Ben had a raging hard-on. Betsy gave Ben a sexy look, lowered herself to her hands and knees, and cooed softly: "Do what you want to me."

The shrill ring of the telephone almost knocked Ben off his chair. *Damn! What incredible timing.* He debated with himself whether to answer it. He glanced longingly at the computer screen before him, knowing Betsy sat poised at the keyboard in front of her computer in a dormitory at the University of Texas two thousand miles away waiting for his response to her seductive wordplay. He quickly typed in "brb," the universal code of on-line computer service users for "be right back."

Ben picked up the telephone on his kitchen wall. "Hello," he said.

"Ben? Fritz Fox here."

Ben's eyes widened. He went limp. "Mr. Fox!" he said. "How are you? They told me not to call."

"Thanks to you, much better," Fritz said. He sounded weak. "Agnes, she told me that you saved my life. For this I am very grateful."

"It was all instinct," Ben said. "I'm just glad I was there."

"Well, if you need my help—" His voice trailed off. "Oy, I'm getting dizzy."

"Mr. Fox? Mr. Fox?"

"Hello?" It was a woman's voice.

"I was talking to Mr. Fox. Is he okay?" Ben asked.

"He's fine," the woman said. "Just tired. Is there a message I can write down for him? I'm his private nurse."

"No. No, that's fine," Ben said. "When is he expected to go home?"

"He'll spend another week in the hospital, then a few weeks at home before we let him think about returning to the office."

"Just tell him Ben said that everything is under control at work."

Ben hung up the telephone, then returned to the computer. "You bastard..." was Betsy's parting message on the screen. He tried to send her a message, but she had already signed off the service.

Ben frowned. It was getting late, nine-twenty. Time flew by when he was playing on RealTime, a live chat feature of the CyberLine computer service. Countless on-line encounters had taught him that it would take hours to romance another balky young cyber-maiden out of her britches.

Few women leaped at the opportunity to reveal their bodies and their minds even behind the cloak of anonymity provided by the computer perhaps thousands of miles from the man trying to use them for his own stimulation. They wanted to feel beautiful, to be seduced with chivalry, wit and romance. They wanted *their* fantasies. And if a guy provided them with Mel Gibson, Richard Gere and Robin Williams rolled into one super-Cyberman, the psychic panties dropped and the sex could be without inhibition, raw and passionate. Ben had learned that sex was in large part in the mind.

Converting that knowledge into finding a living, breathing girl-friend—never mind true love—was a different story. The problem was not a lack of desire. The crushing schedule of an associate at a New York City mergers and acquisitions firm simply left him with little time or energy for such pursuits. Unlike many of the other young associates at Kramer, Fox, he did not have the good fortune, or foresight, to get married before signing on.

His mother constantly reminded him that there was no shortage of available women lawyers at Kramer, Fox, and it did not escape Barbara Kravner's eye that most of them were Jewish. But religion was not important to Ben; warmth, humor, and trust were. Pushiness seemed to be a quality required for a woman to succeed in the aggressive world of mergers and acquisitions; Ben did not find it desirable in a girlfriend. Debby Barnett was an intriguing possibility, but he was still working up the courage to ask her out. *Soon.*

Ben wistfully logged off CyberLine and powered down the computer. He had opened Adams Thompson's safe deposit box that afternoon, and its contents were now spread across a coffee table in the living room of his Upper East Side apartment.

Ben wanted to know, roughly, the size of Thompson's estate before he met with Buddy Frederick on Monday, and he had already fallen behind schedule. Most of Tuesday, Wednesday and Thursday afternoon had been spent responding to what Fritz Fox's wealthy clients thought were routine questions. To Ben's dismay, he had discovered that what was routine to Fritz Fox was not routine to Ben Kravner. It was only after he had found himself researching the simplest questions that Ben appreciated the enormity of the legal knowledge stored in Fritz Fox's ninety-year-old mind.

Ben plopped his lean runner's body onto the couch, his muscles rippling beneath a gray T-shirt and blue gym shorts. He set an open beer bottle on the naked hardwood floor, then surveyed the material on the coffee table with little enthusiasm.

The contents of the safe deposit box appeared uninspiring at first glance. There were deeds to Thompson's condominium apartment on Fifth Avenue and his vacation home in Ellijay, Georgia, title to his Mercedes, and a collection of stamps, presumably rare. A large red accordion-style folder labeled "Personal Documents" raised Ben's hopes, but there were no exotic pictures, diaries or amendments to

Thompson's will, a "codicil" in the parlance of the Trust and Estates lawyer. For a man who had lived alone for twenty-five years, Thompson appeared to have surprisingly few secrets.

Ben sprawled out on the couch and began to read the random collection of bad poetry and tedious essays that filled the folder. He logged each item on a yellow legal pad.

It became apparent to Ben that Thompson had harbored secret passions that he could not reveal through his journalistic writing at the *Herald Times*. The poetry was unremarkable, inspired more by places and things than by people and experiences. But there were several liberal, possibly even radical, essays that were inconsistent with the hard-driving conservative editorials that Thompson approved or wrote in his role at the *Herald Times*.

Ben guzzled the last of his beer and returned the papers to the "Personal Documents" folder. Just as he was about to close up the folder for the night, Ben noticed a compartment that was sealed shut, almost imperceptibly, with clear cellophane tape. His heart rate quickened as he pried it open.

The compartment held a single manila envelope. It was marked "PERSONAL—DO NOT OPEN (DELIVER TO FRITZ FOX, TRUSTEE)" in black ink, and there was a wax seal over the flap.

Ben's mind reeled as his legal training dueled his curiosity. As the executor of the estate, he had the legal right to review all of Thompson's property. He had the responsibility to marshal the estate's assets and collect all relevant papers that might effect the administration of the estate. The envelope could contain legal documents that might supersede the current will and trust on file at Kramer, Fox.

But the envelope requested delivery to Fritz Fox, *Trustee*. Ben was empowered to act on Fritz's behalf, but he wondered if Thompson had left special instructions with Fritz for dealing with the envelope. Maybe he had intended that only his beneficiaries view the contents. But Ben did not recall seeing any such instructions in the trust agreement.

Ben pulled the Thompson file from his briefcase. He re-read the charitable trust, but it said nothing about the envelope or any other specific items of property. But why had Thompson addressed it to Fritz as trustee instead of as executor? Maybe there was another trust.

Ben rummaged through the folder Debby had prepared. Only the will and the Calhoun College charitable trust were in the first subfolder. There were no prior versions of any other trust documents included with the old drafts, either.

The envelope taunted him. Unless there was a specific restriction in the trust agreement, he was permitted, maybe even required, to open it. But he still had doubts. He thought about Fritz Fox. As much as he wanted to be independent, he once again realized how much he leaned upon the Old Man.

Ben dialed Buzz Herzog's number at the office. Buzz picked up the phone on the first ring, cheerfully announcing himself with his signature "This is Buzz," tacitly proclaiming to all the world that, "Yes, it's ten o'clock at night, but *of course* I'm still working."

"Buzzman!" Ben greeted his comrade. "This is Ben Kravner."

"Ben! How's it going, buddy?" Buzz returned the greeting with the vigor of one who had not heard from his friend in months. They had eaten lunch together that afternoon. "I would have thought you T&E guys would be in bed by now."

"Funny. I was just doing some work at home, and I've got an issue I need some quick advice on," Ben said. "Can you do a fly-by on the 28th floor and see if any of the T&E associates are working late tonight?"

"Fat chance, but I'll look. Call you back in five."

Buzz called back faithfully within minutes. "No luck, Ben. All good T&E lawyers are tucked in by now," he said, repeating his earlier insult. "That paralegal you've been eyeballing is still typing away in her cubicle, though."

Ben ignored Buzz's attempts to draw him into a duel of wits, one that he was sure to lose. Any attempt to defend himself would be met by a multi-flanked retort and an instant victory for Buzz. And if he returned the barbs, Buzz would turn vicious, either doubling his attack or launching a stealth campaign against him personally or T&E lawyers generally over the next several days. He had seen Buzz in action enough to simply wave the white flag immediately.

"Yeah, well, maybe I'll give her a call," Ben said. "Go home and get some sleep, big guy."

"You got it, buddy," Buzz chuckled, secure in the knowledge that he was sharing a mutual joke, that the possibility of Buzz Herzog, superstar, leaving the premises before midnight on a *weekday* was so unfathomable as to reduce the mere suggestion of it to humor.

Ben's heart began pounding as soon as he set down the receiver. Would Debby think his late night call an awkward romantic advance and brand him a fool? Nonsense. He was being prudent. Just making sure that he had not missed something obvious. That's what lawyers do.

"Hello," Debby answered. There was a twinge of surprise in her voice. As a paralegal toiling on an hourly wage, she enjoyed the over-time pay, but had little need to brag about her late hours.

"Hi, Debby, this is Ben Kravner."

"Uh-huh. What's up, Ben?"

"Buzz Herzog told me that you were the only one still around. I'm going through the Thompson file, and I found a sealed envelope that's marked 'PERSONAL—DO NOT OPEN, DELIVER TO FRITZ FOX, *TRUSTEE.*' The trust agreement doesn't refer to the envelope. Are there any other files?"

"Nope, I gave you everything," Debby said. "Maybe the instructions are inside the envelope."

Ben was skeptical. "Why would he do that?" he asked.

"Sometimes clients do dumb stuff," she said. "We're tuned in to the difference between *trustee* and *executor*, but they're not."

"So you think I should open it?" Ben asked.

"Don't see why not," she said. "You're the executor. How else are you going to figure out what to do with it?"

"Yeah, maybe you're right. Thanks, Debby, I'll see you tomorrow."

"Righty-oh," she said and hung up.

Ben's anxiety morphed into excitement as he carefully sliced open the seal with a kitchen knife. What would his prize reveal? What could be so important that it needed to be sealed even within the security of Adams Thompson's safe deposit box? This last thought raised doubts in Ben's mind once again, but there was no turning back now.

Ben slid a single piece of tattered, yellow paper out of the envelope. His excitement gave way to both disappointment and relief. There was no codicil leaving Thompson's fortune to a secret lover. There were no instructions for Fritz Fox. But the paper did not appear controversial, either. It was a handwritten poem—perhaps one of the historical doc-uments Dean Frederick had mentioned.

The poem contained several references to the millennium—a source of much excitement these days, but an odd topic in a document written so long ago. The Poem appeared to contain a riddle:

Seven grieving brothers and sisters two
Forever curse the Office of Tippecanoe;
Vengeance is ours for the falsely condemned
From now 'til the coming of the Millennium.

Our pasts now clouded, our futures clear
Shrouded names mask the secret we bear,
From mouth to mouth the Key shall descend
The final object unlocked only in the end.

Each one strike at Vengeance pure,
The next to come in twenty more;
Each a task 'fore the Millennium Meeting,
Then Vengeance shall be much less fleeting.

Scattered to the winds for eight score year
Our progeny, unmasked, will reappear;
Midnight of the Great Year's dawn,
First meet upon the Old School's lawn.

And the Final Vengeance will be ours
When they claim the cursed Office's powers;
A pestilence rained upon the wretched people
Who watched our Jimmy hang from a steeple.

We, The Royal Order of the Millennium Knight
Swear to bring to bear our collective might
To avenge our departed brother's restless soul
And once again make our family whole.

Two clues immediately struck Ben as critical to deciphering the
poem's mystery. First, there was an incident long ago that triggered the
passionate rage so vividly expressed in the poem, and it involved the
Office of Tippecanoe. "Tippecanoe" sounded familiar, but recollection
failed him.

The second important clue was the reference to The Royal Order of
the Millennium Knight. If such an organization existed and planned to
exact some form of vengeance at the turn of the millennium, there

would probably be evidence to that effect. Ben wondered when the millennium actually turned, on January 1, 2000 or January 1, 2001. Since there was no year zero, he figured it was 2001, but questioned whether the grieving and raging brothers and sisters had thought the matter through.

Ben logged back on to the Internet. There were several good search engines that returned a list of sites on the World Wide Web using key words specified by the user, ideally in some order of relevance. With the rise of the Internet to prominence in the last five years, a search could produce thousands of hits. Ben entered a single word: "Tippecanoe."

This search produced only thirty web sites, most with some connection to Tippecanoe County, Indiana. There were sites for the Tippecanoe Ancient Fife and Drum Corps, the Tippecanoe Door & Window Company and the Tippecanoe County Emergency Management Agency. Bed and Breakfasts. Computer management companies. The history of Lafayette, Indiana. He tried the Fife and Drum web site. It contained a history of the French presence in the region, but nothing that struck Ben as even remotely interesting.

He tried a different search engine. Because of the vastness of the World Wide Web and the unique way in which each of these programs worked, they almost always produced different results. The second search produced almost two thousand hits. The program sorted these by likely relevance, though, and Ben perused the first several web sites on the list. Again, most of them were related to Tippecanoe County, Indiana.

He brought up the web page for the Tippecanoe County Historical Association. Tippecanoe County had been the site of a major battle in 1811 between the United States and a confederation of Indian tribes that was attacking western settlers. A small army organized by the governor of the Indiana territory, General William Henry Harrison, repelled the Indians in a bloody battle and destroyed their settlement.

Then the story got interesting. General Harrison was the unsuccessful Whig Party candidate for president in 1836. He ran again for the presidency in 1840, and the Tippecanoe Battlefield was the site of a massive rally. Harrison and his vice-presidential nominee, John Tyler, capitalized on the political slogan, "Tippecanoe and Tyler, Too!" to win the presidency, but Harrison died after only a month in office.

The campaign slogan was the snippet of information that eluded Ben's recollection earlier, an item of trivia from a junior high school text

book stored in deep memory. Tippecanoe was almost certainly William
Henry Harrison, unless Adams Thompson had taken an unusual interest in Tippecanoe County politics. Was the "Office" of Tippecanoe the
presidency, the governorship of Indiana, or one of the many other
offices held by Harrison over the years? Probably the presidency. Why
else would this poem have captured Adams Thompson's interest?

It was already midnight, but Ben was hooked. The final paragraph
of the poem sounded like bluster, but if The Royal Order of the
Millennium Knight existed, there might be clues on the Internet. Ben
recalled seeing several chat rooms catering to millennium watchers.

He clicked an on-screen button with his mouse, and his PenPal list
appeared on the monitor. The list indicated whether each PenPal was
logged on to CyberLine.

"BlueSatin" had initially presented herself as a statuesque blonde,
with blue eyes and a figure to die for. But Ben was not in the mood for
cybersex on the night he first met her, and further probing revealed a
stocky young brunette desperately in need of affection. She lived in a
small Ohio town and worked in a tire factory. They frequently com-
miserated about their loneliness and exchanged ideas for improving
their social lives. She was not logged on tonight.

"PeggySue" was a 32-year old ski instructor in Colorado, a single
mom and a frustrated artist. Ben had only recently befriended her, but
the relationship seemed promising. PeggySue was not logged on, either.

"Quixote" was logged on, but they had not spoken for over three
years. Quixote was a ghost from Ben's past, his mentor, his friend, his
soulmate. He might not have survived his first year at Harvard Law
School without her. But then she had graduated, and he had ruined the
friendship. Ben had seen love in her eyes, and he had panicked. Three
and a half years had passed since then, and he still had not found that
kind of love again. He wistfully monitored Quixote's on-line presence
using the PenPal list, but never had the nerve to reconnect with her on
CyberLine.

"Lisa C" was not logged on. Like Ben, she had a quick wit, and the
two of them could talk for hours about nothing or about the problems
of the world with equal facility and enjoyment. At 27, she was a year
older than Ben, and often used that as the clinching argument in their
debates. Their chats were laced with that undercurrent of sexual tension
that situation comedies on television seem to strive for nowadays. In a

way, he was infatuated with her—at least as much as one could be with someone who might be a figment of someone else's imagination.

That was the problem with CyberLine, he thought. It was a wonderful tool to release one's inhibitions and explore alternate selves. But everybody else in cyberspace was exploring, too. Ben never knew who he was dealing with, man or woman, friend or foe, sincere or deceitful. Sometimes he did not even know who *he* was, anymore. Was he the kind, honest, hard-working gentleman that he tried to present to the outside world or the sexual predator who roamed cyberspace like an untamed lion?

He had always thought a person was defined by how he presented himself to others. Everybody had crazy impulses. Character was determined by the ability to control those urges. Others judged you by your choice of behavior, not the decision-making process that you endured privately. Did acting out alternative behaviors on-line change who he was because he was showing other people the inner workings of his mind? Or was cyberspace just a new medium for testing behavior before displaying it in the real world?

Ben was pleased to see that the one person in cyberspace he was certain he did know was on-line. "WoodythePecker" was a young lawyer in San Francisco, three years older than Ben, who was going through much of the same turmoil as Ben in starting a career in the big city. But Woody was gay and in the closet, in mortal fear of exposing his inner self to his family, friends and co-workers, as well as exposing himself to AIDS.

Woody had revealed himself without fear to Ben, not in search of a cyber-lover, but in search of a friend. Ben and Woody had shared horror stories about experiences at their law firms and had confided about personal relationships that were or might be.

Woody was the only cyber-friend that Ben had met in person. They had known each other for over a year, and Ben had spent a weekend with him this past summer. They had attended a Giants baseball game, toured underground San Francisco and talked. By the end of the weekend, Ben considered Woodrow Barnsworth Taylor III his closest friend in the world. He trusted him completely and often consulted him on legal as well as personal issues.

Ben sent Woody an instant message:

MasterBen: Woodman!

WoodythePecker: Ben! How's it hanging, man? We haven't talked in ages...

MasterBen: Life has turned upside down, Woody.

WoodythePecker: Tell me more, dear…

MasterBen: My boss had a heart attack today. I helped revive him, but he'll be out for weeks.

WoodythePecker: You must have been freaked out!

MasterBen: It was like an out-of-body experience. Like somebody else was controlling my actions. Anyway, guess who's running the T&E Dept in his absence?

WoodythePecker: No way!

MasterBen: Way! Did you hear about the Thompson murder? I'm handling that estate.

WoodythePecker: That's a huge project for any lawyer...for a second year associate to get a case like that, they are sending you a nice message, my friend...

MasterBen: I'm not sure they've thought about it that much—nobody else wants the job (smile)...Anyway, the plot thickens...

WoodythePecker: He gets the girl, too? :)

MasterBen: Nah…"the" girl still eludes me...But I found a mysterious poem locked in Thompson's safe deposit box. It has several references to the millennium even though it seems to have been written over 150 years ago. Have you heard of a group called The Royal Order of the Millennium Knight?

WoodythePecker: The millennium is the hot topic these days, but I haven't heard that one before...sounds a little creepy...what are they up to?

MasterBen:	I don't know if Thompson's poem is real or imagined, but it seems to be written by this group. The poem says that they're planning some dire act of vengeance as the millennium turns…
WoodythePecker:	Well, there are a lot of wackos out there. I've heard worse. Religious fanatics who think the world is coming to an end. We live in strange times.
MasterBen:	(Laughing) Well, if they're an underground organization, the web would be a way for them to meet discreetly...
WoodythePecker:	Could be worth taking a flier...Good luck, my friend, and congratulations on the big assignment!
MasterBen:	Thanks, Woody...

Ben scanned the RealTime rooms for topics relating to the millennium. There was no shortage. He started in a room created by CyberLine entitled "Millennium Chat." There were 24 members in the room; none of the names struck Ben as distinctive. He observed the discussion for several minutes. He found these public chats to be boring for the most part. There were frequently long pauses before anyone spoke. Most of the activity occurred behind the scenes in private messages between members.

One participant in the room, WilyCoyote, was unsuccessfully trying to solicit a date for the millennium, offering dining and dancing in the Rainbow Room, a posh restaurant atop Rockefeller Center with gorgeous panoramic views of Manhattan. Another, ReverendJim, warned that "The End is Near" and demanded that all sinners repent before the judgment day, which he thought, not surprisingly, was to come at the turn of the millennium. A few others shared their plans for the millennium, with their sparse conversation broken up by the occasional "age/sex check"—a request for all members in the room to disclose their age and sex.

After he could stand it no more, Ben took his chance.

MasterBen:	Has anyone heard of The Royal Order of the Millennium Knight?
Jock69:	KKK branch?
MasterBen:	I don't think so. Have you seen any chats discussing anything like that?
Jock69:	Nah.

Ben waited a few more minutes, but the discussion degenerated back to minutia. He exited the room and went to the list of member-created rooms. A separate list was devoted to millennium chats—Millennium Parties, Millennium Prophecies, Millennium Predictions and other similar headings. Ben entered several rooms, learning nothing new, before he came upon Millennium Prophecies Uncensored.

There were eleven others in the room. A member named Doomsayer666 seemed to be leading the discussion.

Doomsayer666:	I believe in the asteroid theory and that there is nothing that we can do to save the world. We need to devote resources to developing a space colony to preserve some small remnant of the human race after it hits.
Freddy2000:	Neat! How long to develop one?
Doomsayer666:	I have friends in the defense industry that say that NASA's already building one and may be in the testing phase.
WhitsEnd:	How many people can it hold? (And do they have room for me!) :)
Doomsayer666:	My sources say that the prototype can accommodate about 10,000 people. It's like a small town.
Dreamweaver35:	Hey, y'all. Joined in late—explain this asteroid hokum.
Doomsayer666:	There are two parts to the theory. The first is the growing body of scientific evidence

that suggests that it's only a matter of time, under the laws of probability, that an asteroid will collide with the earth and destroy it. The second part is a prophecy supposedly hidden in code in the Bible that predicts that the earth will be destroyed in either the year 2000 or 2006.

Dreamweaver35: Heard about that Bible thang a ways back. Supposedly forecasted the assassination of the Israeli prime minister a few years ago. My bet: hokum!!!

Doomsayer666: I'm more concerned about the statistical probability of getting slammed.

WhitsEnd: So how many of these space colonies are they planning to build? (And will they have room for me!) :)

Doomsayer666: They'll cost billions. They'll probably only build one. It would take months to ferry 10,000 people out to deep space. They'll need a new transportation system before they can get serious about fully populating that thing.

WhitsEnd: How will they decide who gets to go?

Doomsayer666: I don't know—how would you do it?

BeamMeUp: Bev Hills 90210 cast 4 sure

Doomsayer666: Very mature, Beamer

WhitsEnd: A lottery...

Freddy2000: The president should decide...set up a commission to do it fair, you know?

Doomsayer666: But limiting the pool to only the best and the brightest perhaps?

WhitsEnd: No way! That rules me out :)

BeamMeUp: Me, too

Freddy2000:   Me, three

Doomsayer666:   I'll take my chances...

Freddy2000:   I'm not so sure that Beamer was on the wrong track...a few attractive specimens to breed future generations sounds cool to me...

TomTom24:   You guys are scary!

TomTom24:   Can you spell H-I-T-L-E-R?

Doomsayer666:   Come now, Tom, surely you can see the difference between mass genocide and a process of selecting the survivors of a catastrophic event?

TomTom24:   But why should any one person or group of people get to pick the criteria? Random sampling would be more fair.

Doomsayer666:   But on the theory that 90% of the country is average or below, a lottery would probably result in only a small portion of the pool being even above average and true genius may be totally excluded...If only 10,000 lives can be saved, we should focus on preserving as much of society's accumulated knowledge as possible.

Freddy2000:   Yuk! Sounds like a place run by eggheads!! Save the artists, athletes and beauty queens and throw the nerds overboard!!!! ;)

MasterBen: This discussion is fascinating, folks, but could I possibly interrupt with an unrelated question?

Doomsayer666:   Fire away, Ben.

MasterBen: I've heard about a group that calls themselves The Royal Order of the Millennium Knight...Nobody seems to know about them...any ideas?

Doomsayer666:   Can't say that I've seen anything like that...

Freddy2000:   Sounds like a serious group...let me know
                      if you find them.

MasterBen: Okay...thanks anyway guys.

Ben exited the room and was ready to quit for the night. It was almost one o'clock in the morning. Within seconds, though, Ben received a private message.

WhitsEnd: Hi Ben. I don't know if these are the guys
                      that you're looking for, but there's a group
                      that meets regularly in a private room
                      called Millennium Nights. They were there
                      about half an hour ago.

MasterBen: What do they talk about?

WhitsEnd: I don't know. Password protected. I sent
                      messages to these guys asking for the
                      password, but they either ignored me or
                      got nasty.

MasterBen: Do you remember the names of any of the
                      guys that hang out there?

WhitsEnd: They all had similar names, like some kind
                      of club. One of them was The General.
                      He's one mean sumbitch.

MasterBen: Yeah, I don't know if those are the guys
                      I'm looking for, but thanks anyway, Whit.

WhitsEnd: Happy hunting.

Ben was not hopeful, but he left the millennium chats and entered the private rooms. This area was set aside for members to create their own rooms on any topic. Private rooms had the advantage of accommodating more than two members if a group wanted to carry on a private meeting, like a family get-together, a club meeting, or, more often, a virtual orgy of one form or another.

The private rooms were easy to use if you knew where you were going and were an invited guest. But it was difficult to find a room if you were just randomly snooping into the affairs of the cyber elite. In fact, it was almost pointless to do so, because most rooms were password protected, and the casual surfer could not view the discussion. The member on the outside could view a list of members inside, though, and private messages could be sent in a typically vain effort to gain entry.

It took Ben ten minutes to find the Millennium Nights room. As anticipated, the room was password protected. He tried to enter a few standard passwords, like "sesame" or "enter," on a whim, but without success.

Ben called up the list of room participants. WhitsEnd had been right. They did seem like a club, but none of the names indicated to Ben that he had fallen upon The Royal Order of the Millennium Knight. The Heir Apparent. The Caretaker. The Spy. The General. The Senator. The Speaker. The Doctor.

Ben logged off CyberLine without attempting to contact them, frustrated with his night's work.

FIVE

THE SEVEN REMAINING MEMBERS of The Royal Order of the Millennium Knight were in the Millennium Nights room that night, as they were every Thursday beginning at midnight. Of course, The Assassin was absent. And now The Publisher was gone, too. The Publisher's activities at the *Herald Times* had been critical in promoting a mood of racial divisiveness across the country, and he and his father had also been an important factor in the rise of the political fortunes of The Heir Apparent, The Senator and The Speaker. But those were not the primary concerns of The Royal Order now.

The Heir Apparent: Spy, was there anything among The Publisher's personal effects that could compromise The Royal Order? Was his copy of The Poem recovered?

The Spy: NY apt and GA house searched. No record of Royal Order. Computer clean. Poem probably in safe deposit box—lawyers control.

The Senator: Has contact with the lawyers been established? We cannot have them nosing around in our affairs.

The Caretaker: A NY lawyer called me. We're meeting on Monday in Atlanta. Assuming The Publisher followed our rules, the lawyers will not be permitted to read the Poem. It should be in a sealed envelope held in trust for Calhoun College, but we might

not get it until they sort out the estate. I'll
ask him about it when we meet.

The Heir Apparent: Hell, do we know anything about this
lawyer?

The Spy: Name: Benjamin Franklin Kravner. BFK
graduated Harvard Law School 1998.
Smart kid. Unconnected. Middle class.
Background clean.

The Heir Apparent: Caretaker, was there any indication that
he found The Poem? Was he nervous or
evasive?

The Caretaker: We only spoke briefly. The boy seemed a
little nervous and excited. You've all seen
young kids when they first enter business
or politics. They try to sound important,
like they belong, but they don't quite have
the act worked out yet.

The General: The Publisher's death is a major security
breach. Don't dismiss anyone.

The Heir Apparent: What do you suggest, General?

The General: Make sure that the envelope was not
unsealed. Caretaker should test the
lawyer on Monday. If he thinks the kid
knows too much, we eliminate him.

The Senator: That's a little harsh, General. If our plan
unravels now, there is still no evidence of
any crime. If we start killing outsiders,
we're all facing the death penalty.

The Heir Apparent: Let's let The Caretaker evaluate Mr.
Kravner on Monday and talk about how to
proceed next week. We'll probably retrieve
The Poem without incident.

The Speaker: I suggest that we burn all remaining
copies. At this point, they're historical
relics and more trouble than they're worth.

The Heir Apparent: Agreed. Any objections? Other business?

The Spy: Security issue #2: Pub's death may not have been random act.

The Speaker: The black militant groups?

The Spy: 3 possibilities: (1) Blacks militants: violent protests in NY, and Pub received death threats

The Spy: (2) random act (NY is NY)

The Spy: (3) Pub contacted last week by somebody claiming to be Assassin.

The Heir Apparent: That's impossible!

The Senator: You told us that The Assassin was eliminated last year. The San Francisco newspaper confirmed it.

The Spy: Pub received e-mail. They set up meet at Pub's apt Friday 9PM. I arranged to be there, but no Pub or Assassin.

The General: Why are we first hearing about this now?

The Spy: Didn't want to alarm. And if Assassin did pass on mission to confederate, I wanted to determine how connection missed last year.

The Speaker: Is there anyone who could have assumed the duties of The Assassin?

The Spy: Only known child was daughter. Assassin divorced and out of touch. Unwilling participant, anyway—wouldn't inspire child or anyone else to participate.

The Senator: Could any information have passed through his estate?

The Spy: Poem recovered. Computer disk clean. Apt searched. No safe deposit box. Estate administration monitored. No documents escaped us.

The General: Could Publisher have concocted this story? I've had my doubts about his resolve.

The Spy: Conceivable. Or another leak from within.

The Doctor: A rogue Knight?

The Spy: We've all provided evidence of our allegiance over last 5 yrs, but the pressure mounts. Like Senator implied, we've yet to cross point of no return. Maybe fear of death penalty will boost our courage.

The Senator: I hope that you are not questioning my loyalty to The Royal Order!

The Spy: I question everybody's loyalty.

The General: If one of us wanted to hunt Publisher, or any of the others, there would be no reason to set up a meeting. This Assassin is an outsider—either an angry confederate of the true Assassin or a willing accomplice whose attempt to join us was thwarted by Publisher's murder.

The Speaker: Well, we may have passed the point of no return after all. If this Assassin is out for revenge, we're all targets.

The Heir Apparent: But if this person has assumed The Assassin's role, but doesn't know our identities, I'm at risk. The next president was supposed to be The Assassin's target.

The Senator: Your likely opponent has not proposed a vice president yet. Perhaps I should start throwing my rather considerable weight around to get on the short list—just as a back-up plan, of course.

The Heir Apparent: That's premature. Hell, as much as I loathe any alternative that leaves me exposed with a target painted on my forehead for four years, I'm not about to throw the election because there's a remote chance that some jackass has assumed The Assassin's role. Spy, what are the odds of tracking down this imposter?

The Spy: Needle in haystack. No leads. E-mail to Pub from phony account.

The Heir Apparent: Does anybody else have any cheerful news?

    The Knights fell silent. The Heir Apparent adjourned the meeting in the customary way: "May God Bless Jimmy MacDougall and each of his descendants and may his Persecutors suffer eternal Damnation." Each of the other Knights responded, "Aye," as was their ritual, and then they exited the Millennium Nights room. It was half past one o'clock on Friday morning.

SIX

DEBBY WAS LINGERING outside Ben's office on Friday morning when he returned with his third cup of coffee. It was eleven o'clock. "Good morning, Ben," she said.

Her voice was laced with disappointment. She was wearing a loose fitting, white knit sweater and a tan skirt. Ben gave her the once over and had approving thoughts.

"Hi, Debby," he said, with all the cheer he could muster, aided by his standard blend of caffeine and adrenaline. The sacks under his eyes felt like lead weights.

"How's it going?" she asked. "You look awful."

"Thanks," Ben said, feigning a scowl. "It's my Friday look—if your eyes are droopy enough, you might not get that weekend assignment."

"I thought for sure you'd come by and tell me what you found in your secret envelope last night," she said. "You piqued my curiosity. You did open it, didn't you?"

"Oh, yeah, I'm sorry," Ben said. The exotic scent of her perfume wafted through the air. He squirmed almost undetectably. "I ran this morning. Got in late, then had a few messages to handle first. The envelope turned out to be nothing—just some weird poem. I'm getting the impression that Adams Thompson was a bit of a flake."

"I wonder why he sealed that up," Debby said.

"Well, it's not as sexy as a codicil or a diary, but it seems to contain a cryptic riddle," Ben said. He got another whiff of Debby's perfume and felt his loins stir. He forced himself to think of fat naked men, reversing his instinctive reaction before it could take its full course. "It smacks of a conspiracy."

"Wow," Debby said. "Can I see it?"

"Sure," Ben said. He set his coffee down on his desk and sat down.

Debby positioned herself beside him rather than taking one of the chairs on the other side. Ben felt her warmth. His mind began to lose focus as the blood rushed to points south, depriving his brain of oxygen. He fished through a pile of papers awkwardly, searching for the poem.

"Here it is," he said trying not to betray his state of emotional disarray. He held the paper up for Debby to take.

Debby shifted her weight towards him and read without grasping it. The barely perceptible movement sent a plume of perfume in Ben's direction, further stoking his inner fire. He silently marveled how, no matter how sophisticated we became as a culture, no matter how formal and business-like we behaved, we were still basically animals, ready to act on our basest instincts at any time, any place. *Fat naked men.*

"This is amazing," Debby said. "Have you figured out what it means?"

"I have some ideas," Ben said hesitantly.

"Like what?"

Ben peered out the window at the East River for a split second. Caffeine. Adrenaline. Perfume. Testosterone. His bloodstream was a living, breathing chemical factory.

"I think it has something to do with William Henry Harrison," Ben said calmly. "He was elected president in 1840 and his nickname was Tippecanoe. He must have done harm to the brother of the people who wrote the poem. Or maybe not. Maybe Thompson made it all up."

"So why all the references to the millennium?" Debby asked.

"I haven't figured that out yet. It sounds like the descendants of this guy were supposed to carry out a vendetta at the turn of the millennium. Do you see the reference to The Royal Order of the Millennium Knight at the end?"

"Uh-huh."

"Last night I tried to see if anyone on the Internet had heard of a group with that name. I only spent about an hour, but didn't have any luck."

"Cool idea. Do you spend a lot of time on the Net?" she asked.

Ben blushed. "A bit."

"Don't be embarrassed," Debby said. "I'm addicted. I hang out in the CyberLine chat rooms almost every night."

"What name do you go by?"

"Different names. I get worried about stalkers so I change it every now and then. Lately I've been using 'DebbyDoes' if you want to chat some time."

Ben smiled. "Hmm. I'm not going to walk into that trap and ask what it is that Debby does."

"Thank you very much. I'll leave it to your imagination." Her eyes twinkled. *Fat naked men. Fat naked men.*

"So did you find anything interesting last night?" Debby asked.

"Not really. Just a bunch of wackos. The 'end is near' type of crap. I don't know what all the fuss is about. If there is a God, I doubt he planned for the Earth's destruction based on the Roman calendar. And if he did, why not the year 1000? What's so special about 2000?"

Debby laughed. "Good point. I'd argue about the existence of God and whether God is a he or a she, but somehow I think that's a discussion for another time."

"How about over lunch?" Ben asked without missing a beat. He surprised even himself.

"Very smooth," she grinned.

The wind off New York Harbor made the December chill even more bracing as Ben and Debby ventured out from the warmth of One Water. The pair were bundled for the nippy weather, Ben in a gray, herringbone coat and Debby in a bright blue down ski jacket and an orange wool scarf. They hunched their shoulders in the cold, and turned right, down State Street, with Ben leading the way.

"Where to?" Debby asked. Her long, frizzy hair blew wildly in the wind.

"We can grab a hot dog in Battery Park," Ben said. "Then maybe take a walk on the esplanade near the World Financial Center."

"Cool. I've never been there."

"Really? How long have you lived in the city?" Ben asked.

"Just a few months," she replied. "I was working out West, in San Francisco, and I needed a change. I moved here after I got this job."

"I love San Francisco," Ben said.

"It's nice. I lived there all my life, though, and it was time to move on."

"You know, I was in San Francisco the day Jerry Garcia died," Ben said. "I was on a bus passing by the corner of Haight and Ashbury when I heard the news. All the old hippies were out there crying and dancing."

Debby laughed. "You don't strike me as the Dead Head type," she said.

"Ah, there are many things about me that you don't know," Ben said mysteriously, raising his eyebrows with a suggestive double pump.

Debby punched him in the shoulder playfully. "Aw, Ben, cut it out."

They turned into Battery Park at the Bowling Green entrance and ordered two hot dogs and two knishes from a vendor with a cart near the gate. Ben picked up the seven dollar tab. He found those situations awkward, but with Debby it was easy. No feminist banter about splitting the check. No half-hearted reaching for her purse.

The park was quiet in the winter months. Most of the people of the street sought out warmer environs. There were still some tourists waiting for the ferry ride to tour the Statue of Liberty and Ellis Island and a few other business people braving the cold, but the park was an escape from the bustle of downtown Manhattan.

Ben and Debby walked with their food down close to the waterfront and sat on a bench overlooking the harbor. The scent of hot dogs, the sea air and Debby's perfume proved a tantalizing combination.

"So, what made you join a big New York firm?" Debby asked, as she wiped a speck of mustard from her lower lip.

"It was the thing to do," Ben said. "I went to Harvard Law School. The big firms were lining up to recruit us, and my family lives in the New York area."

"The 'burbs?" she asked.

"Yeah. Westchester," Ben said. "Middle class neighborhood."

"Any brothers and sisters?"

"Nope. Just me," he said. "I call once a week, but the conversations are always the same. My mom and dad are dying for grandchildren."

Debby laughed. "Can't help you there."

Ben grinned. "That wasn't a proposal," he said. *Although not the craziest idea I've heard today.* "Some day, but I'm not sure enough about what I want to do with my life to settle down."

"Making partner at Kramer, Fox isn't part of the master plan?" she asked.

Ben looked out across the harbor. The sunlight danced off the choppy blue water. Two yellow Staten Island ferries passed in opposite directions about a mile out. His feelings about Kramer, Fox were still in turmoil.

"Who knows?" he said reflectively. "The partners don't seem terribly happy."

"They're filthy rich," Debby said. "I help Mr. Fox with his accounting. Some of these guys are making millions."

"Money's not everything," he said. "Some people thrive on the lifestyle and love the pressure of the deal, but I grew up in a more relaxed world. I miss it."

"Didn't you know what you were getting into?" she asked.

"With eyes wide shut," he said. "Nice Jewish boys are taught at an early age that they're destined to become doctors or lawyers, and I get sick at the sight of blood."

Debby laughed. "That's it, when all else fails, blame your parents."

"Oh, I didn't mean it like that," Ben said sheepishly. "But somehow the law became the default career path and nothing inspired me enough to vary from it."

"So have you figured out what you really want to do?" she asked.

Ben shrugged. "I wish I knew," he said. "Some days I delude myself into thinking I can be great. That I can take my Harvard degree and my big ideas and make a difference in people's lives. Other days I hear my mom's voice in my head and wonder if life is about raising a happy family."

"That's pretty heavy. Most guys just recite the party line," she said, then furrowed her brow and mimicked a gruff, male voice. "'Anything for the team.'"

Ben grinned. "I guess I'm still in shock over the Fritz thing," he said. "Maybe I speak too much."

It was not a small concern. He had become so accustomed to discussing his personal thoughts and dreams on CyberLine, behind the veil of anonymity, that he occasionally found himself revealing more of himself than was perhaps appropriate.

"Not at all," Debby said. "It's refreshing."

"Enough about me," Ben said. "Tell me about your family."

"I much prefer happy family stories like yours," Debby said. Her eyes grew distant. "My dad was killed in a car accident about a year ago and my mom is in a nursing home with Alzheimer's."

"Oh, man, I'm sorry," Ben said. He looked away.

"Yeah, me too," she said. "I never knew my dad. My mother left him when I was five and remarried. He was driving drunk. Crashed his Ford into a concrete barrier at the bottom of one of our famous hills." She sighed. "Let's start walking, okay?"

They strolled along the waterfront, quietly, to the north entrance of Battery Park, past the parking lots along the West Side Drive and on to the high-rise apartment towers of Battery Park City, a community of upscale condominiums built on the western tip of lower Manhattan. Ben led Debby towards a playground. Several preschoolers ran amok while their mothers and nannies huddled with their takeout coffee mugs along the sidelines.

"This is my special place," Ben said. "Sometimes when it gets hectic at the office I come out here and watch the kids play at lunchtime."

"I can see how that could turn your day around," Debby said. "There's no sound more heartwarming than kids laughing and playing."

"Yeah," Ben agreed, then, smiling, pointed at one particularly energetic little boy, who was gleefully evading his harried mother. "Unless they're your own."

Debby giggled. "I wouldn't know."

"I should hope not."

"Oh, why's that?" Debby asked. "Would you think less of me if I had a child?"

"No, I guess not. I was just being flip," Ben said defensively. "Have you ever been married or had a kid?"

"No," she said, hesitating slightly. "I was in a serious relationship before I left San Francisco, but we were never engaged."

They walked north along the esplanade, an asphalt roadway that connected Battery Park City and the World Financial Center with spectacular views of the Hudson River along the way. A few joggers braved the icy winds whipping off the water. Ben instinctively turned his back to the wind, walking backwards about a step in front of Debby.

"Did you break it off?" Ben asked. He realized that the question might have been too intimate when Debby glanced down at the ground. "I'm sorry—is that too personal a question?"

"No, I don't mind talking about it," Debby said. Her smile appeared forced. "We'd been going out for about three months. I broke it off when I left for New York."

"How did he take it?"

Debby cast her eyes downwards, again. "I didn't tell him I was leaving."

"What!" Ben said, louder than he had intended.

"I was upset with him. Haven't you ever left a relationship by just not calling?"

It did not take Ben long to mentally check off his relationships with women. "Yeah, once, I guess," he admitted. A wave of guilt rippled through him as he recalled the incident with Quixote, his old friend at Harvard. He had behaved badly and regretted it ever since. "But we were just close friends. I mean, we never slept together. What did this guy do?"

Ben's eyes met with Debby's, as she contemplated one of the many split second decisions faced in any budding relationship. She turned and withdrew to the wrought iron fence overlooking the Hudson. Ben joined her at the rail. They stood quietly, listening to the gentle, rhythmic sound of water lapping against the sea wall.

"It's kind of hard for me to talk about," Debby said, finally.

"I'm sorry, I didn't mean to pry," Ben said. He smiled and changed the subject. "How 'bout those Knicks?"

Debby laughed. "Believe it or not, I'm a Warriors fan. One of a handful."

"You like basketball?" Ben asked.

"Sure. Does that surprise you?"

"I guess it shouldn't. I must be one of those mythical male chauvinist pigs."

Debby laughed, again. Ben was glad that he had so smoothly changed the mood back to upbeat, but was curious about what Debby's old boyfriend had done to deserve such an abrupt and final brush-off.

Debby also appeared relieved to put the topic of her past romances behind them. "The unicorn was mythical; the male chauvinist pig is very real and not even approaching extinction," she quipped.

"True enough," Ben chuckled. "Along with its close cousin, the Feminazi."

"I was actually into feminism at San Francisco State," Debby said. She put a hand on Ben's arm before he could react. "But don't get all defensive on me. I've reformed. I think that a woman should be independent, but in a kinder, gentler way. Like a partner, not a competitor."

"Kinder, gentler, huh? You're not a closet Republican, are you?" Ben joked. He knew that it was a much safer question than might first appear. Kramer, Fox was a well-known Democratic institution. Fritz Fox himself had close ties to President Norton. He had been offered the ambassadorship to Germany during Hank Norton's first term, in 1992, but had declined.

"Yeah, right. Fritz would have a baby before he hired a Republican paralegal. He was *not* very discreet in the interview on that topic," Debby said.

Ben tried out his new Fritz Fox imitation. "Vell, vell, vell, vat a surprise."

Debby flashed a toothy grin. "Not bad," she said. "You even have your hair flying all over the place like the Old Man."

Ben smiled, and looked down at his watch. "We should head back," he said.

They continued their small talk as they meandered through the narrow lanes on the west side of the tip of Manhattan. As they approached One Water, Debby broached the subject that had been on their minds for the last half hour.

"Ben," she started hesitantly. "Thanks for not pressing too hard about my old boyfriend. It's an emotional subject for me. I'll share it with you some time, but not just yet."

"It was rude of me to ask about it," Ben said. "I'd like for us to be friends, but, hey, if you don't ever want to talk about it, that's okay, too."

The issue made him a tad wary, but Ben was energized by how well he and Debby had clicked. The conversation had flowed almost as easily as on CyberLine. So often his real life infatuations ended in disappointment. He paused as he summoned courage from his reserves. Rejection was easier to accept on-line. There was no risk when you were anonymous; then, again, the payoff was not nearly as great, either.

"Listen," he said. "I'm going to look through Thompson's apartment tomorrow afternoon. It's right near Washington Square. Do you want to get together afterwards for some Mexican food in the Village?"

"Hmmm...sounds like a date," Debby said, smiling.

"Something like that," Ben grinned.

"Would it be okay if I came earlier and went through the apartment with you?" Debby asked. "That poem is weird. I'd like to stay involved if you don't mind."

"Not at all. I'd like that," Ben said sincerely. "I need a sounding board on some of this crazy stuff. I can't talk to Myra or any of the other partners. They'd think I'm either a pain in the ass or unprofessional."

Ben started to shift topics, again, as they climbed the steps of the concrete podium on which One Water rested, but Debby was distracted.

"Hold on a second," she said. She approached a man of the street who was standing on the low cement wall that lined the perimeter of the podium.

He was a tall, black man with long, matted hair and an overgrown beard. His powerful build was wrapped in a tattered army overcoat and capped with a black beret. He was shouting religious aphorisms to passersby who, with the sole exception of Debby, ignored him. He stopped when he recognized Debby. Ben warily followed.

"Merry Christmas, Hubert," Debby greeted the man warmly. He stepped down from the wall and smiled broadly. His large teeth were stained yellow. Ben guessed that he was about forty.

"And Merry Christmas to you, Miss Debby," Hubert said, bowing theatrically. "What brings you out on this cold afternoon." He blew on his hands and rubbed them together.

"Just walking with my friend, Ben," she said, pointing back to Ben. Ben acknowledged the introduction with a friendly salute. Hubert tipped his beret. Debby fumbled through her purse for a moment. She took out a twenty dollar bill from her wallet and slipped it into Hubert's hands discreetly.

"Buy yourself some gloves for the winter," she said as she turned towards the building. Hubert thanked her, then climbed back up onto the wall, resuming his religious banter.

When they were out of earshot, in the building lobby, Ben asked, "Why did you give him so much money? He's just going to get drunk with it."

She shrugged. "Maybe he will, maybe he won't. He always says 'hello' to me. I usually give him small change when I see him, but it's Christmas."

"Is he a drunk?" Ben asked.

"I don't think so. He just dropped out from society in the Sixties," she said. "He's a bright and funny guy who chooses to be homeless. I think he lives somewhere beneath the South Ferry subway station." She pointed across the street, to a building adjacent to the Staten Island Ferry terminal.

Ben was tempted to come back with a sly retort, but he let it go. She could hardly be faulted for her generosity. They crammed into a crowded elevator, with Debby's bundled body nestled snugly against Ben. The subtle aroma of her hair and perfume wafted upwards. *Fat naked men.*

SEVEN

THE VICE PRESIDENT'S low-profile leather chair was tilted back, his arms were folded behind his head, and his feet rested on the enormous partners' desk that had once been used by his hero, Theodore Roosevelt. "Be the voice of Black America," Tony Fabrizio said.

"That's exactly the role I've been trying to avoid for the last three years," LaRosa Smith said from her perch on a black Windsor chair opposite Fabrizio. The workspace was one of three distinct areas in the Vice President's cavernous office in the Old Executive Office Building. A casual sitting area was on the far end of the room, and a long mahogany conference table occupied the middle. "I want to be your advisor, not your *black* advisor."

"C'mon, Rosie. Everybody's an equal in my world, you know that, but we each bring a different perspective to the table," Fabrizio said. "If I need to peer into the minds of men, Italian-Americans or homely folks, I'm the guy. If I need insights into women, African-Americans or the beautiful people, I count on you."

LaRosa smiled broadly; her face was all cheekbones. "You could charm the coat off a mink," she said.

Fabrizio winked. "It comes with the job," he said.

"Okay," LaRosa said. She pondered what the Voice of Black America should tell the next President of the United States. She unconsciously played with the freshly cut hair on the back of her neck. It was a new look for her—short in the front, tapered in the back—and she was not yet accustomed to the bristly feeling.

"I think African-Americans are losing their patience," she said. "It's been more than thirty years since Dr. King was killed, and racial discrimination is still an issue, a very big issue. Black America expected more, faster, but recently it seems as if we're drifting backwards."

"How do you think that will impact the election next November?" Fabrizio asked.

"Honestly, I think race is going to be *the* issue in the election," she said. "And not just for African-Americans. It's a tense situation out on the streets. African-Americans are becoming increasingly willing to engage in violent protest, and mainstream America finds that threatening. Everyone will be looking to the candidates for solutions."

"It's like a chess match, though," Fabrizio said. "Every move we make will be countered by JJ Alexander."

"JJ's tough," LaRosa agreed. "His record on civil rights is excellent. With a Republican candidate like him, we don't own the race issue."

"It's frustrating," Fabrizio said. "How do you run a campaign when you agree with your opponent on most of the issues?"

"I hate to say it, but it'll probably come down to superficial issues and traditional territorial voting," LaRosa said. "Abortion will be a big one. JJ's probably locked up the South with his pro-life stand. Texas might have been a toss-up, but since it's JJ's home state, it's almost not worth campaigning there."

"But New York and the northeastern states are my backyard," Fabrizio said.

LaRosa thought that it sounded more like a question than a statement. "I agree," she said. "There are other smaller states that can still have an impact, but I think this election is going to be decided in California. And that worries me."

"We're only running slightly behind in the polls there," Fabrizio noted.

"There's a young, conservative demographic emerging on the West Coast that JJ may be able to tap into big time," she said. "They're into youth and beauty, and—"

"And I'm on the All-Ugly Team," Fabrizio interrupted, grinning. He jutted his large, square chin skyward and mugged for the nonexistent cameras. "A face only a mother could love."

LaRosa laughed. "Let's just say we might need a runoff in a beauty contest between you, Joe Torre and Rodney Dangerfield," she said.

Fabrizio winced. "Ouch."

LaRosa enjoyed the relaxed relationship with the Vice President. Many politicians preached about racial and sexual equality; Fabrizio practiced it. He said what was on his mind, but his mind was naturally disposed to valuing people for their talents, not their physique or their pedigree. He never gave the impression that he was censoring his thoughts to avoid offending the sensitivities of those around him.

"Seriously, it doesn't seem right, but JJ will win votes in California with that Heisman trophy and his All-American good looks," LaRosa said. "We need to play a little defense, if you'll pardon me stealing one of JJ's football puns. I think it's time to choose your vice president. Someone who'll help you win California."

"I already have a few ideas," Fabrizio said cautiously. "But you sound like you have a suggestion."

LaRosa had given this a lot of thought. "Tom Stevenson," she said without pause. Stevenson was the Democratic senator from California, the minority whip. He was the antithesis of the swarthy, thick-boned Fabrizio, who looked like a hoodlum and occasionally lapsed into the language of the streets. "He's blonde, he's got those wonderful square Scandinavian features, he's articulate—"

"And he's got great hair," Fabrizio said sarcastically, rolling his eyes.

LaRosa smiled sympathetically. "I know, I know. It's superficial as hell, but he's made for TV, and he's made for California," she said. "Politically, you two are a good fit, though, and he's got the best civil rights profile in Congress."

"I don't know, Rosie," Fabrizio said. "We're from different worlds. I like his politics, but he's a blue blood. I want a VP I can think out loud with. I don't want someone who's going to joke about my dumb-ass ideas with his bridge buddies at the end of the day."

LaRosa hesitated before responding. She had hoped, maybe unrealistically, that Fabrizio would buy into Stevenson without a fight. "There's another reason I think you need Stevenson," she said, averting his gaze. "But I had hoped to avoid this discussion."

"You know my rules—everything on the table," Fabrizio said. "No secrets, no lies."

No secrets, no lies. *Just spit it out, girl.* LaRosa knew that confidence was as important in politics as in sports. Think like a winner, the public sees a winner; think like you're on the ropes, the public sees a loser. Fabrizio thought he had a mandate from the Democratic party, and he was projecting the image of a presidential frontrunner. She did not want to deflate that confidence. But the signs were in the tea leaves, and she was Fabrizio's resident seer.

"Did you read the Op-ed piece Stevenson wrote in the *Post* last week in response to the *Herald Times* editorial?" LaRosa asked.

"You mean the one that got that Thompson fellow killed?" Fabrizio asked.

"Yeah. The *Herald Times* argued that the New York Board of Education's proposal to create a metropolitan area school district to force integration of the public schools was 'unnatural,'" she said. "Stevenson replied that—wait, let me read it exactly."

LaRosa reached into her purse and pulled out a folded newspaper clipping. She unfolded it, then read: "While I personally applaud the Board of Education's efforts, I can respect the opinion that forced school bussing across district lines is too expensive and burdensome to students. However, I find it intolerable that a respected institution such as the *Herald Times* could imply that the mixing of the races is unnatural."

"Yup. He handled it well," Fabrizio said. "But I have other ideas that might position us even better on the race issue. I'm no slouch on civil rights, either—I don't *need* Tom Stevenson."

"It's more than the issue itself, Tony. It's the tone of Stevenson's response, the timing," she said, then hesitated. *No secrets, no lies.* "He's leveraging his reputation as *the* civil rights guy in Congress in a year where civil rights is going to be *the* issue in the presidential election. He's going to make a run at you in the primaries. I can feel it in my bones."

Fabrizio's jaw dropped. He swung his feet off the desk and began pacing along an imaginary line. "No way, Rosie. There's no love between us, but he's a party man. We need to present a united front to beat JJ in November. No way."

"I'm as sure about this as I was about Illinois," LaRosa said.

Illinois had elevated LaRosa from political greenhorn to legend in 1996. Fresh out of Harvard Law School, she joined Hank Norton's presidential re-election campaign as a low-level staffer. She proved herself amazingly astute at gauging public opinion, and she rose through the ranks to become a key advisor to Norton's campaign managers by the end of the summer. Many on the staff credited her personally with carrying Illinois by orchestrating an all-night vigil by Norton in a South Chicago housing development on the eve of the election.

Norton carried Illinois by less than 20,000 votes, and Illinois turned
out to be the difference in the election. When LaRosa Smith talked,
Tony Fabrizio listened.

"Shitfuck," Fabrizio said. He tended to combine his two favorite
oaths when he was upset.

"Calm down, Tony, Stevenson's not that bad," LaRosa said.

"Fuckshit," he said. LaRosa fought the urge to laugh. With his
bushy eyebrows, dark sacks under his eyes, and droopy jowls, Tony
Fabrizio was a human cartoon. She had sat in the same chair for three
years—at first stunned, then amused—watching him cuss and stomp
back and forth like a target in a carnival shooting game. A path was
worn in the rug behind his desk from seven years of pacing.

"You'll still have me to bounce ideas off," LaRosa said. "You can
send Tom to funerals and put him in charge of the environment after
you win the election."

Fabrizio glanced skywards. "I had ideas, Rosie. This changes everything."

"Well, who did you have in mind?" LaRosa asked, wondering why
he had not discussed his plans with her before today.

Fabrizio stopped pacing. "I wanted to do something big—really
big—for the millennium election."

"An African-American?"

Fabrizio grunted. "Maybe. Maybe a woman."

LaRosa shut her eyes. She had abandoned her teaching career and
attended Harvard Law School to advance the causes of African-
Americans and women. She had already exceeded her expectations by
becoming Tony Fabrizio's right hand, his sounding board on critical
issues. But now she had an opportunity to influence history. Her next
words might determine whether America elected its first woman or
African-American vice president. *Shitfuck.* No secrets, no lies. *Fuckshit.*

"You know that no one would love to see an African-American or
woman vice president more than I would," she said. *You can still shift
gears, girl.* "But Tom Stevenson could beat you in the primaries, and JJ
Alexander *will* beat you in November if you can't carry California. You
need Tom Stevenson as your VP."

LaRosa fidgeted with her hands, observing Fabrizio's reaction. He
resumed pacing. He projected the image of a thick-skinned tough-guy,
but LaRosa knew that he was trying to hide the hurt.

She looked at her watch. Seven-fifteen. LaRosa had promised to cook Friday evening dinner for her mother. She had been ailing of late, and LaRosa tried to visit at least twice a week.

"Can I go ahead and put out some feelers with Stevenson's staff, Tony?"

"You think he can beat me?" he asked.

"Yes. Even if he doesn't, a nasty campaign will hurt you against JJ."

"Then what's in it for Stevenson?"

"Together you'd make a great team. He'd be better positioned for a presidential run in eight years."

"And you don't think a black or woman candidate will help me beat them?"

LaRosa shook her head. "Nope. Might even hurt."

Fabrizio paced the imaginary line, back and forth, back and forth. Finally, he stopped and simply said, "Set it up, Rosie."

EIGHT

BEN'S EYES DRIFTED between the computer screen on Adams Thompson's desk and stolen glances at Debby as she browsed through Thompson's book collection. It had been an enjoyable Saturday afternoon, mixing business with pleasure. They had inventoried the contents of Thompson's plush apartment together, all the while engaging in the idle banter of new found friends.

Ben tried to focus on the financial data on the computer, a top-of-the-line IBM Thinkpad laptop housed in a docking station. Thompson had demonstrated himself to be well-organized in his financial affairs, and it had soon become apparent to Ben that Calhoun College was about to receive a substantial windfall. He pressed a button on the keyboard to copy the data files on to a floppy disk.

"It's getting late," Ben said. It was almost half past six. "Are you hungry?"

"You bet," Debby said.

"It looks like Thompson's a CyberLine subscriber," Ben said. "All you have to do is guess his password, and then we can go."

"Okey dokey," she said. "What's his screen name?"

"The Publisher," Ben said.

"Try 'Herald Times,'" Debby said.

Ben entered it. "Nope."

"How about his middle name or his initials?"

Ben tried them both. "Nope, again."

"I don't know. Try 'Sesame' or 'Open Sesame.'"

"One step ahead of you, d'Artagnan," Ben said with his best French accent. "I already tried them."

Debby smiled back and touched his shoulder. She tried out her own accent. "Ah, I love it when you speak zee French to me."

"Oo-la-la! My pet, my sweet!" He puckered his lips in an exaggerated way.

She laughed. "Stick to the Musketeers, Ben. They're far sexier than Pepe le Pew," she said.

There was an extra bounce in Ben's step as they strolled the short distance down Fifth Avenue to Washington Square in the glow of the streetlights. There was something about connecting with a *live* friend, a psychic energy, that could not be replicated on CyberLine.

"Have you spent much time in the Village?" Ben asked as they passed under the giant Washington Arch, which marked the northern entrance to the Square.

"Not much," she said. "I still haven't met too many people in New York yet. I hang out mostly near my apartment on the Upper West Side."

"You should check out the city," Ben said. "I've only been down here a year and a half, but it feels like my backyard already."

"You didn't spend much time down here when you were growing up?" she asked.

"No, we stuck pretty much to Westchester," he said. "You know. Cub Scouts. Little League. Neighborhood picnics. Newspaper routes. Nintendo. Cutting grass. Grass growing."

Debby giggled. "You make it sound so exciting."

"I guess you don't know any better when you're a kid. It was safe, predictable. Everybody had their quirks, but basically everybody was the same. White. Middle class. Not quite the living dead or the Stepford Wives, but essentially boring."

"I see. So now I take it you're leading the life of the daring young sophisticate?" she said, smiling.

"Hardly. I love the city, but I've been too busy to take advantage of it," Ben said. "I think I was intoxicated by its finer points when I was a summer intern. The bright lights. Broadway. Bars. Parties. Perpetual motion. Every time you go out you don't know what or who will catch your interest. There's always an element of unpredictability, of danger. It makes life interesting."

"I'd love to see more of it," Debby said.

"Stick with me, kid," Ben said. His Humphrey Bogart imitation was passable. At least Debby recognized it.

"I think this is the beginning of a beautiful friendship," she shot back. They both laughed. Debby caught Ben off guard with a hip-check, knocking him off balance for a moment, but warming him to his core nonetheless. He found her playful habits endearing.

The smell of Middle Eastern food permeated the air as they exited Washington Square at the corner of West 4th and MacDougal Streets. An assortment of restaurants and bars occupied the brightly colored storefronts along MacDougal.

Ben stopped in front of *Sausolito's*. Instead of walking in, he led Debby down a short stairway below street level. A dozen wooden picnic benches lined the right wall of the dining area. The only lighting came from orange glass candleholders on the tables. About half of the benches were filled, mostly with college students. A handful of older men sat at the bar off to the left. Ben and Debby opted for a table in the back corner.

A waitress brought them menus. They ordered a pitcher of margaritas, no salt. Debby leaned over and whispered, "How did you ever find this hole in the wall?"

"A friend," Ben replied. "It isn't much to look at, but a starving wetback would kill for their guacamole."

Debby looked away. Ben sensed that he had offended her. The waitress brought the pitcher of drinks and took their order.

"Did I upset you?" he asked after the waitress left.

"Don't get me wrong, I can cuss with the best of them," she said with an awkward smile. "But I don't like ethnic slurs. I never found bigotry to be an attractive quality."

"I'm sorry. I'm really not a bigot, at all," he said. "I guess I was trying to be a little more colorful to impress you in my own humble way."

She smiled. "Humility," she said. "Now that's one of your most impressive characteristics."

"Hmmm. And what might my other impressive characteristics be?" Ben asked.

She paused as if deep in thought. Ben held his breath. She spoke in a slow, measured cadence. "You're intelligent. You have a great sense of humor. You're not *bad* looking."

Ben exhaled and laughed. It was more of a snort. "I can live with that," he said.

"Okay, now I'll put you on the spot, Mr. Wiseguy. What do you find impressive about me?" Debby asked.

The waitress returned with their appetizer. "Saved by the guac!" Ben said.

"Oh, you're not going to get off that easy, Benny boy," she chuckled.

Ben grimaced. "I've always wanted a nickname, but Benny brings to mind an image of an old Jewish guy with a Yiddish accent," he said.

Debby chuckled. "So what did your friends call you when you were a kid?" she asked.

"Just Ben," he said. He paused to scoop some guacamole with a tortilla chip. "I was one of those kids who couldn't find a nickname that fit."

"What would you want to be called if you could pick one?" Debby asked. She followed his cue and began eating as they spoke.

"You'll laugh."

"Try me."

"Hawkeye."

She laughed. "Hawkeye Kravner. King of the wild frontier. How did you come up with that one? Last of the Mohicans?"

"Nope. I was actually named after the lead character in the TV show M*A*S*H," he said. "Do you remember Hawkeye Pierce?"

"Sure. I watched the re-runs all the time."

"His name was Benjamin Franklin Pierce. *He* was nicknamed Hawkeye after his father's favorite character in literature, Natty Bumppo, from The Last of the Mohicans," Ben said. "I'm a child of the Seventies. My father named me after a TV character, but without the cool nickname."

"Believe it or not, I know what you mean," Debby said while munching on a loaded chip. "There's something about being tagged with a nickname that means you've been accepted. Mom moved around a lot after the divorce. At first I made new friends every time we moved. But it hurt so much to leave them each time, I stopped trying to make new ones."

"That's tough. What did you do?" Ben asked.

"I spent a lot of time alone. I like to draw, and I got pretty good at it," she said.

"Maybe some time you can show me your etchings."

"Very funny, Hawkeye."

Ben grinned his crooked grin. "I like it. I like it," he said.

The waitress delivered two pewter trays piled high with tacos, burritos, refried beans and rice. Debby looked at the plate uncertainly. Ben sensed that she might be wary about using her hands, so he hoisted a taco to his mouth. Debby eagerly followed suit.

"So what about you? Did you have a lot of friends?" Debby asked between mouthfuls.

"Until junior high," Ben said. "A string of best friends all moved away over a two-year span. I started to grow a hard shell after that, too."

"Really? You seem to have so many friends in the office," she said.

"We joke around," he said.

"Did you have a lot of girlfriends in high school?" Debby asked.

"A few good friends, but not too many dates," Ben said, blushing. "I didn't date much until college."

"Me, neither," Debby said. She smirked. "But I made up for lost time then."

Ben felt a surge of warmth. *Say something you idiot.*

After not too long had passed, Debby pushed her plate aside, crossed her arms and leaned forward on the table. "Sooo, you were going to tell me my impressive characteristics?"

"You're finished already?" Ben asked.

"Just taking a break," she said, smiling. "But don't you try to change the subject, again. Tell me about me."

Ben exhaled deeply. *Think before you talk.* "Well, you're intelligent. Confident. Down-to-earth. You have a quick wit. A beautiful smile," he said, gazing into her eyes. He hesitated just a split second. Testosterone. *Take a chance.* Adrenaline. *What if she rejects me?* Alcohol. *Take the path with heart.* "And eyes I could stare into forever."

Debby smiled brightly. "That's such a sweet thing to say," she said softly.

A feeling of controlled euphoria overtook Ben. *She didn't reject me.* "It's all true," he said.

They continued eating and talking until both of their plates, and the pitcher of margaritas, were empty. As Ben paid the check, it occurred to him that it had been a very long time since he could remember speaking so comfortably with a woman. But this was not the time to allow Quixote to haunt him. Three and a half years of pain and guilt was enough. *It's time to move on.*

The cold blast of air that hit them when they stepped outside took some of the edge off their after-meal stupor. Ben's euphoric feeling remained, enhanced by the margaritas. Debby stretched and yawned.

Ben wanted to kiss her. She patted her stomach. "Full belly, empty head," she said.

"Me, too. Feel like walking it off?" he asked.

"You bet," she said.

They walked and talked, down MacDougal Street, right on Bleecker. In and out of shops. It seemed so natural when Debby gave Ben her hand to hold as they turned up Sixth Avenue. A short time later, in a bookstore, was the moment love overtook him.

They were simply standing close, near the magazine rack, each flipping through pages of a different magazine. The bookstore was crowded. There were people on either side of them and behind. He could feel her heat. They silently began to breathe more deeply, rhythmically, in unison. The room became larger, the other people distant, as if an invisible stage had suddenly, slowly, mystically lifted them above the fray to a place of their own. Ben's mind was blank. They stared at the pages in front of them, but the flipping had ceased. For a magical moment, Ben did not know how long it lasted, they were joined by a force that he had never before experienced. It was electric.

Someone dropped a book with a loud bang. Ben blinked. The stage lowered. Ben and Debby flipped the pages of their magazines almost in unison. He still felt her warmth. His nerves still tingled from the residue of the energy that had surged through him. He was happy. *Did she feel it, too?*

Their hands were magnetically drawn together when they stepped out on to the street. They walked, in comfortable silence, towards West Fourth Street. It was almost eleven o'clock.

"It's getting a little late for me, Ben," Debby said. "I think I should grab a cab and call it a night."

Ben did not want the night to end. He hesitated awkwardly. *Tell her how you feel.* The alcohol was wearing off. "Okay, I'll flag one down," he said.

She frowned and looked away. A flash of panic whipped through Ben's being. "What's wrong, Deb?" he asked.

"I can see in your eyes that you're way ahead of me," she said, her voice cracking. "Can we go someplace quiet for a cup of coffee?"

Ben's heart sank. "Sure. There's a 24-hour diner right around the corner," he said.

The short walk was uncomfortable for Ben, the apparent connection broken. They sat in a booth in the back of the diner and ordered decaf. Debby seemed to have trouble finding words.

"What did you mean when you said I was ahead of you?" Ben asked. He tried not to let his hurt show.

"You had a look I've seen before," Debby said. "A puppy dog look."

A puppy dog look. Ouch. This was why CyberLine was so safe. There were no faces to read. Instinct was irrelevant. If you got rejected, you logged off, no regrets, no pain. Face to face, your soul was bared.

"I felt something tonight," Ben said sadly. "I thought you did, too."

She averted his eyes. "Ben, I'm not ready to be courted, again," she said. "I could use a friend now, but I'm not looking to fall in love."

But I felt your heat. You want me as badly as I want you. "It wasn't just me," Ben said.

"I like you a lot, Ben. But I'm not ready for another relationship yet."

"Does this have something to do with that boyfriend you left behind in San Francisco?"

"Yes."

"Are you married to him?"

"No!"

"Then what?"

She looked away, again. She peered out the window for what seemed an eternity to Ben. She turned back and stared directly into his eyes. Resolute.

"I had an abortion."

Ben let the words sink in. It was an issue he had debated with Quixote in the lunchroom at Harvard. They had both believed in a woman's right to choose, but he had angered her because his view of this painful, emotional issue for a woman was too academic. Now he saw the grief in Debby's features, and he understood.

"Did he support you through it?" Ben asked gently.

Silence. She cast her eyes down. "Oh, God," Ben said. "You didn't tell him, did you?"

Silence. "How could you not tell him?" Ben asked softly.

Finally, Debby spoke. "I was angry. I wanted to get out of San Francisco and leave everything behind."

"Were you in love with him?" he asked.

"I don't know. Maybe. Who knows? I'm not, anymore," she said. "That's not the issue."

"So what is the issue?" Ben asked.

"I can't have any entanglements at this point in my life," she said. "I need to sort out my emotions without creating a lot of new ones."

"What are you feeling?" Ben asked.

"Guilt. Anger. Confusion."

Why did women have to be so damn emotional about everything. They needed to take a more academic view if they wanted a choice. It was a survival tool. People would never eat if they thought about the cow's sad, droopy eyes before they gobbled down a cheeseburger.

"A fetus in the early stages isn't a life," Ben said. "The Supreme Court has basically said so."

The tears welled up in Debby's eyes now. She paused for several seconds before speaking. "I've always believed in a woman's right to choose," she said, avoiding Ben's gaze. "And I never once was concerned that a life was being taken. But then I felt something growing inside me, and it was alive. Maybe it didn't have thoughts or emotions, but it was growing and it had life."

"Sometimes we have to make hard choices," he said, his voice cracking slightly. *Be a man. No tears.* "What kind of a life would the baby have had if you didn't want it? You would've blamed it for ruining your life."

"Maybe, maybe not," she said. "I could have put it up for adoption. It was a selfish choice."

"I don't see it that way," Ben said. "You fixed a mistake before it could have a major impact on your life."

"It was alive, Ben," she said tearfully. "I killed it."

"It may have been growing, but it wasn't alive," Ben said earnestly. "Not in the way we care about. A plant grows. It has life, but it has no soul. The same with animals that we kill for food. There's something distinctly human that we're trying to protect."

He reached across the table and took both of her hands into his. There was nothing academic about what he was feeling now. "We have life," he said. "I can feel your emotion, your soul. A fetus has no thoughts, no emotion, no life. It doesn't know that anything is being taken from it."

Debby tried to smile. Her lips moved in all the right ways, but her eyes betrayed her sadness. "Thanks for talking to me," she said. "I haven't told anyone else about this. It helps to talk, but I just need time."

"If that's what you need, then I'll support you," Ben said. "I'll be there whenever you need a friendly ear."

"Or a hug?" she asked.

"You bet," he said.

She smiled. "Hey! That's my line."

They hailed two cabs. One took Debby up the West Side, the other took Ben up the East. Ben hugged Debby tightly before they parted. *There was hope.*

NINE

IT WAS MONDAY MORNING in Atlanta, but Ben did not have Georgia on his mind. In fact, little but thoughts of Debby passed through his consciousness since Saturday night. He was disappointed that their romance had taken an abrupt detour, but he would be a friend until she was ready for the relationship to blossom into something more. He kept replaying the scene in the bookstore and wondered how he could possibly have misread her feelings.

Ben's taxi arrived at Calhoun College promptly at nine o'clock. The Administration Building was a former plantation house in the traditional Southern style, a white clapboard mansion that could have been a stand-in for Tara in *Gone With the Wind*. A dozen other buildings, added over the years, were scattered among the dogwoods and pines that dotted the expansive campus.

Dean Frederick's assistant, Kimberly, met Ben at the reception desk and accompanied him to an interior conference room on the third floor of the Administration Building. Kimberly was Ben's image of classic southern beauty. She had long, blonde hair and wore a short, pale green dress that clung to her shapely figure. Ben could feel her aura of sexuality from several feet away. Her lips screamed to be kissed.

Ben felt guilty about his reaction, albeit involuntary. He was physically attracted to Debby, but the feeling that swept over him in the bookstore on Saturday night was the result of a longstanding infatuation, strengthened by the emotional bond that had developed over the past week. There was no emotional connection with Kimberly. It was pure animal instinct, unaided by unnatural scents.

"Buddy will be right in," Kimberly said with a drawl that made Ben's heart melt. "Can I get you a cup of coffee or a lemonade?"

"A lemonade would be *just* fine," Ben said. *Idiot.* His inflection no doubt sounded like a feeble attempt at a southern accent. He sometimes felt like Woody Allen's chameleon-like character, Zelig. A man whose averageness was made even more so by his innate capacity to adopt the salient characteristics of the people he was with at the time.

Ben meandered around the massive cherry conference table that occupied the room while he waited for Kimberly. The decorator had worked hard to create a dramatic impression. The table was surrounded by ten high-backed, black leather chairs. Ten portraits, framed in gold leaf, were hung inside large oak panels on three of the windowless walls. A framed glass enclosure was suspended in the center of one panel behind the head of the table; it contained a coat-of-arms, a Scotch plaid kilt—orange background with wide black and blue bands and a thin white stripe—and what appeared to be medieval weaponry. A built-in oak cabinet, with bookshelves on top, comprised the fourth wall, near the door.

Ben was thumbing through a picture book of Southern art he had selected from the shelves when Kimberly returned with a tall glass of lemonade. "Buddy should be up any minute now," she said, leaning over next to Ben and placing the glass and a coaster on the table beside him. Ben bathed in her aura.

"Is there anything else I can get for you?" she asked.

"No, thank you," Ben said, hoping that his manner did not betray his thoughts of all that she *could* do for him.

The door to the conference room swung open moments after Kimberly left, and a tall, wiry man with a full head of sandy hair plowed in, smiling broadly, his arm extended in greeting. "Good mornin', Ben," he said. "I'm Buddy Frederick. I'm glad you could make it down here today."

"Hello, Dean Frederick, it's nice to meet you," Ben said, rising to shake the Dean's hand.

"Please, call me Buddy—everybody does."

"Fair enough." Buddy Frederick was a good-looking man, Ben guessed that he was in his early forties, yet there was something about his presence, an insincerity, that made Ben uneasy. His body language did not match his words. He was like someone at a cocktail party who did not want to be there. A smirk seemed permanently etched on his face.

"Is this your first visit to Atlanta?" Dean Frederick asked.

"It's my first visit anywhere south of the Mason-Dixon line," Ben said.

Dean Frederick gave Ben another one of his well-practiced winning smiles. "Maybe after we finish our business I can take you to lunch and show you some of our fine town," he said.

"That would be great," Ben said, practicing his own winning smile. "Will I have time to visit Mr. Thompson's summer home in Ellijay?"

"That's a bit of a haul, about two hours northwest of here," Dean Frederick said. He paused. "I have a meeting this afternoon, but let me ask Kimberly if she can look after you instead."

"Super." Ben offered another winning smile. His jaw ached. He was at the same time panicked, excited and guilt-stricken about the prospect of spending the afternoon alone with Kimberly.

"You're all set," the Dean said when he returned, motioning Ben to sit. "So let's get down to it. Tell me about Adams Thompson."

Ben glanced at his notes, then launched into the short presentation he had prepared, borrowing liberally from the repertoire of Fritz Fox. "I'm prepared to tell you about Mr. Thompson's will and the bequest to Calhoun College, but I was hoping to gather some information, too," Ben said. "I didn't know Mr. Thompson personally, and I like to piece together the various parts of my client's life as I administer the estate. I may be the only person who ever has that opportunity, and I think of it as a tribute to his life to review it in its entirety."

"Adams would like that," Dean Frederick said. "In fact, I chose to meet in this room because it had some significance to my old friend."

"How so?" Ben asked.

"Let's deal with the dry stuff first, then I'll give you a history lesson that fascinated ol' Adams," the Dean said.

"Fair enough," Ben said. "Well, let me start by saying that the will does not become effective until it's probated by the Surrogate's Court for New York County as Mr. Thompson's last will and testament. We'll prepare a probate petition, which will set out the interests in the estate of Thompson's beneficiaries and any other persons adversely affected by the probate of the will. Mr. Thompson had no living relatives. If he had died without a will, the sole beneficiary of his estate would've been the State of New York. We'll serve legal process on the New York State Attorney General. If there are no irregularities in the will and the State doesn't contest its validity, the Court will issue letters testamentary to our firm, as the executor, and we'll proceed with the administration of the estate under the supervision of the Court."

"Which means we get the money," Dean Frederick said, his smirk threatening to break into a full-fledged grin.

"You get the money."

"Any chance the State will challenge the will?" Frederick asked.

"Most challenges are by disgruntled family members," Ben replied. "It's unlikely that the State would contest a bequest to a charity or an academic institution."

"How large an estate did ol' Adams have?"

"Marshaling the estate's assets will be our most time consuming task. We've gathered some documentation and started—"

"Ballpark it for me," Frederick interrupted.

Ben pushed his legal pad to the side and leaned back in his chair. "Thompson's Fifth Avenue apartment and the furnishings will probably be valued at well over one million dollars," he said. "I don't know the value of the house in Ellijay. He has a Mercedes. My preliminary and unofficial estimate of his liquid assets is about five million dollars."

"Mmm, mmm. There's a lot of fine work we can do with that kind of money," the Dean said. "We'll do my old friend proud. When do you think the College will see any of it?"

"It's hard to say. Probably a few months."

"What about any historical documents? Did you find anything in Adams's papers?" Dean Frederick asked.

Ben shifted in his chair. "What do you mean?"

"Adams and I shared a love of history," the Dean said. "He was a collector of historical documents. He also told me that he had written some essays. I'd like to get those items as soon as possible so that we can set up a memorial exhibit. If his writings are significant, we might even consider establishing a program of study based on them."

Ben considered whether he should say anything about the sealed envelope or the poem. *Better not.* "He had some personal papers in his safe deposit box," Ben said warily. "I don't know if I'd recognize anything of historical significance if it hit me in the face, though."

Dean Frederick chuckled. "Maybe not. But if you can send me those documents, I sure would appreciate it," he said. "Adams mentioned something about leaving some of the more valuable ones in trust for the college."

Don't panic. Ben wondered if he had missed something in the trust document. Did Dean Frederick know about the poem or was he just fishing? "I'll have to check into that," Ben said as calmly as he could. "Fritz Fox, my boss, had a heart attack last week, and we're a little disorganized. But I don't think we can distribute anything from the estate until the Court issues the letters testamentary."

"I understand," Dean Frederick said, the disappointment evident on his face. "I'm sure you'll do your best for us."

"There's one other request that Mr. Thompson made in a letter accompanying the will," Ben said. He reached into his briefcase and pulled out an urn. "He asked that we give you his ashes. The letter said that you'd know where to scatter them."

"I'm sure he meant the lake behind his home in Ellijay."

"Would you like me to do that for you this afternoon?" Ben asked.

"No, it's a personal tribute that I'd like to pay to ol' Adams myself," Dean Frederick said. He took the urn and held it up sideways, in both palms, bouncing it gently. "Well, you wanted to know about Adams Thompson?"

Ben felt the tension flow from his body at this signal that his first public performance was over. "Very much so," he said.

Ben prepared to listen politely, but images of the lovely Miss Kimberly were already teasing the fringes of his conscious mind. He knew from experience that those fantasies would soon consume him, reducing the Dean to nothing more than a talking head.

Dean Frederick jumped up and retrieved a jug and two glasses from the oak cabinet. "This Scotch whiskey is almost 170 years old," he said, pouring about two fingers' worth into each glass. "And there's a marvelous story that goes with it. One that fascinated Adams.

"We call this room the MacDougall Room," the Dean continued. He circled his arm around the room in a sweeping gesture. "These portraits are of the ten children of James Earl MacDougall, II and his wife Ann. That's Jimmy, the oldest, to the right of the coat-of-arms. Alex. Freddy. Kate. Tommy. Glenn. Andrew. Danny Boy. Stewart. And little Colleen. Georgia was settled by the Scots, and the MacDougalls immigrated here around 1830. This jug was one of several that they brought with them from Scotland."

In the blink of an eye, Ben's mental picture of Kimberly was snuffed. Something was *definitely* wrong. The math was easy. Jimmy.

Seven brothers and sisters two. The Dean knew about the poem. He tried to maintain a relaxed and interested look while he calculated his quickest escape route.

"They staked a claim to three hundred acres of prime north Georgia farmland and turned it into one of the most productive cotton and tobacco plantations in the South," Frederick continued. "James died in 1838, and young Jimmy took over the leadership of the MacDougall clan. Are you familiar with the history of the South around these times, Ben?"

"Not the details," Ben replied. "Everybody knows that slavery was a big issue then."

"It was a passionate issue for Jimmy MacDougall. They had a problem with runaway slaves, and he dedicated himself to preserving slavery as an institution. His activities caught the attention of none other than John Calhoun, the legendary senator from South Carolina, the leading proponent of slavery in Congress and the benefactor of this fine college.

"Calhoun had presidential aspirations," the Dean said. "But he supported Martin Van Buren's bid for re-election in 1840 to maintain Democratic party unity. Van Buren was a Yankee, a New Yorker, but he defended the Southern States' right to permit the institution of slavery. William Henry Harrison was the Whig Party candidate."

Ben noticed Frederick scrutinizing his reaction to the mention of Harrison. He forced himself to maintain his composure. "What was Harrison's position on slavery?" Ben asked.

"That, Ben, was precisely the question on John Calhoun's mind," Dean Frederick said, waving his right index finger in the air. "Harrison was a Yankee with southern roots. He was careful not to take a stand on the slavery issue. He sought support by offering food, hard cider and catchy campaign slogans rather than intelligent positions."

"I remember that from one of my high school history classes," Ben said. "They called it the Hard Cider Campaign."

"I'm impressed," Dean Frederick said, pressing his lips together tightly. "Well, Calhoun realized that Harrison was winning the hearts of Americans with the fervor of his campaign, and he was certain that deep down in his Yankee heart Harrison was an abolitionist. At Calhoun's bidding, a band of about two hundred Southern Democrats, including Jimmy MacDougall and two of his brothers, trekked on horseback to a massive rally at the site of Harrison's greatest military victory—the Battle of Tippecanoe."

Ben once again thought he noticed the Dean studying him. *Gotta throw him off.* Ben snapped his fingers. "Tippecanoe and Tyler, Too," he chuckled. I nearly drove my parents mad repeating that slogan. I couldn't get it out of my mind."

"Well, Old Tip drove the Southern Democrats mad, too," the Dean said, smiling. "And they were determined to force him to take a stand on the slavery issue at the rally."

"Were they successful?" Ben asked.

"No," Dean Frederick said. "In fact, the day ended in tragedy. Harrison moved through the crowd all afternoon, pausing to shake hands and sip cider with his well-wishers. Jimmy and his boys prepared to taunt Harrison as he approached, but Jimmy recognized a Negro man standing near Harrison as a runaway slave from the MacDougall plantation. He rushed towards the slave, and Harrison, with his knife bared, then stabbed the Negro to death."

"My God," Ben said. "Did Harrison think it was an assassination attempt?"

"If Harrison knew that his life had never been in jeopardy, he didn't say," the Dean continued. "He presided over a kangaroo court that convicted Jimmy of murder and sentenced him to die by hanging."

Ben swallowed hard. There could be no doubt. Jimmy MacDougall was the subject of the poem found in Adams Thompson's safe deposit box. But what did it all mean? Why was Dean Frederick telling him this story?

"When Jimmy's brothers returned to the MacDougall plantation and related their misadventure to their mother, she fainted from grief," the Dean continued. "She died a week later, some say from a broken heart, others say she took her own life. In either case, the MacDougall clan was never the same."

Dean Frederick shook his head. "I have this vivid picture in my mind. The nine remaining siblings gathered at the grave site, dressed in the family tartans," he said, pointing to the frame on the wall that held the plaid garments. "The sounds of 'Amazing Grace' playing on the bagpipes, wafting in mournful elegance through the forest."

"That's such a haunting image," Ben said. He wondered why the MacDougall family portraits and tartans were displayed here. He tried to recall the words to the poem. In his present state, he could only remember that it was about vengeance and the millennium.

"They all left the plantation some time after that. Nobody knows exactly why or what became of them. Adams and I have tried to track them down, but records were not great back then, and we could not find a trace of them. There is an uncorroborated story that all of the MacDougalls' slaves were killed in a fire that was intentionally set, and the MacDougalls fled under false identities to escape prosecution."

So that was it! They had murdered their slaves to avenge Jimmy's death. Helpless men, women and children. Killed in the most gruesome manner imaginable. Ben clenched his teeth. "How many people did they murder?" Ben asked.

"There were over fifty," the Dean said. "None survived."

"Why are you honoring these people as if they were heroes?" Ben asked incredulously, gesturing at the ring of portraits around the room. "And why was Adams Thompson so fascinated by them?"

Ben realized that his tone had been sharper than he had intended by the expression of surprise on Dean Frederick's face. An image of Fritz Fox shaking his head disapprovingly suddenly appeared in Ben's mind's eye. *We save this indignation for the courtroom.*

The Dean rocked gently in his chair. "I think Adams Thompson was mesmerized by the sheer emotion that overwhelmed an entire family," he said calmly. "They gave up their wealth and somehow disappeared without a trace. Did they become outlaws in the Wild West? Or run off to Europe or South America? Nobody knows."

Ben stroked his mustache. Could the poem have been Thompson's fictional account of the legend of the MacDougalls? That would be a rational explanation for it. Perhaps the only rational explanation. Still, something strange was happening. The Dean was testing him. He wanted to know if Ben had seen the poem. *Why?*

"As for these portraits 'honoring' the MacDougalls," the Dean continued. "The plantation was deeded to John Calhoun on the condition that it be converted to an institution of higher education with the objectives of developing new agricultural techniques and perpetuating the institution of slavery. The slavery clause was illegal after the Civil War, of course, and was annulled. A second condition was that these portraits be hung in a prominent location to forever preserve the MacDougall name. We hardly ever bring guests up here, but I felt the occasion of Adams's death warranted it. I hope I haven't caused you any undue embarrassment."

Ben blushed. He had offended his first client. "I'm sorry," he said. "I have a tendency to shoot off my mouth at the first sign of perceived injustice. I didn't mean to be disrespectful."

"No worries here," Dean Frederick said. "The MacDougalls are an interesting story, but no great source of pride for us." He leaned forward and put his hands on his knees. "Shall we drink a toast to our friend Adams?"

"I could use a drink," Ben said with a crooked grin.

The Dean slid one of the Scotch glasses to Ben and lifted the other. "To Adams George Thompson, Jr.—may his name go down in history side by side with the legends he loved," the Dean said.

Buddy Frederick drained the Scotch in one gulp. "Hear, hear," Ben mumbled, then followed suit.

Kimberly was waiting outside in her red Jeep with a packaged lunch when the meeting ended. Ben was drained. Kimberly still held an allure to him, but the sexual energy that had initially overcome him had petered out. He looked out the window and ate his sandwich quietly as they drove. The silence seemed to make Kimberly uncomfortable.

"How do you find Atlanta?" she asked.

As tired as he was, Ben could not resist. "I usually go to Savannah and make a right," he said, smiling.

Kimberly rolled her eyeballs skyward, shook her head and grinned. "Everybody's a comedian."

"Sorry. You led with your chin," he said. "Actually, I think Atlanta's beautiful. I love the way the forest comes right up to the city."

"Yeah. I've lived here all my life and wouldn't think about living anywhere else," she said.

"It's different than I anticipated," Ben said. "Most of my expectations were formed from TV and the movies."

"Well I hope your first southern encounters were more like scenes from *Gone With the Wind* than *Hee Haw*."

Ben laughed. He tried on a southern accent. "Frankly, Miss Kimberly, I'm finding the South to be quite charmin'."

She snickered. "Well, Mr. Ben, I never, ever would have figured you for a snake oil salesman. You New York lawyers seem like all business. Always so serious."

Ben looked out the window, as Kimberly steered the Jeep onto the highway. "I feel like a kid playing a grown-up game sometimes," he said softly.

"What do you mean?" she asked.

"One day you're a kid goofing around with your friends, the next day you're in a suit and tie. You feel as if you're supposed to be serious and business-like, but inside you're still this goofy guy," Ben said. "Like I'm staying at the Ritz-Carlton this trip. The first thing I did was bounce on the bed a couple of times and then stood there grinning like an idiot when I peed in that shiny marble bathroom. I don't know why I'm telling you this."

Kimberly smiled. "It's because I'm easy to talk to."

"Maybe so," Ben said. "So, how do you like Atlanta?"

"It's the only place I've known," she said. "I've got my little apartment in Buckhead. Lots of restaurants and night clubs nearby. It's easy to meet people. I can't complain. What about you—do you have your own place in New York?" she asked.

"Uh-huh. I live in a high-rise in Manhattan. Buckhead sounds similar, except we've got forty levels stacked on top of each other."

"I couldn't live like that," she said. "I need space. Sometimes I take my Jeep and drive to the Chattahoochee River and just hike along the trails by myself for hours."

"That's cool. I think we all need space. That's probably why New Yorkers are so cranky," Ben said.

She laughed. "Well, you're not so bad for a cranky New Yawker."

"Not a bad accent for an amateur. By the time you get home tonight you'll be speaking New York like a native."

"Oh, God help me, no," she said. "I'll have to watch Andy Griffith and Dukes of Hazzard re-runs for a week!"

They chattered on for the next hour and a half. They exited the highway as the mountains approached, and drove along the fringe of the Blue Ridge for about forty miles before reaching Thompson's Ellijay home.

The cabin was small. It had only one level. The front door opened into a living room, with a blue plaid sofa facing a fireplace. A striped oval area rug covered the hardwood floors between the sofa and fireplace. A glass sliding door on the back wall opened to a deck outside. The kitchen was off to the right; a single bedroom was to the left.

A desk in the bedroom revealed nothing of value. A copy of the CyberLine software was loaded on a computer, but there was nothing else of interest.

Kimberly was watching television on the sofa when Ben emerged from the bedroom. "Find anything interesting?" she asked.

"No, it looks like we both wasted our time," he said. "It was just something that needed to be done."

"Well…it doesn't have to be a total waste," Kimberly said coyly, as she slunk towards Ben.

He felt her aura coming. A surge of testosterone restored his earlier energy. He tensed. "What do you mean?" he asked. *Idiot. Be a man. Don't make her spell it out.*

"I saw a hot tub out back. We could fire it up for a bit, then come back in and warm up."

The blood rushed from his brain and elsewhere to a single point. Not even thoughts of fat naked men could help now. *What about Debby?* He smiled weakly. "I didn't think to bring swim trunks," Ben said. *Idiot. You're not committed to Debby. She said she's not ready to fall in love.*

Kimberly giggled. She came up close to him. Real close. He was consumed by her sexuality. "This is the South, silly; y'all won't get arrested for some good old-fashioned skinny-dippin'."

She leaned in and kissed him gently on the lips. His body was on fire. She slid her hand up the inside of his leg. "C'mon, let's have some fun, Ben. I can feel you want to."

He did not pull away. *But I'm in love with Debby.* Kimberly kissed him again, this time firmer, longer. *But she doesn't love me.* He placed his hands on her back and pulled her closer. *It's been four months.* He could feel her panties and her warmth through the thin green dress. Their tongues met, their breathing quickened, his hard-on pulsated. Kimberly pressed her pelvis into him gently.

Ben's psyche became a battlefield as the passion escalated. *God, I want her. Lift up her dress and be a man. But Debby. Just fuck her. Debby will never know. We're just friends, anyway. But there's still hope. It's been four months—fuck her, dammit. I need to build trust. Now or never, fool, make your move.*

Ben pulled away. "What's the matter, Ben?" Kimberly said with an exasperated, almost desperate tone. Her hair was disheveled.

"I'm sorry, Kimberly. I just can't. I want to. God, I want to. But I'm starting a new relationship with someone and I can't start it like this. I'm so, so sorry."

Kimberly sat down on the floor, leaning against the back of the sofa. "Oh Lord, I'm so embarrassed. I thought we had a connection."

Ben sat down next to her. They were both still breathing heavily. "I've never felt so connected to anyone in my life," he said. "You turned me on the second we met."

"Really?"

"Absolutely."

"This doesn't happen very often."

"You're perfect. A guy would have to be nuts not to want you. I'm nuts! Hell, I'm a fucking raving lunatic."

"Yes you are. But you're a sweet fucking raving lunatic." She smiled.

The ride back to Atlanta was quiet. Kimberly asked some questions about Debby. Ben asked some questions about Atlanta. They were both knocked out from the battle between their hormones and their minds. Kimberly kissed Ben sweetly on the cheek when she dropped him off at the Ritz, and he promised to call her if he was ever back in Atlanta. It was a quarter past five o'clock.

There was a message for Ben to call the office. Quitting time for the secretaries at Kramer, Fox was five-thirty.

"Ben! Geez, Louise! Where have you been?" Carol, his secretary, said. It was unusual for her to be so excited.

"Just taking care of business down here," Ben said calmly. "What's up?"

"Your office was trashed this morning! We've been trying to get you all day."

"What happened?" Ben asked.

"Somebody broke in over the weekend. It's a mess. There are papers everywhere."

"Shit! Who did it? What were they looking for?"

"The police were in there," Carol said. "We can't tell what they took yet. The police want to talk to you."

"Okay. I have an early flight tomorrow morning. Can you transfer me to Debby Barnett?"

Debby was eager to talk. "Ben! Are you okay? Did you hear about your office?"

"Yeah. Carol told me. I'm fine. Did you get a chance to look in there? Could you see if they were going after anything in particular?"

"It's a mess. They wouldn't let me in until about an hour ago. Leo was down there, but nobody else," she said. She lowered her voice to a whisper. "Was the poem on your desk?"

"No. I have it with me in my briefcase," he said.

"Good," Debby said. She sounded relieved. "You've got to put it back in the envelope."

"What?" Ben said.

"I started cleaning up the mess in your office," she said hesitantly. "I found the second trust agreement you were looking for. I must have accidentally filed it with the tax memos when I was rushing to put together the package for you."

Ben closed his eyes. This was big. He had breached his duty as trustee. "Fritz will be livid," Ben said.

"I know," Debby said. "I'm really sorry. I'll tell him it's all my fault."

"We'll figure out how to deal with it tomorrow," Ben said. "Strange things are happening down here, too. People care about that poem a little too much. I can't wait to talk to you tomorrow."

"I've been thinking about you all day today," she said. "Were your ears ringing?"

"More than you can begin to imagine."

TEN

AT THE SAME TIME KIMBERLY FREDERICK left Ben Kravner at the Ritz-Carlton on Monday evening, Cal Stewart sat at his squeaky clean desk admiring her likeness in a series of photographs that he had received from a private investigator. He was amazed at what The Caretaker would ask his daughter to do in the name of The Royal Order—although she seemed to be enjoying herself in these pictures. He slipped the photos into a manila envelope and sealed it. He printed the name "Dr. Raymond Allgood" in block letters on the front.

Stewart glanced at the wall clock and clenched his teeth. It was only a short walk across the campus of the National Institutes for Health to the Director's office, but Allgood was late once again. Stewart was going to enjoy watching him squirm. *Last time that uppity Nigra shows me up.*

He rotated in his chair and glared through the wall of glass that overlooked the expansive NIH grounds. *In one year they'll all be squirming.* It was a prospect that was at the same time gratifying and troubling.

Cal Stewart learned of his role in the fate of the Negro race in America on his thirteenth birthday. It had been an exciting moment. One that still resonated in his mind, still made his heart pound. His father's eyes had been ablaze, his voice filled with pride. The Stewarts, the entire MacDougall clan, were destined for greatness.

Francis Stewart had evoked the memories of the great Scottish heroes of generations past. William Wallace, Robert Bruce, the Stuart kings and all of the brave Highlanders who perished at Culloden fighting for justice. The MacDougalls would have their own justice, he had proclaimed. The presidency would fall. The Negro race would be vanquished forever.

Vanquished. It was the word that had been passed down to each of the members of The Royal Order by their fathers. But the concept made him uneasy. He feared that his more powerful cousins had a far different vision of the Final Vengeance than he had.

He would be satisfied if blacks were simply put back in their place. Eliminate affirmative action. Permit discrimination. Just let nature take its course. Their natural inferiority would assure that justice prevailed in the end. Let them start the civil war.

But some of the others advocated a stronger approach. The General seemed eager to initiate war. And The Spy, who Stewart perceived as the most unbalanced of the lot, fervently believed that nothing short of the racial cleansing of the land would satisfy the spirits of their fore-fathers. He could not read the thoughts of The Speaker, The Senator and The Caretaker.

Stewart took some comfort that The Heir Apparent, their leader, appeared to take a more moderate view. Ever cautious not to break the alliance that had been crafted over a century and a half, The Heir Apparent had advocated triggering a brief war, with blacks accepting a subordinate role under the terms of surrender. At least he was not call-ing for the butchering of innocent men, women and children.

Dr. Allgood arrived fifteen minutes late. He smiled and gripped Dr. Stewart's hand heartily. The tall, broad, black man towered over Stewart, whose scholarly hunch made him appear even shorter than his five-foot, seven-inch frame.

"Cal, good to see you. Sorry I'm late," Allgood said. His deep, boom-ing voice enhanced his commanding presence. "I had a call from Dr. Hobert in Paris that I had to take. It's late there. They're doing some exciting research on the role of retroviruses on the etiology of AIDS, and they've made some discoveries that may provide a link to identifying the role of viruses in the development of human cancer. They want to know if we can still get funding to participate in the research next year."

"You know the budget has been fixed for some time now, Ray," Stewart said.

"This sounds like a real break-through project, though. I don't think we want to miss out on it."

"Write up a proposal, and we'll talk about it." Stewart was irritated. This was supposed to be his meeting. "Listen, have a seat. I called you because I have a personal favor to ask."

Dr. Allgood sat. He ran his hand through his close-cropped hair, which had only recently begun to gray at the temples. "Sure. What's up?"

"A friend of mine runs a small college in Atlanta," Stewart said. "They're trying to develop their medical program, and he asked me if we can throw some extramural research funds their way to finance a cancer research study next semester."

"What's the objective?" Allgood asked.

"They're investigating the long term carcinogenic effect of certain FDA-approved pharmaceuticals."

"So they want to track case studies?" Allgood asked.

"No. Their theory is that there are too many uncontrolled variables in the general population. They want to use life prisoners at a Georgia penitentiary."

"You know as well as I do that we can't support potentially danger-ous research on prisoners," Dr. Allgood said. He leaned forward. His eyebrows furrowed downward. "Are you testing me, Cal?"

Stewart leaned back in his chair. He raised his open palms in a ges-ture intended to soothe. "Calm down, Ray. I think this is important research. We may have to run a little wide of the rules, but we can pull it off."

"No way, Cal. If they wanted to start in January, they should have applied last February like everybody else."

"I can use the Discretionary Fund," Stewart said. "If you make the request, I'll grant it."

"The application still needs to pass through OPRR," Allgood said. The Office for Protection from Research Risks was charged with pro-tecting humans and animals from overzealous research scientists.

"But I make the final judgment as to whether an activity is covered by the policy on human experimentation."

"There are special rules for prisoners," Allgood said. "There's no way you can approve this project."

"We both know there are shortcuts. Help me out here, and I'll see what I can do to fund your virus research."

Allgood folded his arms and stared at Stewart angrily. "That's not fair," Allgood said. "My project is cutting edge; yours is illegal. Plain and simple."

"Ray, I'm afraid you have to help me on this one," Stewart said.

"Look, I'll find another way to get in on the virus research," Allgood said. "I'm sorry, Cal. I take the law seriously."

"This is not about tit-for-tat," Stewart said. "You're going to help me whether or not I help fund your precious research."

Allgood looked stunned. "I will not participate in this conversation any longer," he said, rising from his chair.

Uppity Nigra. "Sit down, Dr. Allgood!" Allgood froze in his tracks. Stewart knew that the sharpness in his voice was out of character; it felt good. Allgood glowered at Stewart. He did not sit.

"If you want my resignation, you'll have it in the morning," Allgood said.

Stewart slid the manila envelope across the desk. "You'll want to see this before you do anything rash," he said. "You have a family to think about."

"What's this?" Allgood asked.

"Take it back to your office and think about it," Stewart said. "You'll get an application in the mail this week from Calhoun College. Approve it, then send it to me. I'll work it through the process. Before you sign it, though, I want you to make one change. The prison population in Georgia is disproportionately African-American. We can't risk having a nearly all-white institution like Calhoun College doing experiments on blacks with all of the racial unrest we've seen lately. Limit the test group to white prisoners. They can use blacks in the control group."

"You're insane. You'll have my resignation in the morning."

"You may tender your resignation if you desire, but I strongly suggest that you review the contents of the envelope before you make your decision."

Allgood's jaw was firmly locked. Fire danced in his eyes. He snatched the envelope from the desk and stormed out of the room, slamming the door behind him.

It was after six o'clock. In a bad movie, Cal Stewart thought, his sinister laugh would have echoed through the empty hallways of the NIH displacing the fading echo of the slamming door. But he was not a theatrical man. Instead, he just smiled. It was a sinister smile.

ELEVEN

A VETERAN REPORTER STEPPED FORWARD from the pack gathered outside the Russell Senate Office Building, the most prestigious of the three Senate office buildings in the Capitol Hill complex.

Aw, hell. JJ Alexander cursed to himself. His thinning, gray-streaked, blonde hair billowed in the frigid breeze as he crossed Constitution Avenue. It was five o'clock on Monday afternoon, and the 56-year-old former football star was in no mood to talk to the press.

"Senator Alexander, can you comment on the rumor that Tom Stevenson will be announced as Tony Fabrizio's running mate within the next few days?" the reporter asked. The pack encircled Alexander.

Goddam wolves. "I have time for two or three questions," Alexander said. A bouquet of microphones and tape recorders were thrust in his face.

"Do you fear a Fabrizio-Stevenson ticket?" the same reporter asked.

Alexander laughed heartily. "Hell, I'm no stranger to fear," he drawled. "I played quarterback in the NFL against the Purple People Eaters in Minnesota. I *feared* Carl Eller and Alan Page. I fought in the jungles of Vietnam and was a POW for two years. I *feared* the Viet Cong. But Tony Fabrizio and Tom Stevenson? Naw, I don't fear them. They're pussycats compared to the demons I've faced."

He pointed to a middle-aged woman in a red parka. "Senator Alexander, there's been speculation that Fabrizio's staff might be the source of the Stevenson rumor in an attempt to cut off an ambush," she said. "Who do you think would be a more formidable opponent next November, Fabrizio or Stevenson?

Alexander resisted the urge to roll his eyes. *That's right, sweetheart, you're so smart you're going to make me look like a dumbass country boy on national TV.* "Tony Fabrizio and Tom Stevenson are both fine gentle-man, and either would be a worthy adversary," Alexander said. "But, hell, the American people are ready for real change—a Second American Revolution—and I'm prepared to give it to them. Fabrizio and Stevenson represent Democratic politics as usual. Spend, spend, spend, spend, spend. You give me any Democrat you want in November, and I'll kick his ass."

The press corps erupted in laughter; they had their clip for the six o'clock news.

"Last question, folks," Alexander said, then pointed to an older man in a wool overcoat.

"Senator, would you consider Governor Hodges or Senator Gibbons as a running mate to neutralize the Stevenson factor?" the man asked.

Alexander was skeptical of the value of any woman on the ticket, but he viewed Cindy Hodges as an insincere bitch. The thought of sharing the Republican ticket with her turned his stomach. Harley Gibbons was a space cadet. That might help in California, but would cost him the rest of the country.

"I've had informal conversations with several candidates for the vice-presidential slot, but I can't comment on that right now," he said. "Thank you very much, folks. I've gotta run."

Alexander hurried up the steps, ignoring the flurry of questions that ensued, then rushed through the metal detectors just inside the door. An alarm sounded.

"Damn. Must be that metal plate in my head from Vietnam," Alexander said. He winked at the Capitol Police officer stationed at the security checkpoint, then stepped back through the metal detector.

Alexander knelt down and lifted up his right pants leg. He pulled a Smith & Wesson .22 caliber revolver out of a black leather ankle holster, and handed it to the officer. He purchased the weapon after a Congressman, Bert Rice, a kid from Oklahoma, was held up at knifepoint three weeks earlier. The pistol was light on firepower, but it gave Alexander a sense of control in a town that seemed to be spinning out of it.

"Sorry, Phil," he said to the security officer. "Sooner or later I'll remember I'm carrying that damned pea-shooter."

"No problem, Senator," the officer said, returning the weapon to Alexander after he passed through the metal detectors without triggering the alarm. Congressmen were permitted to carry firearms in federal buildings; staff and visitors were not.

Alexander climbed the marble staircase to the third floor. He waved a hasty greeting to his clerical staff, then closed the door to his office, Russell 315, one of the largest in the building. The room was lavishly decorated, befitting the Senate Minority Leader. The Texas state flag was displayed prominently by the door. An entire wall was devoted to photographs of Alexander with distinguished colleagues and guests. A royal blue sofa was strategically placed opposite the photo gallery.

Alexander plopped into his worn leather chair. An antique walnut desk abutted the window, offering an unobstructed view of the Capitol Building across Constitution Avenue.

The weary senator stroked his chin. Powers greater than nature seemed to be forcing his hand. Perhaps the spirits of his departed ancestors were sending him a message from the great beyond. Within the same week, the troubling rumors about Tom Stevenson had emerged, and he had learned of the unexpected reappearance of The Assassin.

JJ Alexander had learned that his destiny was to be president on his thirteenth birthday when his father crowned him as The Heir Apparent. Everything he had done since then—Green Beret, star quarterback, Congressman, Senator—had been carefully crafted to achieve that glorious moment for his father. George Alexander was almost ninety now, in poor health, but he was determined to live to see The Royal Order claim their ancestors' Final Vengeance. And, dammit, JJ Alexander was not going to fumble the ball in the closing minutes of the game!

It was funny, he thought, how our fathers made the rules and each of us played out the game no matter how at odds with our basic nature. He had overcome an intense fear of death, by sheer force of will, to return home from war a hero. He had played football to build his popularity on a national scale despite a loathing of physical violence. He had excelled in the world of politics even though his natural quiescence and intellectual curiosity would have better suited him for a career in academia or science.

He had transformed himself into what his father wanted him to be. And by the time The Royal Order of the Millennium Knight convened in 1995, Alexander had been well-situated, as the Senate Minority Leader, to land the Republican vice-presidential nomination in 2000— at least as well-situated as anyone could have been.

But when the Knights had begun to fill in the details of the rough game plan envisioned 155 years earlier, they had realized that their ancestors had not thought this conspiracy all the way through. It was difficult enough to place a candidate in a position to win a presidential election; it was nearly impossible to arrange a successful vice-presidential nomination. There were too many factors outside of their control. The nomination depended on the political needs and whim of the presidential candidate, and the ticket's success depended upon his strength, not his running mate's.

The Knights had desired more certainty. They had agreed that The Heir Apparent should run for the nation's top job in 2000 rather than seek the vice-presidential nomination. Only The Assassin, who was supposed to be prepared to murder the incoming president—and had no way to identify friend from foe—had stood in his way. It was only after The Assassin had been neutralized that JJ Alexander formally had declared his candidacy.

Alexander balled up a piece of paper and squeezed it in his right hand. Now, with The Spy's announcement that The Assassin's role may have been assumed by a person unknown, Alexander faced a difficult decision. He was not a risk-taker. Life in the White House would be intolerable knowing that at any moment The Assassin's bullet could be whistling through the air, bearing down on his skull.

But this risk was different than the one he had faced in 1995. The stakes were the same, his life, but in 1995 the probability that The Assassin would strike had seemed high; now the odds were difficult to assess. Who was the person who claimed to be The Assassin? It was only remotely possible that The Assassin had passed down his duties to an accomplice before his death.

Alexander wondered if one of his brother Knights was trying to frighten him into abdicating his role, so that the scoundrel could steal the glory and make a run for the presidency himself. The Knights were passionate, ambitious men. They wanted to make the plot work. For Jimmy. For their fathers. For themselves.

Perhaps one of them had the same surreal fantasy that Alexander played over and over in his mind like a motion picture. A shot rings out. The new president falls. Fade to black. A single bell chimes ominously. Cut to The Heir Apparent triumphantly taking the oath of office on the Capitol steps clad in the traditional tartan of Clan

MacDougall. As the bagpipes play in the background, that powerful image yields to flashbacks of historical scenes, one fading into the next in a hazy slow motion.

Alexander pounded his fist on his desktop as the vivid images flashed through his mind. He wanted the fantasy. He wanted that moment of triumph in which he would feel the fiery blood of Jimmy MacDougall coursing through his veins. But he did not want to play Russian roulette. The re-emergence of The Assassin was a new variable and called for a new plan.

There were only two options—maybe a third, but that alternative was bold and unprecedented. The other Knights could encourage another Republican candidate to challenge for the presidency, with Alexander accepting a vice-presidential nomination late in the primary season. Or he could continue his campaign, running the risk that The Assassin was a real threat, relying upon The Spy to eliminate the peril as he had so ably done once before. Neither alternative offered the assurance Alexander craved.

He cocked his arm behind his ear, then launched the ball of paper across the room directly into a small trash can. *Touchdown!* The third option tugged at his heartstrings, but the window of opportunity was closing. It was bold, but that made it beautiful. It was unprecedented, but the millennium milestone cried out for change.

He could almost hear the whispers of his ancestors' spirits, challenging him, cheering him, emboldening him. He needed more time to ponder such a daring step, perhaps consult with his cousins, but the Stevenson rumor was forcing his hand.

Alexander continued to churn these thoughts in his mind, unconsciously running his hand through the remnants of his hair. At about five minutes to six o'clock, almost quitting time for his staff, he called in his top aide, Trey Wallace, over the intercom. Alexander barked out a simple command: "Trey, get me a meeting with Tony Fabrizio tomorrow afternoon."

TWELVE

BEN KRAVNER was something of a celebrity when he waltzed into the offices of Kramer, Fox at eleven o'clock Tuesday morning. He had enjoyed a relatively low profile at the firm for his first year. Now people stared. They whispered. He shut the door to his office until the police arrived.

The police were clueless. The Kramer, Fox offices were protected by electronic key locks. The firm's central computer system logged the comings and goings of all personnel. Any one of two hundred employees who dropped in over the weekend could have slipped into Ben's office undetected. Any one of them could have held a door open for an outsider without a trace of a memory.

Ben and Carol worked feverishly all morning to return his files to some semblance of order. It was not until mid-afternoon that he was able to see Debby.

She gave Ben a warm hug behind closed doors. "I was so worried about you all day yesterday!" Debby said.

"It was one crazy day," Ben said.

"Do you think that the break-in is related to the Thompson case?" she asked.

"Last week I thought the poem was a dead man's folly," Ben said. "But Dean Frederick told me a wild story yesterday that has me looking over my shoulder."

"What did he say?"

Ben reviewed the notes on his legal pad and related a shorthand version of the tale of Jimmy MacDougall.

"Spooky," Debby said. "So you were right about the Harrison connection. Did the Dean know about the poem?"

Ben pressed his tongue against the inside of his cheek as he reflected on the question that had been plaguing him for the past twenty-four hours. Why *did* the Dean tell him that story? "I'm not sure," he said. "He asked about historical documents found among Thompson's belongings, then used some of the buzz words from the poem. I sensed that he was trying to gauge my reaction."

"You didn't tell him about it, did you?" she asked.

"No. I thought about it, but decided not to," Ben said. "Lucky thing, too, since it turned out that I shouldn't have broken the seal."

"I'm so embarrassed about that," Debby said sincerely. "What are you going to do?"

"It's a difficult ethical issue," Ben said. "If a lawyer knows that his client plans to commit a crime, he has an obligation to disclose that information. The poem talks about acts of vengeance. Thompson may have written it as a fictional explanation for the MacDougalls' disappearance, but I'm not satisfied yet. I want to approach this poem like a legal document. Analyze it line by line. If we think a crime is contemplated, we're obligated to disclose it. If not, I'm not sure about the ethics. We made a mistake. Maybe we can find the seal in Thompson's apartment and re-seal the envelope."

"I'm game," Debby said eagerly. She settled into one of Ben's guest chairs.

Ben read the first verse of the poem aloud:

"Seven grieving brothers and sisters two
Forever curse the Office of Tippecanoe
Vengeance is ours for the falsely condemned
From now 'til the coming of the Millennium."

"We already know that Tippecanoe was William Henry Harrison," Debby said.

"And Dean Frederick's story confirms that the Office of Tippecanoe is the presidency," Ben added.

"Did Jimmy MacDougall have seven brothers and two sisters?" she asked.

"Yeah. Portraits of the ten MacDougall children were hanging in Dean Frederick's conference room," Ben said.

"What do you think the 'vengeance' line means?" Debby asked.

"The Dean mentioned a rumor that the MacDougalls set fire to their slaves' bunkhouses," Ben said.

"Maybe they blamed the runaway slave that Jimmy killed for the whole incident and punished the others for it," Debby said.

"Hmmm. But the line before suggests that they're cursing the Office of Tippecanoe," Ben said. "The vengeance seems directed at the presidency."

"From now 'til the coming of the Millennium," Debby said. "A 160-year curse if it was written in 1840."

"The Dean made a big deal about the MacDougalls' Scottish ancestry. We drank from a jug of Scotch whiskey that he told me the MacDougalls brought over from Scotland when they immigrated," Ben said. "Weren't the Scots big into curses and spiritual things?"

"You think this is all about hocus pocus?" Debby asked.

Ben shrugged. "I don't know," he said. "People vent steam in different ways. Some people kick the cat, others hit a golf ball really hard. If writing poems and placing curses stops a guy from shooting up a schoolyard, God bless him. Let's read on:

"Our pasts now clouded, our futures clear
Shrouded names mask the secret we bear,
From mouth to mouth the Key shall descend
The final object unlocked only in the end.

"The Dean said that he and Thompson tried to track the MacDougalls down, but couldn't find a trace of them," Ben said. "They must have adopted false identities."

"Maybe they were embarrassed by the incident and wanted to start new lives," Debby suggested.

"Or maybe they were running away," Ben said. "If they killed their slaves, they'd be fugitives."

"Would they be?" she asked. "If slaves were property, couldn't they destroy them without being guilty of a crime?"

"Interesting question," Ben said. "That might explain why they thought Jimmy was wrongly condemned. If he killed his own slave, it might not have been murder in their eyes."

"Okay. So we don't know why they ran away and changed their names," Debby said. "What was 'the secret we bear'? The shame of Jimmy's crime? The murder of their own slaves?"

"Could be the curse that they put on the presidency," Ben said sarcastically.

"This does sound far-fetched," Debby said. "Maybe they had a wee bit too much of that Scotch whiskey when they wrote the poem."

Ben laughed. "Now that's the most logical explanation I've heard yet."

"But it wouldn't be any fun," she said, smiling.

"True enough," Ben agreed. "A real mystery would be more exciting."

"Can you read the last two lines of the verse again?" Debby asked.

"From mouth to mouth the Key shall descend

The final object unlocked only in the end," Ben read.

"Yeah. That's where it gets mysterious," she said. "What's the 'Key' and the 'final object'?"

"Listen to the next verse," Ben said. "It smacks of conspiracy:

"Each one strike at Vengeance pure,

The next to come in twenty more;

Each a task 'fore the Millennium Meeting,

Then Vengeance shall be much less fleeting."

"It sounds like each of the MacDougall brothers and sisters was to get one chance at personal revenge," Debby said.

"But the weird thing is that it was supposed to be spread out from the time the poem was written until the millennium," Ben said. "They couldn't have expected to live that long—unless they're vampires or planned to wreak vengeance from beyond the grave."

"The Scottish curse thing again." Debby made a spooky sound. "Ooooooo."

Ben did not laugh. He was already reading ahead. "Or maybe they were leaving it to their descendants."

"Spoken like a true trust and estates lawyer."

"No, really," Ben said. "Listen to the next verse:

"Scattered to the winds for eight score year

Our progeny, unmasked, will reappear;

Midnight of the Great Year's dawn,

First meet upon the Old School's lawn."

"You're right," Debby said. "Their progeny, their descendants."

"Their progeny *unmasked*," Ben said. "They weren't just hiding from mankind, they were hiding from each other!"

"What do you mean?" she asked.

Excitement was beginning to enter Ben's voice. "Let's go back a couple of verses," he said. "Their names are shrouded. They're 'scattered to the winds' for 160 years. Then they're 'unmasked' as the millennium turns. 'From mouth to mouth the Key shall descend.' There's some sort of code for them to find each other. That's 'the Key'!"

"Do you think the Old School is Calhoun College?" Debby asked.

"It's gotta be," Ben said. "They're supposed to meet at Calhoun College, their old home, on December 31, 2000."

"To do what?"

"Party!" Ben bobbed his head and rocked his arms in an exaggerated dance move.

Debby rolled her eyes. "C'mon, Ben. The poem was cryptic. What was that last line?"

"First meet upon the Old School's lawn?"

"No, the last line from the verse before."

"Then Vengeance shall be much less fleeting?"

"Yeah," she said. "It sounds like they had something big in mind."

"You're right," Ben said. "Here it is. Second to last verse:

"And Final Vengeance will be ours
When they claim the cursed Office's powers;
A pestilence rained upon the wretched people
Who watched our Jimmy hang from a steeple."

"Jesus," Debby said.

"They were plotting a coup!" Ben said.

"From 160 years before?"

"It's insane," Ben said. "You may have been right—they must have been drunk when they wrote this."

"Or, like you said, the poem may have been written by Thompson or another amateur historian with a vivid imagination," Debby said.

"More likely," he agreed. "Nobody could carry off a conspiracy for 160 years. No way."

"Well, if anybody could do it, it would be the Scots. They're stubborn, and they're passionate," Debby said. "I've got a little Scottish blood myself. It wouldn't be easy, but I could see a strong Scottish clan passing down a curse from generation to generation."

"Even if they could inspire future generations to execute a conspiracy, how could they possibly be in a position to pull off a coup 160 years later?" Ben asked. "We're talking about nine separate families here. Seven generations. Maybe three to five kids in each generation on the average. You'd think that at least one person out of three hundred would realize the insanity and end it!"

"It does sound far-fetched," Debby said. "But isn't it fishy that Dean Frederick knew about this story and was testing you? Or that Adams

Thompson would give five million dollars to Calhoun College without any real connection to it? Yeah, it's nuts. But would it be the *most* insane thing that you ever heard?"

Ben thought for a moment. "Yes. It would be," he said. "Let's try the last verse:

"We, The Royal Order of the Millennium Knight
Swear to bring to bear our collective might
To avenge our departed brother's restless soul
And once again make our family whole."

"It doesn't add anything," Debby said.

"Just the cool name for their group," Ben said. "Let's recap and see if we can make sense out of nonsense."

Ben reviewed his notes. "A man named Jimmy, perhaps Jimmy MacDougall, was executed around 1840," he said. "His siblings were convinced that he was wrongly condemned, and they blamed William Henry Harrison. They planned an act of vengeance directed at the presidency every twenty years, maybe one act for each sibling or their kin. The siblings' families were to act independently until the millennium, when they're supposed to identify each other by deciphering the Key and meet at Calhoun College to carry out their Final Vengeance."

Debby twisted in her chair. "It doesn't sound so impossible when you put it all together like that," she said.

Ben leaned back and placed his feet on his desk. "Something's bothering me," he said.

He did not speak for two or three minutes. Debby doodled on her legal pad. Finally, Ben spoke. "If the conspiracy was real, we should be drowning in evidence of it," he said. "But we're not. It's *possible* that someone is orchestrating the racial conflicts we're seeing lately, but we're not on the brink of war."

"But they have over a year," Debby said. "They could be setting up for a coup when the millennium turns, and we wouldn't necessarily know about it until it happens."

"And Thompson has been right in the middle of this race crisis with his racist editorials," Ben said. "You're right. We can't rule out that something is being planned now. But what have they been doing for the last 160 years? If they were targeting the presidency, wouldn't we know about it?"

"A few presidents have been assassinated," Debby said.

"But there's no connection," Ben said. "And it hasn't happened every twenty years."

"Well, which presidents were assassinated?" she asked.

"Kennedy, Lincoln. I think there were a couple of others, too," Ben said. "But Lincoln was killed in 1865 and Kennedy in 1963. John Wilkes Booth and Lee Harvey Oswald. Almost 100 years. No connection."

"Can you do an Internet search to find the others?" Debby asked.

Ben logged on to the World Wide Web. He entered a search: "Presidents."

The search engine returned 864 hits. The first web site on the list was exactly what he was looking for—short biographies of the American presidents, from George Washington to Hank Norton.

"Let's start with Harrison," Ben said. He skimmed the biography on the computer screen, summarizing for Debby as he read. "He was elected in 1840 and inaugurated in 1841. Wow. He died after only a month in office."

"Was he assassinated?" Debby asked.

"Nope. He died of pneumonia. Caught a bad cold at his inauguration."

Debby smirked. "A likely story," she said.

"Zachary Taylor was the next president to die in office," Ben said. "He was elected in 1848 and died in 1850 after eating cherries on July 4th at the Washington Monument."

Debby shook her head in disbelief. "Where do they come up with this stuff? Cherries?"

"It's in the book. You can look it up," Ben said. "Lincoln was next. Then James Garfield. Garfield was elected in 1880 and was assassinated only six months after he was sworn in."

"A pattern emerges."

"Not so quick," Ben said. "Let's see. William McKinley was assassinated in 1901, less than one year into his second term. Okay, the pattern breaks apart here. Warren G. Harding died of a heart attack in 1923, three years into his presidency."

"It could have been made to look like a heart attack," Debby said, straight-faced.

"Okay, wise guy," Ben said. "FDR was next. Can they fake a cerebral hemorrhage, too?"

"You never know," she said sweetly.

"Anyway, Kennedy was the last president to die in office."

"But Reagan took a bullet in the chest."

"True enough."

"Okay, oh Skeptical One," Debby said. "Look a little harder at the pattern. Just look at dates; forget about whether it was an assassination or an alleged natural death."

"Okay, Commander," he said, bowing his head and raising and lowering his arms rhythmically in mock reverence.

"Okay, okay. I forgot you're the boss," she said. "Pretty please let's look at the pattern."

Ben jotted some notes on his legal pad. "1841, 1850, 1865, 1881, 1901, 1923, 1945, 1963," he said. "Let's check the years between deaths. Nine, fifteen, sixteen, twenty, twenty-two, twenty-two, eighteen."

"But there were eight deaths. 'Each one strike at Vengeance pure.' Seven brothers and two sisters. Maybe one more death after the millennium," Debby said. "Kind of scary, huh?"

Ben stared out the window thoughtfully. The sun had set. He scribbled some more notes. "Okay, I'm intrigued," he said. "Look at the election years of the dead presidents instead of the year of death. 1840, 1848, 1860, 1880, 1900, 1920, 1940, 1960. Let's say Zachary Taylor died a natural death from bad cherries and Ronald Reagan somehow escaped destiny. Reagan was elected in 1980. Eight presidents. Twenty-year cycle."

"This is freaking me out now," Debby said.

"Let's not be too hasty," Ben said. "There are still holes in this theory. It could be coincidence."

"It's a little too neat for me," Debby said. "What holes do you see?"

"Well, for starters, three of the deaths were natural deaths," Ben said. "Pneumonia. Heart attack. Cerebral hemorrhage."

"Let me play devil's advocate here," Debby said.

"A role that suits you well."

"Ha. Ha. A heart attack could be simulated by poisoning. A cerebral hemorrhage could be caused by poisoning or a blow to the head," she said. "Or maybe the powers-that-be knew the presidents were murdered and covered it up. Political cover-ups have been known to happen."

"What about pneumonia—can that be simulated?" Ben asked.

"It's harder to come up with an explanation for that," Debby admitted. "But then again Harrison was the first president to die in office. If he was murdered, maybe they used his bad cold as an explanation to avoid alarming the public."

Ben shook his head. "Okay. I can't believe I'm saying this, but a conspiracy is within the realm of possibility," he said. "Not very far inside, but I can't say it's *totally* absurd. But let's say that the mission of the descendants of each MacDougall sibling was to kill a president elected every twentieth year. Lincoln and FDR were elected in the twentieth year, 1860 and 1940, but they didn't die until their *next* term. If they hadn't been re-elected, the would-be assassins would've failed."

"I don't have an answer for that one," Debby said.

Ben tilted his head back and stared at the ceiling. "I guess it can't be easy to arrange an assassination," he said after a long pause. "Maybe it's not so surprising that one or two failed. If this *is* real, they did fail in 1981. If we're looking only for plausibility, those failings don't rule out the possibility of a conspiracy. Hell, it was wartime during both the 1860 term and the 1940 term. The killers could have been drafted."

"So what next, my captain?"

"Dinner." It was after seven o'clock. "Can you order some Chinese?"

"You got it," Debby said, unfazed by the request. There was nothing unusual about asking a paralegal to order dinner from one of the dozens of takeout restaurants serving the owls of Wall Street.

Debby was gone for about ten minutes. Ben was focused intently on the computer screen when she returned. "What are you looking at?" she asked.

"I'm hunting for connections," Ben said. "I was researching vice presidents."

"Find anything?" she asked.

"I don't think so," Ben said. "It's so hard to tell because we don't know the identities the MacDougalls assumed. John Tyler was Harrison's vice president. Andrew Johnson succeeded Lincoln. Then Chester Arthur, Theodore Roosevelt, Calvin Coolidge, Harry Truman and Lyndon Johnson."

"LBJ I could believe," Debby said.

Ben snickered. "Maybe so. But I can't see Teddy Roosevelt being involved. He's related to FDR. There's also no way that the MacDougalls could have infiltrated the vice-presidency in 1841 or as soon as 1861."

"What about the known assassins?" she asked.

"Let's check." Ben scanned through the biographies again, jotting down notes as he read. "John Wilkes Booth killed Lincoln. Garfield was shot by Charles J. Guiteau. Leon Czolgosz killed McKinley. Lee Harvey Oswald was presumed to have shot Kennedy, but the conspiracy theorists have had a heyday with that one. John Hinckley, Jr. shot Reagan. There's more research we could do, but my intuition tells me that we're not going to find any links."

Ben's skepticism was returning. Was this all coincidence? Could the poem have been written after the fact in an effort to support fact with fiction?

"Ben?" Debby said hesitantly. "What about next year's presidential campaign?"

"Tony Fabrizio is a lock for the Democrats," Ben said. "There's little chance that he's descended from Scots. And his record speaks for itself. If racial unrest is part of this conspiracy, Fabrizio is not involved. Same for JJ Alexander."

"What about Stevenson?" Debby asked."

"I saw that rumor on the news," Ben said. "He says all the right things, and his civil rights record is top drawer. But there's something slimy about him that I don't like. That doesn't make him likely to lead a coup, though."

A messenger knocked on the door. Their food had arrived. They broke off their discussion and moved to a conference room to eat. They rehashed their thoughts about the poem and the conspiracy. No further progress was made.

Ben turned quiet as they were cleaning up and preparing to quit for the night. The episode with Kimberly had confirmed what he had already begun to suspect. His feelings for Debby were more than infatuation. He wanted to share that revelation with Debby, but he no longer trusted his instincts in matters of the heart.

"Penny for your thoughts," Debby said, as if she could read his mind.

"I was spacing out," Ben said. *Coward.* Great men visualized their dreams and made them reality. If she rejected him, the world would not stop spinning. They would still be friends. There would still be hope. If he remained silent—

"No. There is something on my mind," Ben said.

"Shoot."

Ben peered out into the hallway. He closed the door to the conference room even though nobody else seemed to be around. "I was thinking about Saturday night," he said. His heart pounded. "I really enjoyed your company."

She smiled and touched his arm. "I had a great time, too."

"I want you to know that I understand what you're going through, and I want to be there for you," Ben said. The words swirled through his mind, but fought mercilessly to avoid the perilous leap from his tongue. He swallowed hard, opened the window of his brain's inhibiting wall, then let his soul pour out. "I'm falling in love with you. I'm willing to settle for being your friend until you work out your issues. But I want you to know how I feel."

She kissed him softly on the cheek. "You're a good friend, Hawkeye Kravner," she said. "We'll just have to take things as they come."

BEN ARRIVED HOME SHORTLY before ten o'clock, after stopping to run some errands. He was relieved to find that his apartment had not been broken into over the weekend. He was tired, but thoughts, emotions and images flashed through his mind. *Could the conspiracy be real? It was insane. Debby. Jimmy swinging from a steeple. Nine drunken MacDougalls. I told her I love her. Shit. Harrison, Lincoln, Garfield, McKinley, Harding, Roosevelt, Kennedy, Reagan. Alexander and Fabrizio. Vice Presidents. Stevenson. Do I really love her? Kimberly. Her lips. Damn. Why do I act from my heart instead of my head? She called me Hawkeye.*

No, sleep was not imminent. He knew that he could convince Debby to follow the passion she felt on Saturday night, if he could only articulate the words. *Visualize the dream, make it reality.* It had been difficult enough to tell her he loved her; it was too hard to tell her that she should love him back. It was so much easier to think of all that he could have, should have, said now that he was in the solitude of his apartment.

Then Ben had an idea. He composed an e-mail.

Dear Debby,

I know you said you want to take things as they come, but I felt something magical between us last Saturday and I know you must have, too. Whether it's convenient or not, our paths have crossed at this time in our lives.

I saw you reading a book of Robert Frost's poems in Thompson's apartment on Saturday. One of my favorites is <u>The Road Not Taken</u>. I'm sure you know it. Like Frost's lone traveler, the choice we make at this crossroads in our lives can make all the difference in our future.

> *I shall be telling this with a sigh*
> *Somewhere ages and ages hence:*
> *Two roads diverged in a wood, and I—*
> *I took the one less traveled by,*
> *And that has made all the difference.*

Won't you follow your passion, your heart, and take the road less traveled by with me?
Ben

Ben read the message again and again. Finally, he sucked in a deep breath, said a silent prayer to a God in whom he did not believe, and clicked the send button.

Satisfied that he had done all that he could to relieve the pressure on his left brain, Ben's attention shifted to his right brain problem. He was not at all convinced that the Poem was evidence of a crime. Yet his intuition told him that Dean Frederick was hiding something. If he expected a sealed envelope, then a sealed envelope he would get.

Ben dug the envelope with the broken seal out of his desk drawer. He transcribed the Poem onto a legal pad. He opened the package of manila envelopes he had purchased on the way home, and carefully wrote the words "PERSONAL—DO NOT OPEN (DELIVER TO FRITZ FOX, TRUSTEE)" on the front of one in black marker, exactly as printed on the envelope he had found in Thompson's safe deposit box. Then he inserted the original Poem. He would have to find the wax seal in Thompson's study and finish the job tomorrow.

Ben tossed the old envelope back in the desk drawer and placed the new envelope in his briefcase. Tomorrow it would be tucked safely in the firm's vault.

Ben still needed to talk. He logged on to CyberLine and took the shortcut directly to RealTime. It never occurred to him to pick up the telephone. There was nobody to call. Woody was on-line.

MasterBen:	Woodman!
WoodythePecker:	Ben! How goes the battle?
MasterBen:	My head is spinning...
WoodythePecker:	The millennium thing? A babe?
MasterBen:	Two babes, the Millennium Knights, every-thing...
WoodythePecker:	Two babes! Tell me details, dear
MasterBen:	This never happens to me. I haven't got-ten laid in four months. I was alone with this beautiful blonde in Atlanta yesterday and she started coming on to me.
WoodythePecker:	Did you do her?
MasterBen:	I wanted to so badly, but I started dating another woman this weekend.
WoodythePecker:	Oh really...how was your date?
MasterBen:	We had a great time...I think I'm falling in love...
WoodythePecker:	Cool deal! Did you do her?
MasterBen:	Nope. She really turns me on, but I think we need to take it slow...
WoodythePecker:	An old-fashioned girl? I think I'm going to cry.
MasterBen:	(Laughing out loud) No...I don't think that's it...she has some issues to work through...
WoodythePecker:	That sounds like trouble. Maybe you should have porked the southern belle. It may be awhile before you have another chance!
MasterBen:	It didn't feel right...We were already going at it hot and heavy and I had a bout with my conscience...

WoodythePecker:	I hear that. It's like the little cartoon devil on one shoulder and the angel on the other <smile>
MasterBen:	(Laughing) Exactly. Fuck her! No! Fuck her! No!
WoodythePecker:	(Rolling on the floor laughing)
MasterBen:	Anyway, if you can pick yourself off the floor, let me change the subject just a little...what do you know about dead presidents—ones that died in office?
WoodythePecker:	Uh oh, history test...let me think...Lincoln, McKinley and Kennedy were killed. Did any others die in office besides FDR?
MasterBen:	Not bad. Garfield was also assassinated. William Henry Harrison, Zachary Taylor and Warren G. Harding died naturally... Do you see any pattern in their deaths?
WoodythePecker:	Let me think...
WoodythePecker:	Not really...you have a theory I take it?
MasterBen:	Think about when they were elected... Harrison in 1840, Lincoln in 1860, Garfield in 1880, McKinley in 1900, Harding in 1920, FDR in 1940, Kennedy in 1960...
WoodythePecker:	You know, I did hear about that...in high school...I had a civics teacher who called it the 20-Year Jinx...he joked that Reagan only had a few months left in his second term...gee, I haven't thought about that in years, especially since Reagan seems to have broken The Jinx...
MasterBen:	I never heard about it until I read that poem I told you about.
WoodythePecker:	Just one of life's great coincidences, I figure...you can't find any real connection, can you?

MasterBen:	Nothing obvious, but the poem suggests that in 1840 the brothers and sisters of a wrongfully condemned man set out to wreak vengeance on the presidency over a 160-year period ending at the turn of the millennium...
WoodythePecker:	Freaky...how does the poem say they do it?

Ben entered the poem on his computer and sent it, verse by verse, to Woody.

WoodythePecker:	It seems a little over the top, man...could Thompson have dreamed this up?
MasterBen:	I don't know...the paper it was written on is tattered, but I really can't say how old it is…
WoodythePecker:	Have you ever read *Foucault's Pendulum* by Umberto Eco?
MasterBen:	No, what's it about?
WoodythePecker:	The book is dense, but the gist of it is that an intellectual and his cronies in modern Italy stumble upon a handwritten poem supposedly written by a leader of the Templars, an elite band of knights that were forced underground during the Middle Ages. The poem was barely legible in spots, but the intellectuals interpreted it as saying that the Templars had a plan to scatter and remain underground for hundreds of years only to emerge at a designated date and location to take over the world.
MasterBen:	Wow, when was the book written?
WoodythePecker:	Late 1980s
MasterBen:	So did the Templars get outed?

WoodythePecker: It turned out that there was no conspiracy... the paper was probably just an ancient grocery list...but the cool plot twist was that by snooping around and investigating the legend of the Templars, the intellectuals aroused the interest of a group of pseudo-Templars that had formed a cult group. The pseudo group then met at the place and time that the intellectuals predicted, awaiting the arrival of the real Templars. The intellectual leader ends up getting killed at the scene. Slow reading, but recommended.

MasterBen: Well thanks for spoiling the ending, Woodman! <grin> Is there a Cliff Notes version?

WoodythePecker: I don't THINK so...

MasterBen: So you think that my poem might be a hoax?

WoodythePecker: It seems incredible, don't you think? I mean, maybe Thompson or somebody else dreamed it up after-the-fact to explain this wild coincidence...

MasterBen: I don't know...I'm at a point where I think that there's some plausibility, but I don't know what to do next...The partners don't want anything to do with me. Fritz is home, but he'd think I'm nuts, anyway, and I don't want to tell him that I opened the sealed envelope...

WoodythePecker: What makes you think that it's plausible?

MasterBen: The reason I was in Atlanta yesterday was to talk to the dean of Calhoun College— the sole beneficiary of Thompson's estate. It's getting late and I don't want to get into all the details, but he made me suspicious...

WoodythePecker: Did you discuss the poem with him?

MasterBen: No way...but it seemed like he might know about it, and he was testing me... he made me very uncomfortable... my instincts told me to shut up and listen...

WoodythePecker: Got to go with those instincts, man.

MasterBen: I'm getting tired. I'll keep you posted on the babe watch...

WoodythePecker: Please do! You know I live vicariously through you, dear. Let me know if anything intriguing turns up in the dead presidents caper, too. If I don't hear from you next week, I'll send the authorities after your pal, the dean!!! <wink>

MasterBen: You jest, but my office was trashed when I was in Atlanta...

WoodythePecker: Do you think it was related?

MasterBen: I don't know...my renowned instincts think it might be...I'm not working on any other high profile matters, but they didn't take anything and my apartment wasn't trashed when I got home tonight...If they were serious about finding the poem, they would have broken into my apartment…

WoodythePecker: Makes sense, but I'd still be careful. It might have just been easier to break into your office.

MasterBen: I've got my guard up, but I'm thinking it might have been an overzealous reporter looking for a scoop...I'm sure he was dis-appointed...

WoodythePecker: But still, there is much to be said in favor of zealousness!

MasterBen: Uh-oh, Woody's got a new word...look out

WoodythePecker: And I've got three extra hours to try it out!

MasterBen: Buenos noches, mi amigo

WoodythePecker: Adios!!!

THIRTEEN

IT WAS SEVEN-FORTY-FIVE on Tuesday evening. The Vice President was in his shirtsleeves, his suit jacket slung over the back of his chair.

"What do you think JJ wants to talk about so desperately?" Tony Fabrizio asked, as he paced back and forth behind his desk, carrying a 25-year old "I Love My Dad" coffee mug in his right hand.

LaRosa Smith sat in one of the black Windsor guest chairs, her feet resting on Fabrizio's desk. "I don't have a clue," she said. "I'm sure he's heard the Stevenson rumor, but there's no reason for him to discuss that with you. But if he just wanted to talk about legislation or Senate business, he wouldn't have been in such a tizzy to set up a meeting on short notice. Trey Wallace was insistent that we do it today. Something's up. Something unusual."

"Maybe he thinks he's dug up some dirt on me or Hank that could influence the election."

"Yeah, right," LaRosa said, grinning. "The only bigger choirboy in D.C. than you is Hank Norton. I *wish* you guys had a few small skeletons in your closet—it would make my job more interesting."

Fabrizio laughed. "I'll bet you didn't know that I actually was a choirboy," he said. "My parents wanted me to study for the priesthood, but I would sneak away to play baseball or flirt with the girls."

LaRosa knew just about everything about Tony Fabrizio, although that historical nugget had escaped her. Fabrizio had grown up in the Bensonhurst section of Brooklyn, a primarily Italian neighborhood and a breeding ground for the Mafia. Fabrizio's father despised the "gangstas," as he had called them, and Tony was the heir to his father's moral outrage.

Fabrizio had put himself through night school, first at Brooklyn College and then Brooklyn Law School. He had married his high school sweetheart, Emily, after he had obtained his law degree and accepted a job as an assistant district attorney for the Eastern District of New York in Brooklyn. He had received favorable publicity for prosecuting a string of organized crime cases that resulted in the heads of three crime families receiving life sentences in federal prison.

The Mafia had first tried to corrupt Tony Fabrizio. When that failed, they had terrorized him. In 1970, two Mafia henchmen kidnapped his daughter, Christina, then only three years old, and had threatened to kill her if Fabrizio did not drop a federal racketeering case against Dominick Brunelli, a boss in the Petrillo crime family.

The kidnapping case became the top priority for the New York Police Department and the FBI, as well as Fabrizio's many friends on the streets of Bensonhurst. With the assistance of a number of key informants, some from competing mob families that found crimes against children reprehensible, the kidnappers had been discovered within four days. Fabrizio had participated in the raid, in which both kidnappers were killed.

Television cameras had caught a surprised and emotional Fabrizio carrying little Christina, tired, tearful, but safe, out of the wreckage. The story had made the national news. Fabrizio had gone from locally respected crimebuster to national hero overnight.

Fabrizio had leveraged his fame to political advantage. He had served as New York State Attorney General for six years, then successfully ran for Governor of New York in 1976 at the age of 36. He had remained as Governor, and one of the most popular elected officials in U.S. history, until 1992, when Hank Norton pegged him as his vice-presidential running mate. Throughout his political career Fabrizio had maintained the highest ethical standards and treated all of his constituents and colleagues with fairness, kindness and respect, whether Democrat or Republican, black or white, rich or poor.

Fabrizio's intercom buzzed. "Senator Alexander is here to see you, Tony."

"Send him in, Claire," Fabrizio answered. Protocol dictated that he put on his jacket to receive guests. LaRosa saw him scowl at it as if the jacket wrote the rules. He left it folded over the back of his chair. This was his turf; he wrote the rules. The worried look that he wore all afternoon disappeared. His back stiffened. His eyes narrowed as he focused himself on meeting any challenge presented by his old adversary.

LaRosa sulked towards the door. This meeting was to be a private one, at Senator Alexander's request. She was miffed, and she gave Alexander a chilly greeting on her way out.

"THANKS FOR MEETING WITH ME on such short notice, Tony," Alexander said. His well-practiced Texan drawl was in high gear. He would have followed protocol and addressed Fabrizio as "Mr. Vice President" if LaRosa had remained in the room, but Alexander knew that Fabrizio disliked the formality. The two rivals had worked together for seven years, with Fabrizio presiding over the Senate and Alexander a key player in the Senate Republican leadership. They had developed a level of comfort and personal trust that was rare among political foes.

Fabrizio motioned for Alexander to sit in the chair that LaRosa had just vacated. "I have to admit to being curious about what could possibly be so urgent," he said. "But I've known you long enough to know that you wouldn't have asked for the meeting if you didn't think it was important."

"I'm not going to beat around the bush," Alexander said, hesitating for a moment in a way that he had practiced time and again over the weekend.

"You never do, JJ," Fabrizio said. "You never do."

Alexander leaned forward and locked eyes with the Vice President. This had to be perfect. "Tony, I've got cancer. Hell, I haven't even told Missy about it yet, and if you leak it to the press, damn it, I'll deny it."

Fabrizio's jaw dropped. He shifted in his chair uncomfortably. "JJ, I'm truly sorry, and you know that I'd never do that," he said sincerely. He foundered for a moment, trying to find words. "How does this affect your plans?"

"It doesn't necessarily have to. My doctor thinks he can keep it under control in a way that I can maintain my privacy and my dignity. Hell, I could live for another twenty or thirty years."

"That's terrific," Fabrizio said, grinning. "I'm looking forward to kicking your backside next November, and I don't need you running any half-assed campaign to do it!"

Alexander laughed, then returned to the serious tone that he had so carefully rehearsed. "I'll give you a run for your money if you want it, and, damn it, I think I can beat you, with or without Tom Stevenson," he said, pausing for effect. "But I don't *know* that I'll beat you, and if you're honest with yourself I don't think you *know* that you'll win, either."

"You're right, JJ, I don't *know* it, but that's half the fun of the battle," Fabrizio said.

"I know what you mean. I've fought a lot of tough battles in my time, on the football field and in the political arena, and there's no greater feeling of power than winning a close one," Alexander agreed. "But the cancer has made me sit back and think about why I'm doing this—running for president, I mean. I enjoy the trappings of power as much as anyone, but you know me—I'm not one of the old guard wheelers and dealers or one of these young Turk right-wing fundamentalists who want to create a puritan society. I've dedicated my life to public service and making this country safe and fair for everyone. I love this country, and when I leave it, I want to leave a lasting legacy. I want to be remembered."

"Nobody has created a greater legacy than you have, JJ," Fabrizio said.

"Name five great Americans who've made their mark in the Senate," he said. "We work as a collective body. Yes, I'm confident that I've provided sound leadership. But at the end of the day I've produced nothing that's mine. We've passed some good, solid programs, but the problems we face today are still pretty much the problems we faced thirty or forty years ago."

"Well, you've got your chance right now," Fabrizio said. "Put together a package that people want and sell it, sell it, sell it. If your platform is better than mine and the people buy into it, then God bless them and God bless you."

"I've done just that, Tony. I'm calling it 'The Second American Revolution.' But I don't have the confidence in the American people to see beyond the catch-phrase. Hell, I'll have my 'Revolution' and you'll have your 'New Deal' or 'Square Deal' or 'Real Deal,'" Alexander said. "Even though I believe in my program and in myself, I don't *know* that I'll beat you. And with this cancer thing, I don't know if I'll get another chance."

"JJ, I'm not sure what you're getting at here. I agree with most of what you said, but the political process is what it is. If you win, you have your chance to create your legacy, but I'm going to do everything fair that I can to beat you. I'm truly sorry about your illness, but I can't let that influence the way I run my campaign."

"I don't want you to give up your legacy," Alexander said. He knew his delivery had to be perfect. He had to *ooze* sincerity. "I'm proposing a *real* second American Revolution. I'm suggesting that we use the occasion of the new millennium to usher in real change. Together, we can marshal the best resources from both political parties and develop a program that makes a difference to the people of this country without the squabbling and posturing of politics as usual. I'm offering unification. We run on the same ticket. You're the president; I'm the VP. We both get our legacies. We both make a real difference in people's lives."

Fabrizio seemed stunned. Alexander waited for a response, allowing the drama to build. "I don't know what to say," Fabrizio said. "I'm truly at a loss for words."

JJ grinned. "I didn't expect you to respond immediately. Hell, I wanted to think this through myself for a few more weeks, but the Stevenson rumors forced my hand," Alexander said. He leaned forward and spoke in hushed tones. "All I ask is that you keep this quiet. Discuss it with your advisors, but keep it close for awhile, turn it over in your mind a few times. Think what it means for you, and think what it means for the American people. From my end, I'm prepared to move forward with this immediately."

Fabrizio stood and began pacing behind his desk. "Tell me a little more about your Second American Revolution," he said.

Alexander sat back and crossed his legs. "As a young man, and a Texan, I was influenced by Lyndon Johnson's quest for the Great Society," he said, following Fabrizio with his eyes. He knew the Vice President well enough to realize that he was listening seriously. "LBJ started to bridge the gulfs between the rich and the poor, blacks and whites. Somewhere along the way we got lost. Attitudes have improved some, but the gulfs have gotten wider."

Fabrizio stopped to face him. "Have you thought about the details yet?" he asked.

"I don't want to talk details," Alexander said. Honesty was one thing, giving away the farm was another. "Not yet. But we need to think big. We're trying to build a bridge with toothpicks. We need to step back, kick the steel and put this baby together the right way."

Fabrizio stepped around the desk and extended his hand. "I'll give it a good, hard think, JJ. But this is not a decision to be made lightly, and I can't make any promises."

Alexander shook Fabrizio's hand firmly and looked him in the eyes with that practiced trust-me look. He said, "That's all I ask."

Not ten seconds after the door closed behind Alexander, Fabrizio was on the intercom: "Rosie, get your ass in here!"

FOURTEEN

THE JINX was on Ben Kravner's mind as he rode the elevator to the 25th floor of One Water on Wednesday morning. The mystery of the 20-Year Jinx was intriguing, but a conspiracy by one family over 160 years was too fantastic to believe. Even if the MacDougalls' rage had survived for a generation, maybe two, how could it possibly have meaning to their descendents seven generations removed?

Ben closed his eyes and tried to imagine himself in their place. Paul Kravner was a gentle man, so it was hard to envision, but what would he do if his father had told him at an impressionable age that it was his destiny to kill? *The same thing I did when he told me it was my destiny to be a lawyer.* Could it be possible? Seven generations. Nine family chains. Was the bond between father and son that strong? *Seven dead presidents.*

The more Ben thought about it, the less certain he became. There were no apparent connections between the deaths. *But why did Dean Frederick tell me about the MacDougalls?*

Ben contemplated his next move. He could not go to the police or the FBI. His only evidence, the poem, had been illegally obtained. Even brushing that concern aside, the conspiracy theory was too wacky to bring to the authorities without hard proof. It was simply a bizarre coincidence.

Fritz Fox was still out of the picture. The Old Man probably would not have much to add to the process, anyway, and he would doubtlessly think Ben foolhardy for wasting time on such trivial and non-legal pursuits. He might even fire him for opening the sealed envelope.

Ben figured he would revisit Thompson's Fifth Avenue apartment later in the morning. He had inventoried the contents on Saturday, but a more thorough search for evidence of a conspiracy now seemed appropriate.

It was not to be.

"Ben!" It was Carol. He had almost slipped into his office undetected.

"Good morning, Carol. How's it going?"

"Good." She held up one finger while she finished chewing a bite of her bagel. "You've got a message from the police. Detective Johnson."

"Is that the cop I spoke with yesterday?" Ben asked.

"I don't think so. That was Detective Jamieson."

"That's right. Johnson's the one in charge of the Thompson murder," Ben said. "I'll call him. Thanks." Ben stopped for a cup of coffee and read the morning mail before calling the detective.

"Lawyers and bankers. Gotta love 'em," Detective Johnson said when Ben introduced himself on the telephone. He had a heavy Bronx accent. "Sure wish I could start work at ten in the A.M."

"I had a few other pressing matters to take care of before I returned your call," Ben said. "Coffee, mail, you know the drill."

"Whatever. Look, we've got a lead in the Thompson murder. You're listed as the contact in the file."

Ben perked up. "That's right. What have you got?"

"We picked up a wino trying to buy booze with Thompson's canceled credit card. Can you come down to the station?"

It was a gray, wintry morning. Ben took a taxi for the short ride to the Sixth Precinct in Greenwich Village. The uniformed officer manning the metal detector in the lobby directed Ben to Detective Johnson's desk on the second floor.

The station house was relatively new. The lighting was good, and it did not yet have that stale, dank smell that characterized most of New York's aging precincts. Unlike the crowded police offices portrayed on television, the desks were separated by partitions, affording the detectives a small amount of privacy. Like the television precinct houses, there was a low din of background noise—telephones ringing, fluorescent lights humming, a drunken suspect shouting for his lawyer, some random laughter, and sundry conversations taking place at varying volumes.

Ben found Detective Johnson preparing paperwork and chewing on a sandwich. His face was punctuated with a wide, red nose. He was a large man, not fat. His shirtsleeves were rolled up, exposing muscular forearms. He looked to be about fifty.

"Bologna?" Ben asked, as he knocked lightly on the partition.

"Salami. I just got promoted," Johnson said. The Bronx accent suit-ed him. "You must be the wise guy lawyer."

Ben extended his hand. "Ben Kravner."

Johnson wiped his hand on his pants and shook Ben's hand. "Charmed, I'm sure. Have a seat, Kravner."

"Do you think the guy you picked up killed Thompson?" Ben asked.

"We're going to hold him as a suspect. The guy's homeless. A drunk. I don't think we'll pursue the credit card charges if he doesn't look good for the murder. That's him over there shouting for his lawyer. A real sweetheart."

The man was black-skinned, rail thin, with graying hair, probably about sixty years old. He was dressed in a tattered overcoat.

"He doesn't look like he could have overpowered Thompson. Thompson was a hefty guy," Ben said.

"Yeah. I don't think he's good for it, but we have to check it out," Detective Johnson said. "He says he found the wallet in a dumpster on East 8th Street, a few blocks from the murder site."

"Did you find the murder weapon?" Ben asked.

"Yeah. Sure. Mr. Green did it in the library with a candlestick."

"I'll take that as a 'no.'"

"Good guess, Sherlock."

"Did he have the wallet or just the credit card?" Ben asked.

"We found the wallet in his shopping cart. We dusted for finger-prints. Nothing helpful. I was about to tag it and bag it for evidence."

"Can I see it?" Ben asked.

"I'll need it back, but I thought you might want to look through it." The Detective handed Ben the wallet and directed him to an empty desk.

The wallet was still intact. No money, of course, but it still held Thompson's driver's license, a few credit cards, health insurance card and other standard fare. There were a number of business cards. Ben scanned the names, but nothing struck him as interesting. There were no photographs.

A spare car key was hidden in a compartment in the back of the wallet along with the insurance identification card for the Mercedes. The insurance card was stuck to the side of the compartment. When Ben yanked it out, another slip of paper fell to the floor.

Ben picked it up and read it. He then experienced what one of the partners at Kramer, Fox jokingly called a "clong." A shot of adrenaline. The bulging of the eyes. The sickening feeling of one's stomach accelerating into the throat. The moment when terror first strikes. At Kramer, Fox a clong usually was immediately preceded by the realization that an irreversible error in judgment had been made. There was about to be one ticked off client. Maybe a lawsuit.

Ben's client was dead. But simultaneously with his clong came the realization that the Poem was not a dead man's folly. The Jinx was real.

FIFTEEN

LAROSA SMITH RARELY SHOWED EMOTION at work, but she was having trouble containing her excitement. "I've thought about it half the night," LaRosa said. "JJ's proposal is a blockbuster!"

"It's just so...unsporting," Tony Fabrizio said. They were in Fabrizio's office on Wednesday morning. He was in his customary repose, feet on desk, chair tilted back, arms behind head. A Danish sat half-eaten on a plate atop his desk.

"I know the gamesmanship of politics is important to you. It's important to all of us," LaRosa said. "It's one of the few public arenas where those who are too old or too uncoordinated or too female to play professional sports can compete. But JJ is a formidable opponent. You're not going to win big. You may lose. If you accept his offer, it's in the bag."

"I don't know, Rosie. The two party system is such a basic component of our political heritage. People want choices. If both parties reject us, we could end up on a third-party ticket with twenty percent of the vote. A lot of folks vote along party lines without thinking."

LaRosa thought Fabrizio was being too conservative. If she did nothing else in her four-year stint as the Vice President's chief advisor, she had to convince him that this was the opportunity of a lifetime.

"As long as you don't go crazy and throw the incumbents overboard, the Democratic Party will be thrilled," she said. "We are the Democratic Party, and we're the big winners here. We have a chance to influence Congress to adopt sweeping legislation that can make a difference in people's lives. If we can avoid partisan politics, you and JJ may go down as the greatest leaders in American history."

"But can we avoid partisan politics?" Fabrizio asked. "How do you think the Republicans will react?"

"Privately, they might be angry," LaRosa admitted. "But they'll have no political choice but to support you publicly. Nobody has stepped up yet to seriously challenge JJ in the primaries. You both have unbelievably strong ratings in the polls. The Republicans will hop on your bandwagon rather than support a sure loser."

Fabrizio frowned. "I still think people want choices," he said, shaking his head. "What if the Republicans do something dramatic to create an exciting alternative. Maybe a woman or black candidate. Cindy Hodges or General Maxwell."

"Cindy Hodges couldn't even carry California, her home state. America may be ready to elect a woman president, but she's not it. I don't know of any women who are ready for the office right now.

"General Maxwell's a good man," LaRosa continued. "And he might have a chance against an extreme opponent, but you and JJ aren't going to lose the African-American vote just because you're running against an African-American. I'm not saying African-Americans are color blind, but you've both built strong support over many years. And even if this becomes a racially charged election, you still *are* in the majority."

"So you'd have me play the race card?" Fabrizio asked.

"It's not playing the race card. A lot of whites will support you simply because you're white and running against an African-American candidate, but that makes them racists not you. I know you. You won't pander to them."

"I don't think I've pandered a day in my life," Fabrizio said, smiling.

LaRosa grinned. "I doubt you have."

"You keep avoiding the biggest issue," Fabrizio said. "Are the American people ready to abandon the two-party system? Will they view our collaboration as a ploy, some sort of breach of trust, a way to create a political monopoly?"

"With different players that would be a real risk. But the message you and JJ are sending is 'revolutionary change, not evolutionary change,' and you both have the political record and respect to sell it. You're not preachers, you're doers. The American people are sick and tired of politics as usual. All talk, no action. Gridlock. Damn it, Tony, you pick the cliché. This is a once in a lifetime opportunity. With all of the excitement surrounding the millennium, this is the perfect time to sell a revolution."

"Keep going, Rosie, you're on a roll," Fabrizio said, grinning.

LaRosa's relationship with Fabrizio had not always been so easy. When she had first accepted the job as his Chief of Staff, she had been uncomfortable. She had known that politics was still essentially a man's game, and a white man's game at that. She had been defensive, always out to prove she belonged on her merits. She had suppressed her femininity and playfulness and accentuated her African-American heritage.

She almost had lost her job. Not because she was too black or not sexy enough, but because she had not been herself. Rather than fire her, Fabrizio had taken her aside for a heart-to-heart chat. Fabrizio told her that for the relationship to work, he had to be able to trust her totally. She had to be willing to let down her guard and be herself. He had to know that her advice came from her heart. *No secrets, no lies.*

It had not been an easy transformation for LaRosa. For thirty-two years she had fought for acceptance. It had been hard to recognize when the battle was won. While she had been slow in reaching the critical insight, she was a fast learner. She let out her natural sense of humor. She spoke her mind. She abandoned the tribal dress in favor of more professional attire. Occasionally, she dared to be sexy, not because she was flirtatious, but because her sexuality was a part of her.

The relationship with Fabrizio, once awkward, had become easy. Their friendship had blossomed. He had grown confident that her intuition was grounded in a strong heart as well as an astute political mind.

And now LaRosa's intuition was telling her that Fabrizio was sitting on a gold mine. "Sorry, boss," she said. "This is an awesome opportunity for you and for the country. It's the type of situation we dreamed about in lunchroom debates in law school. 'What would you change if you were president and you didn't have to deal with partisan politics?'"

"Look, Rosie, I respect your instincts," Fabrizio said. "And I'm a dreamer, too. But experience tells me that there's a catch. We're not dealing with school kids here. Cancer or no cancer, I'm not sure why he's giving up his one chance to be the Big Dog."

LaRosa stifled a smile. "What's so funny?" Fabrizio asked.

"Nothing really. You reminded me of something an old professor of mine used to say. 'The view is pretty much the same whether you're the second dog on the team or the last.'"

Fabrizio snorted. "That's my point," he said. "Why would somebody who has dedicated his life to being the best at whatever he does be willing to settle for a view of my backside in his final race?"

"Sometimes you just have to stop thinking," LaRosa said. "Once he signs up as your running mate, it's over. What does he possibly have to gain from throwing the election at that point?"

Fabrizio reflected on that thought for a moment. "What about Stevenson. Have we made any implied promises to him?"

"Absolutely not. Like every other politician, he's probably overconfident and *thinks* he's got it. But, look, he knows the give and take of politics. He'll sit back and marvel like everyone else in Washington how the hell you pulled this rabbit out of your hat."

"Do you still think he might make a run for the presidency this year if he's not my VP?" Fabrizio asked.

"No," she said confidently. "He couldn't beat the two of you together, and he's too smart to try."

"Hmmm. Where have you left things with Stevenson's chief?"

"The next step is a personal meeting between you and Tom," LaRosa said. Fabrizio was rocking gently in his chair. "So, what are you thinking?" she asked.

"Let's hold off Stevenson and ponder it," Fabrizio said. "We're in no rush."

SIXTEEN

BEN LOCKED THE DOOR to his office. He pulled out the slip of paper from his pocket. His hands shook. It was a list. "The Heir Apparent. The Speaker. The Senator. The General. The Spy. The Publisher. The Doctor. The Caretaker. The Assassin." Names he had seen only briefly almost a week earlier in the Millennium Nights room on CyberLine. The Royal Order of the Millennium Knight had convened. *The Jinx was real.*

"Holy shit!" Debby said, after Ben shared the details of his frightful discovery. "How could they possibly pull it off?"

Ben shook his head incredulously. "I can't believe it," he said. "But kids are easily influenced by their parents. Usually, we think about unintentionally passing down bad habits to the next generation, but why couldn't somebody take advantage of that bond?"

"The Hatfields and the McCoys," Debby said.

"Huh?"

"The two hillbilly clans that fought for years," she said. "I think that feud crossed a generation."

"But seven generations? It's too fantastic to believe, but somehow they did it," Ben said.

"So now what?" Debby asked.

"We need to figure out who these guys are and gather evidence of the conspiracy," Ben said. "We still can't disclose this to anyone else. I'm the only connection between the List and the Poem. I saw those names in the chat room. We know the conspiracy is real, but we have no proof."

"When you think about it, the List isn't connected to the Poem at all," Debby said. "Adams Thompson is the only link between the two."

"And 'Millennium Nights' is similar to 'Millennium Knight,'" Ben noted. "But we'd get laughed off the planet if we brought this to the police. We've got to take our intuition and develop hard evidence."

"So how do you propose we do that?" Debby asked.

"Maybe guess possible suspects based on the List," he said. "We know The Publisher. If the Knights were successful, then the Speaker of the House, John Daniel, must be The Speaker. The Heir Apparent is probably a candidate for vice president."

"Stevenson is an obvious suspect," Debby reminded him.

"Right," Ben agreed. "There are only one hundred senators. We need to narrow that pool. There are too many generals to guess The General. Doctors, too. The Spy could be someone in the FBI or the CIA. We should consider if any of their top officers could be involved."

"What about The Caretaker and The Assassin?" Debby asked.

"I don't have a clue how to identify them," Ben admitted.

"Maybe the dean at Calhoun College?" Debby asked. "You said he seemed suspicious."

"He could be The Caretaker," Ben said. "That's a good thought."

Debby's mind seemed to be clicking. "And the List might be part of the 'Key' that the Poem mentions," she said excitedly.

"Maybe. But I don't understand how knowing only the nicknames would help the Knights find each other, though," Ben said. "We can't do it."

"True."

"But you're right to think in terms of the Key," Ben said. "That's probably how they found each other and set themselves up in the Millennium Nights room."

"What did the Poem say about it, again?" Debby asked.

Ben removed his transcribed copy of the Poem from his briefcase. He had taken to locking it there whenever he was not using it. He had stopped at Thompson's apartment on the way back from the police station and re-sealed the envelope. It was now in the firm's vault.

"Our pasts now clouded, our futures clear, shrouded names mask the secret we bear, from mouth to mouth the Key shall descend, the final object unlocked only in the end."

"It was supposed to be passed down from mouth to mouth," Debby said.

"That'll make it difficult. It probably won't fall into our lap like the List did," Ben said.

"Maybe we can figure it out if we think like the MacDougalls," Debby suggested. "They were about to scatter across the country. They knew that they wouldn't make contact again for over 150 years. How would you develop a code to permit their descendants to find each other?"

"Maybe a secret message in the newspaper," Ben said. "No, it would've been hard to predict if there would be one newspaper that would be convenient for all of them."

"Maybe if they had picked a date in advance and agreed to use the largest newspaper in a big city, like Atlanta or New York," Debby said.

"That's possible. We'd never be able to decrypt that," Ben said. Did they have classified ads in the newspapers back then?"

Debby shrugged. "Gee, I don't know," she said.

"Let's think of other possibilities," Ben said.

"Maybe an agreed meeting place on a specified date?"

"They would have to be confident that the place would still exist after 150 years," Ben said. "And it would have to be a place where they wouldn't get lost in a crowd."

"That rules out national landmarks, like the White House or the Washington Monument," Debby said.

"Calhoun College is a possibility," Ben suggested.

"But they already used that as the site of their Millennium Meeting."

"Yeah, that might be too obvious," Ben agreed. "There's no way we're going to guess that, either. I don't think we're going to be productive trying to guess the Key without some other clues."

Debby smirked. "Which will drop from the sky like manna from heaven?"

"You're starting to hang around me way too much," Ben said. "The sarcasm thing is rubbing off."

"I'm trying it on, and I think it fits."

"Fair enough," Ben said. "Anyway, the only other place that I can think of to find clues is the Millennium Nights room. Maybe we can figure out when they meet, and then try to find a way to observe what's going on in there or try to make contact with one of the Knights."

"When did you see them in the room?" she asked.

"It was the day before we went out to lunch. Thursday night, I think. It was after midnight."

"Maybe we can take shifts and monitor the room," Debby suggested.

"We'd need a 24-hour watch," Ben said. "We'll need help."

Debby hesitated. "I don't think we should talk about this with anyone else," she said. "Do you?"

"Well, I've been talking on-line with a friend of mine," Ben said.

"On-line! Are you crazy?"

"It's not like that. Woody's my best friend in the world. I've met him in person."

"You're the boss," Debby said. She did not sound entirely convinced.

"Anyway, Woody's the only one. I know he'll help us," Ben said. "I have three other friends on-line. I won't provide details. I'll only tell them that I need help monitoring the room and that it's important. They're good friends. They'll help."

"That's the two of us, then, and four of your Net buddies. Four hours each," Debby said. "How do you want to organize this?"

Now it was Ben's turn to hesitate. "Can you keep a secret?"

"Of course."

He turned to his computer and double-clicked. "I have a copy of CyberLine on my computer here." The firm had a policy against installing personal software on the firm's computers.

Debby laughed. "Ooooo. Ben's been a bad boy," she said. Ben blushed. "Oh, Ben, it's no big deal. Everybody does that. I have CyberLine installed upstairs on my computer, too."

"These are my PenPals," Ben said, pointing to the screen. The list included WoodythePecker, BlueSatin, Lisa C., PeggySue and Quixote.

"Sounds like a motley crew," she said.

"I can count on them for help—except Quixote. Let's divide the day into four-hour slots. Since I saw them in the room around midnight, I want the 10 p.m. to 2 a.m. shift. Do you have a preference?"

"I can monitor the room from my desk while I'm doing other busy work," Debby said. "Is 10 a.m. to 2 p.m. okay?"

"It's yours. I'll send e-mails to the others, and we'll see if they can help."

"Sounds like a plan," Debby said. "Who's Quixote?"

Ben blushed, again. "An old friend I haven't spoken to in a couple of years."

Debby started to ask another question, then stopped. She started to leave, then she came back and shut the door. "I got your e-mail last night," she said.

Ben tensed. "I didn't feel like I said everything I wanted to say last night before we left," he said.

An uneasy smile crossed her lips. "It's hard to talk about emotions, especially when we're both such sensitive people," she said. "I love <u>The Road Not Taken</u>; it's one of my favorite poems. You're already one of the closest friends I've ever had, but I've got to work out my problems before I'm ready to take our friendship to the next level."

Ben forced a grin. "You can't blame a guy for trying," he said.

"Still friends?" she asked.

"Still friends."

AS BEN HAD HOPED, his CyberLine PenPals were eager to help. By the time he left work on Wednesday at eight o'clock, the arrangements had been made for a 24-hour watch on the Millennium Nights room.

Woody, a night owl by nature, needed no prodding to accept the 2 a.m. to 6 a.m. shift, which ended at three in the morning San Francisco time. Lisa C., who was also in Manhattan, covered the Millennium Nights room from six to ten in the morning, when Debby took over the watch. BlueSatin was working a night shift at the tire factory, and she agreed to take the two o'clock afternoon watch. PeggySue picked it up at six o'clock in the evening, and Ben rounded out the day from ten to two in the morning.

Ben was too excited to wait until his ten o'clock stint. He logged on to CyberLine at eight-thirty and went directly to the RealTime private rooms. Since he did not have the password, he could not observe as users entered and exited the Millennium Nights room or the conversation within. However, the name of the room appeared on a list of private rooms, which indicated how many members were in the room at the time. It was currently empty.

If there had been members in the room, they could be identified by clicking on a button that provided a list of occupants. Once the member was identified, a private message could be sent. If any of Ben's friends found the room in use, they were instructed to try to engage one or two of the occupants in an innocuous conversation. Ben was more interested in determining the times that they met, at this point, but thought it would be interesting to see how the Knights reacted.

Ben's PenPal list was active. Woody, Lisa, and Peggy Sue were logged on. Ben added DebbyDoes to the list, but she was not on-line. Ben sent Peggy Sue a message.

MasterBen: Hi PeggySue. How goes the first watch?

PeggySue: 8:45 and all is well.

MasterBen: (Laughing) No activity?

PeggySue: Nope. I've been checking every five minutes.

MasterBen: Fair enough. Anything interesting going on in your life?

PeggySue: Not really. It's the busy season at the ski club and I'm exhausted. I love my job, but I'm too tired to paint when I get home.

MasterBen: That's too bad. I'll pray for an early melt.

PeggySue: (Smile) Don't do that! The ski lessons pay the bills. I'll get over it and paint in the spring.

MasterBen: Since I'm on-line, anyway, do you want me to cover the rest of your shift?

PeggySue: I don't mind doing this at all, but if you're doing it, anyway, a bubble bath would be nice! <smile>

MasterBen: Sounds good to me...Wish I was there to wash your back <devilish grin>

PeggySue: Good night, Ben...you horny devil.

MasterBen: 'Nite, PeggySue...thanks again for helping out with this.

PeggySue: No worries. I'll check in with you tomorrow.

Ben tried Lisa next.

MasterBen:	Hi, Lisa...how goes the battle?
Lisa C.:	Hey, Ben! How's your witch hunt going?
MasterBen:	Another friend is taking the first shift right now...at least she was until a bubble bath called...
Lisa C.:	Some friend!
MasterBen:	I'm teasing...she had a tough day on the slopes of the Colorado Rockies and I'm ready to start my watch early, anyway...
Lisa C.:	Sounds like a tough life...skiing, bubble bath...it would be just awful if she had to curl up by a roaring fire with something warm, too.
MasterBen:	(Laughing) She's a ski instructor...I'm sure she works very hard...and I already volunteered to be that something warm but got shot down <smile>
Lisa C.:	So...is your witch hunt business or pleasure?
MasterBen:	This one's all business...I'll tell you about it when it's all over. Right now I think it's better to play this hand close to the chest...I mean vest.
Lisa C.:	(Laughing hysterically) You're incorrigible.
MasterBen:	But I'm cute.
Lisa C.:	Like an iguana.
MasterBen:	Ow, that smarts...We really should get together some time...just for coffee...I'm not so bad looking and we already know we get along great...We probably know each other better than a married couple...
Lisa C.:	We do know what the other likes sexually...
Lisa C.:	And iguanas do make nice pets...

MasterBen:	Oh, man...you had me getting all hard there for a minute...\<grin>
Lisa C.:	Now there's a challenge...\<smile>
MasterBen:	So, will you at least think about it?
Lisa C.:	C'mon, Ben...we've been through this before...what if we aren't attracted to each other? I don't want to lose you as a friend...you're one of my best buddies in the whole world \<blushing>
MasterBen:	(Laughing) I know, but you can't blame a guy for trying...I'm starting a new relationship and I want to give it a chance, anyway...
Lisa C.:	Someone from RealTime?
MasterBen:	No. I haven't ever dated anybody from online. She's from work. A paralegal at my firm...
Lisa C.:	What's she like? \<turning light shade of green>
MasterBen:	She's cool...you'd like her...smart, confident, good sense of humor, pretty...
Lisa C.:	Did you have sex with her?
MasterBen:	No...she really turns me on, but she has issues...
Lisa C.:	A likely story \<smile>
MasterBen:	No, they're real...but I promised not to tell...
Lisa C.:	I don't even know who she is...
MasterBen:	It wouldn't feel right...
Lisa C.:	Your call, Ben. Your hand must be getting quite a work out while you wait...
MasterBen:	\<blush> Maybe I need a surrogate...what are you doing Saturday night?

Lisa C.:	(Laughing) Mouse at play while the cat's away?
MasterBen:	I'm very faithful <puppy dog hurt look> You should have seen the babe I turned down when I was in Atlanta on Monday...
Lisa C.:	Do tell...
MasterBen:	She works for the client I was visiting... she was all over me!!!
Lisa C.:	Literally?
MasterBen:	Yeah...One step away from lifting her dress and it's a home run...but I pulled away...what an idiot...
Lisa C.:	That Jewish thing again?
MasterBen:	I think it was part guilt, part something else that I haven't experienced before...
Lisa C.:	Impotence? <grin>
MasterBen:	Funny (not laughing) No, I think there's a bond between me and this other girl and I want to build trust between us...if I had sex with Kimberly, I'd have a secret and there would be no trust...
Lisa C.:	I think I'm still going with my impotency theory <grin>
MasterBen:	Okay, you caught me <sheepish grin>
Lisa C.:	So it sounds like you're pretty serious about this gal?
MasterBen:	We had a moment on Saturday night when I knew I was in love and this thing with Kimberly on Monday confirmed it...
Lisa C.:	Does she love you back?
MasterBen:	I don't know for sure...she's not looking for love because of the issues in her life...but there is a connection...I feel it...

Lisa C.:	Cool...I'm happy for you.
MasterBen:	In the meantime, I have all this excitement at work to keep my idle hands busy...
Lisa C.:	I almost forgot...Have you been checking the room?
MasterBen:	Yep...Nothing doing...I've got to check in with another buddy, though...thanks for listening tonight, Lisa! <smile>
Lisa C.:	You bet, that's what friends are for...sweet dreams, Ben

Ben returned a parting note, and then contacted Woody. His mind was racing.

MasterBen:	Woodman!
WoodythePecker:	Benmeister! You must have been making your rounds—I noticed you came on-line some time ago.
MasterBen:	You got it...the information superhighway is lit up tonight...
WoodythePecker:	So are you going to keep me in suspense about your discovery today?
MasterBen:	The 20-Year Jinx is real!
WoodythePecker:	Don't mess with me, man...what did you find?
MasterBen:	The police found Thompson's wallet... There was a list of names—they were the same nicknames that I saw in the Millennium Nights room in RealTime last week...
WoodythePecker:	Are you sure? These cyber-names tend to blend together after awhile...
MasterBen:	I'm sure. You wouldn't forget these names if you saw them, either: The Heir

Apparent, The Caretaker, The General, The Senator, The Spy, The Speaker, The Doctor and The Assassin.

WoodythePecker: Wow, nothing like a little melodrama...

MasterBen: I thought it was a bizarre club when I first saw them in RealTime...but tie it together with Adams Thompson, the plot described in the Poem, and the Millennium Nights/Knights link and I think we've got ourselves a conspiracy...

WoodythePecker: Don't be too hasty...Maybe Thompson and his buddies organized the bizarre club based on the Poem.

MasterBen: Like in that book you told me about...

WoodythePecker: *Foucault's Pendulum.* They may just be a group of conspiracy theorists waiting for the descendants of the MacDougalls to reappear at the dawn of the millennium.

MasterBen: The voice of reason speaks...

WoodythePecker: (Laughing) I'm not saying stop investigating...you're right, the odds that the Jinx is real have increased...but don't go making an ass of yourself...keep it quiet for awhile...

MasterBen: That's my conclusion, too...I can't go to my boss or to the police with the evidence I've got now...I want to monitor the Millennium Nights room with the help of you and some other friends and try to crack the Key...we need to know who the conspirators are to make any kind of case...

Ben and Woody discussed the various ways that the MacDougalls might have created the Key. They did not come up with any new ideas. Ben continued to monitor the Millennium Nights room as they spoke. There was no activity. Woody took his turn at the helm when Ben logged off at two o'clock, Thursday morning.

SEVENTEEN

THE FIRST 24-HOUR WATCH on the Millennium Nights room had been fruitless. Ben anxiously began his second watch at ten o'clock Thursday evening. It was one week since first contact.

They began to appear one by one at the midnight hour. The Doctor. The Speaker. The Heir Apparent. The Caretaker. The Senator. The Spy. The General was the last to arrive at ten past twelve.

Ben did not want to contact the Knights as MasterBen. These were intelligent men. If Dean Frederick was one of them, they might already be suspicious of him. He signed off CyberLine, then logged on again using one of the other cyber-names he had reserved, CurvyCarol. He sent a message to The Doctor.

"What are you boys up to in that room? It sounds so mysterious and sexy…"

There was no reply. He tried The Speaker with the same message. Again, no reply.

THE KNIGHTS HAD DISPENSED with formalities and were preparing to discuss the status of their plan.

The Speaker:	Is there a woman bothering anybody else right now?
The Doctor:	I ignored her and she seems to have gone away.
The Speaker:	I know this happens from time to time, but I'm sensitive about security these days.
The Heir Apparent:	Ignore her. Nobody can see in here. If

anybody is unlucky enough to guess the password, The Spy can arrange another accident.

The Spy: Only too happy to oblige.

The Senator: We all appreciate your subtle and rather dark sense of humor, Spy, but let's remember what we spoke about last week. So far no innocents have been harmed. If we start arranging "accidents," we add a great deal of personal risk. Let's be sure a security breach is real before we act.

The Spy: Point taken.

The General: Now she sent me a message.

The Heir Apparent: Like I said, ignore her. We have several items we need to cover tonight. Caretaker, tell us about your meeting with the lawyer.

The Caretaker: I played my little game with him in the MacDougall Room. I'm not sure what to make of him. He didn't mention the Poem. Either he hasn't found it or he realizes that he's stumbled on to something. He tensed when I was telling Jimmy's tale, but I couldn't tell if it was from recognition or general anxiety. He's very young. He's only been doing this for a year, and his act is not very smooth yet.

The General: What does your gut tell you?

The Caretaker: I'm sure my gut is not as finely tuned as yours, General. He seems like a bright kid, but inexperienced. Professional. He even resisted the charms of young Kimberly.

The Doctor: That's quite an accomplishment.

The Caretaker: Careful, good Doctor, she is my daughter.

The Doctor: And a lovely lass she is, sir. And I believe

her photos will be helpful in getting our little research project underway.

The Heir Apparent: That's good news, Doctor. If all else goes
as planned, you may have the honor of fir-
ing the shot that starts the war.

The General: I want to hear more about the lawyer. Spy,
have you discovered anything new?

The Spy: Office telephone tapped. Nothing interesting. Apt not wired; no tail. Caretaker, do
you think that's warranted?

The Caretaker: Yes.

The Heir Apparent: Why?

The Caretaker: Caution. Like I said last week, The
Publisher's copy of the Poem should be
sealed and subject to a trust. The kid
didn't say or do anything inconsistent with
that and a case of the jitters. But there's a
lot at stake. I don't have enough confidence in my instincts. Let's keep an eye
on him for a few weeks and see if he does
anything suspicious.

The General: I agree with The Caretaker.

The Heir Apparent: Any problem with that, Spy?

The Spy: No. Call it drug stakeout. Report to detail
comings/goings.

The Heir Apparent: Good. Any progress in finding our friend,
The Assassin?

The Spy: None. If killed Pub, he disappeared. Police
picked up drunk trying to use Pub's credit
card, but not killer.

The Heir Apparent: I think we all anticipated that The
Assassin would not be found based on
your last report. In fact, I've acted based
on that assumption. I met with Fabrizio on

Tuesday and made him an unusual proposal. I suggested that we join forces. He'll be the president, I'll be the VP.

The Senator: Have you gone mad? How did he react?

The Heir Apparent: Hell, I've thought deeply about this. Hear me out. First, if I win the presidency, I'm The Assassin's target. That's not an option that I relish.

The Heir Apparent: Second, Fabrizio seems to be leaning towards Stevenson as a running mate. My candidacy is vulnerable if Fabrizio carries California, and Stevenson can help him do that. Even if Fabrizio doesn't go for my proposal, he might delay announcing his choice. Time is my ally in California.

The Heir Apparent: Third, I think the American people would leap at a bipartisan ticket. It's a bold and symbolic way to usher in the new millennium. Fabrizio's reaction was as expected. He was stunned. For now, he agreed to think about it.

The Heir Apparent: Finally, you have to appreciate the drama of it. I triumphantly assume the presidency after Fabrizio's tragic death. It's the way our ancestors envisioned it.

The Senator: Perhaps "mad" was too harsh a word. But don't you think you were a little hasty? What will the Republican leadership think?

The Heir Apparent: The Speaker is a key member of the Republican leadership. I expect his support. The Republicans won't be thrilled, but they don't have many alternatives. Once we're in power and Fabrizio is dead, I don't care if my working relationship with Congress is difficult. Our legacy will not be civil rights legislation, it will be civil war.

The Speaker: But what if The Assassin doesn't material-ize?

The Spy: Wait six months, otherwise I'll handle it.

The Heir Apparent: My hopes exactly.

The Senator: What if Fabrizio doesn't agree to your pro-posal?

The Heir Apparent: Then we need to re-evaluate our plan. I won't assume the presidency if The Assassin is not located. I'll throw the ball-game.

The Spy: We've all worked too hard to give up at first sign of adversity. Remember the penalty for treason...

The Heir Apparent: Don't threaten me. Let's not forget whose responsibility it was to eliminate The Assassin. The objective chosen for me by our ancestors was to be elected VP in the millennium election. I've taken steps to make that happen. If that's not possible, then we may have failed to achieve the crowning glory our ancestors envisioned, but we can still claim their Final Vengeance.

The General: What are you proposing?

The Heir Apparent: We can still trigger the civil war even if I'm not the president. We won't be able to stand and triumphantly declare our tri-umph from the presidential pulpit, but we may still be able to dictate terms if we're victorious. It will take some planning, but we'll just have to roll with the punches.

The Doctor: I think teaming with Fabrizio is a terrific idea. I like the drama. The final presiden-tial assassination is such an integral part of the plan.

The Speaker: It adds a lot of pressure on me. The Republican leadership will go ballistic.

The Heir Apparent: I'm sure you'll do your best. We've all had to make sacrifices and take risks.

The Senator: May I make a proposal?

The Heir Apparent: Of course.

The Senator: As one of the senior Democrats in the Senate, I may be able to use my influence to gain the inside track for the vice-presidential nomination. Tom Stevenson is popular, but I have almost twenty years seniority.

The Heir Apparent: I appreciate your willingness to pinch hit for me, once again. But I've already approached Fabrizio, and I feel that it's my obligation to take my best shot at the presidency. I do think that you can use your influence to help in another way, though, Senator.

It was about half past one o'clock on Friday morning. The discussion in the Millennium Nights room continued for several minutes. Ben had abandoned his early efforts to gain the attention of the Knights. He maintained his watch to determine their quitting time. The room emptied by the time Woody was ready to take over at two o'clock. Ben suggested that Woody take the night off.

EIGHTEEN

CHRISTY KIRK PAID HER BREAKFAST BILL at the hotel restaurant. The cashier smiled and thanked her with a sugary Southern accent. Christy mocked her, replying "Yeah, y'all have a good day, too," with an exaggerated Brooklyn accent, which was all the more cruel in that she was born in St. Paul, Minnesota and had developed only a slight New York twang after seven years in the city.

"Next time try decaf, darlin,'" came the angry retort from the cashier.

Christy looked at her watch, standing outside the Dunhill Hotel on Tryon Street in downtown Charlotte—or "uptown Charlotte" as the local chamber of commerce had been promoting it. Her meeting was in ten minutes. She crossed the tree-lined street, passing the Nationsbank Corporate Center, the sixty-story monument to Southern regional banking that towered over the quaint, low-rise cityscape like a giant phallus.

Christy's short auburn hair blew in the balmy December breeze. She did not think of herself as an unattractive woman, but she found that her intensity, often betrayed by her eyes without a spoken word, caused some people to take an instant dislike to her. She could be charming when she wanted to be, but she had taken some delight in cultivating the image of the steely-eyed bitch. It kept people at arm's length. It was safe.

Security was a feeling that Christy Kirk had rarely enjoyed in her twenty-five years. Her father was a respected businessman in St. Paul, an insurance salesman, who always seemed to have a kind word for everyone. Until he came home.

Christy and her mother had been subjected to an almost endless barrage of physical and verbal abuse. They could do nothing right in

Willie Kirk's eyes. An "A" on Christy's report card should have been an "A+;" a "B" was an unforgivable offense. Her friends were not good enough. She was too thin. The house was never clean enough. Something was always wrong with dinner. And his reaction was always loud or violent, regardless of the magnitude of the infraction.

Christy had sought escape, first in the fantasy world she had created in her journals, then in the real world of the Ivy League, courtesy of a scholarship to Columbia University. She had arrived in New York determined to prove her father wrong, to show him that her life had value. She had studied hard, played little, and graduated in the top ten percent of her class, earning her a place in the graduate program at the prestigious Columbia School of Journalism.

It had been there that Christy had first captured the attention of Adams Thompson, Jr., where he had been an adjunct professor. A reporting job at the *New York Herald Times* was a prize that few college recruits snared, but Christy had set her sights on it.

Most *Herald Times* reporters had served long apprenticeships at newspapers in smaller cities and towns, learning their craft, the wheat separated from the chaff. Only the best even aspired to the *Herald Times* or the *Washington Post* or the handful of other top tier newspapers in the country.

But Christy had shown Thompson that she had the qualities of a great reporter, the tenaciousness to dig for the difficult stories and the courage to write them. She had gotten the job.

Thompson had put on a gruff act, but Christy knew that he was fond of her. He made sure that she was assigned stories that a rookie reporter had no business writing. When she had upset the wrong people, somehow he made the problems go away. She had initially thought of him as one more instrument to help her achieve the fame that she craved, but now she missed him. His interest in her had been almost paternal. He had made her feel safe.

But now Thompson was gone, and Christy was determined to prove that she could fend for herself. In the week and a half since she had stormed out of Roger Martin's office at the *Herald Times*, Christy had plunged into her story, at each step hearing Roger's dire warning echoing in her ears.

She had found that white supremacists made the firemen, sanitation workers and longshoremen she had toyed with seem like Boy Scouts.

They were the radical fringe, people with a predisposition towards violence and questionable mental stability.

Christy had started her research with Roger's folder, which contained
several hundred newspaper clippings from around the country, apparently the product of Roger's vast collegial network. She had been aston-
ished not only by the extent of the racially motivated activity, but also by
its fragmentation. Hate came in boxes of many different shapes and sizes.

She had categorized the white supremacy groups into four broad
groups—Ku Klux Klan, Neo-Nazis, Skinheads and Christian
Identity—but still others, like the enormous National Association for
the Advancement of White People, an offshoot of the KKK, and the
violent Army of God defied such classification. The one common bond
among most of the groups, and even that was not clear to her, was their
ties to the Religious Right. They almost universally justified their
hatred of people of color and Jews as divinely ordained.

Roger's folder had included only limited material about the black
separatist groups, the House of David and the Nation of Islam, but had
included extensive clippings about the massive build-up of activity by
the NOMAADs, the National Organization for Mutual African-
American Defense. Unlike the other groups, the NOMAADs did not
appear to be inspired by hate or religion. They simply saw the increasing militarization of the white hate groups, and they were determined
to defend themselves.

Christy had then turned to the Internet to try to tie the material
together, but she had given up in frustration. She found hundreds of
web sites devoted to individual hate groups. Their propaganda was
almost always difficult to understand and sometimes nonsensical.
Nothing appeared to link the groups. She had decided to talk with real
people first, form a general impression, maybe figure out their motivation, and then try to make sense of the white supremacy movement.

Christy had focused her attention on three organizations, all with
significant ties to the Carolinas, for no other reason than convenience.
She was not sure whether she was still employed by the *Herald Times*,
and she did not want to run up a large expense account. If those interviews panned out, she could expand her contacts to higher levels.

The White Knights of the Ku Klux Klan had chapters in three small
towns in central North Carolina within a fifty mile radius of Winston-
Salem, all of which appeared to have unusually active memberships.

The Aryan Alliance was a Christian Identity group with headquarters in Charlotte and a paramilitary compound in the western part of the state, southeast of Asheville. It had chapters in twenty-six states.

The NOMAADs were headquartered in Washington, D.C. and had chapters in all fifty states. They had a major training facility ten miles north of Greenville, South Carolina, not far from the North Carolina border and the Aryan Alliance camp. It was the closest NOMAAD facility to any major white supremacy compound that she had been able to identify.

Hate groups did not advertise in the Yellow Pages, but Christy had been able to track down contacts from the newspaper clippings and the Internet sites. She had started with what she hoped would be the easiest interviews, the leaders and members of the three rural KKK chapters. Her plan had been to cut her teeth on them, learning the right questions to ask and the "hot buttons" to avoid when she reached the higher levels of the white supremacy movement, the contacts she ultimately hoped to quote to support her story.

The Klan meetings had been eye-opening. She had expected hooded rednecks with potbellies and a handful of teeth among them. But this was the new Klan. A more moderate Klan. A middle-class Klan. At least that was the way they had presented themselves. Christy had done some digging, asked some direct questions and discovered a different story.

The Klan had been originally founded in 1866 in Pulaski, Tennessee by Nathan Bedford Forrest, a former Confederate general. They had engaged in lynchings and other tactics of intimidation, disguised in white sheets, to discourage Southern blacks from exercising their newly acquired voting rights. The Klan had largely disappeared by the early 1870s, only to reappear in ebbs and flows beginning shortly before World War II.

Membership had declined again in the 1970s as integration began to be accepted, spawning the more laid back Klan popularized by David Duke. This was the image the Klan was still trying to sell, but Christy discovered that they had in fact entered into a new era.

Today's Klan was distinguished by an increasing paramilitary presence within many factions and ties to the Christian Identity movement. While they outwardly portrayed themselves as more restrained than the traditional Klan image, they were every bit as violent and then some. The National Association for the Advancement of White People had splintered from the Klan because of disagreements over ideology and Klan-sanctioned violence.

Still, even among the Klan factions, Christy found that there was no centralized leadership. Two of the three leaders that Christy had met claimed to be on a mission from God. The other had claimed to be God's son. All three chapters engaged in paramilitary training, but even within that small region in central North Carolina there was no plan to combine their efforts.

Christy had left the Winston-Salem area more concerned about isolated terrorist attacks on black and Jewish targets, but less worried about unification of the white supremacy movement into a significant fighting force.

Christy found her destination, a four-story brick office building on West Tryon Street. She was anxious about this morning's meeting. Franklin Verdant, the Chairman or the Imperial Wizard or the Grand Pubah of the Aryan Alliance, was no redneck. The Aryan Alliance had chapters in twenty-six states and had doubled its membership in the past five years to more than fifty thousand men, women and children. Verdant had not risen to power by buying drinks and slapping backs. He was an intelligent, passionate man whose life was centered on hate and violence.

For once, Christy felt as small as she looked as she stepped off the elevator into the richly decorated offices of the Aryan Alliance. Then she closed her eyes and slipped into character.

The receptionist was expecting her, and she was hustled into a small conference room, no more than ten feet square. Unlike the reception area, little attention had been given to the decor of this room. A round, mahogany table surrounded by four padded swivel chairs filled most of the tiny space. A glass pitcher of water and four cups were on the table-top. The barren walls were painted an undistinguished shade of white.

Before Christy could become bored with her surroundings, the door burst open, and a tall, imposing man with a deep, booming voice introduced himself as Franklin Verdant. Verdant had a game face that made even Christy cower. He was bald except for a ring of salt and pepper hair around the base of his scalp that drooped into a neatly trimmed beard and mustache. His wrinkled brow and dark, bushy eyebrows were slanted downwards into a permanent, imperious scowl. He was elegantly attired in a navy blue suit, red silk tie and blue candy-striped shirt with French cuffs and gold cufflinks.

Verdant glowered at her. "I expected somebody more mature," he said.

Christy knew that this was a critical moment. Her eyes locked with his. "I can call the newsroom and get you a 45-year old, faggot-assed liberal if you really want one," she said. "Or you can stick with the toughest bitch in New York. Your choice."

Verdant sat down. His expression, better suited for leading Mongol hordes into battle than polite conversation, remained unchanged. "You've got fifteen minutes. Talk, bitch."

Christy had been promised an hour. She suppressed an urge to grumble. They could argue in fifteen minutes if he needed to flex his muscles again. "How many chapters are there in the Aryan Alliance?" she asked.

He leaned forward. "Look, if you're half as good as you think you are, you know the answer to that question. It's on our web site. Now skip the bullshit and ask me what you really want to know."

Okay. So he was going to play it tough. *I can deal with that.* "You'll answer any question I ask you?"

"I'll answer any fucking question I feel like answering," he boomed. "But I will not waste my time with bullshit."

Christy was unfazed. "What are the basic principles of the Christian Identity movement?" she asked.

"Web site." He was not going to give an inch. She knew the basic tenets—that Northwestern European whites are God's "chosen people" and the true Israelites and the Jews and other non-Aryan peoples are the children and followers of Satan, intent upon taking over the world. It made better copy if she could get him to say it.

"Can you just sum up how you understand those principles and how they've guided your life?"

He placed his palms on the edge of the table and raised himself. "Do you think I'm stupid? I'm not going to give you a quote that you can take out of context and make me look like an ignoramus. You think that just because my beliefs aren't shared by the majority they're foolish. Just remember this—Jesus was an outcast in his time, too."

"So, you think you're like Jesus?" Christy asked.

Christy knew immediately that she had crossed a line. Verdant's ears flushed and his eyes narrowed to little slits. "Look, Princess Bitch, I can have you hog-tied, fucked and left for dead in the woods outside town within an hour. Are you ready to take this seriously or is this interview over?"

Christy suppressed the wave of fear that tried to rock her self-assurance. Verdant wanted her to be intimidated. *Fuck you, Nazi asshole. Nobody bullies the Bitch.* "You seem to rely heavily on your web site," she said. "What role is the Internet playing for your group?"

Verdant settled back into his chair. "The Internet is the one medium where we can compete with the liberal national media," he said. "We're constantly being portrayed as ignorant rednecks. People can read our web site, uncensored, and see what we're about. It's been an outstanding recruiting tool."

"If you're so concerned about the national media, why did you agree to this interview?" she asked.

"The *Herald Times* is the only shop I would even consider talking to," Verdant said approvingly. "That editorial on school integration took some guts."

Christy had wondered why it had been so easy to schedule the interview. He expected a glamour piece. Quote or not, that was not going to happen. "Do you use the Internet to communicate with other like-minded groups?"

Verdant poured himself a glass of water from the pitcher on the table. "We use the Internet to communicate within our own group," he said. He took a sip, then placed the glass on the table. "We have a Rapid Response Team, a group of volunteers who are contacted via e-mail to respond to special situations, whether alerting members of an emergency or gathering information from them."

"What kind of emergencies have arisen?"

"Just as an example, an arrest warrant was issued for one of our members. We used the Rapid Response Team to locate him and arrange for safe passage from state to state. He has eluded the authorities for over a year now."

Christy thought she knew who he was talking about, but that was not the story she wanted. Now that she had the Nazi talking, she needed to know if he was goose-stepping alone or in partnership. She leaned forward and asked the real question on her mind, again, this time more directly. "Does your group have close ties to other Christian Identity groups?"

Verdant made a steeple with his fingers. "I speak with other leaders in the Christian Identity movement and similar organizations," he said cautiously.

Christy tapped her heel nervously against the leg of her chair. It was easier to bathe her terrier than draw information from Franklin Verdant. "Has there ever been any discussion of merging the groups?" she asked.

"There's always talk," Verdant said evenly. "Sometimes I initiate those talks. We'll need a strong centralized government to carry out our critical tasks during the first few decades of the Aryan world—the racial cleansing of the land, the eradication of racially destructive institutions, and the reorganization of society into a new world order."

Verdant spoke of genocide as if it was an item on a task list, right after washing the car. Christy searched his eyes for a soul. She found none. "So why does there appear to be so little cooperation between the Christian Identity groups?" she asked.

"Because I believe that I'm destined to lead—and so does Rolf Sanders of the World Church of the Creator, Sam Diggs of the Aryan Kingdom, and Frank Sims of the National Socialists. One day when the Apocalypse looms near, God will decide. For now, I'm content to spread the word to as many true believers as I can."

Christy was getting close. She could feel it. He knew something. And this pit bull was going to get it out of him. *Bite and don't let go.* "Is the Apocalypse coming soon?"

Verdant responded coldly and to the point. "I'm a warrior, not a prophet." He rose and stalked out without another word or gesture.

Christy looked at her watch. Exactly fifteen minutes had passed. She was drained. And Verdant had been willing to let his guard down for the *Herald Times.* She needed to prepare more carefully for her interview at the NOMAADs' South Carolina compound next Wednesday. Who knew what hog-tying or mayhem they had planned for her.

NINETEEN

THE VICE PRESIDENT was agitated. "I hate that pompous old fart," Tony Fabrizio said. He was in his shirtsleeves, pacing back and forth behind his desk. It was Tuesday morning. His customary half-eaten Danish lay on a plate on the desk.

"Calm down, Tony," LaRosa said. She was reclining in one of the guest chairs, her feet resting on Fabrizio's desk. "It's probably just Senate business. He might want to call in one of his chits for some prime Carolina pork."

"I doubt Ty Andrew would waste a chit on pork barrel legislation," Fabrizio said. "He's the Pork King. Geez, we're cutting back on military funding and somehow he managed to attach a provision for a $40 million refurbishing of Camp Lejeune to the anti-crime bill last month."

"Every dog has his day." LaRosa said. "He was the Senate *Minority* Leader for twelve years. You can't blame him for enjoying himself a little as the Majority Leader now that we're back in power."

"I can forgive his mastery of the art of politics," Fabrizio said. "I can't forgive his personal weaknesses. He's a hypocrite, a womanizer and a bigot. One minute he's out in front of the microphones professing his support for civil rights legislation, the next he's in the Senate cloakroom with his Southern cronies telling racist jokes and bragging about his latest sexual conquest."

"That's not an image I need right after breakfast," LaRosa said, as she swung her feet off the desk. "He's got to be the ugliest old goat in Congress. He gives me the creeps. I always get the feeling he's looking at my ass when I turn my back on him."

Fabrizio winked. "Well, I'm not sure I would hold that against him."

LaRosa rolled her eyes skyward. "Thanks, Tony. I love you, too," she said, her voice laden with sarcasm. She stood to go. "I think I'll leave you two good old boys to do whatever it is that you do when there are no woman folk around."

Fabrizio snorted. "That's me, the last of the good ol' boys."

FABRIZIO ROLLED DOWN HIS SHIRTSLEEVES and put on his jacket after LaRosa left. There would be no relaxation of protocol with the Senator from North Carolina.

"Mr. Vice President," the Senator drawled, extending his hand and smiling, revealing his crooked, tobacco-stained teeth. "Thank you so much for meeting with me this morning. I know you are a very busy man."

"You know that my door is always open for you, Senator Andrew," Fabrizio said, smiling warmly. LaRosa was right; Ty Andrew was not an attractive man. He was 69 years old, fifty pounds overweight, with a shock of dyed black hair combed from left to right across an ever-widening bald spot. His large, wrinkled face was losing its battle with gravity. He stank of body odor and tobacco.

"That's very kind of you, Mr. Vice President. And how is that lovely wife and daughter of yours?"

"They're doing wonderfully, thank you," Fabrizio said. "And how's Mary Lou? I was very concerned to hear that she was in the hospital last month."

"She's doing just fine, thank you. She gave us a little scare, but she is recovering nicely. I will be sure to tell her that you were inquiring about her."

"Please do that. Have a seat, Senator." Fabrizio waved him to one of the Windsor chairs by his desk. Fabrizio stood until the slow-moving Senator seated himself. The chair strained under Andrew's weight.

Senator Andrew coughed and cleared his throat. Then he pulled out a handkerchief and blew his nose with several loud honks. He carefully folded the handkerchief and replaced it in his pocket. "Excuse me, Mr. Vice President, I have been a little under the weather lately."

"Of course." Fabrizio glanced at his watch and resisted the temptation to roll his eyes.

Senator Andrew did not seem to notice Fabrizio's impatience. He continued to charm the Vice President with his highly cultivated gift of gab. "It's been a little colder than usual this winter, don't you think?"

"Maybe so. It's been damp."

"So true. My arthritis has been acting up lately, too."

"Maybe a little sun would do you and Mary Lou some good over the Christmas recess."

The Senator chuckled. "We don't travel much. We will no doubt be spending the holidays in our cabin on the Blue Ridge surrounded by all of our grandchildren. It's been a family tradition for as long as I can remember."

Fabrizio glanced at his watch, again. "Well, Senator, as much as I would love to chat, I have another meeting scheduled in about fifteen minutes."

"Of course. I do appreciate your taking the time to see me this morning, as always. I suppose that I could have waited to bend your ear in the Senate cloakroom, but I have been hearing some disturbing rumors. Most disturbing rumors. I thought that I should ask you about them personally."

"Fire away, Senator. My life is an open book for you."

"I appreciate that. I appreciate the trust that you and Hank Norton have shown in me as the principal liaison between the Democrats in the Senate and the White House," he said, seeming to take particular pleasure in distinctly pronouncing each syllable in the word "liaison." "I think that we have a truly outstanding working relationship."

"I value that relationship, too, Senator Andrew."

"How long have we known each other, Mr. Vice President?"

Fabrizio smiled instinctively. "It's been almost seven years."

"I showed you the ropes in the Senate."

"You did indeed."

"We've made a good team. That's why I am truly disappointed about the rumor that you are considering Tom Stevenson as a running mate. Not that I have anything against Tom. He's a fine man. A good senator. But he's young. He hasn't paid his dues. I hoped that you would at least give me the courtesy of interviewing for the job. I've served the party loyally for over forty years. I've taken some bullets for both you and the President these last seven."

Fabrizio squirmed. "Senator, first of all, I haven't made any final decisions regarding my running mate for next year, although I may make an announcement shortly. You've been a loyal friend to the President and myself. We consider you a powerful ally in the Senate.

Maybe I should have spoken with you as a courtesy, but I'd much rather have you in the Senate where you have done so much good work."

Senator Andrew leaned forward in his chair—Fabrizio thought that it might break under the strain of his shifting girth—and stared the Vice President in the eyes. "We both know that's a truckload of happy horseshit."

Fabrizio recoiled from the sharpness of the Senator's reply. "Senator?"

"Tom Stevenson's a pretty boy that might do you some good in California," the Senator said. "I understand that. But that's not the only factor that goes into these decisions. You need to take into account stature within the Party. Seniority. Leadership. The respect of the American people. Loyalty. I'm not going to be around forever, son, and this is probably my last chance to pay tribute to the great Americans who have supported me throughout my long career. I want you to give some serious thought to a Fabrizio-Andrew ticket in 2000. We'd make a fine team—and I could virtually guarantee you the South."

Fabrizio stood. "Senator, you know I have great respect for your accomplishments, and I'll give your proposal serious thought. In any case, whether you join me on the ticket or not, I hope that we can continue to work together as a team and that I can count on you to deliver the South next November."

Senator Andrew continued to cajole the Vice President for another five minutes before making his slow—and for Fabrizio, painful—exit. LaRosa hustled into Fabrizio's office moments later. Fabrizio had already removed his jacket and rolled up his shirtsleeves. The pacing resumed, now with increased intensity. He was fuming.

"Fuckshit," Fabrizio said. "I was right, Rosie. That old fart is up to no good."

"What did he say?" she asked.

"He says he's paid his dues. He wants to be my running mate."

"He's crazy! He's too old. He's from the South. He smells. He'd be a liability rather than an asset."

"Plus I hate the old fucker's guts."

"That could be a problem, too."

"I didn't need this right now!"

"What did you tell him?"

"I told him I'd think about it."

LaRosa looked concerned. She picked up a paperweight from Fabrizio's desk and toyed with it. "I know his kind. He'll be leaking this to the press by this afternoon if his people aren't already doing it."

"This could tear the Party apart. I cannot run with Ty Andrew. That's not an option," Fabrizio said. "But if I choose Tom Stevenson, Ty dropped some hints that he might not fully support me in the election. We need Ty Andrew to give us any hope in the South."

She fidgeted with the paperweight. "He might make life miserable for you in the Senate, too. He's a vindictive old snake."

"You've got something on your mind, Rosie. Spit it out."

"I know you wanted to ponder JJ's proposal over the holiday break, but I think you need to respond more quickly," she said. "Both Stevenson and Andrew would understand the enormity of this opportunity."

Fabrizio stopped pacing. "Why do you think I need to move so fast?"

"If you let Ty Andrew get too far out in front of this train, it may be hard to pull him back into the station. Given just a little time, he's going to take his campaign to the press. And you don't want to publicly bruise that humongous ego of his. He'll start pulling strings and calling in favors, and before you know it, you're going to have to say 'no' to a lot more powerful people than just Ty Andrew. I'm not saying you need to jump into bed with JJ. You know that I think it's an incredible opportunity for you, but it's your call. What you do need to do is make a decision quickly. You've got to do something before Ty gets rolling."

Fabrizio listened, then resumed his pacing, silently, stroking his chin. Finally, he stopped and sat down at his desk. He put his face into his hands. But he could not rub out the stress lines. "Shitfuck," he said. "I'll sleep on it, Rosie. I'll make a decision tomorrow."

TWENTY

THE ENTRANCE TO CAMP TUBMAN, the NOMAAD training facility, was unmarked, and Christy Kirk almost drove past it in the Wednesday afternoon fog. She had rented the dark green Chevy Cavalier that morning in Charlotte, where she had spent the last five days preparing for her interview with Colonel Thomas Hardy, the commanding officer at Camp Tubman. The training camp was in the rolling hills that marked the fringe between the Blue Ridge Mountains and the Carolina Piedmont, adjacent to the Cowpens National Battlefield, part of the federal National Parks Service.

It was already almost three o'clock, the scheduled time for the interview. Camp Tubman was only an hour's ride from Charlotte, but Christy had taken a wide detour to sneak an unofficial peek at the Aryan Alliance compound, which was nestled in the mountains of western North Carolina only fifty miles from the NOMAAD facility. She had been disappointed, though. Unlike Camp Tubman, the Alliance compound was surrounded by a security fence, eight feet high and topped with two feet of razor wire, and the main entrance had been guarded by armed sentries. She had tried to find a safe observation point in the mountains above the compound, but had been thwarted by rain and thick fog.

Christy drove quickly through the woods along the narrow dirt road leading into Camp Tubman. A low chain link fence appeared off to the right amidst the trees, beyond which appeared to be an empty picnic area. The road then banked sharply to the left, up a steep ridge, and the fence broke to the right following the base of the ridge in the other direction. The woodlands transformed into brown pasture as Christy ascended the hill; the pastoral image dissolved the moment she reached the crest.

The ridge descended abruptly into a rolling valley about a half mile wide, bounded on both sides by a thick forest of oak, hickory, chestnut, and pine. The compound, which covered about fifty acres, buzzed with activity despite the gloomy weather.

Dozens of long, white shingled buildings dotted the valley, many still under construction. The crack of rifle blasts and hammers slamming into wood reverberated throughout the encampment. Several groups of men, all black, clad in gray cotton sweatsuits with the NOMAAD insignia plastered across their chests, jogged in military formation across different sectors of the compound. Puffs of purple smoke rose from the far side of the camp, on the other side of a meandering stream, presumably from a firing range.

Christy checked in at the main building ten minutes late. Colonel Hardy had left instructions for her to find him on the firing range.

Christy was surprised when Thomas Hardy greeted her with a smile. After her experience with Franklin Verdant, she had expected the worst. At first glance there was little to distinguish Hardy from the corps of gray clad troops taking target practice. But Christy had done her homework. She knew that behind the smile and the fleece facade lay the fierce heart of a warrior more than the equal of Franklin Verdant.

Hardy had graduated first in his class at West Point and had been routinely promoted from second lieutenant to colonel over a twenty-year Army career. The Army was desperate to promote black officers to top leadership positions, but Hardy had abruptly cut short his flight to stardom in 1996 when he joined the NOMAADs. At forty-five years old, six-feet tall, buzz cut, straight back, no fat, he was still a military man.

"Miss Kirk, so good of you to join us," he said cheerily, pumping her hand vigorously. "Let's sit over by the athletic fields so we can have some privacy."

"I'm sorry I'm late, Colonel Hardy. I had a little trouble finding the place."

"Happens all the time. The men call me Colonel Tom, by the way, and I kinda like it," he said grinning broadly.

Christy smiled. There was an earthiness about Tom Hardy that instantly, and unexpectedly, put her at ease. She made a mental note not to let her guard down. "Not exactly text book military procedure," she said.

"These men are all volunteers," Hardy said. "We don't even pay expenses. We put them through an intense two-week basic training program and encourage them to come back for advanced training whenever they can make the time. There ain't no reason to make this any harder on them by imposing ridiculous rules and procedures. We try to keep it friendly."

"How many men can you accommodate at one time?" Christy asked.

"Right now, about two thousand. There are about five hundred recruits on the grounds today. We have facilities under construction for three thousand more, and we're negotiating to acquire that pasture beyond the highway over there," he said, pointing south. "We'd like to house ten thousand when we're all through."

"Wow. That sounds like more than a training camp. Are you planning to recruit a permanent army?" she asked.

Colonel Tom hesitated before answering. He looked directly at her. Christy had seen those eyes before—in the mirror. Tom Hardy was a pit bull, the jovial packaging notwithstanding.

"I'm under instructions to talk straight with you," Hardy said. "But I've got to admit that I disagree with that decision. I'm very aware of your newspaper's editorial positions. A few weeks ago we were organizing rallies against you."

"That editorial and all the ones before it were written by Adams Thompson, and he's dead," Christy said. "Even if he were alive, I'd pull the story before I allowed them to turn it into a glamour piece for the white supremacy movement. I'm collecting information on the paramilitary build-up by both white and African-American groups. I haven't reached a conclusion yet, but if tensions have reached a new level and armed conflict is a real possibility, that's news, and I'll report it as I see it."

"That's fair, that's fair," he said, bobbing his head. "The answer to your question is yes. We've been growing our membership at a fast pace. Some are just financial contributors, most are eager to participate in protest rallies, and a high percentage are willing to fight if necessary. If the threat we see materializes, we're prepared to engage the white hate groups in war."

Christy's heart began to pound as she scribbled shorthand notes on her pad. The story was real. There were so many questions to ask. "Is the threat imminent?"

"I'm just an old soldier," Hardy said. "I can tell you that my orders are to train these men as fast and as well as I can, given the resources I've been provided. General Collins and his staff are more focused on the big picture. They're in a better position to tell you whether there's an immediate threat and how we'd respond to it. Clearly, there's been an increase in the activities of the white hate groups, and we are concerned. Very concerned."

"Can you help me set up a meeting with General Collins in Washington?" she asked.

"I can try."

Christy continued to fire questions at him, and Colonel Tom answered each one patiently and directly. He was strong on factual questions, but deferred to General Collins on most strategic issues.

The NOMAADs' membership had recently crossed the one million mark, and training facilities were accessible to members from all fifty states. Over fifty thousand members had undergone basic training. Camp Tubman was the second largest training facility; the largest was Camp Douglass in upstate New York.

Funding came primarily from the membership, but Hardy hinted, off the record, that they had a special relationship with the federal government. Camp Tubman, which covered fifty acres, had been carved out of the 900-acre Cowpens National Battlefield, a Revolutionary War historic site, and was leased on favorable terms from the National Parks Service.

The Colonel walked Christy back to her car when they had finished. "There's one other thing you can tell me," Christy said after he offered to make himself available.

"Fire away."

"Why are *you* doing this?" she asked. "I've done my research. You were a highly decorated officer in the Army. In five or ten years you could've been top brass. Why did you give it up? Why are so many African-American men giving up time away from their families and jobs to do this?"

He paused thoughtfully. "People join us for different reasons. We are not and never have been a 'black hate group.' The founders saw a threat from the radical fringe. Since the mid-1990s, we're seeing large scale acts of domestic terrorism, dramatic increases in the memberships of white supremacy groups, and a build-up of paramilitary activity by those groups. We don't know if or when any of them intend to strike African-American targets, but we want them to know that we will respond with deadly force if they do."

Christy noted that he had deftly avoided answering the question from his personal perspective. She sensed that he was holding something back, but forced herself to be patient. "Go with the flow"— Christy Kirk's second rule of journalism, right after "Go for the jugular." "So you're trying to create an army to deter them from attacking first?" she asked.

"In a nutshell, yes. But the NOMAADs have become more than that. In trying to meet that challenge, we filled a void that existed since the death of Martin Luther King. Many members joined because they saw us as an impassioned, organized force fighting for the rights of African-Americans, and we have become what our membership wants us to be. We're Dr. King with a stick. Nonviolent civil disobedience is still our first mode of operation. But unlike King, we're willing to fight back if our protests are met with violent resistance."

"But the NOMAADs would never initiate an armed conflict?"

Hardy did not hesitate. "Never."

"If African-American targets were attacked today, how would the NOMAADs respond?"

"Focused counter-attacks. We're not looking to start a race war. We're not a racist organization."

"Isn't that just vigilantism? Shouldn't it be left to the government authorities to prosecute terrorists?" Christy asked.

Christy felt an invisible wall go up between her and the Colonel. "We'll do whatever it takes," he said, signaling with his manner that the interview was over.

Christy had her story, but her sixth sense told her to press on. The real story was still buried in the recesses of Thomas Hardy's mind—no, it was buried in his soul. What had he seen or felt that motivated him to abandon a brilliant military career? Surely he could have done more for his race as a leader and as a role model at the top of the Pentagon hierarchy than as a glorified drill sergeant for the NOMAADs. Before Hardy could politely excuse himself, she laid her suspicions bare with the political agility of a buffalo.

"What are you holding back from me?" she said accusingly, her eyes striving to pierce directly into his soul.

"Pardon me?" the Colonel said, his voice rising for the first time. "I think I've been very open with you—against my better judgment."

"You have been, and I do appreciate it. But there's a bigger story here. I feel it. There's more you want to tell me, but something is holding you back."

"And the truth will set me free—is that it?" he asked.

"Something like that."

"Christy, old loyalties die hard," Hardy said. "You've got a great story. I'll get you in touch with Bill Collins. He's much more eloquent than I am. You'll get some great quotes." He shook her hand, then strode unwaveringly towards the firing range.

Christy's mind churned. *Old loyalties*. It was a clue. There had been a rash of racial incidents in the military in recent years. Could the military leadership have been infiltrated by white supremacists? What did that mean if it was true? She shouted after him.

"It's the military brass, isn't it? You saw something that scared you, didn't you?"

Hardy stopped abruptly and took two steps back towards her. It was a different man. His nostrils flared, his eyes flashed with anger. His voice was controlled but laden with suppressed rage. "Nothing scares me, Miss Kirk. I see a challenge, I meet it head on, I beat it." He turned and stormed away, leaving Christy dumbfounded.

The rented Cavalier chugged up the steep eastern slope of the ridge that hung suspended over Camp Tubman like a giant wave primed to slam into a beach. As the sounds of the NOMAAD compound faded into the distance, Christy wondered how the United States military could possibly be involved in the white supremacy movement and how she could possibly get the scoop.

TWENTY-ONE

BEN KRAVNER had been nervously checking the Millennium Nights room every few minutes for the last two hours. His band of cyber-spies were supposed to have secretly watched the room all week, but no activity had been reported. His friends seemed to be getting bored with the project and were probably avoiding him. He had barely even seen Debby all week.

It was just as well. Ben's intuition told him that tonight was the night. He had spent the week working long hours to keep the T&E Department afloat while he counted down the minutes until Thursday, midnight.

The Knights began entering the RealTime chat room one by one. Same night, same time, three weeks in a row. Once again, The General was the last to enter, at about ten minutes past twelve.

Ben did not attempt to communicate with any of them. He continued to check the room from time to time to determine how long the meeting lasted, but he could not view the discussion.

The Heir Apparent: Gentlemen, I have some important news this evening. However, I'd like to defer that discussion until we've completed all other business. Spy, has your surveillance of the lawyer produced any results?

The Spy: Slow week for BFK. Goes to work 9-10am. Runs to work most days. Lunch in office, one day went for walk. Leaves office after 9pm. Eats dinner in apt. One telephone call all week—parents Sunday evening. Nothing alarming. Stayed home all week-

	end, except for daily run. Spends time on Internet in the evening, mostly womanizing. Continue to monitor, but no reason for concern.
The General:	Any further thoughts on the whereabouts of The Assassin?
The Spy:	No leads. Looking at Assassin's family. Did last year, but double-checking. Ex-wife: mental institution. Her husband: working stiff in Oakland. Daughter: SF law firm. Nothing unusual.
The Heir Apparent:	Well, finding The Assassin is no longer of critical importance...

The Heir Apparent explained his remarks, and then the Knights adjourned. Ben observed that it was a short meeting, pleased to be able to retire early, but frustrated with his inability to progress the case against The Royal Order of the Millennium Knight.

TWENTY-TWO

THE WHITE HOUSE PRESS CORPS was buzzing on Friday morning. Tony Fabrizio had called a press conference for ten o'clock. The word on the street was that he planned to announce a running mate. The Stevenson rumors had been flying for two weeks, but there were whispers that Ty Andrew might be under consideration. The Indian Treaty Room in the Old Executive Office Building was filled to capacity. There was excitement in the air. TV cameras waited to roll.

At exactly ten o'clock, LaRosa Smith emerged from Tony Fabrizio's office, two floors below the Indian Treaty Room. She was dressed in her best suit, a form-fitting gray pinstripe jacket and skirt. She was wearing a little makeup, which she normally eschewed. She enjoyed seeing a male intern do a double-take and nod approvingly as she hurried towards the stairs, her heels clicking on the black and white checkerboard marble floor.

She could hear the excited din from the waiting press corps as she climbed the grand, spiral staircase. Bob Elfman, one of the Secret Service agents assigned to Fabrizio, and an incorrigible flirt, was guarding the door to the Indian Treaty Room. He winked as he held the door open for her. "Bet you're not wearing any panties under that skirt, Rosie."

LaRosa winked back at him. "You win," she said without breaking stride. Elfman's jaw dropped.

The television cameras started to roll as LaRosa strode into the room. Light poured in through a skylight and three large windows overlooking the White House. The podium was set up along the right wall, in front of the doorway to an adjacent conference room.

This was LaRosa's short moment to step out from behind the scenes, and she was savoring every minute. She stood at the lectern, silent, surveying the crowded room, waiting for the reporters to quiet. Ordinarily, a press conference of this magnitude would be held in the roomier, more modern briefing room in the East Wing of the White House; however, Fabrizio preferred the historical setting.

The Indian Treaty Room was an exquisitely appointed, two-story room with a nautical motif. Seahorses and dolphins were built into the black cast iron railing that encircled the second floor balcony; an old-fashioned compass face was imbedded in the mosaic tile floor; and important stars for navigation were painted on the dark, 34-foot high ceiling. The echoes of one hundred voices bouncing off the stars slowly faded.

"Thank you," LaRosa said. She was completely at ease. "Ladies and gentlemen, today is an historic day, and I am proud to introduce to you the Vice President of the United States, Tony Fabrizio!"

Agent Elfman waved for the Vice President to enter. LaRosa stepped down from the podium. Cameras flashed. Fabrizio was resplendent in a navy blue, double-breasted suit and a bright red tie. He smiled radiantly. The press corps applauded warmly. Fabrizio gripped the sides of the lectern.

"Ladies and gentleman of the press, my fellow Americans. When I announced my candidacy earlier this year, I had high hopes of bringing about real change. But I ask you, 'What is real change?' The phrase has become trite, just another buzzword for politics as usual in Washington," he said. Then his voice deepened. He became more animated, using his hands to emphasize his points. "Politics as usual is not good enough for Tony Fabrizio, and it's not good enough for the American people."

LaRosa marveled at Fabrizio's skills as an orator. She put the words on paper; he made them sing. She watched how he moved his hands, shifted his facial expressions, changed his tone of voice. He was a magician with the spoken word.

"I receive thousands of letters and e-mails every week," Fabrizio continued. "The single most important issue on the minds of Americans is the issue of race. While opportunities for African-Americans have improved over the last forty years, there is a climate of racial unrest in America today. The gap between educational opportunities available to White America and Black America is a wide one. Our inner cities are crumbling. Crime is increasing. While many African-

Americans are escaping poverty, for millions of others the cycle of poverty goes on.

"There is nothing inherently magical about the millennium," Fabrizio continued. "But there is something about landmark dates that makes us reflect upon where we have been and where we are going. We want to do magical things to mark the moment in history."

Fabrizio paused, as if to let the words hang poignantly in the air. "My fellow Americans, I ask you to make history with me. I have a special friend waiting outside in the hall who will be my choice as the next vice president of the United States. Together, we hope to abandon evolutionary change in favor of revolutionary change. To bring people of all races together as one nation, under God, indivisible, with liberty and justice for all."

LaRosa knew what was coming, but she still found herself holding her breath. "Ladies and gentlemen, I introduce to you the father of The Second American Revolution," Fabrizio said. "Jefferson John Alexander!"

A collective gasp rose from the press corps. JJ Alexander confidently strode into the room. He smiled broadly and waved to the television cameras. For a brief moment, there was total silence. Then a cough at the rear of the crowd reverberated throughout the cavernous room.

Alexander's voice was powerful and full of emotion. "'I have a dream,'" he began. "Words spoken by Martin Luther King just over thirty years ago. Dr. King followed his dream with a rare intensity and passion, a fire that he breathed into a nation of his children, a passion that nearly took America to the brink of revolution, one small step short of the promised land. A passion that has slumbered, if not died, in the years after Dr. King's tragic death."

LaRosa had not previewed Alexander's speech. She felt the emotion building within herself as he spoke. *This was the right choice, girl.*

"Tony Fabrizio and I share a dream. We want to awaken that passion in each American. We may never again find a leader who is a father to each of us. We cannot wait for a solitary man to breathe fire into our hearts and souls and lead us to the promised land. We need to make our own promises. We need to dream our own dreams. We need to find the passion within ourselves to create the America of our dreams and breathe that fire into our children so that our dreams can become a reality. One father to each son, each son an essential link in a chain,

joining America together, one link at a time. Ordinary men can together achieve greatness if driven by sufficient passion."

LaRosa choked up. *Was it really a Republican who was going to take us
to the promised land?* She looked across the crowded room. The press corps
was spellbound. She wondered how mainstream America would react.

"Building this dream is not a task for politics as usual. We need to
focus on our common goals rather than our differences. If we are to
realize our dream of a truly united America, we need to shunt partisan
politics aside and work together to achieve our objective. We ask for the
support of the American people and the Democratic and Republican
parties in making this millennium election one that will go down as
one of the great moments in world history. Thank you. I'm sure that
you have many questions for the Vice President and me."

Tony Fabrizio stepped forward to join Alexander at the podium.
The press room erupted. Cameras flashed. Arms flew into the air. A
hundred voices shouted to be heard. Fabrizio pointed to an elderly
women in the front row. "I believe the young lady from the Canfield
News Service gets the first question."

Harriet Canfield rose and looked down at her notes. "Thank you,
Mr. Vice President, Senator Alexander. Have you discussed this
announcement with the Democratic and Republican Party leadership?"

Fabrizio and Alexander looked at each other. Alexander extended
his open palm, inviting the Vice President to field the question.
Fabrizio stepped up to the microphone.

"We informed the party leadership of our plans this morning immediately before the press conference," Fabrizio said. "We did not invite
the party leadership to participate in this decision for a number of obvious reasons. Secrecy was paramount. If this merger, for lack of a better
word, fell through, we could not afford to have it leaked to the public.
We sincerely hope that both the Democratic and Republican parties
will support our historic bid, but we are committed to our program
even if forced to run on a third-party ticket."

Fabrizio pointed to a reporter in a blue blazer and khaki pants in the
middle of the room.

"Martin Haspel, *Washington Post*," the reporter said. "What exactly
is the program that you are proposing?"

Alexander stepped to the microphone. "We're calling it The Second
American Revolution. We have not worked out the details. Our pro-

gram will be based on our shared belief that the issues underlying the race problem in America run deeper than the overt discrimination and unequal opportunity existing today. Our goal will be to bring real opportunity within reach of all Americans, regardless of their color or economic standing."

Alexander pointed to the next questioner.

"Thank you, Senator. Bob Belladonna, *New York Herald Times*. The two-party system has been an important part of the American political process since its inception. Aren't you concerned that a critical element of our system of checks and balances will be lost if there is a unification of the parties?"

Fabrizio stepped front and center once again. "That's an excellent question. JJ, jump in if I misstate your views on this," Fabrizio said. "I don't agree that the two-party system is part of our system of checks and balances. The Constitution provides for three branches of government—the Executive, Legislative and Judicial Branches. Any legislation that we propose under The Second American Revolution still must pass both houses of Congress and must survive any judicial challenges to its constitutionality."

Alexander stepped up to the lectern. "I also want to make it clear that we are not asking that the Democratic and Republican parties be merged. There are still many ideological differences that we feel provide the American people with alternative voices in Congress. There'll be thousands of votes that Congress faces each term that will not affect our programs."

"That's exactly right," Fabrizio agreed. "What we're asking for is the people's mandate. We think that as a nation we can agree that there is one single issue that demands to be the national priority. By joining our candidacies, we're asking the American people to set aside the thousands of smaller issues that we face and on which we differ, and focus on the single vision of a united America that we share. If we continued to run separate campaigns, we would without doubt begin to focus on our differences rather than our common goal, and America would suffer."

Fabrizio pointed to a blonde woman on the left side of the room. "Sylvia Sanders, *Los Angeles Times*. Which one of you first approached the other?"

Fabrizio and Alexander exchanged glances and a private wink. They smiled, and each pointed at the other. "He did," they said in unison.

The press corps erupted in laughter, and in one rehearsed moment the tension evaporated from the room.

The press conference continued for another thirty minutes. LaRosa watched as the reporters filed out of the room at its culmination, apparently torn between gossiping with their colleagues about this unprecedented event and formulating a catchy lead for the story of a lifetime.

TWENTY-THREE

T HE NATION WAS ELECTRIFIED by Tony Fabrizio's announcement on Friday morning. But on Friday evening, Ben Kravner absently stared out the window of the "5" train, the Lexington Avenue Express, oblivious to the excited chatter around him.

The train was packed with commuters. The voices of two Asian women standing beside him and babbling in a foreign tongue disrupted his thoughts. Nine days had passed since his discovery of the List convinced him that The Jinx was real. He had been frustrated by his inability to match names to the nicknames on the List. But the announcement of JJ Alexander as the vice-presidential nominee fit. It was the perfect way to assure election as the vice president. JJ Alexander was The Heir Apparent.

He shot a dirty look at the Asian women. He tried to push further away from them, without success.

Ben was sure that The Jinx was real, yet he had no hard evidence and no reasonable prospects of uncovering any. He was convinced that The Royal Order of the Millennium Knight met every Thursday night at midnight in the Millennium Nights room on CyberLine, and at no other time. He had no way of observing the happenings in that room. The Knights were not volunteering any information. And he did not have the Key.

The train stopped at Union Square station at 14th Street. More people tried to press onto the already overcrowded train. *Argh. This train was never going to get uptown.* An old Hispanic man with booze on his breath pushed close to Ben. Ben's nerve endings jangled. He plunged his free hand into his pocket to protect his wallet. He felt his key chain.

On impulse, Ben fought his way past the crowd plowing in and exited the train. He carried the key to Adams Thompson's apartment on his key chain. He and Debby had thoroughly reviewed the contents of the apartment, but perhaps Dean Frederick's tale might add relevance to an item that had seemed unimportant during the first search. At least he would be able to hear himself think.

The apartment looked different at night. The dark walls created an eerie pall in the dim artificial light. Ben's heart beat faster as he tip-toed through the apartment. Convinced that he was alone, except perhaps for the spirit of Adams Thompson, he hurriedly ate his dinner of takeout Chinese food in the kitchen before undertaking a more thorough search.

The significance of the painting over the fireplace, the burning of Atlanta, was clearer now. Although born a Yankee, Thompson was a rebel at heart. Ben also spent more time in Thompson's bedroom, searching his personal possessions for secret hiding places and documents that might have escaped his eye on the first trip. He was not hopeful, though, as he assumed that the apartment had been searched and stripped bare of any incriminating evidence by the Knights or those in their employ. He found nothing new.

The result was the same, not surprisingly, in Thompson's office. The IBM ThinkPad computer again caught Ben's eye. He envied the docking station, the ability to take the computer on the road but have access to the best peripherals when at home. Ben switched it on. Friday night and nowhere to go. He logged on to CyberLine as a guest, using his own cyber-name, MasterBen. There was an e-mail message from Woody waiting for him.

Benmeister!
Did you see the press conference today? I think I know the
Key. Be on-line at 10PM your time.
Woody

Ben's mind spun. It was nine o'clock. Too late to try to get back to his own apartment. He turned on Thompson's oversized television. CNN was running clips from the press conference. He studied them carefully, but the insight he craved eluded him. He half-heartedly flirted with a number of uninspiring cyber-maidens as the minutes slowly ticked towards ten.

Anxiety and paranoia gripped Ben when Woody did not appear on time. Could the Knights be monitoring his Internet communications like in the movie *The Net?* Was that really possible? *No. Only in the movies. I hope.*

His conviction that such high drama was reserved for the big screen was confirmed fifteen minutes later.

WoodythePecker:	Benmeister!
MasterBen:	You're late.
WoodythePecker:	Well, don't get all surly on me, man. Traffic was brutal.
MasterBen:	Sorry, Woodman...Paranoia is setting in. I feel like I'm being watched. Do you remember the movie The Net? I started to wonder if they had made you disappear...
WoodythePecker:	(Laughing) Sorry, my friend. All rumors of my demise to the contrary, I am very much alive. What makes you think you're being watched?
MasterBen:	I don't, really. I'm just self-conscious about my big secret...So, don't keep me in suspense—you figured out the Key?
WoodythePecker:	I think so, but we need to fill in some gaps. Did you see the press conference today?
MasterBen:	I watched some clips tonight. It looks like JJ Alexander is a strong candidate as The Heir Apparent.
WoodythePecker:	Right. Now think about who our two primary suspects are...
MasterBen:	Adams Thompson and JJ Alexander.
WoodythePecker:	That's Jefferson John Alexander. It clicked when Tony Fabrizio announced his name. Adams and Jefferson.
MasterBen:	Presidents!
WoodythePecker:	You got it, my friend. I'm guessing that all of the Knights were named after presi-

dents. I did a little checking at work. Harrison was the ninth president. There are nine names on the List. They probably used the first nine presidents.

MasterBen: Washington, Adams, Jefferson. Madison and Monroe, I can never remember which comes first. Who's next?

WoodythePecker: John Quincy Adams, Andrew Jackson, Martin van Buren and then Harrison.

MasterBen: Still, that's only first names...That's not enough of a clue for them to find each other among millions of people...

WoodythePecker: There's got to be more to the naming convention, but we have something to work with now.

MasterBen: I'm not sure it works...Dean Frederick at Calhoun College has to be involved in some way, probably The Caretaker...but his first name was Tompkins.

WoodythePecker: Hmmm. And we thought The Speaker had to be John Daniel. Let me look him up on the Web.

WoodythePecker: His first name is Johnson. Johnson Martin Daniel.

MasterBen: Our theory is starting to fall apart. Andrew Johnson didn't become president until 1865. The naming convention had to be adopted in 1840.

WoodythePecker: Think about other prominent people with the right first names—Washington, Madison, Monroe, Adams, Jackson, Van Buren and Harrison.

MasterBen: Harrison must be a popular name, but I can't think of any politicians with those other names.

WoodythePecker: Adams and Jefferson is just too big a coincidence.

MasterBen: Our two suspects that don't fit the pattern are Tompkins James Frederick and Johnson Martin Daniel. Their first names look like last names and their last names are common first names.

WoodythePecker: What else did Adams and Jefferson have in common?

MasterBen: They signed the Declaration of Independence...

WoodythePecker: True...But a lot of people signed the Declaration of Independence. They were also both vice presidents. Adams was George Washington's VP and Jefferson served with Adams. That's still an exclusive club of nine!

MasterBen: Let's take a ten minute break and check the Web for info on the VPs.

Ben hurriedly typed in the search terms he wanted. He made several typing mistakes in his excitement. And the Web seemed painfully slow. Finally, he collected the information that he sought. A tone sounded, indicating that Woody had sent an instant message.

WoodythePecker: Holy shit!

MasterBen: I think we have them, Woodman!

WoodythePecker: I saw something else when I wrote down the names. Look at the presidents together with the vice presidents:

George Washington/John Adams
John Adams/Thomas Jefferson
Thomas Jefferson/George Clinton
James Madison/Elbridge Gerry and George Clinton
James Monroe/Daniel Tompkins
John Quincy Adams/John Calhoun

Andrew Jackson/John Calhoun & Martin van Buren
Martin van Buren/Richard Johnson
William Henry Harrison/John Tyler

MasterBen: Adams, Jefferson, Tompkins and Johnson were all VPs.

WoodythePecker: But look at the whole names. Adams George Thompson, Jefferson John Alexander, Tompkins James Frederick, and Johnson Martin Daniel. See the pattern in their first two names? The first name is the last name of a VP, then the second name is the first name of the president that VP served under.

MasterBen: You're a genius!

WoodythePecker: Let's put the rest of them together...

MasterBen: Clinton Thomas, Gerry James, Calhoun John, Van Buren Andrew, and Tyler William. And we're missing The General, The Senator, The Spy, The Doctor and The Assassin.

WoodythePecker: I'll bet The Senator is Ty Andrew. His name was in the newspapers this week.

MasterBen: I can't associate any of the other names. But all of the suspects have last names that are or could be first names— Thompson, Alexander, Daniel, Andrew and Frederick.

WoodythePecker: They must be connected to the presidents in some way. Maybe Alexander Hamilton...I think he was the first Secretary of the Treasury. There must be a pattern. Cabinet officers or something.

MasterBen: I don't think so—I think I know where to find the other four names...

Ben was ecstatic. At last, progress. He cleaned up quickly after he explained his theory to Woody, leaving everything in Thompson's apartment as he found it. He took a taxi home. He tore off his coat and immediately booked a flight with his travel agent for Monday. It was late, but he was too keyed up to sleep. He wanted to share his news with Debby. He debated whether to wait until Monday or call her on the telephone. He could not wait.

"Hello," she answered.

Debby sounded tired, but not as if she had been asleep. He was relieved that she was home and not in the arms of another man. "Hi, Deb. It's Ben. I didn't wake you did I?"

"Hello stranger! No, I've been up reading. Have you been avoiding me?"

"I've been feeling a little emotional lately," Ben said.

"I know. I've been confused myself."

"I think I've discovered something important in our little mystery," Ben said, the excitement evident in his voice.

"Really? It looked as if we'd hit a dead end," she said.

"I don't want to talk about it on the telephone," Ben said. "Can you meet me for a cup of coffee?"

Thirty minutes later Debby was at Ben's door. "It's late for me, Ben," she said, handing Ben her coat. "Just one cup of coffee and the scoop on your new discovery."

Ben had missed Debby's scent. "Coffee's almost ready," he said happily. "Have a seat in the living room and I'll tell you about the Key."

Ben brought the coffee in two minutes later. Debby was sitting on a contemporary sofa backed up against a window; Ben was suddenly conscious that it did not match the black leather recliner centered in the middle of the room. The top-of-the-line big screen TV looked cheap next to the inexpensive audio equipment stacked on a makeshift cinder block rack, a stale remnant of Ben's college days. Ben's Aptiva sat on an old—in the decaying rather than the antique sense—wooden desk on the left. The walls were barren, save for a framed print of an Ansel Adams mountain scene over the desk.

"So, what's the scoop on the Key?" Debby asked, apparently oblivious to the surroundings.

Ben poured her a cup of coffee. "The Key is a naming convention. My computer friend, Woody, cracked it after watching Vice President

Fabrizio announce JJ Alexander as his running mate on TV today," Ben said. "Each Knight's first name is the last name of one of the first nine vice presidents. His middle name is the first name of the president under which the vice president served. John Adams served under George Washington. Adams George Thompson. Thomas Jefferson served under John Adams. Jefferson John Alexander."

Debby pressed her lips together. "Impressive. How did you figure out the Knights' last names?" she asked.

"The names of the Knights that we think we know sort of fell into our lap. Thompson. Alexander. Dean Frederick fits the pattern. So does John Daniel, the Speaker of the House, and Ty Andrew, The Senator. They were easy enough to guess once we saw the pattern in the first two names. We're still missing four Knights. The General, The Doctor, The Spy and The Assassin."

Debby shifted in her chair uncomfortably. "So you still don't know how to identify them? We can't take a half-baked theory like that to the authorities," she said.

"I think I know how to identify them."

"How's that?" Debby asked.

"I think the last names are the first names of the nine brothers and sisters of Jimmy MacDougall."

Debby thought about that for a few seconds. "Thompson. Alexander. Frederick. Daniel. Andrew. You're right, all common first names. Do you know the others?" she asked.

"Not yet," Ben replied. "But those portraits in the MacDougall Room at Calhoun College had name plates. I booked a flight to Atlanta for Monday."

TWENTY-FOUR

B EN COULD NOT SLEEP after Debby left on Friday night. Her scent lingered in the apartment. His mind darted between thoughts of romance and the Key. The answer to the riddle was in the MacDougall Room. Dean Frederick had rattled off the names two weeks before in such dramatic fashion, but he could not remember them. Seven brothers and sisters two. Dean Frederick would be suspicious if Ben asked to meet in the MacDougall Room again. Ben struggled unsuccessfully with a plan for a half hour, then left it to his subconscious to work it out, as his conscious mind drifted back to love.

Ben logged on to CyberLine. Lisa C. was his only PenPal on-line. Before he could send her a note, a tone sounded. Ben smiled. It was Lisa.

Lisa C.:	Hi Ben.
MasterBen:	Hi, Lis! How's it going? <smile>
Lisa C.:	Okay. You sound cheerful.
MasterBen:	Cheerful enough. I finally got a lead in that case I'm working on at work!
Lisa C.:	That's cool.
MasterBen:	So, what's new with you?
Lisa C.:	I'm a little anxious. I've got something on my mind.
MasterBen:	Do you want to talk about it? You've been there for me when I've needed a friendly ear...

Lisa C.:	Actually, it's about you...
MasterBen:	Really...How long do I have to live, doc? <smile>
Lisa C.:	I'm not so sure you'll be smiling after this...
MasterBen:	Uh-oh...what's up?
Lisa C.:	You have to promise me that you won't abandon me. I need you...
MasterBen:	You're scaring me, Lis...what have you done?
Lisa C.:	I haven't been completely honest with you...
MasterBen:	Are you a guy?
Lisa C.:	No!
MasterBen:	That's the only thing that would really tick me off...
Lisa C.:	You may change your mind. I've been less than truthful about a few things—three to be exact.
MasterBen:	Okay, hit me...I'm a big boy...
Lisa C.:	I love you.
MasterBen:	I'm stunned...Flattered, actually. In a way, I think I've known that and I've loved you, too...
Lisa C.:	You'll understand better after you hear the second lie.
MasterBen:	Bracing myself <smile>
Lisa C.:	I'm Debby.
Lisa C.:	Say something, Ben! Are you still there?
MasterBen:	I'm feeling several different emotions right now...In one sense, I'm elated...I've been

in love with you for two weeks and have been tearing myself up inside because you haven't returned my love...

Lisa C.: I'm sorry <hanging head down>

MasterBen: I don't know if that's good enough. I've been open and honest with you, both as a cyber-friend and as a real life friend. You've been spying on me. I've told you some of my deepest secrets, some of them about you, and you've just sat there behind the anonymity of the computer. Probably laughing at me.

Lisa C.: It's not like that at all, Ben! I never wanted to hurt you. It's much more complicated than that, and falling in love with you has made it more complicated still.

MasterBen: You can't use that abortion crutch to justify anything. I trusted you. You betrayed me.

Lisa C.: There was no abortion.

MasterBen: Was that your third little secret?

Lisa C.: No.

Lisa C.: There's no easy way to say this.

MasterBen: Just spit it out. It can't make things much worse.

Lisa C.: I am The Assassin's daughter.

TWENTY-FIVE

B EN STARED BLANKLY at his computer screen as Lisa C., a/k/a
Debby, tried to provoke a response from him. It was an exercise in
futility. Ben was dazed. The screen had become a blur. He abruptly
jabbed the power button with his index finger as if the computer would
bite it off if he allowed his finger to tarry a moment longer than necessary. Debby's pleas evaporated into the cyber ether.

Ben sat at his desk, stunned, his face buried in his hands. His mind
was clicking at a dizzying pace. One insight followed after another.
Debby C.—her name plate at work. Deborah Colleen Barnett. Her
mother had remarried. Colleen. Her father's last name was Colleen.
One of the sisters. Debby had set him up.

He had known Lisa months before he had become involved with
Debby. She must have found his CyberLine nickname on his computer at work. Or through more nefarious means. *Who knows what she's
capable of doing?* Why was she setting him up? She must have guessed
that he would work the Thompson estate. Or maybe she even suggested it to Fritz Fox. The Thompson *estate*. She needed information from
the Thompson estate. *She needed the Key.* And Ben had given it to her.

She had trashed his office—that's why no one had seen an intruder.
She had intentionally misplaced the trust document and tricked him
into opening the sealed envelope. She was The Assassin. She had
assumed her father's duties after he had died. Now she could join the
others. The Royal Order of the Millennium Knight. The Thompson
estate. Estate. *She killed Adams Thompson.* Was she killing them or joining them? *Oh God, she knows where I live!*

Ben grabbed his coat and raced from his apartment. It was dark. An
icy rain was falling. He looked up and down the street from the shad-

ows of his building. No sign of Debby. The rain was coming down in buckets. All of the passing taxis were full. He kept looking, in fear, for Debby's frizzy hair bobbing in the distance. His mind's image was different than the one that had come to fill his daydreams. Her blue eyes no longer sparkled; they pierced. Black leather jacket. Confident, purposeful stride. Semi-automatic pistol tightly gripped in her right hand. Demonic smile. She was The Assassin. She had become a nightmare.

Finally, a taxi stopped. Ben told the driver to just drive. He slumped in the back seat.

Ben tried to gather his thoughts. Maybe he had enough information to go to the police. The Poem. *Damn.* He had left that back in the apartment, in his briefcase. The List. The Key. Thompson's murder. The Assassin. He could tell a coherent story. The worst they could do was lock him up as crazy, an option that did not seem all that bad at this moment. Detective Johnson would not be sympathetic. He wanted to solve a murder. He did not want to hear conspiracy theories.

The FBI. They were educated. They had federal jurisdiction. They might listen. Ben asked the driver to pull over near a telephone booth. When he returned, he directed the driver to Federal Plaza in downtown Manhattan, the home of the FBI's New York field office.

The FBI does not sleep. Maybe in Missouri, but not in New York. A uniformed guard asked Ben to sign his name in a log book. Ben hesitated, then signed in as "Benjamin Pierce." It was 12:15 a.m. Ben's name was the only name on the page. The guard directed him to the 23rd floor.

The elevator bank on the 23rd floor was separated from the FBI offices by a glass door. It was locked. The reception area on the other side of the door was unattended.

Ben tapped on the glass lightly. He felt his heart beating. Nothing. He looked around the elevator bank. A doorbell on the right wall was partially concealed by a large plant. He pressed it. Thirty seconds. Nothing. He turned to go, but stopped when he heard the sound of a door opening.

A young man, about Ben's age, signaled for Ben to wait. The man reached behind the half-wall at the reception desk. A buzzer sounded, and Ben pushed the glass door open. The man smiled. He was wearing a white shirt and black suspenders. He had the build of a linebacker. Thick neck. Broad shoulders.

"What brings you out on such a bleak night?" the man asked. His voice was friendly, reassuring.

Ben's heart was beating faster now. He had trouble finding his breath. "I need to talk to an agent," he said, his voice cracking.

"Come with me. I'm Agent Franco. Mike Franco," he said, extending his hand. He directed Ben towards the door to the left. "You seem agitated. What's wrong?"

"You might think I'm crazy. I think I've walked into the middle of an incredible con—"

The color drained from Ben's face. A framed photograph on the wall of the reception area was now in full view. A metal plate identified the man as the FBI Director—Gerry James Kate. *The Spy.*

"What's wrong?" Agent Franco asked.

Ben hesitated. "Nothing. I made a mistake coming here." He turned to leave.

Agent Franco put his large hand on Ben's shoulder. "We can help. Talk to me." He sounded sincere.

Ben peered into Franco's eyes, searching for a friend. Then Ben looked away. He walked towards the glass door. "I'm sorry. I made a mistake."

Ben strode purposefully through the lobby downstairs. The guard called for him to log out. Ben kept walking. The guard called again. Ben ran for the door. The guard rose from behind his desk, but did not give chase. Ben ran from the building and disappeared into the dark, rainy night.

He did not stop running for ten blocks. He found himself on Broadway. Not the bright lights and non-stop action of the Great White Way in midtown. The dark, dank Broadway that connects the city that never sleeps to the hollow canyons of Wall Street. Warehouses. Seedy businesses. Erie silence. Ben was out of breath, soaking wet, and cold to the bone. He bent over, hands on both knees, trying to catch his breath.

A loud noise broke the quiet, startling him. He sprung up, primed to continue his flight. It was only a street person; he had dropped an empty bottle.

It was nearly two o'clock in the morning when Ben approached his apartment building. A car passed. The street was empty. He was tired. Wet. Cold. Numb. His mind had ceased to function. His only thought was of a hot shower.

Then a movement in the shadows jolted him back to an alert state. A figure, clad in a trenchcoat, was lurking in the darkness near his building's vestibule. Fear consumed him. He turned to run.

"Ben! Wait!" It was Debby. There was desperation in her voice.

Ben wavered. Fight or flight. Something made him look back. She had taken a step toward him, into the light. She looked sad.

"Ben, don't go. Let me explain," she pleaded.

"Did you kill Adams Thompson?" he asked.

"No! Ben, *please*, I love you. I need to talk with you."

Ben slung his wet coat over the shower rod in the bathroom. He was confused. It had been a long day. His emotions had run the gamut. Love. Fear. Anger. Hate. Now he was just weary. He changed his clothes in the bedroom.

Debby was still standing near the door when he returned. Her trenchcoat was folded over a chair in the kitchen. She was wearing only a plain black T-shirt and blue jeans and was trembling, fighting back tears.

"Are you cold?" Ben asked. She nodded. "I'll heat up the coffee."

They sat down at the kitchen table. "What can I say to get you back, Ben?"

She looked very small. There was no sparkle in her eyes, but they did not pierce, either. She looked afraid. Lonely. Desperate. "I don't know. Why don't you start with the truth?" There was a sharpness to his tone that he had not displayed to her before.

"I deserved that," she said. "The truth is a long story."

"I think I may have heard part of it already. Give me the short version."

She sighed, then slumped in the chair. "My father was Van Buren Andrew Colleen. Everybody called him Andy. What I told you about him before was all true. He was killed in a car accident about a year ago. Drunk driving. I had not seen him in over twenty years. My parents were divorced when I was five, and mom remarried a few years later. Her second husband, Philip Barnett, adopted me. I kept Colleen as my middle name. After you told me about the naming convention today, I figured that you would probably make the connection once you learned that Colleen was one of the sisters."

"You probably give me too much credit, but maybe so. Go on."

"My mom is in an institution with Alzheimer's. My father never remarried. I was my father's only known relative when he died. Not that there was much of anything to inherit, but I had to go through all his things."

"Did you find a copy of the Poem?" Ben asked.

"No. I didn't find anything to do with the conspiracy. But I did find some letters tucked away in an old book. They were from my half-brother. My father must have had an affair while he was married to my mother. I don't think my mother ever knew about his son, but my father kept in touch and saved the letters. My brother lives in LA. I tried to contact him, but his phone was disconnected. When I tried to find him at the return address on the letters, his landlord told me that he hadn't seen my brother for awhile, either. He disappeared shortly after my father's accident. I went through his things. That's when I found photocopies of the Poem and the List."

"What's your brother's name?"

"Van Buren Andrew Stone."

"So *he's* The Assassin?"

"Yes. I think so."

"Did your brother's letters say anything about it?"

"There was one letter assuring my father that he would complete his 'mission.'"

"How did you figure the plot out?" Ben asked.

"Same way you did," she said. "But I couldn't figure out the Key, and I didn't know any of the history behind the Poem."

"What made you go after Adams Thompson?"

"My brother had scrawled some notes on his copy of the List. I think he was trying to make contact with the other Knights, but didn't know how to do it. He had written down Thompson's name and one other. The publisher of *The Washington Post*, James Symington. It made sense that one of them would be The Publisher. The Publisher would need to run a newspaper established in a major east coast political center to have any significant influence. I ruled out Symington. I easily traced his roots back to the 1700s. Thompson's trail ended in the mid-1800s."

"So what were your intentions?" Ben asked. "For God's sake, you set yourself up with Thompson's *estate* lawyer. It doesn't sound like you were going to invite Thompson for tea."

"Look, Ben, you can look down your high and mighty nose at me if you want. My brother is prepared to kill the next president of the

United States. I'll do whatever it takes to protect my country and my family name. My intentions were to talk to Thompson. Believe it or not, I had set up a meeting with him on the night he died. If he was uncooperative, I was prepared to kill him. I never got that chance."

"How do I know I can trust you?" Ben asked angrily. "You pretended to be my friend. You set me up months ago when we met 'by chance' on CyberLine even before you were working at Kramer, Fox. I told you things that I haven't told anyone else. God, I even told you about you! If I wasn't so completely drained I would be too embarrassed to face you."

Tears trickled down Debby's face. "I never meant to hurt you," she said. "I needed to use you. Can't you see that? I needed to know everything about you so that I could manipulate you to help me. I didn't know that I would fall in love with you."

Ben closed his eyes tightly. He had so wanted her to be in love with him. His nerve endings pulsated. "It was supposed to be anonymous," he said. "I gave you everything. There's nothing about me that you don't know. I have never felt so exposed in my life."

"I know and I wish I could take it all back," Debby said sincerely. "But I can't. The only thing I can offer you is my heart."

She stood up awkwardly, brushed away a tear, then put her hands on Ben's shoulders. She kissed him gently on the cheek from behind. "Make love to me, Ben."

TWENTY-SIX

BEN RAN HIS HANDS down the curve of a naked body that was as beautiful as he had dreamed. Only it was Kimberly's body, not Debby's. It was Monday, not Saturday. Ben kissed her. Her lips sizzled with sexual electricity; their tongues jousted passionately, playfully. He let his hand graze her inner thigh. She moaned. Their naked bodies danced, slowly, in unison, to the rhythm of love. She stroked him gently.

"Do me now," she whispered in his ear.

"I want them to watch," Ben said. There was a firmness in his voice. He slapped her on the rump. "Get up on the table. On your hands and knees."

Kimberly smiled her naughty smile, then climbed up on the large cherry table, slowly, in a well-practiced routine designed to titillate. Ben watched hungrily, then followed her up on the table top. She arched her back, her tail tilting upwards. Ben bent down to kiss her.

"Now," she said.

Ben put his hands on her hips and slowly entered her. She moaned, then he thrust himself into her with a force born of both passion and pain. He closed his eyes and soaked in her sexuality. He was already pulsating. He knew he would not last long. *Ten strokes.* He wanted to last ten strokes.

"Harder," she pleaded.

Ben opened his eyes. He scanned the room, as he pumped himself into her. His eyes focused on the portrait behind the head of the table. Jimmy. He pumped again, harder this time. She moaned. His gaze shifted to the next portrait. Alexander. And again. Frederick. He could feel his own anger and sexuality peaking. He thrust himself into Kimberly again. Kate. Again. Thompson. Again.

"I'm cumming," she groaned.

He pumped harder. Glenn. Ben groaned as he reached the moment of orgasm. He pumped again, exploding into her. Andrew. Again. They both moaned. Daniel. Again. Stewart. Again. And little Colleen. He had drained himself. His gaze lingered on the portrait of Colleen.

Ben rolled off Kimberly and lay face up on the table. Ten names forever etched into his mind, forever associated with sex more potent than he had imagined possible. Kimberly dropped to the table, prone, facing Ben with her head resting on her right hand.

"That was amazing," she said. "I didn't think that I would ever see you again."

Ben rolled over to face her. He smiled. "I couldn't stop thinking about you. That new relationship didn't work out and I was kicking myself for not finishing what we started two weeks ago. I had to see you again."

Kimberly looked into Ben's eyes with disbelief. "You mean you came down here just to see me?" she asked.

"Yep. And it was worth it." He kissed her breast and snuggled close to her. He was getting aroused, again.

"Cool. I thought you were down here to visit, Daddy."

Ben looked confused. "Who?"

Kimberly laughed. "You didn't know that the Dean is my father?"

Ben did not know what to say. He tried to maintain a calm demeanor, but he could tell from Kimberly's reaction that his horror was evident.

"Don't worry," Kimberly said coyly. She seemed to be enjoying his discomfort. "I won't tell him you were here. It will be our little secret." The naughty smile came so easily to Kimberly's lips. "Of course, there's a price for my silence."

She rolled over, on her back, bending her legs at the knees. They made love once more on the table under the watchful gaze of the brothers and sisters MacDougall and then twice at Kimberly's apartment.

Ben caught the early flight back to New York on Tuesday morning. He slept soundly on the plane.

TWENTY-SEVEN

BEN HAD WAVERED between going into the office and going into hiding when he arrived in New York on Tuesday morning, but he elected to maintain his normal routine. He was at risk, but so far the risks seemed manageable. Just the same, he had taken the precaution of withdrawing five hundred dollars from the bank in case the urge to take flight suddenly overcame him.

The FBI had seen his face on Friday night, but they did not know his name because he had the foresight to sign in under an alias, Benjamin Pierce. Kimberly, The Caretaker's daughter, could hurt him if she told the Dean that Ben had been in Atlanta on Monday, but she had promised secrecy. He trusted her. The Caretaker himself had seemed suspicious two weeks ago, but nothing had come of it. Ben had spoken with him once since then on the telephone, and the Dean had been cordial and relaxed. Only Debby and Woody knew that he had discovered the conspiracy.

Now, after spending the morning catching up on a few neglected matters, Ben was daydreaming. He reclined in his green swivel chair, his feet resting on the credenza. The midday sun was obscured by a dense cover of clouds. A dull ache in his abdomen was a pleasing reminder of the prior night's extended sexual activities.

Ben's once clear mind was now muddled. A month ago his existence had been simple, bordering on pathetic, he thought. He came to work; he went home. Some might describe his job as dull, but the newness of it provided a sufficient challenge for his understated passion. He had a perfectly acceptable fantasy sex life in cyberspace. No complications.

Now he was in a quandary as two real life lovers competed for his affection. He had not made love to Debby in the wee hours of Saturday morning, but he still had strong feelings for her. Ben had sent her away, angrily, but with enough tenderness to leave open the possibility of a reconciliation. Her intentions that night had been good. He questioned her motivation in stalking Adams Thompson, but he might never know that whole truth. The answer was in Debby Barnett's mind, a complex labyrinth that she exposed to him bit by bit, as was convenient for her.

Ben's sexual escapade with Kimberly confused the situation. She had a lack of inhibition that he had only before experienced in RealTime. He could have fun exploring his wild side with her. A smile crossed his face as he relived a particularly vivid and memorable moment.

And then there was the small matter of the fate of the nation. The type of serious business that should be left for the consideration of great men with white hair. Twenty-six year old boys playing with adult toys should have the luxury of mentally replaying their sexual adventures during their lunch hours without interruption. Images of burly young Scotsmen in kilts had no place invading visions of Kimberly's lithe, compliant body, but there they were, in Ben's mind's eye, alternating with likenesses of sweaty, cigar-smoking politicians like JJ Alexander, John Daniel and Ty Andrew.

Ben sat upright and swiveled to face his desk.

His dalliance in the MacDougall Room at Calhoun College had confirmed that the naming convention had indeed been applied to all of the suspected Knights. The last name of each of them was the first name of one of the brothers and sisters MacDougall. Adams Thompson—The Publisher. JJ Alexander—The Heir Apparent. Buddy Frederick—The Caretaker. Ty Andrew—The Senator. Gerry Kate—The Spy. John Daniel—The Speaker. Van Buren Andrew Colleen—The Assassin.

It had been simple for Ben, with the assistance of the Internet, to fill in the two remaining gaps. The descendents of Glenn and Stewart had not yet been identified. The first names dictated by the naming convention were Clinton Thomas and Calhoun John. Internet searches for Clinton Thomas Stewart and Calhoun John Glenn had not been fruitful. But a search for Clinton Thomas Glenn had revealed the Chairman of the Joint Chiefs of Staff. The General. And a search for Calhoun John Stewart had produced the Director of the National Institutes of Health. The Doctor.

There could be no doubt. The Jinx was real. The question in Ben's mind now was how to save Vice President Fabrizio from his fatal rendezvous with The Assassin and the nation from The Royal Order's Final Vengeance, whatever that might be.

The Assassin was under deep cover. The other Knights were powerful men. The FBI was The Spy's house, and it had jurisdiction over federal conspiracies. The New York police would send him special delivery to the FBI.

No, Ben knew he had to set his sights higher. He needed to go directly to the White House. But an anonymous young lawyer could never get an audience with the President or even his staff, especially if he was not willing to disclose his intentions in advance. They would laugh at him if they even listened long enough to find it amusing.

Ben knew that he needed help, someone who could bring him instant credibility and White House access. He had two choices.

The first was Fritz Fox. He was a close friend of the President, one of a handful of Washington outsiders who could obtain an audience with Hank Norton without disclosing his agenda. There was no shame in approaching Fritz now. He had labored for three weeks to build his case while the Old Man convalesced. Fritz was due back in the office in three days, on Friday, to attend the staff Christmas Party.

The case was not perfect. The Poem supported the theory that the Knights were planning to kill the next president, but it did not prove it. The naming convention, the Millennium Nights room and the ties to the MacDougalls chipped away at reasonable doubt, but proving those elements of the case might be difficult. If the Knights thought they were under suspicion, they would probably hide as many vestiges of their plot as possible. It would take a team of federal investigators to bring down The Royal Order.

Ben's primary doubt was the handling of the sealed envelope. Under the terms of the trust, it never should have been opened. The Poem would not be valid evidence in court. Debby's photocopy from her brother's apartment was useless, too. They needed to tie the Poem to Adams Thompson and the List.

Still, if the President was made aware of the conspiracy, the Knights could be stopped. Ben's worry was that Fritz would refuse even to review the illegally obtained evidence. The President needed to know about The Royal Order of the Millennium Knight.

Ben sighed. He turned to his computer and clicked on the CyberLine icon. His PenPals had all been helpful. Woody's insights in particular had been critical to solving the riddle of The Royal Order. But now Ben was focused on the one listed cyber-name that he had not called upon for assistance. Quixote. His old mentor and friend from Harvard. And now a Washington insider.

If Ben could regain Quixote's trust, he could bypass Fritz Fox's unwavering ethical standards and alert the President to the imminent threat. But he and Quixote had parted awkwardly and had not spoken for over three years. They had unfinished business that Ben was afraid to revisit. He stared at the computer monitor, frozen in a state of indecision. No, Quixote was the option of last resort.

Debby crossed Ben's mind. He missed having her as a sounding board. She had a good practical take on these issues. He dialed the telephone.

"Hello," Debby answered. She sounded weary.

"Hi, Deb. It's Ben."

Silence. Ben heard her swallow. "Hey, Ben."

Ben detected sadness in her voice. "We need to talk," he said.

"Okay. Should I come down there?" she asked.

"No. Not here. Let's meet after work for a drink."

They met in the bar of the restaurant in the lower lobby of One Water. Few of the lawyers from Kramer, Fox ever drank there. It was too convenient, too easy to be spotted. The lawyers only went there for a quick lunch with a summer intern or a prospect on a job interview— obligatory occasions, rarely pleasurable. But at six o'clock on a Tuesday, it was sufficient for Ben's purposes.

Debby seemed distant, small. Her eyes were swollen from tears shed some hours ago. Ben touched her arm when he pulled out a chair for her. He wanted to hug her, to tell her that the events of the past weekend were all forgotten. But he could not lie or lead her on. It would take time if they were to become friends again. But his abdomen burned. No longer from the remnants of the prior night's sex, now with the embers of another fire not quite extinguished. It was a subtle emotion, not easily labeled. A gust of wind could fan it or snuff it.

They talked about nothing while they waited for their drinks. Ben initiated real conversation after the waiter left. He looked directly into Debby's eyes. "Look, Deb, I'm sorry about the other night. You put me through the wringer. The last few weeks have been a heart-wrenching ordeal for me, and I couldn't handle all those emotions in one night."

Her eyes grew misty and searched for a point upon which to fixate. She found a place beyond Ben's right shoulder. "You pushed me away with such disgust," she said. "It tore my heart out."

"I'm sorry."

She sipped her margarita. She started to speak, but stopped herself. She tried again. "What do you think of me now?"

"I don't know. I really don't know," Ben said. "I think I'm afraid."

She looked directly at him now. A tear rolled down her cheek. She choked up trying to get out the words. When the words came, she pleaded for him to believe her in a sad, hoarse whisper. "I'm not a killer, Ben," she said. "I haven't spent my whole life training to be The Assassin. I walked into this conspiracy just like you did."

"I did *not* walk into anything—you set me up," Ben said harshly. He softened his tone. "But that's not what I meant. I feel like a part of our friendship is still there, and I'm afraid that if we talk too much about it, we'll lose it. That something might be said that can't be taken back."

"I can understand that," Debby said. "You do believe me then?"

Their eyes met. "Yes, I do."

"Good," she said trying to smile and sound perky. She wiped her eyes with a cocktail napkin. "Then where do we go from here?"

Ben shifted forward in his chair. He spoke softly, so as not to be overheard. "I miss you as a sounding board. I think there's enough evidence to take our story to Fritz, but some things still bother me."

"Like what?"

"Like the sealed envelope. The Poem is the only evidence of wrongdoing. Otherwise, there's just two strange coincidences—presidents elected every twenty years dying in office and powerful men with names linked in an odd way. There's no connection between the two."

"But you said that you have an ethical obligation to disclose the crime," she said.

"Yeah, but the evidence is still tainted," Ben said. "It wouldn't be admissible in court."

"Do we care?" she asked. "We want to expose the conspiracy. Stop them from killing. So what if they don't go to jail?"

"Can anyone really be sure they won't do it if they don't get locked up?" Ben asked. "And what if Fritz takes a hard line? He might not even look at the Poem if I tell him it was in the sealed envelope. Or he might look at it and think it too fantastic to even consider."

"Well, you know what the practical answer is," she said.

Ben rolled his eyes. The practical answer. Non-lawyers were so quick to dismiss the law. "You mean destroy the envelope and the trust document?" Ben asked. "That's not gonna happen."

"Why not? Wasn't it unethical to re-seal the envelope?" she asked.

Ben sipped his beer. "I don't see it that way," he said.

"Oh, please. You were just protecting your ass."

"To be honest, I don't know if there is a right way to handle that issue," he said. "You deceived me. The envelope never should have been opened. I tried to make it right."

"But you copied the Poem," she said.

"Just fulfilling my obligation to confirm that a crime was contemplated," Ben shot back.

Debby leaned forward. "You've got all the answers, don't you? If Fritz doesn't read the Poem, the next president *will* die and these monsters will be running the country. But Ben Kravner's precious ethics will be intact. You *have to* destroy those papers. There's no other way. You can be a hero or a coward. Your call, Ben."

Ben felt his ears flush. His tone became sharper, his voice still a whisper. "So it's black or white? What about the rule of law? People have a right to privacy. We can't just take the law into our own hands because we have a gut feeling that somebody did wrong. That's why the Bill of Rights protects people against unauthorized searches. That's why you hear about murderers getting released on technicalities. Because the police acted on the basis of their intuition instead of their brains."

"We need to stop them from doing something terrible," Debby said. "*You* need to stop them."

"Why does it have to be me?" Ben asked. "Why didn't you go to the police or send an anonymous letter to the President? You knew about the Poem all along."

Debby smirked. "Fair point. I was afraid, too. I didn't know who was involved in the conspiracy. It was obviously powerful men, and I needed someone powerful and smart to beat them."

Ben shifted his eyes skyward. "Right. Second year lawyer. Mighty Mouse is here to save the day."

Debby took his hand in hers. He swallowed hard.

"Look, you were just a way to get to Fritz Fox. He has the White House connections," she said.

Ben's jaw tensed. He looked away.

"But don't sell yourself short," she said. "You put the pieces together. You did more than I could do. More than I expected you to do. You're easy to underestimate, Hawkeye Kravner, and it may be that characteristic that lets us pull this off."

Ben wondered whether he should tell Debby about Quixote. No, while that path would avoid a confrontation with Fritz, the ethical issue would still need to be addressed. And he would have to wrestle with the demons that had haunted him since they had parted.

Ben chewed on his lower lip while Debby patiently sipped her drink. Somehow, just lying about the envelope and the trust had not entered his decision-making calculus. It came so easily to her. But could she be right this time?

Ben recalled a favorite class in law school. Tragic Choices. The law, life, was full of them. Dilemmas that had no easy answers. One kidney, two dying people in need of a transplant. The rights of a fetus versus the rights of a mother. Pull the plug, or not. Whose responsibility was it to answer the unanswerable questions? Great men with white hair, not young lawyers. *Not Ben Kravner.*

Great men. Ben looked across the table into Debby's blue eyes and recalled a day not all that long ago when they had stared out at New York Harbor sharing their dreams. *Dammit, it was time to start being great.* This was his decision. He had opened the envelope. He had pursued the investigation of the Poem. The ethical judgment was his to make. It was unfair to place that burden on Fritz Fox. It was unfair to place it on the President of the United States. These monsters had to be stopped.

"Okay," Ben said with some bitterness. "I'll burn the papers. You're right. The fate of the nation is more important than a small thing like my honor and integrity."

"You're doing the unselfish thing, Ben. There must be some honor in that."

Ben slumped into his chair. Difficult decisions drained him of his energy. He sipped his beer. *Tragic choices.* He hoped he had made the right one.

TWENTY-EIGHT

DISCOVERING THE PASSWORD to the Millennium Nights room had become Ben's obsession. He was desperate to find one incriminating item that was unrelated to the Poem before he met with Fritz Fox, and words from the mouths of the Knights themselves seemed like his only hope.

Ben had collected all of Thompson's passwords for his various accounts, searching for patterns. He had called his banks, his credit card companies and even CyberLine and some of the other computer services to which Thompson subscribed. The banks and credit card companies had been cautious, but had yielded the information when Ben personally appeared at their offices with Thompson's death certificate. The computer services had been more lax about their security, but little was at stake.

By Thursday afternoon, Ben had assembled almost two dozen passwords and, working on his computer at Kramer, Fox, had tried thousands of letter and symbol combinations, some obvious, some following logically from the patterns evident in Thompson's known passwords, some obscene. None had worked.

The end of the business day was approaching, and he was running out of ideas. He sat staring blankly at his computer, deep in thought. The Knights would be meeting that night in the Millennium Nights room. He knew that this was his final opportunity to bolster his case before he spoke with Fritz Fox tomorrow morning.

Then he had one last idea. He dialed the telephone. He punched several keys on the telephone pad as he navigated through the maze of a voice response system. Finally, a live person, a young woman, answered.

"CyberLine, may I help you? This is Tina speaking."

Ben tried to sound important and confident. "Yes, I spoke to a woman named Donna earlier today about a problem, and she was very helpful. Can I speak with her, again?" Ben had enjoyed flirting with Donna while she helped him find Adams Thompson's CyberLine password.

"We have several hundred operators on duty today, sir. Do you know her last name or her extension?"

"No, I'm afraid not. Is there any way you can search your database by first name and cross-check against the operators on duty today?"

The operator sighed. "Hold on, sir," she said, crossly.

A local radio station played in the background while Ben was placed on hold. One full song and part of another were completed when the line began to ring. "CyberLine, can I help you? This is Donna speaking."

"Donna! This is Ben Kravner. You helped me earlier today." Silence. "You helped me find a password for a man who had passed away."

"Right! I remember. Did you find what you needed?"

"Well, actually I need your help, again," Ben said. "Mr. Thompson left behind a letter requesting that we notify his on-line friends of his death. One of the RealTime chat rooms that he had identified is password protected. Is it possible for you to leave a message in the chat room for me or give me the password?"

"I'm not sure if you understand how the chat rooms work, Mr. Kravner. You can't leave a message there. You type a message and only the people in the room at the time will see it."

"Oh," Ben said innocently. "Can you tell me the password so that I can pass on Mr. Thompson's message tonight? His discussion group meets at midnight."

"I'm not supposed to do that. I wish I could help you."

"C'mon, Donna, this was a dying wish," Ben pleaded. "It's only old war buddies getting together. It's not like I'm trying to steal money."

"I don't know—"

Ben sensed her resolve weakening. He spoke softly. "Look, I'm a lawyer. I'm trying to do my job. You sound very sweet, and I know you're trying to do *your* job, but what's the harm here? I can try to talk to your boss or go down to the local CyberLine office with a copy of the death certificate, but it's the end of the day. The funeral is tomorrow, and I want to give these guys a chance to pay their last respects. I have no other way of contacting them. Can you *please* help me?"

There was a long pause. Ben held his breath. "Okay. But I could get in trouble for this. Please don't say anything to anybody."

Ben's heartbeat quickened. "I promise. Scout's honor."

He heard her keyboard clicking. "The password is T-i-p-T-y-2000."

Ben pounded the air with his fists. TipTy2000. Tippecanoe and Tyler, Too! It made sense. He had even tried similar passwords, but did not guess this abbreviated combination. He had trouble containing the excitement in his voice. "Thanks, Donna. I never would have guessed that in a million years. You're a lifesaver."

Ben opened the CyberLine program on his computer. His heart was racing now. He lightly pounded his desk with his fist while he waited for the program to load. Every step of the program seemed to be moving in slow motion. He mistyped his own password. Finally, he reached the RealTime area. He scanned the room list for the Millennium Nights room. He clicked on it. The program requested the password. He typed in "TipTy2000."

The pop-up window for the room opened. Ben let loose a jubilant sigh of relief. The room was empty, as expected. But it would begin to fill in six hours, at midnight, when The Royal Order of the Millennium Knight entered one by one. Finally, he would be able to peer into the minds of the enemy!

But his jubilation was short-lived. As he began to structure a plan, he realized that he could not invisibly observe the proceedings in the Millennium Nights room like a phantom Knight. Once he entered the room, his cyber-name would be visible to all others in the room. Once discovered, the Knights would abandon the room in favor of another or change the password. Or worse. If the Knights learned that he was aware of their plot, they would hunt him.

Ben realized that he would get only one chance to participate in the proceedings of The Royal Order, and the stakes were high. One wrong move, and he would put his life in jeopardy. Maybe the lives of many others.

The key was avoiding detection. Ben had an idea. He tried to create a new cyber-name, one that used a number of blank spaces and then a single typographic symbol, a dash. The CyberLine program accepted it. He tried entering a chat room with the nearly invisible cyber-name.

The chat room's electronic host announced that "   -" had entered
the room. *Damn.* He slammed his fist into his desk. *That was stupid.*
Of course, the host would announce the entry of a new member into
the Millennium Nights room. The Knights would detect an intruder
instantly.

There was not much room for creativity. The only way to eavesdrop
undetected would be to enter the room using one of the Knights'
cyber-names or under the guise of a nearly identical name. And that
would be risky. If one of the names was duplicated, he would be discovered. The ruse would only work if he took on the identity of one of
the Knights and then arranged for that Knight to be detained. At midnight on a Thursday night. The odds looked long.

Ben glanced at the List, hoping that manna would fall from heav-
en, again. "The Heir Apparent. The Speaker. The Senator. The
General. The Spy. The Publisher. The Doctor. The Caretaker. The
Assassin." He could try using a lower case "t" in "the" for any of them.
But that might be too obvious. He only had one chance.

There would not be much point in trying to detain the political
honchos. He did not have a hook. Not even Quixote's political contacts
could help him there. That ruled out The Heir Apparent, The Speaker
and The Senator.

He stared at the next name on the List. The General. He typed it
on his computer screen: "The General." The number "1" replaced the
letter "l." It was virtually undetectable. He sat there in awe of himself.
Manna from heaven.

Now all that Ben had to do was detain the Chairman of the Joint Chiefs
of Staff from attending what was probably the most important meeting of
his week at midnight on a Thursday night. Ben looked at his watch. It was
already seven o'clock. This would take more than divine intervention.

He struggled for ideas. Maybe a family emergency. He quickly
researched Clint Glenn's profile on the Department of Defense web
site. He had a wife and two grown children. It would be hard to man-
ufacture a family crisis that warranted his immediate attention. And if
Glenn had even the remotest suspicion that someone had intentionally kept him away from the meeting, there was a high risk that the
Knights would change the password. Too risky.

Ben was too powerless to create a national emergency. Too cowardly, or too intelligent, to try kidnapping The General or killing him. He

ran through a number of scenarios in his mind, none of which seemed promising or practical. Ben slammed the door to his office on his way out at eight o'clock. The excess adrenaline pulsing through his bloodstream found a home in his nerve endings. He felt every one of them.

Ben watched helplessly on his computer at home as one by one the Knights entered the chat room just after midnight. The Heir Apparent. The Doctor. The Spy. The Speaker. The Caretaker. The Senator. Each appearing in seemingly random order within two minutes of the midnight hour. Ten minutes later The General entered the room.

Ben pounded his right fist into his left palm. *Gotcha!* A pattern had emerged. Ben had observed the Millennium Nights room for three weeks now. Each time The General had been the last to arrive. Each time he had been ten minutes later than the others. Coincidence? There were too many coincidences.

Perhaps General Glenn had a standing appointment on Thursday nights that did not allow him to be home until ten minutes past midnight. More likely he was an arrogant man, thumbing his nose at his comrades by making them await his arrival. In any event, the pattern was Ben's only hope. Too late for this night, but an idea to test the following week if none better sprung to mind. The Knights appeared to be in no hurry.

The weekly meeting of The Royal Order of the Millennium Knight was called to order upon The General's arrival, outside of Ben's view but within his grasp. Ben wisely exited the program and went to bed. There was no point in subjecting himself to temptation.

The Heir Apparent: Gentlemen, I gather that you have all seen that my plan is proceeding even better than anticipated. Thank you, Senator, for what I suspect was an Academy Award-winning performance for the Vice President's benefit.

The Senator: I've got to admit it, you were right. That Yankee pigfucker hates my guts. I could see it in his eyes. I don't know why I had not seen it before.

The Heir Apparent: Hell, everybody else in the Senate could. Whenever you would make one of your speeches from the middle podium on the Senate floor, Fabrizio would be rolling his eyes behind you on the upper podium. Well done, Senator.

The Senator: Only too glad to be of service.

The Heir Apparent: Now that the key component of our plan appears to be moving forward so smoothly, again, I'm hoping that this is a short meeting. Are there any issues that need to be discussed this week? Spy, any word on The Assassin?

The Spy: I'm afraid so. Major security problem: Assassin's daughter turned up in NY working at Fox's law firm. Involved with BFK.

The Heir Apparent: What do they know?

The Speaker: Fox is a personal friend of the President. This could be the end of us!

The Spy: Stay calm. Let me recap, but assure you that the situation can be contained. BFK's office phone tapped 3 wks, since Friday, 12/3. Visual surveillance and home phone tap after our meeting on 12/9. No suspicious communications or behavior 12/3 – 12/16. On Friday, 12/17, BFK visited Pub's apt for 4 hrs. No evidence of activities. Returned to his apt and booked flight to Atlanta for Monday, 12/20.

The Heir Apparent: Caretaker, did he visit with you on Monday?

The Caretaker: No.

The Spy: Wait. More activity over weekend. BFK phones Deborah Barnett midnight 12/17. Deborah Colleen Barnett—Assassin's daughter. BFK says he discovered something important in "our little mystery" and invited her to his apt. No evidence of discussions at BFK apt, but believe he didn't know she's related to Assassin. She's paralegal at Kramer, Fox assisting on case. Romance developing.

The Senator: Has Miss Barnett taken on the role of The Assassin? Did she kill The Publisher?

The Spy: Wait for all facts, then draw conclusions and develop rational course of action. After DB left apt, BFK on Internet. DB interrupted him using alias. She befriended him on-line under alias and carried on both on-line and live relationship. For some reason, DB confessed to BFK on-line. BFK terminated connection to Internet. Agent reported BFK ran out in frenzy and hailed taxi. Any guesses where he goes?

The Senator: The young lady's apartment?

The Spy: FBI Manhattan Field Office. Agent says BFK nervous—he ran out, possibly spooked by my picture. Guard says BFK failed to sign out. Used assumed name, by the way. Surveillance team picked him back up at his apt. DB there waiting. BFK appeared frightened. Entered apt together. No evidence of activities in apt. DB exited less than hour later. Appeared upset.

The General: Have you been monitoring Miss Barnett's activities since then?

The Spy: Received report this AM. My appraisal incorrect. Saw no need for daily reports.

The Heir Apparent: We're only human, Spy. No need to fall on your sword. Please continue.

The Spy: DB surveillance begins this PM. Daily reports. Notify you by e-mail if special

	meeting required. No unusual BFK activity Sunday. In Atlanta Monday PM. BFK met by young woman later identified as Kimberly.
The Caretaker:	What! She didn't tell me anything about this.
The Spy:	Agents report quite taken with each other. Long dinner, 3 hrs in Admin Building. No evidence of activities, but agents have theory. Retired to Kimberly's apt late in AM.
The Caretaker:	Gentlemen, I apologize for my daughter's behavior. I'm going to take care of this myself tomorrow.
The Heir Apparent:	Caretaker, we understand that you're embarrassed, but I think it best that you do nothing to alarm your daughter. If you're too harsh, she's only more likely to run to Kravner and confirm any suspicions that he already has about our group.
The Caretaker:	She knows nothing. That said, I understand your point, and I will not confront her.
The Spy:	BFK brief phone call with DB at office on Tues. Reluctant to speak on phone. BFK spent time on Internet visiting chat rooms etc., but report has no detail about random contacts that did not result in substantive discussion. Those are the facts. My conclusion: BFK and DB have identified our group and deduced at least part of our plan. DB probably hostile. Recommendation: eliminate risk immediately.
The Senator:	I repeat my long-standing concern about killing outsiders. Once we commit murder, we all face the electric chair.

The Spy:	You're behind the times, Senator. They kill murderers—and traitors—by lethal injection these days. Treason is what we face if BFK and DB disclose their concerns to someone who'll listen.
The Doctor:	Spy, most, if not all, of the evidence you presented could be explained by Mr. Kravner's over-active libido, which would not be so unusual for a young man in his mid-twenties. What makes you so sure that they're on to us?
The Spy:	Events of Friday, 12/17 offer most support. Heir Apparent announcement. Frenetic activity by BFK. Several hrs in Pub's apt. Books flight to Atlanta.
The Doctor:	He might have been on the telephone having phone sex with Kimberly. He books the flight to finish what they started.
The Spy:	But calls DB. Refers to "important discovery" about "mystery." DB confides she's Assassin's daughter—assumes he already knew about Assassin. BFK runs to FBI. Then flees FBI when sees my pic. BFK knows. Heir Apparent's announcement triggered something in his mind. Maybe he figured out the Key.
The Caretaker:	If he was in the Administration Building with my daughter, he may have been using her to fill in the last part of the Key from the portraits. I'm with The Spy—put the Jew lawyer on ice.
The Doctor:	I'm afraid you've convinced me. The connection to Miss Barnett is too strong. The fact that he ran to the FBI means he's looking for outside help. He thinks he's solved the riddle.
The Speaker:	What about Miss Barnett? What do you think her role is in this affair?

The Spy:	If she hooked up with Pub's estate lawyers, she probably killed him to gain access to his personal papers. She was probably the one who sent the e-mail to Pub claiming to be Assassin. On-line relationship with BFK pre-dates her employment with law firm. She set him up from the beginning.
The Speaker:	Why would she need to do that?
The Spy:	Our ancestors decided that The Assassin should not have the Key. Maybe she somehow came across a copy of the Poem and nicknames, but could not determine our identities. Figured out Pub's identity, then hoped to find the Key in documents left to his estate.
The General:	But what do you think her intent is now that she has determined our identities?
The Spy:	If she killed Pub, she must be considered a lethal enemy.
The Speaker:	But what if she was just trying to link up with us? We don't know for sure that she killed The Publisher. Someone made the point a few weeks ago—she did not have to contact him to kill him. He was one of the most hated men in America after publishing that editorial—any Negro with a knife could have murdered him.
The Spy:	That was before we knew she had contacts with Pub's estate lawyers. She was obviously setting up Pub to be killed.
The Senator:	I've been listening patiently to all of the evidence, and I have to agree with The Spy's conclusions. However, I repeat my reservations regarding killing these two young people. Surely, such worthy conspirators as ourselves can devise a way to neutralize this security threat without killing.

The Spy: Senator, I wish you could see me rolling my eyeballs.

The Knights continued to deliberate over the fate of Ben and Debby for another half hour. In the end, they all agreed. The threat required immediate action.

TWENTY-NINE

A N ICY BREEZE WHIPPED off New York harbor on Friday morning. Ben scowled as he scurried up the stairs from the Bowling Green subway station. Snow flurries had just begun to fall. The television weathermen, with their annoying Santa caps and incessant cheeriness, were forecasting a white Christmas.

Ben glanced at his watch as he marched down Whitehall Street. Five minutes before ten. He would have to hurry for his ten o'clock meeting with Fritz Fox. He was eager to see his old friend, and perhaps even more eager to share the burden that had weighed on his mind for these past weeks. Yet he was nearly ill with anxiety. He was still not sure if he could lie to Fritz Fox about the sealed envelope.

Ben took the elevator directly to the 28th floor. The halls were quiet. Most of the secretaries traditionally took a half day of vacation to prepare for the Christmas party, which began at noon. It was the only time during the year when the lawyers and staff socialized together, and the secretaries enjoyed dolling up for the affair.

Ben stopped at Debby's cubicle. She was not at her desk. He thought it had been assumed that she would join him for the meeting with Fritz. She was an integral part of this mystery, and he was counting on her moral support. Her absence increased his edginess.

Ben, still clad in his overcoat, walked around the corner and down the South Corridor to Fritz Fox's office. Fritz was on the telephone. He looked like his old self. Ben signaled with his hand that he would return in five minutes; Fritz acknowledged with a smile and a wave.

Agnes had not seen Debby all morning. She had not called in sick. Ben frowned. She had probably taken the morning off. *Unbelievable.*

Ben went back to Debby's cubicle. He put his briefcase down in the corner and slung his coat over one of the guest chairs. He punched four digits on her telephone keypad.

"Ben Kravner's office, Carol speaking."

"Hi, Carol. It's me. I'm in the office. I have a meeting with Fritz."

Carol hesitated. Then she spoke in hushed tones that could not hide her distress. "Geez, Louise, Ben! There are two FBI agents down here looking for you. Are you in some kind of trouble?"

Adrenaline jolted Ben's heart rate into high gear. The FBI. Gerry Kate. Had he been identified when he visited the FBI field office? Had Kimberly squealed? Did they have Debby? "What do they want?" Ben asked. His voice cracked.

"They wouldn't say," Carol whispered. Ben heard a man talking in the background over the telephone. Then he heard Carol's muffled voice. "Ben, they're going to come up to you. Are you in Mr. Fox's office?"

Ben slammed the phone down. He grabbed his coat and briefcase. He heard a commotion on the internal staircase down the East Corridor to his left, as he scrambled out of Debby's cubicle. No time to think. He ran to his right, around a corner and then down the South Corridor past Fritz Fox's office.

Agnes looked up, shocked. Ben did not stop to explain. He sped around the corner to the West Corridor and ducked inside the T&E file room. He closed the door quietly. He heard heavy footsteps bearing down around the corner in the South Corridor behind him. He was breathing hard. His heart was pounding. The footsteps continued past the file room down the West Corridor.

Ben knew he did not have much time. Carol said there were two agents. One of the agents would be watching the elevator bank and the other would be circling the floor. It would only be minutes before the agent would circle back, this time searching more carefully. He cracked open the file room door and peeked out. The West Corridor was empty. He heard Agnes talking excitedly on the telephone.

The hallway containing the main elevator bank and the stairwell bisected the floor, running parallel to the North and South Corridors and intersected with the West Corridor about thirty feet from Ben's hiding place. The stationary FBI agent would probably be guarding the center hallway, so that neither the elevator nor the stairwell was a viable escape route.

Then Ben remembered the freight elevator. It served the bottom half of the building, the first 28 floors, and rested on either the first floor or the 28th floor when it was not in use. Ben would need to cross the center hallway, and the FBI agent's field of vision, to get there, but the agent would be on the other side of a glass security door.

There was a fifty-fifty chance that the elevator would be on the 28th floor. Even if it was, the agent would catch him if he could get through the security door quickly, either with an electronic card key or if the receptionist buzzed him through. Ben could not remember if anybody was manning the reception desk. In any event, it was his only option.

Ben tossed his coat and suit jacket into the corner behind the file room door—better to appear natural, like he was going to the men's room. The agents had not seen him yet. Maybe he could slip quietly out of the office. Out of his worst nightmare. He retrieved his copy of the Poem and the List from his briefcase and put them in his pocket.

Ben peeked out from behind the door, again. The West Corridor was still empty. He heard a strange man's muffled voice coming from the South Corridor. The second agent was in Fritz Fox's office around the corner. Now or never.

Ben ventured out tentatively. His heart raced. He composed himself, then strode purposefully down the corridor. He turned right, into the center hallway. A light-haired man in a dark suit, about Ben's age, guarded the internal stairwell on the far side of the elevator bank. The reception desk was empty. The agent and Ben locked eyes through the glass door. Ben tried to appear nonchalant, but to no avail. The agent sprang to alert.

"Stop where you are!" he shouted, drawing his gun.

Ben bolted into a narrow hallway to his left. The freight elevator was one hundred feet ahead, in an alcove off to the right. Two seconds later he heard the agent rattling the glass door. He did not have a card key.

Ben heard a shout. Then pounding feet. The freight alcove was ten feet in front of him. He looked back. The second agent, older and heavier than the first, had just entered the hallway. He shouted for Ben to stop. Ben had a five second lead.

Ben lunged into the alcove as he braced for the sound of a gunshot. Nothing. Four seconds. Ben pressed the elevator button and prayed. Fifty/fifty chance. The footsteps were getting closer. Three seconds.

The doors opened. Ben rushed in, pressed the button for the loading dock with one hand and smashed the "Close Door" button with the other. He heard the agent shout, again. Two seconds. The door started to close. Ben slumped to the floor in the corner of the elevator, his knees to his chest. He held his breath. One second. He saw the glint of the agent's gun. The door slammed shut with a loud clank. The elevator hesitated. Ben heard the agent smash the elevator button repeatedly. Ben did not let his breath go.

"Shit!" Ben heard the agent's muffled voice say, followed by a loud bang on the door. The elevator jerked and began to descend.

Ben let out his breath. He felt beads of sweat rolling down his forehead. Dark stains blotched the underarms of his white shirt. His heart was still pounding. He wiped his face with his sleeve. The elevator descended slowly. Ben cursed out loud. It was slower than the public elevators. He was not free yet.

He thought about getting off at another floor. No, there would only be more agents later, not less. He had only one chance at escape. Now. His one advantage was that the agents did not know the building or where he was going to exit.

The freight elevator could stop on all floors, including the main lobby, the lower lobby, which was home to a number of small shops and a restaurant, and the loading dock. The loading dock was in the rear of the building on South Street. Ben watched the light above the elevator door tick off the floors as it descended. He clenched his teeth tightly as the elevator approached the lobby. It did not stop.

The doors opened at the loading dock with a loud clank. The sound echoed for a few seconds, then silence. He held the elevator door with one arm and peered out. The loading dock was empty. The staff was off for the holiday. He walked out hesitantly. He had not been down there before.

It was a large room, about fifty feet square, with concrete walls and floor. A metal desk and a folding chair were arranged to create a makeshift office adjacent to the elevator. Various tools and a number of keys hung from a piece of pegboard that was attached to the wall behind the desk. The foul odor of yesterday's trash lingered.

Ben searched for an exit. The roll-up aluminum gate to the loading bay was closed and locked. There was a small metal door with a window next to it. It was locked, too. Ben pressed his face against the win-

dow. South Street was empty. Ben startled when he heard the freight
elevator jerk into action, then panicked. The dumpster. He could hide
in the dumpster. But then what? They weren't going to quit until they
found him.

Ben scanned the keys on the pegboard. There were dozens. But each
had a tag. Ben glanced skyward and thanked a God in whom he did
not believe for not limiting the ranks of the obsessive-compulsive to
lawyers. He tossed several aside until he found one labeled "Loading
Bay Door." He heard the freight elevator stop. There was a pause for
about two seconds, then it started again.

Ben ran for the door. The lock was a double-sided deadbolt. He
fumbled with the key and the lock. The key fit. The freight elevator
door opened with a loud clank just as Ben darted through the doorway
into the frigid air. He slammed the door and started to run, stopped,
then ran back to lock the deadbolt with the key. Curiosity made him
look back in through the window. He saw the light-haired agent sprint-
ing towards him, only a few feet from the door. Ben lost his balance and
fell over backwards.

Ben righted himself, as the agent rattled the door. Their eyes met
through glass for the second time. Ben's heart pounded, but he forced
a crooked smile and dangled the key for the agent to see. The agent
scowled angrily and stepped back. Ben saw the gun through the window and ran.

The sound of the shot and glass shattering exploded in his ears. He
leapt off the loading dock to the gravelly street, falling on his hands and
knees. Pain shot through him.

Ben crawled to the base of the loading bay and sat for a second with
his back to the cement wall. He rose tentatively as he heard the agent
cursing and breaking away the remainder of the shattered glass. Ben
was not shot. No bones were broken. His pants were ripped at the
knees; his knees had only minor scrapes. He pulled out his shirttails
and wiped his bloody hands.

The agent was suspiciously quiet. Ben peered over the top of the
wall. A shot rang out. Chipped cement sprayed into the air six inches
from Ben's head.

Ben had seen enough. The agent was trapped in the loading area.
Ben sprinted down South Street towards the Staten Island Ferry terminal. The cement podium blocked the agent's view and his line of fire.

The icy breeze ripped into Ben's face. His muscles tightened. His hands and knees ached. His bloody shirttails danced in the wind.

South Ferry was only a block away, across Whitehall Street from the main entrance to One Water. There would be people there. The Staten Island Ferry. The subway to the World Trade Center and points north. Ben looked over his shoulder. Nobody followed. He jogged into the street and ran behind a line of buses parked along the curb.

Ben emerged from behind the buses. He ran towards the ferry terminal, across Whitehall Street, when a piercing shout froze him. "Stop right there, Kravner, or I'll shoot!"

It was the older FBI agent. He was on the podium in front of One Water, fifty yards away. About a dozen people were milling around the plaza in front of the ferry terminal. They all stopped, paralyzed, watching the drama unfold before them. Ben raised his arms high. The agent was approaching slowly, arms extended, gun drawn.

Ben felt the ground rumble below him. A subway train was pulling into South Ferry Station. The station entrance was twenty yards to his left, just beyond the ferry terminal. He did not have long to react. He heard Fritz Fox's voice in his head. *Go for it, Marathon Man.*

Ben dropped his arms and sprinted towards the entrance. The people around him scattered. The agent, unwilling to risk a shot with so many bystanders, lowered his gun and ran, on an angle, to cut Ben off. Ben had a twenty-yard lead when he burst through the glass doors of the subway station. He lost some ground scrambling to hop over the turnstiles. The agent hurdled the turnstiles only moments behind him.

Ben dashed down the steps to the subway platform two at a time, shouting for the handful of arriving passengers to move aside. He stumbled into the wall by the landing at the base of the first flight of stairs. A large mosaic of a ferry boat decorated the wall. Ben turned to see the open doors of the waiting northbound "1" train one flight below.

A chime sounded; the doors were about to close. Ben began to move towards the stairs. A shot rang out. Ben dropped to the ground in the fetal position, knees to his chest, head buried in his arms.

The shot shattered a tile on the ferry boat mosaic above Ben's head. The FBI agent crouched at the top of the stairs, arms extended, gun pointed down at Ben. "Get up!" he yelled.

Ben's heart pounded; his breathing was labored. The stairs and the platform below were clear. There was nowhere to run or hide. The doors to the train closed, and it pulled out from the station. *It was over.*

Ben scrambled to his feet. Then, suddenly, a man's blood-curdling shout reverberated throughout the station. The agent's head reflexively turned; he kept the gun trained on Ben. A look of horror crossed the agent's face. He tried to swing the gun around.

Ben stared in disbelief as a burly figure barreled into the FBI man. The agent's arms flew up into the air, a shot careened off the ceiling tile, then he reeled helplessly down the stairs, landing hard on his left side. He screamed in agony.

Ben stood, horrified, his back pressed against the wall at the bottom of the stairwell. The agent writhed in pain near Ben's feet, his left leg bent at an unnatural angle midway between his ankle and knee, both hands cupped over his left ribs. He was breathing irregularly and coughing up blood. The gun was perched four steps above, just outside the reach of the disabled G-man.

A hulking black man in a tattered army overcoat and a black beret stood, silhouetted, at the top of the stairs, both hands on his hips. It was Hubert, the man of the street whom Debby had befriended. Ben saluted him and nodded his thanks. Hubert tipped his beret and walked away, shouting: "Repent, sinners! Repent! The time has come to repent for all of your sins! The end is near!"

The ground began to tremble. It signaled not the imminent realization of Hubert's apocalyptic predictions, but rather the arrival of another train. Ben stepped over the fallen agent and retrieved the gun from the steps. He had never handled a firearm before. The steel was colder, heavier than he expected. He climbed the stairs, tentatively, not sure what awaited him at the top.

The station was deserted. There was a faint smell of gunpowder in the air. A small crowd gathered outside. Hubert was preaching to his new audience, which, for the most part, ignored him. Ben heard a police siren in the distance. He saw the light-haired FBI agent aggressively pushing his way through the crowd, his gun drawn.

"Stand clear of the moving platform," a recorded message warned. The South Ferry platform was curved, a small part of a large loop of track that enabled the southbound "1" train to turn around and head northbound. An electronic "gap filler" extended the platform to meet the train near the opening doors so that riders were not required to leap across the gaps between the curved platform and the straight trains.

Ben crouched below floor level on the first flight of stairs and peered through the railing at the platform below. He shook his head, wondering what surprises the arriving train held for him. *Probably a National Guard battalion on a field trip to Staten Island.* The gap fillers extended, and the doors opened. Nobody exited the train, perhaps because it was so close behind the one before it.

Ben swallowed hard. His survival instinct was taking over. He did not want a shoot-out. Up until now he was at least standing on the moral high ground. If he killed a cop or a bystander, there would be no hope of reclaiming his life, a goal which he already felt slipping from his grasp.

He heard the chime from the "1" train. He could catch it if he ran. But it was at least a five-minute ride to the next stop, Rector Street, and the police or the FBI might have time to radio ahead for help. He would not be difficult to identify, coming off an empty train and running about in his bloodied shirttails in the snowy weather.

But the train was his only hope. Fifty/fifty odds? He had already been lucky twice today. He hustled down the stairs, past the FBI agent still moaning on the landing, and bolted for the train.

"Wait!"

Ben froze. He raised his arms up over his head, the gun dangling harmlessly from his index finger.

"Put yo' arms down, jackass."

Ben lowered his arms and sighed. It was Hubert. The "1" train pulled out. The loud screech of metal on metal cut through Ben like the sound of fingernails on a blackboard.

"Cops'll be crawlin' all over that train," Hubert said. "You've gotta take the Lex."

"I can't get to Bowling Green without going outside," Ben said. "The cops are already out there."

Hubert laughed. "Stick with Hubert, man. You're in my house now. Ain't nobody gonna catch you in my house. There's an old shuttle track 'tween South Ferry and Bowlin' Green. Nobody uses it but me."

"You mean we've got to get down on the tracks?" Ben asked. His eyes were like saucers.

"Unless you wanna do lunch with the cops, man."

Hubert lowered himself on to the tracks, avoiding the electrified third rail. "No sweat," he said, extending his hand to Ben.

There was no other way out. "Give me a second," Ben said.

Ben ran back to the stairs. He glared at the FBI agent on the landing one flight above. "I don't know what you were told, but I have not committed any crime!" Ben shouted. "I'm being stalked by your boss, Gerry Kate. I'm going to toss your gun on the tracks, and then I'm going to disappear. I am not armed! Do you hear me?"

The agent grimaced, but signaled his understanding. Ben retreated to the edge of the platform, then heaved the gun as far as he could down the tracks to the north. Then he climbed down from the platform, rejecting Hubert's hand. He looked north, up the southbound track. No sight or sound of an approaching train. Then they sprinted in the opposite direction, around the loop, into the subterranean darkness.

THIRTY

THE CHIMES sounded. The doors to the "5" train, the Lexington Avenue express, closed. Ben stood, one arm grasping the steel pole running from the floor to the ceiling in the center of the aisle. An elderly woman sat alone in front of him. Ben saw fear in her eyes. He tried to smile. She stood up and staggered to the other end of the car as the train lurched forward.

Ben noticed several people staring at him. He grimaced, and realized why, when he saw his reflection in the window. There were streaks of soot on his face from his jaunt through the subway tunnels with Hubert. His hair, already on the long side of business-like, was unkempt. The tension in his forehead forced his eyebrows to slant towards his nose, combining with his mustache and intense brown eyes to give him an angry, almost evil, appearance. It was a frightening image even to himself.

He suddenly felt vulnerable on the train. His appearance, or a suspicious passenger, could draw the attention of a cop on a platform. Ben exited at the next stop, Brooklyn Bridge/City Hall.

A blast of arctic air greeted him at the stairwell. It was snowing. A thin white layer coated the lawn of City Hall Park. He crossed Chambers Street and ducked into an abandoned storefront to shield himself from the wind.

Ben was disappointed that he did not feel relief after his dramatic escape through the subway system. His adventure was only beginning. The FBI, with the assistance of the New York City police, would be looking for him everywhere. He could not go back to his apartment. He could not stay with his friends or family; he could not even call them. The FBI would no doubt be tapping the telephones of everyone that he knew.

Then he thought about Debby. His heart sank. She had not let him down. Somehow the FBI had caught on to them both, and now she was their prisoner. Or dead.

For now, Debby's fate was beyond his control. He had to find a way to survive and get his message to the White House.

Ben cupped his hands and blew on them for warmth. He desperately needed a coat and gloves, but was reluctant to dip into his cash reserves. He opened his wallet. He still had the five hundred dollars he had withdrawn from the bank on Tuesday. Now he worried that it was not enough. He assumed that the FBI would be able to locate him the instant he tried to use his credit cards or a cash machine. The five hundred dollars might have to feed, clothe and shelter him for longer than he cared to predict.

Ben saw a pay telephone on the corner of Broadway and Chambers. He dashed out from his protected alcove. He thumbed through the Yellow Pages.

Ben jogged into the Salvation Army thrift shop on the northern fringe of Chinatown, breathless and beyond cold, fifteen minutes later. His face was so numb that he could not feel it. The clerk, a hefty, middle-aged, African-American woman, looked Ben over. She had a lazy eye, so that it was difficult for Ben to follow her gaze.

"Are you in trouble, son?" she asked.

"I'm cold," Ben said, rubbing his hands together. It hurt his jaw to speak. "I need a coat and gloves."

She walked out from behind the counter. She put her hands on her hips and shook her head with exaggerated displeasure. "Looks like you need a new shirt and pants, too. What sort of trouble have you got yourself into, son?"

Ben shrugged. "I got into a fight. My coat was stolen."

"Well, I suppose that's your story and you're sticking to it. Let's see what we can find."

"Nothing too fancy," Ben said.

The woman laughed heartily. "Well, I don't think that will be a problem."

They picked out a pair of light brown twill pants, slightly worn in the knees, a white polo shirt with a small purple stain under the collar, a red ski jacket that had no apparent defects and a pair of black leather gloves with the fingertips worn away.

"You can change behind the screen in the back and then clean yourself up a bit in the washroom," she said.

Ben changed and washed, then returned to the counter. The clerk was speaking with a poorly dressed, elderly man. As Ben got closer, he heard her giving directions to a shelter. The man left, and the woman turned back to Ben. She put her hands on her hips and looked up and down at him with her exaggerated movements. "Mm, mm, mm. Now aren't you a fashion statement."

Ben smiled for what seemed like the first time in days. He noticed with some relief that most of the feeling had returned to his face. "What do I owe you, ma'am?" he asked.

"Well, let's see," she said. One eye looked directly into Ben's, the other looked over his shoulder. "Two dollars for the pants. One dollar for the shirt. One dollar for the gloves. That coat is in pretty good shape. Let's say twenty dollars for the whole enchilada."

Ben looked in his wallet. He hesitated. Five hundred dollars. It would not last long. He pulled out two twenty dollar bills. "Here's forty. I put the old stuff in the trash in the back. Thanks for your help."

"Well, thank you, sir. Now you have a merry Christmas."

Ben pushed the front door open, then went back to the counter. "I heard you giving directions to that old man. Is there a shelter nearby?" Ben asked.

"Well, there are two in lower Manhattan," the clerk said. "The nearest one is on Spring Street, near Lafayette. That's only a five minute walk. The other one is a little bigger. It's up in Gramercy Park—19th Street between Third and Lex." She gave him an odd look.

"What's wrong?" Ben asked.

"Well, son, our shelters do fine work, but they do get crowded this time of year, and they don't always attract the best element of society, if you know what I mean. You might want to put that big, old wallet of yours in your shoe if you're planning to spend tonight in a shelter."

Ben sat down on the floor and put all but twenty dollars of the cash in his shoes. "I'm not sure what I'm doing tonight, but better safe than sorry," he said. "Thanks, again."

The mid-afternoon chill was bearable with the new coat and gloves. Ben felt less conspicuous in the old clothes. In a city of eight million people, it would be next to impossible for the FBI to pick him out on the streets. It would take a mistake for them to find him. He could not afford even one.

It was time to formulate a plan. Ben ticked off his objectives. Expose the conspiracy. Evade the FBI. Find food and shelter. Save Debby. The last thought surprised him. The hollowness in his heart confirmed his suspicions—he still had feelings for her. Was it love? Whatever the emotion was, he knew he could not let it control his consciousness. Following the path with heart was satisfying, but led to mistakes.

His top priority was to expose the conspiracy. The options were the same as they had been that morning, but were now riddled with obstacles. Fritz Fox was still his best alternative. But the Knights knew that. They would be waiting for him to make that mistake. Did they know about Quixote? Probably not, but it would be even more difficult for Ben to establish that connection now. Quixote's telephone number was unlisted. He was a fugitive. No credibility. No computer. Sour history. Fritz was still the better choice. Ben had to find a way to contact him without detection.

Or did it really matter if he was detected? Fritz would protect him and listen to him. Ben just needed to stay alive long enough to talk to him. *Stay alive.* That thought sent a chill through his body. The FBI agents had shot at him. He had information that could destroy some of the most powerful men in the country. Their first defense had been to weaken his credibility, but that could not be their only defense. Their mission and their lives were in jeopardy. For the first time, Ben realized he was not running for his freedom—he was running for his life. And he would jeopardize the life of anybody that he involved.

Ben knew that the FBI would be monitoring Fritz's telephone. Fritz would be endangered if he called. Fritz would insist upon a meeting with Ben to see all the evidence before he called the President. He would want to look into Ben's eyes and know that this was not the desperate ploy of a fugitive. If Fritz delayed, as he must, he would die. Gerry Kate would see to that. A thought trapped in Ben's subconscious teased him, then took flight.

He was at the corner of Delancey and Lafayette. He needed a place to think. He jingled the keys in his pocket. His apartment was out of the question. He could not involve friends or relatives. The Salvation Army shelter was a few blocks to the south, but it would be noisy and crowded. He needed a quiet, safe place where he could focus on his thoughts and not be constantly alert to his surroundings. He needed a library.

The New Amsterdam branch of the New York Public Library was a warm and welcome refuge. The library's main room was divided into two areas. Directly across from the entrance, rows of low bookshelves encircled a magazine reading area with eight wooden tables, four chairs each. A second area, to the left, was devoted to computers. Two computers were dedicated to the card catalogue, but there were six other computers available for public access to the Internet. Ben filed that information away for later use. First things first. Coffee.

The coffee from the vending machine had a metallic taste, but the caffeine provided the anticipated jump start. Ben settled into a hard chair in the magazine reading section. It was a small area, about the size of his living room. An elderly woman and a middle-aged man were seated, separately, at the tables; another two women circulated among the bookshelves. No one took notice of Ben.

Ben's mind, now more focused than outside in the cold, returned to the problem of contacting Fritz. He went over his options. Telephone. The FBI would be listening. Best case: Fritz believes Ben, realizes the immediate danger and calls the President. *Unlikely.* Worst case: Fritz demands a meeting, the FBI tracks him and kills them both. The Royal Order remains undetected and bad things happen. *Unacceptable risks.*

The thought that teased him earlier finally surfaced. The *FBI* would be listening, not Gerry Kate personally. Kate was no doubt using the FBI as his personal tool, but his agents could not be privy to the conspiracy. *Could they?* When Ben spoke with Carol on the telephone that morning, she did not say what the agents wanted. Kate must have created phony charges.

Ben sipped his coffee. He could call Fritz and tell him enough about the conspiracy and the involvement of Gerry Kate to put the agent monitoring the call on alert. It was risky. The agent might think it was a ploy and report it to Kate. But the agent would not kill Fritz. *Would he?* What if Kate had recruited a special team to assist him in the conspiracy? Ben frowned. He could not take that chance. Not yet. There were still other options.

E-mail. Ben did not have access to his computer, but he could sign up for a free e-mail account on the Web using the library's computers.

But the FBI would be monitoring Fritz's incoming e-mail. Ben would be assured of saying everything he wanted to say, without being cut off, but Fritz would still be at risk. The FBI could intervene before Fritz acted on the message. Ben was not sure about the technology, but wondered if the FBI might even intercept the e-mail before Fritz read it. The telephone seemed the better option of the two.

Personal contact. Ben could not get near the office. Fritz would be leaving for the day soon, anyway. He would be out of the office for the weekend, maybe longer. The FBI—no, Gerry Kate—knew that Fritz was the only way for him to connect with the President, probably the only person that could help him. Kate would make sure that agents were watching Fritz around the clock.

But the agents would only be watching for contact by Ben. What if he found someone else to make the contact for him? Maybe Carol or one of his friends at the firm. *Could he trust them?* He was a fugitive. There might be a reward for information about his whereabouts. He could all too easily imagine Buzz Herzog basking in the glow of the television lights, immodestly describing his role in the capture of the fugitive, Benjamin Franklin Kravner. *Too risky.*

Ben sipped his coffee. If contact was to be made with Fritz, he would have to do it himself. Maybe he could disguise himself. Fritz had walked in Central Park at six o'clock every morning before the heart attack. Ben wondered if the doctors had allowed him to start his regular exercise regime, again.

He would find out tomorrow, Christmas Day. The park would probably be empty. The FBI agents would likely maintain some distance between themselves and Fritz. Ben could pass Fritz a letter describing the conspiracy in detail and include copies of the Poem and the List. There was some risk of discovery, but it was the safest of his alternatives.

Ben's stomach rumbled. His mind turned to food and shelter. The Salvation Army had sounded better earlier in the afternoon when fear and frostbite consumed his thoughts. With warmth and something of a plan, Ben's aspirations became loftier. He would need privacy to transform himself into the new Ben Kravner, one that even his mother would not recognize. He already had a mental picture.

A hotel was a possibility if he believed that his run from justice was to be short-lived, but even in the best case Fritz would need some time to work his magic. It would be hard to find accommodations in New York City for less than one hundred dollars. Paying cash might also arouse suspicion, and Ben's picture would be splashed all over the television news that night.

An idea that had dashed in and out of his mind all afternoon lingered now. Thompson's apartment. No doorman. Privacy. Warmth. A kitchen. Big screen TV. Free. It also contained something he had long coveted and was now desperate to call his own—the IBM Thinkpad in the docking station on Thompson's desk. It offered the opportunity for him to reconnect to the world.

But, like every other aspect of his life now, it was risky. He would be a top priority for the FBI. They would stake out his apartment, his parents' house in Westchester, and Fritz Fox. Did they know that Ben had access to Thompson's apartment? There was too much at stake to take chances. Ben had to assume that the FBI knew everything and was prepared to devote all of their resources to his capture. But even complete knowledge by the FBI would not make fortress Thompson impregnable.

Four inches of fresh, white snow blanketed the city streets. Ben trekked through the concrete tundra from the library to Greenwich Village, staying clear of the main thoroughfares. He remained alert for signs of the FBI or the police, but encountered no one to fear. He found what he was looking for on Bleecker Street, between MacDougal and Sixth Avenue.

Ben entered the second-hand clothing store. The jangling bells interrupted the clerk, a young woman with long, dirty blonde hair, from her reading. She looked up grudgingly from behind the counter at the back of the store.

"We're closing early for Christmas," she said. "Fifteen minutes."

Ben acknowledged her with a sheepish wave. It was a deep, narrow store, with a single aisle. Racks filled with women's clothing lined both walls. The store reeked of incense.

Ben was uneasy handling the women's clothes, even though the store was empty. He quickly found the three items he was looking for and brought them to the back. The woman reluctantly put down her book. Her facial muscles twitched in an ambiguous attempt at a smile.

"They're for my girlfriend," Ben said awkwardly.

The clerk rang up the items on an old manual cash register without comment. A long, brightly colored dress with a woven Aztec pattern.

K-ching. A pair of white boots with fur lining. K-ching. The boots were small, but Ben would be able to squeeze into them. And an olive knapsack. K-ching. The total came to $48.67.

The clerk's facial muscles twitched again after Ben paid her, then she returned to her book. He stuffed the dress and the boots into the knapsack haphazardly, flashed his winning smile in the direction of the back of the clerk's head, and left through the jangling door, content, for once, not to have made a lasting impression.

Ben made stops at a drug store and a sandwich shop, then wandered MacDougal Street looking for a place to change clothes. Despite the snow, the Village was busy with high-spirited Christmas revelers. Ben searched for a quiet place. Finally, he came upon *Sausolito's*. There were a dozen patrons inside. The room was dimly lit.

He went directly to the restroom in the rear. There were two stalls. One was occupied; Ben slipped into the other. He waited for the first man to leave, then placed the knapsack on the sink. He took out one of several disposable razors, a can of shaving cream and a woman's wig that he had purchased at the drug store and laid them out on the counter. He looked in the mirror wistfully. He tugged at the mustache one last time in a rare moment of sentimentality, then lathered up.

Ben emerged from the men's room hesitantly. He was wearing the woman's wig, which was a similar shade of brown to his own hair but was slightly longer than shoulder length, the red ski jacket, the Aztec dress under it, and the white boots. He carried the knapsack under his arm like a purse. He felt like a jackass. Nobody seemed to notice.

It was not a long walk from *Sausolito's* to Adams Thompson's apartment—up MacDougal, along Washington Square Park, and over to Fifth Avenue—but it was a painful one. The boots were tight, but the physical pain was bearable. More difficult to bear were the snickers from the passing revelers, which were frequent enough to confirm that his disguise was far from perfect.

Ben's heart raced as he neared the corner of Fifth Avenue and Washington Square North, one block from Thompson's apartment. His impulse was to walk past the building while checking for lurkers in trenchcoats and sunglasses or other signs of surveillance. But he knew that he had only one chance. He was not going to fool anybody with his disguise if they had a close look at him. *Now or never.*

He entered the semi-circular driveway in front of Thompson's gray brick apartment building. There was no one visible in the doorway or the lobby. He discreetly glanced across Fifth Avenue. A man was lingering in the vestibule of the high-rise across the street. No trenchcoat. No sunglasses. Maybe he was waiting for his date. Ben's intestines liquefied, anyway. *Last chance to run.*

He fumbled with the keys, but was soon out of the floodlights and into the lobby. The elevator seemed to take forever. His body tensed, as he waited breathlessly for the front door to swing open violently with a frightful shout from an armed G-man or for the glass to shatter as a sniper's bullet raced towards his heart. The elevator chime sounded. The doors opened. No shouts. No bullets. The doors closed safely behind him.

Ben tensed again as he entered Thompson's residence. A search of the dark and gloomy apartment revealed no surprises. Ben locked the deadbolt. He left the lights off in case the apartment was being watched. He changed out of the women's clothes. He brought his shaving gear and a scissors from Thompson's office into the bathroom. The only window faced the back of the building. He closed the shades and the door and turned on the light.

Ben ran his fingers through his hair as he looked in the mirror. An odd sadness came over him, but he could not bear to dwell on it. He hacked off large clumps of his long, black locks with the scissors, then completed the job with three disposable razors. He was completely bald when he finished, satisfied that even his mother would not recognize him. And hopefully the FBI.

A wave of guilt overcame him as he thought of his mother. His parents had to be petrified—their peaceful suburban existence thrown into turmoil by invading agents of the FBI, their only child a fugitive, alone in the bowels of New York City. He wanted desperately to get them a message that he was safe, but he did not dare it.

Ben spent the next several hours drafting a letter to Fritz Fox. The bathroom was the only room in which he felt safe to use the light. He sat on the toilet, using a large coffee table book about the Civil War as a desktop.

His heart pounded as he relived the events of the past several weeks, describing them in sobering detail. The discovery of the Poem and his ethical breach in opening the sealed envelope. The meeting with Dean

Frederick in Atlanta and the revelation of the story of Jimmy
MacDougall and Old Tippecanoe, William Henry Harrison. The
recovery of Adams Thompson's wallet and the List. The regular meetings of The Royal Order of the Millennium Knight in the Millennium
Nights room on CyberLine. The decryption of the Key upon the surprising announcement of the merger of the presidential candidacies of
Tony Fabrizio and JJ Alexander. Debby's disclosure of her activities and
her relation to The Assassin. Debby's brother, the potential successor to
The Assassin, who remained at-large. The late-night visit to the FBI
field office. The confirmation of the Key by the first names found on
the portraits in the MacDougall Room at Calhoun College. The nar-
rowly averted ambush by the FBI in the offices of Kramer, Fox.

He warned Fritz of the grave danger of delay, that the FBI was watching his every move. He urged him to contact the President immediately.
He knew that Fritz would be reluctant to act without a face-to-face meeting, but Ben pleaded for Fritz to draw upon their mutual respect, trust
and friendship to find the faith to act decisively. He wrote "Fritz Fox" in
black marker on the front of a business envelope and inserted the letter
and copies of the Poem and the List that he had transcribed.

Ben gathered his hair clippings, the wig and the women's clothes and
walked them down to the building's incinerator. He cleaned the bathroom of all evidence of his transformation. He looked in the mirror curi-
ously. He was amazed at how much difference hair made to one's appearance. He looked like a sixteen-year old. A sixteen-year old skinhead.

It was almost midnight. Ben peered cautiously out of the darkened
window of Thompson's bedroom. The man was still lingering in the
vestibule across Fifth Avenue. Ben's new look would be put to the test
the next morning. He undressed and lay in Thompson's bed.

His mind would not rest. He recalled the layout of Central Park and
visualized the exchange of the letter with Fritz Fox. Fritz would not recognize Ben right away, but he would piece the puzzle together later
when he read the letter. Fritz would believe in him; the letter was from
the heart. The Royal Order of the Millennium Knight would be
exposed. Benjamin Franklin Kravner would save the world.

He smiled in the dark. Benjamin Franklin Kravner. Hawkeye. He
wondered where Debby was right now. He had not thought about her
since early afternoon. She was alive; he felt it in his heart. He would
save her, too.

He rubbed his bald scalp. Like Samson, he had drawn power from his hair. His confidence peaked when his hair was longest. It was his small measure of civil disobedience against the Establishment. But somehow, bald, he felt more powerful than ever before. There was something about the element of danger, the size of the stakes, that made his heart soar. He was daring to be great.

THIRTY-ONE

THE KNIGHTS HAD AGREED to meet in the Millennium Nights room at midnight on Friday to discuss the capture of Ben and Debby. As usual, The General was the last to arrive, ten minutes late. The Heir Apparent deferred to The Spy immediately.

The Spy: DB was apprehended this AM and held in Maryland safe house. BFK eluded agents and still at-large.

The Heir Apparent: It's difficult to convey anger in this medium, Spy, but I think that I speak for the group when I say that this bungling is getting tiresome.

The General: What measures are you taking to find him?

The Spy: He's on most wanted list. Evidence planted on drug charges. Agents instructed shoot to kill.

The Senator: Isn't there any way we can avoid killing him?

The General: I think The Spy acted wisely. Kravner knows his life is in danger now. He's going to disclose the plot as soon as he can. Even a suggestion of a conspiracy of this magnitude might attract somebody's attention.

The Spy: Exactly. We can't take that chance. We're too close.

The Heir Apparent: I agree. Public response to a Fabrizio-Alexander ticket has been overwhelming. The polls show almost 75% approval. The Democrats have endorsed us. The Republican party leadership is miffed, but they meet next week and I don't think they have much choice.

The Speaker: We have, of course, been discussing the matter, and you are correct—the top brass is irate. I'm making some progress trying to convince my colleagues that it would be political suicide to try to oppose the ticket.

The Heir Apparent: I'm confident that you'll succeed. Spy, how can we be sure Kravner won't find somebody to listen to his story? Does Fox know anything?

The Spy: Interviewed Fox. He knows nothing. Still worries me. Thinks highly of BFK. If BFK gets to him, Fox will listen. Fox also personal friend of Prez. Can go directly to White House.

The Heir Apparent: Can you put a surveillance team on Fox?

The Spy: Not enough. We can't completely cut off his communications. BFK is computer literate. He may get message to Fox. Damage irreversible.

The Heir Apparent: Are you proposing that we murder Fritz Fox?

The Spy: No. Silence him for a few days. BFK captured soon. Smart kid, but he'll make mistake. They all do.

The Heir Apparent: Be careful. Old men are brittle, and Fox had a heart attack a few weeks ago. If he dies, people in high places will be interested in the investigation. If the connection is made to Kravner's difficulties, the odds against us multiply. Somebody might be willing to listen to conspiracy theories if The Publisher's lawyer is murdered so soon after The Publisher's death, especially if the lawyer is Fritz Fox.

The Caretaker: What if we frame Kravner for the Fox murder? He won't be able to walk out on the street without getting lynched. That would also make it less likely that anybody connects Fox's death to The Publisher.

The Senator: I'm sorry, but I have to put my foot down here. I have had the pleasure of working with Mr. Fox on a number of sensitive matters, and he is a remarkable gentleman. He has one of the sharpest minds I have ever known, he's highly ethical, and he is a kind and compassionate man. Even putting aside my objections to killing any outsiders, I would sooner betray this group than support the murder of Fritz Fox.

The Spy: Senator, those are dangerous words.

The Heir Apparent: I understand The Senator's point, and I have no doubt of his loyalty to The Royal Order. Fox is an innocent, and any threat he poses can be neutralized without murdering him. Spy, we'll leave the details to you. If you can find a way to undermine Kravner in the process, that's all the better.

The Spy: I'm on top of it.

The General: Does Kravner have any other contacts that need to be neutralized?

The Spy: People have 100s if not 1000s of contacts. Can't "neutralize" all. He'll only communicate with someone if (a) they can help him, (b) low risk of detection and (c) he trusts them with his life. You're all high-powered men. Think how many people fall into that category for you.

The Speaker:	Not many.
The Spy:	Even fewer for BFK. He's young and a loner. Interviews with family, co-workers and neighbors this PM. We have phone and e-mail records. He has friends at law firm, but Fox is only concern. Colleagues unconnected. BFK knows that FBI monitoring all communications into office, so high risk of detection. Any employees contacted by BFK told to contact FBI pronto. Warned that anyone assisting BFK prosecuted for harboring fugitive.
The Senator:	What about family?
The Spy:	Surveillance team monitoring BFK's parents. Only child. Calls every Sunday. May try contact to let know safe, but won't share details. Knows they'll be watched closely and won't involve. Police would contact FBI, anyway. Extended family: middle class, no connections.
The Spy:	BFK is a CyberLine user. No record in RealTime. However, we found e-mail communications with 4 people indicating disclosure of some information. They were monitoring Millennium Nights room.
The General:	They've been eavesdropping on our meetings?
The Spy:	Can't view discussions, but can tell when room in use and who's in it.
The Speaker:	Do we need to set up a new meeting room?
The Spy:	Continue meeting here. BFK can't view discussion. If desperate, might try contact using alias. Opportunity to pick up trail.
The Speaker:	Can you trace him if he's in RealTime?
The Spy:	Not instantaneously. If know cyber-name, can access account through CyberLine.

	Can determine POP, the point of presence, used to access Internet. Won't know phone number, but we'll know locality.
The General:	Does he have a computer with him?
The Spy:	No. One of my hopes is that he uses credit card to buy laptop. He uses computer every day. He'll feel naked without it.
The Heir Apparent:	Who are Kravner's Internet friends? How involved are they?
The Spy:	Two of them were DB. She was duping him under alias. 3 others treated as suspects in drug case. Woodrow Taylor: lawyer in SF. Peggy Sue Jenkins: ski instructor in Aspen. Linda Pinter: works in tire plant in Akron. Electronic and visual surveillance teams monitoring activities. BFK probably only used them to monitor our room. Not likely that he ever met them. BFK not likely to trust anyone over the Internet enough to provide details. These people could be anybody. He knows that. It appears that he frequently adopted aliases, as well.
The General:	We can't take any chances, Spy. We seem to keep underestimating him.
The Spy:	Point well taken, and full surveillance teams assigned. BFK needs to reach out to somebody. My assessment: we have not been compromised yet.
The General:	Are there any other contacts that warrant attention?
The Spy:	All other contacts in past 6 months incidental. He knows can't contact family and friends. Girlfriend in custody. Fox inaccessible by tomorrow. No access to computer. Picture plastered on every post office and precinct wall. BFK has whatever money in

pocket, and he's afraid to use bank and credit cards. He'll turn up frozen to death in back alley or he'll make a mistake. It will not take long to apprehend BFK.

The Heir Apparent: We're counting on it—but we need to develop alternate strategies, too. If Kravner finds a way to get through to somebody with the right connections, everything would be lost.

The General: We could create a diversion. Make sure that the White House is so preoccupied with other matters that nobody will have time to listen to wild conspiracy theories.

The Spy: Particularly from someone on FBI's Ten Most-Wanted list.

The Heir Apparent: What did you have in mind, General?

The General: We need to accelerate our plans. We thought we had another year to let everything fall neatly into place, but that may not be true now.

The Senator: Intriguing thought, General. There's no reason why we can't take the nation to the brink of war now, then push it over the edge when we're ready. If all works according to plan, that will be after The Heir Apparent is inaugurated. But if the plan is foiled by Kravner or otherwise, our Final Vengeance can still be claimed.

The Heir Apparent: The only problem is that we risk losing control over events if we leave time between them. If I'm the president, I can control the government's reaction. We can never be sure how Norton will react to a situation.

The General: That's the cost of gaining an option. If we don't do it, we risk losing everything. If we try something and it fails, we still have time to develop other alternatives. We risk achieving nothing for our life's work if we don't start taking risks to protect the mission.

The Caretaker: I agree. It's time to prove our mettle. If we take these next steps, we go beyond conspiracy and into treason. We have to ask ourselves: are we willing to die for The Royal Order of the Millennium Knight?

THIRTY-TWO

A STRANGE ALARM BLASTED, awakening Ben with a fright. He leapt out of bed in a state of foggy-eyed confusion. Then he remembered. He was on the run. He smacked Adams Thompson's alarm clock. The alarm stopped. Five o'clock, Christmas morning. He groaned. Sleep had been short and fitful.

Ben peeked out the window. A glacial river of pristine snow seemed to flow through the gray canyon of Fifth Avenue into Washington Square Park. Light flurries gusted from the rooftops, illuminated in the glow of the street lamps. There was no sign of the man loitering under the vestibule across the street the night before, but Ben was still wary.

Ben splashed water on his face and took one final curious look in the mirror at his strange new countenance. The teenage skinhead. His parents would faint. He dressed quickly and packed the shaving materials and the ThinkPad in his knapsack. He wore the knapsack on his back, hoping to give the impression of a student on an excursion to the library or a friend's apartment to study. On Christmas Day. At five o'clock in the morning. *No turning back now.*

Ben did not know if or when Fritz Fox would walk this morning. Maybe he had stopped exercising after the heart attack. Maybe he slept late on the weekends. Maybe it was too cold or too wet. But Ben knew that he might not get many more chances. He had already decided that it was too dangerous to spend another night in Thompson's apartment. He had only planned his life as far as this one moment—handing off the letter to Fritz in Central Park. It had to happen. He would will it to happen.

Ben hesitated as the elevator doors opened into the building lobby, then lurched forward with an artificial determination. He felt self-conscious. His hair had been a meaningful part of his identity, and its absence created an odd sensation, like the war veterans who lost arms or legs but still reported feeling in the phantom limb. He had phantom hair. But his self-consciousness went beyond his baldness. He was prey. Like a deer alone and deep in a forest of eight million trees, he was statistically safe, yet knew that the eyes of a hunter could lie behind any one of them. He heard every sound and was aware of every movement.

Ben exited the building, a wicked arctic blast slapping him across the face, the indescribable sensation of phantom hair replaced by a very real numbness. Ben rubbed his gloved hands together and stamped his feet to speed the circulation of blood to his extremities.

Then, suddenly, he heard a sound from across the street. Ben froze and shot a furtive glance at the neighboring apartment building. He saw a small movement in the shadows. A man was in the alley across the street—and he was staring directly at Ben.

Their eyes met. It was the younger FBI agent who had shot at Ben from the loading dock. *Act natural. He can't possibly recognize me.* Ben forced an awkward grin and waved an embarrassed greeting. The agent smirked and blew out a cold, misty breath.

Ben put his gloves in his pocket and made a snowball. He fired it at a street lamp. Missed. He danced through the snow, now accumulated eight inches high, kicking it and soiling its purity. He threw another snowball. Slowly he worked his way the short distance down Fifth Avenue into Washington Square. He looked back up Fifth. The agent was not in sight. Ben ran through Washington Square and all the way to the West Fourth Street subway station. It was half past five o'clock.

The "D" train deposited Ben on Central Park West at 77th Street, adjacent to the Museum of Natural History, twenty-five minutes later. A newspaper was tucked under his arm. The street was deserted.

Ben could only guess where Fritz would enter the park. He recalled Fritz saying that he walked around "The Lake," as if there was only one. Central Park extended from 59th Street to 110th Street and contained 840 acres of wooded and landscaped grounds. Ben knew of three lakes and a pond in the park. The largest, which he thought was the one Fritz meant, extended from 77th Street to 71st Street.

Ben entered the park at 77th Street. He walked south, along a path following close to the western shore of the lake, in search of a place to lie in wait. It was dark, but the path was lit by street lights set about one hundred yards apart. Still, Ben was uneasy. Central Park's reputation as a haven for evil-doers loomed large on his mind, and the shadows of the snow-covered trees cast an eerie pall. Ben went on, his jaw set firmly and his eyes blazing, yet treading lightly and flinching at the slightest sound, an odd combination of temerity and timidity, man and mouse.

A small gazebo along the lakeshore offered a view of the walking path as well as shelter from the wind, but it was too close to the path. Ben would not have time to arrange a chance meeting with Fritz, and he might arouse the suspicion of the FBI agent following him.

Ben passed through a long, vine-covered walkway. It was like a covered bridge, but served no function. A thicket of maple trees separated the walkway and the lake. Ben saw the perfect lookout spot when he emerged on the other side.

The southwestern corner of the lake was formed in the shape of a finger, bending slightly eastward. The path around the lake diverged near the tip of the finger. To the right, the main route continued due east, circling the lake. To the left, another trail led to a small, wooden gazebo nestled in a cove at the base of the finger, where the lake widened. Ben jogged towards the cove.

He climbed carefully down the icy stone steps that curved through a rock outcropping, down an embankment, to the cove. The gazebo offered him an unobstructed view of the main path in both directions. He would be able to see Fritz walking south along the west shore, from across the narrow waterway, where the path emerged from the thicket of maples near the vine-covered bridge. He could also see him walking west along the southern shore if he came around the lake in the opposite direction.

The gazebo, a small A-frame structure with four wooden pillars and two benches, was on flat ground, abutting the lake. The roof was covered with snow. An old oak tree leaned over the lake at a forty-five degree angle, its spidery branches brushing against the gazebo roof. A lone pigeon was perched on a limb. The high-rise apartment buildings on Central Park West rose above the urban forest in the distance.

Ben dusted stray flurries from the gazebo bench, then sat. His eyes darted between the western and southern paths. Only a few die-hard joggers trudged through the snow. From time to time he turned the pages of the newspaper, searching for any mention of the events of the prior day.

Seven o'clock came and went. Ben was almost ready to quit the cold in favor of a cup of coffee someplace warm, *any* place warm, when his heart skipped a beat. His picture was on the "Local News" page.

Ben cringed. It was a bad photograph, one that until then had graced only the lawyers directory at Kramer, Fox. It got worse. The story in the *Herald Times* said that he was wanted by the FBI on federal drug charges and for assaulting an officer. The officer was in serious condition after breaking a leg, a few ribs and perforating his lung in a fall during a shoot-out in the South Ferry subway station. *Kravner should be considered armed and dangerous.* A chill ran down his spine. His fears were confirmed—the FBI was out to kill him.

Ben folded the newspaper violently. It made sense. If they captured him alive, his tales of conspiracy could attract the attention of important people, especially with Fritz Fox by his side. Just then he looked across the lake and saw a familiar figure emerging from the vine-covered walkway behind the thicket of maples.

It was Fritz. He was bundled in a black coat and capped with a fur-lined hat, but his small stature and brisk gait were unmistakable. Joy and relief tried to find expression on Ben's tired, numb face, but his facial muscles were too stiff to accommodate the emotions. He checked the letter in his jacket pocket, needlessly, for the twentieth time. This was it, the beginning of the end of his travails. If he timed it right, he would meet Fritz at the point where the paths diverged in five minutes.

Ben watched the thicket behind Fritz. He expected to see an FBI agent shortly, lurking a respectful distance behind. Ben was surprised to see a man follow almost at once. He was walking briskly, almost running, with a large stick in his hand. The stick could have been for fending off stray dogs, but the man's stride contradicted a benign purpose. He was hunter, not prey.

The man with the stick was too well-dressed to be a mugger. The FBI was not going to give Ben the opportunity to contact Fritz. Ben sprung up from the bench, but was paralyzed by indecision. If he ran, he might be able to reach Fritz before the FBI assassin could complete his task. But then what? Ben was unarmed. The agent would no doubt be pleased to accept him as a prize instead of, or in addition to, Fritz Fox. And Ben knew that if he was captured, there was no one else to stop The Royal Order of the Millennium Knight's march to their Final Vengeance.

Ben watched helplessly as the distance between Fritz and his attacker closed, then was overcome with grief when the two figures disappeared behind a clump of trees near the southern tip of the lake.

Ben buried his face in his gloved hands. He had opened the sealed envelope. He had tried to be the hotshot lawyer, taking on the most powerful men in the nation on his own. Why? The answer sprang to his mind instantly—to impress Fritz Fox, a man who was more like a grandfather to him than a mentor. He had saved him once; now he had killed him.

Ben sat there, stunned, motionless, contemplating his fate. There was nowhere for him to turn. His parents, his friends, his colleagues were all incommunicado. There were apparently no limits to what The Royal Order would do to stop him.

A siren pierced the morning stillness. Surrender to the police was an option. He would be charged with various drug offenses, any remaining shred of credibility would be destroyed, but he would live. It was not his responsibility to save the world. *That was for great men with white hair.*

Great men. One had died today. Would Fritz Fox have surrendered if faced with adversity? *No!* Fritz Fox would have dueled with the devil until justice was done or his last drop of blood had been spilt. And he wanted to be like Fritz Fox.

Ben felt his despondency lift as an icy gust slapped him in the face. There would be no surrender. Fritz Fox's death would not be in vain. There was still one last card to play.

Ben sucked in a deep breath, then metamorphosed as he expelled it, the steaming mist rising high into the air before dissipating. His eyes blazed. His nostrils flared. His jaw set firmly. The anger and sorrow that moments ago had almost conquered him were now the fuel that stoked the fire within. Passion overcame fear. The Royal Order of the Millennium Knight beware—Benjamin Franklin Kravner, Hawkeye, was on the warpath.

Ben gave one final hard look at the clump of trees where he last saw Fritz Fox alive. "They don't know the meaning of vengeance," he said out loud, then bolted east, along the lake's southern shore.

THIRTY-THREE

LAROSA SMITH EMERGED from the bedroom of her Foggy Bottom apartment dressed only in a flimsy white night gown. She let out a loud yawn, arching her back and stretching her lean, sinewy body like a cat. Her head ached; her body was sore.

"Good morning, sleepyhead," a man's voice called out from behind the counter by the breakfast nook.

LaRosa jumped. "I thought you left," she said.

She sat on a wooden stool by the counter, leaning on her elbows, her face in her hands. A muscular man with skin the color of dark chocolate was reading the Sunday *Post* at the kitchen table, munching on a croissant, wearing only purple boxer shorts. LaRosa could not remember his name.

"You were terrific last night," the man said.

LaRosa shook her head. "I don't feel terrific," she said. He had short, kinky, black hair, an undistinguished face, and a gorgeous, hairy chest. Medical student. What was it with her and younger men? And what did she do to warrant a "terrific" rating? *You don't really want to know, girl.*

"We had a lot to drink at the Christmas party last night," the Chest said. "I made coffee." He went directly to the cup cabinet, then poured a mug full for LaRosa.

"Thanks," she said. What was his name? Something with a "J." Jack? James? She sipped the coffee. "Good," she said.

"Want a section of the *Post*? Can I make you a croissant?" he asked.

Now she remembered what she liked about younger men. They were so eager to please an older woman. Older. Another birthday was coming. *Not over the hill yet.* "No. Thanks. I need to wake up a little," she said. "Was it a quiet Christmas in the news?"

"Nothing dramatic on the political front—but you'd already know about anything big by now, anyway, wouldn't you?" the Chest asked.

Was it Julian? Jules? Julian or Jules, she was sure of it. Julie would be too familiar. "Probably," she said. "But I might have slept through an earthquake last night."

The Chest smiled. "You rocked my world, baby," he said.

LaRosa smiled weakly. "Anything happening in the world of sports?" she asked.

The Chest pulled out the sports section of the *Post*. "Georgetown beat Villanova big time," he said.

"How did GW do?" she asked.

"Let's see. George Washington. That's your alma mater, right? They lost to Delaware in overtime. Sorry."

"I went to GW as an undergraduate," LaRosa said. "Class of '88."

"Wow. You look much younger than that."

LaRosa smiled a real smile, the one that transformed her face into all cheekbones. "Thanks. A girl needs to hear that every now and then. I'll be thirty-five in a couple of weeks."

The Chest did a mental calculation. "Three years of law school…so, you've been a lawyer for eight years?"

"No, I taught in the D.C. schools for five years," LaRosa said. "Graduated from Harvard Law School in '96."

"No shit," the Chest said. He fumbled through the scattered sections of newspaper, then skimmed an article on the front page. "One of your fellow alumni was in the news today. Did you know a guy named Benjamin Franklin Kravner?"

LaRosa choked on her coffee. It had been over three years since she had last spoken with Ben Kravner. "Ben?" she said. "What, did he win a big lawsuit or something?"

"No, he was arrested."

LaRosa's eyes widened. "Ben? Are you kidding me?" she asked. "He's one of the most ethical people I've ever met."

"You knew him well?" the Chest asked.

LaRosa looked away. "We were friends," she said. "What did he do?"

"It says that Kravner was believed to be the head of a nationwide organization of young professionals that was involved in illegal activities, including dealing in drugs, all managed over the Internet."

"No way," LaRosa said. "Not Ben. Let me see that article." Time did not change people's basic nature. Money, maybe. But not that much.

The Chest handed her the newspaper. The article reported that Kravner had eluded the FBI in a gun battle, seriously injuring an agent in the process. Then, on Christmas Day—yesterday—he was believed to have attacked his boss, the internationally renowned Fritz Fox, a personal friend of the President, in Central Park, knocking Fox unconscious from behind. Fox was suffering from a broken hip and a concussion, but was expected to recover.

LaRosa put the newspaper down on the counter and ran her fingers through her short, black hair. This was not the Ben Kravner she remembered from Harvard. Intelligent. Funny. Somewhat shy and awkward, but pleasant looking. A diamond in the rough.

"How did you know him?" the Chest asked. "Wasn't he a couple of years behind you at Harvard?"

LaRosa smiled. "Yeah. I was a third year; I was the teaching assistant for his first year Civil Procedure class," she said. "He was my personal project that year."

The Chest's eyebrows raised. "How so?"

"The professor—F. Theodore Donald—was a prick," she said. "He was looking to make an example of one of the new kids during the first week of classes to demonstrate the rigors of law school, and he picked Ben."

LaRosa closed her eyes. "God, he was like a frightened puppy," she continued. "His eyes were so wide that his eyelids looked like they were propped open with toothpicks. Professor Donald used the Socratic Method to pick apart every one of Ben's responses."

"So you felt sorry for him," the Chest said.

"Yeah." She smiled as the memory lingered. She had wanted to hug him. While Professor Donald had viewed his job as breaking down the new law students and then toughening them up in his own image, like a drill sergeant in the Marines, she had seen her role as a nurturing one, providing support and building confidence. Ben had been ready to quit law school; she convinced him to stay. Not only had Ben turned out to be her best student in that class, he had become one of her closest friends. Ever.

"Was he your little trophy white boy?" the Chest asked, unsmiling.

"What!" LaRosa said, stunned.

"Never mind," the Chest said.

"Where did that come from?" she asked.

The Chest hesitated, then spoke. "I'm sorry. It's frustrating, though, when all the fine black women go looking for white meat. Are you ashamed of being black?" he asked.

"What's with all this hostility?" LaRosa asked. "Ben was a friend. I never said we were lovers. And I was with you last night, wasn't I?"

"You were terrific," the Chest said, walking around to the other side of the counter and kissing LaRosa on the side of the neck. "But I never got that dreamy look that came over your face when you were talking about that drug dealer friend of yours."

"That doesn't sound like Ben," LaRosa said.

"But you were lovers, weren't you?" the Chest asked.

LaRosa felt her cheeks flush. She turned away. "No," she said. "We never made love. We were just good friends. Not that it's any of your business."

The Chest raised his arms over his head in an exaggerated gesture of surrender. LaRosa enjoyed the way his muscles rippled. "Okay. You win," he said. He picked his clothes off the living room floor. "I've got to get over to the med school library, anyway."

The Chest, Julian or Jules, dressed and left with an empty promise to call.

LaRosa curled up on her couch and read the *Post* article, again. The Ben Kravner she knew could never have committed the litany of crimes this Ben Kravner was accused of, but that was his picture plastered on the front page.

LaRosa's eyes saddened as she reminisced. Just good friends. Was that all they had been? The lunch room debates. The late night study sessions in their private corner of the Law Library. The bull sessions at Angelo's Pizza and in her apartment and at a dozen other spots around Boston. A void in her heart that had long since been filled, or forgotten, re-opened. She had fallen in love with him.

There had only been two white men—no, two white people—in her life who had not made her feel black. Tony Fabrizio was one, Ben the other. They had made her feel like a partner, an equal in every way, perhaps enhanced, but never detracted, by her womanhood, and never, ever, had she felt that they were conscious of her race.

That made them better than her, she thought, because she could never seem to forget her race. She dreamed of one day not being so self-conscious, but it would take more than two color blind men to change that part of her world.

LaRosa had thought that Ben was color blind, but now she was not even sure of that. Ben had agreed to join her and her family for a celebration dinner after her law school graduation, and she had planned to tell him that she loved him that night in her apartment.

But it had never happened. Ben had not shown up at graduation or at dinner or at her apartment. He had not picked up his telephone that night, either.

LaRosa had left the next day to start her job in Washington for the Norton campaign. She had become engulfed in the war that was the 1996 presidential campaign for the next five months. There had not been time to dwell on the emptiness in her heart. But when the campaign had ended and she realized that she had not seen or heard from Ben in five months, she had cried.

Many times over the last three and a half years she had wanted to ask him why, obsessively wondering if it had something to do with her race. She believed in her heart that it did not—it could not—but there was still the lingering doubt.

She had thought that he loved her, too. If he had hidden his feelings so well from her, maybe he had hidden other character defects. Maybe he was capable of organizing a nationwide drug conspiracy. Maybe he was capable of attempting to murder Fritz Fox.

LaRosa sighed. Ben Kravner was out of her life, and she was not going to let him ruin her weekend. Tony Fabrizio had taken a long Christmas weekend off. It was the first weekend in months that LaRosa had not spent time in the office. The Fabrizio-Alexander campaign was beginning to look like a juggernaut that could not be stopped, and even the compulsive Fabrizio was starting to relax.

LaRosa sat down at her desk and switched on the computer. Christmas dinner with her family yesterday had been wonderful. Not quite as exciting as the party her sister, Sydney, had dragged her to afterwards, but everybody was in a terrific mood because their mother's health and spirits had been much improved.

LaRosa opened her e-mail account to send a few Christmas greetings. She had a number of new messages, most of it junk mail. She cursed the purveyors of this nonsense and began to delete the incoming messages one by one.

Then one e-mail caught her eye. It was not from one of her regular correspondents, but the cyber-name "Sancho Panza" drew her attention. She clicked on the message, which had been sent the day before, and a pop-up window opened. She gasped.

Quixote,

Hi, Rosie. Still tilting at windmills? I've been meaning to write or call for a long time. You probably don't believe me right now—I know I hurt you very much—but it is true. I wish you could look into my eyes and see the truth, as you always could, but as you by now know, I am a fugitive.

I am not a drug dealer. I have uncovered a conspiracy that involves many powerful men, including those with influence over the FBI, and I am being set up. This may sound like the depraved plea of a desperate man, but it is the truth, and you are the only one who can help me warn the President now that Fritz Fox was killed. These men are insane, and your boss, Tony Fabrizio, is in grave danger.

We need to talk ASAP. PLEASE e-mail me with a time and (discreet) place to meet. I will try to be in Washington by Tuesday, December 28. Please do not contact the authorities or discuss this with Fabrizio.

Ben Kravner

LaRosa was breathless when she finished reading the message. Her mind churned; her heart throbbed. Ben's story made more sense than the one in the *Post*. But the note was so vague. A conspiracy? It did sound very much like a desperate attempt at an alibi.

But why contact her? He had to find a way around the FBI. Ben had hoped to use Fritz Fox to get to President Norton, but now he needed another contact in Washington. He thought Fox was dead. Why? If he had meant to kill him, he would have made sure he completed the job. Ben was too smart to screw up like that.

LaRosa paced her apartment. She knew that if she let Ben Kravner back into her life, she would be re-opening a psychic wound that she hoped had long ago healed. No—she knew that it had not healed when she had read the *Post* article that morning. That wound could never heal until she learned why he had so abruptly left her.

She had experienced rejection before; some day she might let some-one close enough to risk experiencing it again. But her instincts had never failed her like they had with Ben. She *knew* that he loved her as much as she loved him. She had to find out if her instincts were fallible.

She sat down at the desk, typed a note, then sent it. Maybe she would discover the truth on Tuesday.

THE SMELL OF FRYING BACON permeated the Bethesda home of Dr. Raymond Allgood. Sunday brunch was both a tradition and a team-building exercise for the Allgoods.

Stanton, a wiry fifteen-year old, washed, peeled and sliced potatoes. Diana diced onions. She was fourteen, but almost as tall as her broth-er and had long, flowing black hair like her mother, Claire. Claire Allgood set the table, prepared a fruit cup of fresh melons, orange and grapefruit slices and cherries, and supervised a gigantic skillet of home-fried potatoes, always cooked to well-done. Ray presided over a con-coction of scrambled eggs, onions, bacon and Louisiana hot sauce that remained a carefully guarded family secret.

The clinking of stainless steel on stoneware was the only sound in the Allgood dining room. It was noon when the last plate had been cleaned, and the current events round of the day's festivities began.

"Stanton, you get to pick first today," Ray said, handing him the front section of the *Washington Post*.

Stanton carefully scrutinized the front page. "Not too many choic-es today," he said. "Looks like black homeless family freezing to death in a car or crazy white lawyer dealing drugs."

"Probably good lessons in both stories," Claire said.

"I'll take Frozen Black Family for $500, mom," Stanton said.

"How did they die?" Ray asked.

"It says here that they were evicted from their apartment and were living in a car," Stanton said. "The heater must have broken. The mother was only twenty-one, and her kids were one and three."

"That's terrible," Claire said. "Didn't they have any family they could turn to?"

"Or a homeless shelter?" Ray asked.

"It ain't clear from the story," Stanton said.

"Well, why do you think that they chose to live in a car rather than find help?" Claire asked.

"And don't say 'ain't,'" Ray added.

"Yes, dad," Stanton said, glancing skyward. "I don't know why they didn't look for help. Pride maybe."

"Would you be too proud to ask for help if you were in trouble?" Ray asked.

"No, but it's an easy question for me to answer because I know I can go to you guys for help," Stanton said. "If you weren't around, I might sleep in a car before I slept in a homeless shelter."

"Why's that, sweetie," Claire said.

Stanton thought about the question for several seconds. "I guess because I'd be embarrassed if my friends found out," he said. "I like that everybody thinks I'm the smartest kid in class. I feel like they look up to me. I'd be afraid to lose that respect if people thought I couldn't take care of myself."

"It's good to have pride," Ray said. "Especially if it drives you to work hard and succeed. But sometimes good people fall on hard times. You can't let your pride stand in the way of your health."

"And you shouldn't look down on other people who are having trouble," Claire said. "It's that kind of attitude towards the homeless that may have killed that family. They shouldn't have been afraid to ask for help if they needed it. We not only need to help those who are less fortunate than us, we need to make them feel good about accepting our help."

Stanton slid the newspaper to Diana. "I guess I'm stuck with the doofy white guy story," she said.

"Diana, we don't speak like that even in the privacy of our own home," Claire said. "Racism goes both ways. We don't want white families snickering and calling African-Americans names at their kitchen tables."

Diana cringed. "Okay, mom," she said. "But they all do."

"That's just not true, young lady," Ray said. "I stood shoulder-to-shoulder with whites and blacks alike during the Sixties fighting for civil rights. I've told you the story a dozen times about the white preacher that risked his life to save mine. There are a lot of good white people out there. What's the story about?"

Diana skimmed the article. "The FBI tried to arrest a lawyer in New York for dealing drugs on the Internet, but he escaped," she said. "Then he tried to kill his boss—Fritz Fox." She giggled at the name.

"Why did he try to kill his boss?" Claire asked.

"It doesn't say," Diana said. "All of his co-workers were shocked. Everybody thought that he was this really straight Harvard guy. He was supposed to be tight with Fritz. It says that he actually saved Fritz's life a few weeks ago when he had a heart attack."

"I've heard of Fritz Fox," Ray said. "He's President Norton's friend. I think he was nominated as an ambassador a few years ago. Hard to believe anybody at his law firm would be dealing drugs."

"Well, these guys have great names, at least," Diana said. "The lawyer's name is Benjamin Franklin Kravner. I still think he looks like a doof."

"What type of law did he practice?" Claire asked.

Diana scanned the article for the answer. "Trusts and Estates," she said. "What's that?"

"They're lawyers who prepare wills and estate plans so that people can pass on their property to their family or to charity when they die," Ray said. "Does the article say how they caught the lawyer?"

"Nothing," Diana said. "It says that the FBI believes Kravner is part of a nationwide ring of young professionals dealing drugs and conducting other illegal activities over the Internet."

"But nobody else was charged?" Ray asked.

"Nope," Diana replied.

Ray raised his eyebrows. "Strange," he said. "Okay, let's wrap this up. It's almost kickoff time. Any lessons from this story?"

Diana and Stanton looked at each other and rolled their eyeballs. They answered simultaneously: "Just say no to drugs."

THIRTY-FOUR

RAY ALLGOOD WAS IN A BAD MOOD on Monday morning. The Redskins had been shellacked by the New York Giants, 42-6, in yesterday's football game, a mound of paperwork was scattered atop his desk at the National Cancer Institute, and a meeting he dreaded was scheduled in ten minutes.

Ray yearned for the days when he had toiled long hours in spartan laboratories doing the cutting edge medical research that he loved. His assistants had pandered to the bureaucrats, like he had become, while he had devoted all of his energy to his life's passion. Even then, despite the long hours in the lab, Ray had always managed time for his family. He adored them. He had even accepted an administrative job he abhorred to spend more time with them. Twenty years of marriage. Four beautiful, healthy babies who were not babies any more. Only one slip up. And now it had come back to haunt him.

Ray grimaced as he replayed that evening in his mind. He was to be the keynote speaker at a conference sponsored by Emory University in Atlanta. He had grown up in a working class African-American suburb in the south side of Atlanta. He had graduated at the top of his class at Morehouse College, a predominantly African-American college in downtown Atlanta that had been at the center of the civil rights movement during his stay there in the mid-Sixties. His character had been formed in Atlanta, and his character had served him well. He had been proud to come home.

He rarely drank, but he had sipped a little champagne at the reception. The flirting with Kimberly had started innocently. She seemed genuinely interested in him, asking a lot of questions, listening eagerly to his answers, transfixed. Or was it he who had been transfixed with her? She was stunningly beautiful. Very blonde. Very white. Was that it? He remembered the feeling of power he had felt laying on top of her, thrusting himself into her white body. His groin stirred as the memory unfolded.

He had not felt guilty. Not too much. He had obtained the unobtainable. White culture bombarded the public with its ideal of beauty—blonde hair, blue eyes, tight little tits and ass—on television, in the movies and in magazines, taunting black maledom: "*This* is real beauty, but *you* can never have it."

Now *he* did have it. A magnificent treasure forever locked in his mind. Even Claire might be tempted to stand back and admire the beauty of his conquest. It was art.

Or so it had seemed at the time. The photographs that Cal Stewart had graciously passed along were not so kind. His face, contorted in some bizarre combination of pleasure, pain and pride, would not play well in Peoria nor at home. His erect sexual organ would not qualify as art in the social circles in which he traveled, even if its homelier half was buried in various points north and south on Kimberly's body in the photographs. His mostly white colleagues would not empathize with the creative impulse that had inspired his mental picture of the forbidden fruit.

He glanced down at the paperwork in front of him, then at his watch. Five to ten. Dean Frederick had requested a personal meeting. He had seemed eager to move the application from Calhoun College along quickly. Somehow Cal Stewart had fast-tracked the whole process, so that Calhoun College would have a check for one million dollars within a week or two—*if* the application was graced with the signature of Dr. Raymond Allgood.

Ray leaned forward on his desk with his face resting on his hands. There was nothing terribly dramatic about the research proposal. Calhoun College researchers would be testing the long term carcinogenic effect of drugs that had already been approved by the FDA to treat other illnesses. It was a worthy objective, and the proposal was well-stated. But experimentation on prisoners was strictly regulated. Doctor Stewart was running circles around the regulatory process. It was a clear abuse of power.

But it was Cal Stewart's power, and Ray Allgood needed to borrow that power, too. The grant for his retrovirus research would be approved right away. Fifty million bucks. It would instantly make the National Cancer Institute *the* major player in a cutting edge project.

It was an exciting opportunity, but that alone would not be enough to push Ray over the edge. It came down to the photographs. Claire would not understand. He would lose her and the kids. He had to sign the papers.

His intercom buzzed. "Dean Frederick is here to see you, Dr. Allgood."

"Thanks, Rosemary. Send him in, please."

Ray rose to greet his guest, a tall, wiry man in his mid-forties, but did not walk to the front of his desk or extend his hand. He forced a smile, but he found it hard to hide his disgust. "Hello, Dean Frederick. I was just finishing my review of your application."

"Please, call me, Buddy—everybody does."

"Very well. Let's get right down to it then," Ray said, motioning the Dean to sit. "I'm sure you're aware that this is a very unusual grant that Calhoun College has requested, both in its subject matter and in the accelerated application process."

Buddy Frederick smirked. "Yes, sir, I understand that," he said with a pronounced Southern accent. "But then again what good are friends in high places if they can't do special favors for each other?"

"I tend to do things more by the book," Ray said curtly; his flared nostrils now hinted more formally at his anger.

Dean Frederick crossed his legs and smiled. "You're right, Ray. Your technique in the missionary position—flawless." He made a circle with his right thumb and forefinger to emphasize the point.

Ray stood, leaned forward, his hands on the desktop, and stared into the Dean's eyes. He no longer tried to disguise the contempt in his voice. "Look, *Buddy*," he said, sneering. "I'm still wavering on this application. I love my family, but I have my pride. I am an ethical man and I despise—*despise*—people who abuse power. Now we can discuss this application like the gentlemen that we pretend to be or you can take your sorry ass back down to Atlanta empty-handed."

Dean Frederick's smirk remained intact, as if permanently etched on his face. "I'm going to get that approval whether it's from you today or your successor tomorrow. The *only* thing at stake here is whether I get the pleasure of destroying your life or not. Your call, *Ray.*"

Ray suppressed a violent urge. He sat down, his breath heavy, but his jaw clenched shut. He was trapped. Nothing would change if he martyred himself. It was the system. *The damned system.* The abusers of power would keep on abusing people and he would be discredited, his marriage over, his beautiful children taken from him. There was no choice.

Ray angrily scrawled his signature on a piece of paper, ripped off a carbon copy, and pushed it across the desktop to Dean Frederick. "It's approved. Doctor Stewart will handle the rest of the paperwork. You'll get a check in about one week."

The smirk spoke. "Aren't you forgetting something?"

Ray glowered at him. "Did I forget to say 'thank you' for shitting in my hat, *Buddy*?"

"My, my, my. I guess you can take the *boy* out of the street, but you can't take the street out of the boy," Frederick said. "No, Doctor Stewart said something about a change you needed to make to the grant proposal."

Ray looked at the Dean quizzically, then experienced a flash of recognition. Dr. Stewart was concerned about experimentation on African-American prisoners to avoid any charges of racially motivated selection of the subjects. The Georgia prison system had a disproportionate number of African-American inmates, and Calhoun College was a predominantly white school. He wondered why Buddy Frederick had not addressed the issue himself in the application, but Ray was seething and in no mood to extend the conversation any longer than necessary.

"Right, I almost forgot," Ray said. He took back the copy from the Dean, marked a note on the original and the copy limiting the subjects to Caucasian prisoners, and initialed the changes. He slid the copy back to Dean Frederick's side of the desk, avoiding the Dean's smirking gaze, then swiveled in his chair, turning his back to the Dean.

Buddy Frederick reviewed the approved application, then Ray heard him fold the papers ever so carefully and place them in his pocket, procrastinating with an unabashed intent to infuriate, a skill long mastered by those masquerading under the guise of the Southern gentleman. Ray silently gazed out the window until Dean Frederick took his leave with a mocking, but unacknowledged, parting remark.

BREAKFAST WAS LATE. She looked forward to meals. She had been locked in the basement of the house since Friday night. Aside from the indignity of having been stripped to her undergarments and hand-cuffed to the center pole supporting the house, Debby Barnett had been treated reasonably well. Three meals a day. No mental or physical abuse. *It could have been vorse.*

Debby smiled as she pictured Ben doing his Fritz Fox impression, with his goofy crooked grin and his sexy long, black hair flying about in the wind that day when they walked along the Hudson. Then she saddened as she wondered where he was and if they were treating him well, also.

She had never meant to fall in love with Ben Kravner, but how could she resist? He was everything her father was not—intelligent, good-natured, sensitive, loyal and oh so loving. He was a romantic searching for a kindred spirit, and she had let him down. How—

Debby startled as the door to the basement swung open abruptly and light rushed into the windowless room. She squinted. The silhou-ette of a man was framed in the doorway.

"Good morning, Miss Barnett. I hope you have found your accom-modations suitable."

She was sitting on the floor, her hands chained around the pole. She put her head close to the pole so that she could shield her eyes from the light, trying to connect a face to the voice. The voice was one she had not heard before. It was not a kind voice. This man was not here to deliver breakfast.

"Who are you and why are you keeping me here?" she said, trying to disguise her fear with bravado.

The door closed. It was dark, again. She heard the dull clap of leather shoes on the concrete floor.

"My name is Gerry James Kate. I am the Director of the FBI and the descendant of Kate MacDougall. You may know me as The Spy."

He stopped, about ten feet away. Something in his voice made her tremble. She was in the presence of evil. The stark reality that the game she was playing had high stakes was sinking in. There was no point in pretending that she was an innocent.

"What are you going to do with me?" she asked.

"As you have already guessed, you and your friend, Mr. Kravner, present a serious security risk to our group. Some of my cousins are queasy about killing. I have no such misgivings. However, you intrigue me. As long as you are cooperative, you will live. If you become diffi-cult, you will die. Do I make myself clear?"

"Yes," Debby said weakly. Her eyes were wide. She fought off a wave of dizziness and nausea to maintain her composure. "What have you done with Ben?"

"Mr. Kravner is none of your concern now. You need to concentrate on keeping yourself alive," The Spy said. "Now, tell me how you happened to learn of The Royal Order of the Millennium Knight."

Debby had thought about how to respond to that question for much of the last three days. Her half-brother, the true successor to The Assassin, was on the trail of the Knights, presumably to join them and carry out the MacDougall's Final Vengeance. She could not let that happen.

"My father gave me an envelope and told me not to open it until after he died," she said. "The Poem was in the envelope."

She heard The Spy pacing, back and forth along an invisible line. "I see. Did he tell you he thought he was in danger?"

"No."

"What did he tell you to do with the contents of the envelope, the Poem, after he died?"

Debby hesitated. "He said to take it to Adams Thompson, the publisher of the *New York Herald Times* and tell him that it was from The Assassin."

"Did you communicate with Mr. Thompson?" The Spy asked.

"I was supposed to meet him at his apartment the night he was murdered."

"How did you schedule this meeting?"

"I sent him an e-mail," Debby replied.

She heard The Spy walking closer to her, then felt his shadowy presence above her. "What did the e-mail say?" he asked. "Before you answer, please keep in mind that e-mail messages leave an electronic trail. These things can be checked."

"I don't remember exactly what I said. It was over a month ago."

She felt his palm gently touching her face. "Come now, Miss Barnett, you're an intelligent young lady. This must have been a very important event in your life. Give me a rough idea. Did you tell him your name?"

A lump formed in her throat. His hand was cold and creepy. She wanted to scream. "No. I requested a meeting and signed it 'The Assassin.'"

"Thank you, Miss Barnett. That's a true answer. Very smart."

"Do I get a cookie?"

"Sarcasm has no place when you're trying to impress someone holding your heart in his hands, Miss Barnett," The Spy said. "Now tell me, if you only wanted to hand Mr. Thompson a piece of paper, why did you so cryptically send him a message from a dead man?"

A dozen thoughts raced through Debby's mind, none of them falling into focus. She felt The Spy's cold hand tracing a line down her neck from ear to ear.

"The perfect lie will not fall from the sky, Miss Barnett. Every lie begets several other lies and sooner or later every liar gets *caught*."

The Spy's open hand came crashing into Debby's face with a loud slap at the instant he finished the sentence. She let out a surprised yelp as she sprawled to the floor, the handcuffs preventing her from sliding further than arm's length away. The horrible taste of brain fluid filled her mouth; a warm trickle flowed from her nose. She sobbed uncontrollably.

"There will be no food for you today, Miss Barnett. I have a busy schedule, but I will be back to *chat* some more later in the week. Maybe we can exchange happy little anecdotes about your father. But I may not be so generous if you lie to me, again."

The Spy stalked out of the room, leaving Debby stunned on the floor to ponder her fate.

CHRISTY KIRK SAT IMPATIENTLY in the Washington, D.C. headquarters of the NOMAADs. She glanced at her watch. Eleven o'clock. She had been waiting an hour already. She made her third trip to the water cooler, studying her watch in an obvious and vain attempt to garner the sympathy of the receptionist.

The NOMAADs occupied an entire floor of an office tower on 10th Street, just south of Mount Vernon Square, where New York Avenue and Massachusetts Avenue intersect. In contrast to the headquarters of Franklin Verdant's Aryan Alliance, the NOMAADs' offices appeared spartan. The receptionist sat behind a large metal desk like the ones in the *Herald Times* newsroom. There was no artwork in the small waiting area, which consisted of four steel-framed chairs with colored plastic seats. The hallways were carpeted in institutional beige.

Still, Christy feared that the interview with General William Collins would be much like those with the other leaders, dripping with attitude. *General*. These people had incredible egos. Grand Dragons, Imperial Wizards, Prophets, High Priests and Generals. While the others had been less than hospitable, at least they had not kept her waiting. *Asshole*.

She opened her notes and read through them for the fifth time. It had been twelve days since her interview with Colonel Tom Hardy. She had spent some of that time building her network of contacts within the Klan and the other white supremacy groups, but she had focused her attention on Hardy's implication that the white supremacists had somehow infiltrated the military leadership. She had made polite inquiries through normal channels, resulting in an interview with the head of the Defense Equal Opportunity Management Institute, who had inundated her with statistics and pamphlets demonstrating the military's prodigious commitment to equal opportunity. He had vigorously denied any suggestion that the white supremacy movement had taken root in the armed forces.

All protestations to the contrary, it had been evident that the military was grappling with a massive race problem. Christy's independent research had documented over one hundred racially motivated assaults on U.S. military bases on American soil over the past two years, including five deaths. Yet she had no way of determining whether these attacks were sanctioned or condoned by the military leadership, which was a tight circle that was virtually impenetrable by a civilian, particularly a female reporter.

The telephone rang at the reception desk. The receptionist smiled at Christy. "General Collins will see you now. I'll walk you down the hall."

They passed several empty offices in the hallway. There were none of the usual office noises—clicking keyboards, telephones ringing, copy machines whirring, snippets of conversation. The receptionist noticed Christy's curiosity.

"We're usually much busier around here," she said. "Something's going on this morning. Everybody's huddled in a conference room on the other side of the floor."

General Collins was in a corner office. He was on the telephone when the receptionist ushered Christy in. He motioned for Christy to sit. "Uh-huh...yes...uh-huh," he rolled his eyeballs for Christy's benefit. "Sounds serious," he said, continuing his telephone conversation.

General Collins was not as she had expected. She had envisioned a large, broad man of military bearing. He had a small frame and an intellectual appearance, an image he seemed to cultivate with a business suit and gold wire-framed glasses with small circular lenses. He had a deep, strong voice.

"Listen, Robert, this is our top priority. By the end of the day we'll have finalized our strategy and you'll have instructions...Uh-huh...Look, I've been keeping a reporter waiting for over an hour, and she looks like she's ready to take a bite out of me. We'll talk again at the end of the day...Right." He hung up the telephone.

General Collins stood and walked around the desk and extended his hand to Christy. "Miss Kirk, I'm very sorry to keep you waiting. A crisis is developing, and I may need to cut our meeting short."

"Well, I appreciate any time you can spend with me," she said, shaking his hand firmly. General Collins motioned her to sit, and he sat in the second guest chair instead of returning to the power chair behind his desk. "What sort of crisis is developing?" she asked.

He frowned. "It's the Army, again. Another racial incident. We have an unconfirmed report that there are serious casualties this time."

Christy's eyes widened. "What happened?"

"Let's wait for the official word on that. I think this interview with you is important to our cause. Let's focus on that."

Christy suppressed a smile as a feeling of pride swept over her. Finally, a serious person. "That's fine," she said. "But this is not a propaganda piece."

He grinned. "I understand that. What's your angle on the story?"

General Collins rocked gently as Christy spoke, listening intently. "The increase in membership in white hate and patriot groups and the rising tide of black militant groups. I'm trying to determine if there's a threat of a real escalation in violence or if this is bluster as usual."

Collins continued to rock, carefully choosing his words before he spoke. "Miss Kirk, you're sitting on a much bigger story than that," he said. Then he placed his forefinger a fraction of an inch from his thumb. "We're this close to civil war. We're sitting on dynamite. I don't know if today's incident will be the spark that sets it off, but it's coming. It may be a month, a year, or tomorrow, but it's going to blow."

Christy was stunned. "How can that be?" she asked. "I thought combat was a possibility when I started my research, but I'm finding that the white hate groups are too fragmented to mount a serious war. Their leaders are all maniacs and egotists."

"A couple of years ago that was clearly true," General Collins said. "But a few things have changed. We've received new information just this week that has made us even more certain that the battle lines are forming."

He jumped up and walked to a whiteboard on the wall to Christy's right. He scrawled four words in large block letters in blue marker: "TACTICS, YOUTH, INTERNET, ORGANIZATION." Christy studied him, taking down notes at the same time. He was confident, smart. He was drawing her in, making her feel like a player. She felt a growing excitement.

General Collins sat, pointing at the board as he spoke. "Tactics. All of the white hate groups initially had similar, maniacal goals. Holy war. Holocaust. Racial cleansing. Coup d'etat. They wanted everything at once, but they were the radical fringe—they never had the support to launch the large scale attacks to which they aspired. They became all talk, no action. They lost the young people who might have had the passion to carry out a holy war."

"So how has that changed?" Christy asked. "I've spoken to several of these leaders. They still have the same goals. They're still the radical fringe."

"To some extent I agree with you. Mainstream Americans will not support them after the fighting begins," General Collins said. "What makes them so dangerous is that *they* don't see it that way. They think that all whites will take arms against African-Americans in a racially charged war.

"Their new tactic is to start small and wait for the groundswell of public support," he continued. "They'll spread propaganda making a target appear to be in the wrong, then swoop in to save the day with a terrorist attack. It's scary. They've been practicing, and they can do it. Oklahoma City. The Atlanta Olympics. The abortion clinic bombings all over."

Christy sat wide-eyed. The professor had captivated his student. He continued, pointing to the second item on the whiteboard. "Youth. The hate groups and the patriot groups have targeted their recruitment efforts at young people. The Skinheads are particularly vulnerable."

Christy interrupted. "I thought the Skinheads were already a neo-Nazi organization?"

"That's a misconception. The Skinhead movement began in Europe in the 1960s. Originally, it was not racially charged at all. It was a sub-culture based on music and violence. Lower class kids of all races being different. But Nazi groups found many of the Skinheads to be willing recruits. Hating Jews and blacks gave them some direction to channel their violence. The Skinhead movement split. Most of them are still in it for the music, the violent way of life. Others formed the hate groups that you see on TV and in the press. The march on Skokie. The racial killings."

"So what's changed?" Christy asked.

"The hate groups have realized what the Nazi extremists knew in the 1970s. Young people are malleable and vulnerable. They want to belong to a group, and they'll follow the leader of their group with a passion, even if they don't really understand what the group is about. They're trying to make it cool to belong. A new wave of white hate rock music is surging across the country and the kids are like mice following the Pied Piper. Not just the violent fringe. Middle class kids. Intelligent kids. Kids that know computers."

Christy smiled. "Which leads us to item three."

General Collins grinned. "So it does. The Internet. Do you use the Net?"

"Sure," Christy said.

"What do you use it for?"

"I do a lot of research for my stories on the Web," she said.

"Anything else?"

She blushed. "The chat rooms."

"What do you find appealing about the chat rooms?" General Collins asked.

"I think I see where you're going with this. The privacy. The anonymity." Christy replied.

"Exactly. You can say whatever is on your mind without fear of repercussions. Even if you would never think to call an African-American in your office a nigger, you can call him nigger on the Net. When people start expressing those repressed thoughts, and find others agreeing and encouraging them, the ideas begin to become more acceptable. The thoughts that we accept ultimately become our beliefs and our beliefs ultimately guide our actions. The white hate groups have discovered this and have launched a massive campaign on the Internet."

General Collins shook his head gravely. "They're socializing racism," he said bitterly. "It took us thirty years to make it socially unacceptable for mainstream America to express racist thoughts in public. It might have taken us another thirty years to raise a generation that did not even think those thoughts, but we were on the way. But now people all across the nation are sharing those repressed thoughts and a whole new generation may be tainted by bigotry."

"But how does that take us to the brink of civil war *now?*" Christy asked.

"They're also using the Internet as a recruitment tool. Again, they're targeting kids. Even young kids. We found one web site that was like a Sesame Street for racists, teaching kids to hate. But even the older kids are susceptible. You've seen the rash of shootings by high school kids over the last few years. Who do you think is putting those thoughts into their heads? The white hate groups and the paramilitary patriot groups are taking on kids as members. They're all fascinated by guns and violence. If they have to say they hate niggers to get to play with them, that doesn't bother them. They see these web sites with cool guns and music, and they're hooked."

"Can you support your assertions with facts? Has membership in these groups been increasing?" Christy asked.

General Collins shook his head. "No. Unfortunately, there is no official headcount. But there is evidence. The Southern Poverty Law Center monitors these groups under their Klanwatch program. You can look it up on their web site. There are now over six hundred hate groups or chapters of these groups."

Christy shook her head in disbelief. "I saw web sites for some of them when I was doing my research, but I didn't realize it was that extensive."

General Collins looked grim. "It's all that and worse." He pointed to the last item on the list. "Organization. You were absolutely right when you said that these groups have been too fragmented to do any cataclysmic damage. But they've always had ties to each other. From time to time a few of the groups get together for conferences with racist speakers. The memberships bond. It's the egos of the individual leaders that prevent the groups from planning a joint exercise. That's why nobody believes we're newsworthy yet."

"That's what my old boss told me when I was pitching the story," Christy said. "He argued that the white supremacy groups are all bluster."

"Exactly," Collins said. "But that may be changing. We've heard rumblings about a 'Super Conference.' We can't confirm it, but a significant number of these groups may be planning to get together. A lot of their leaders are religious men. There's been talk for years of a religious holy war at the turn of the millennium. Prophecies. The hate groups interpret this as a race war."

Christy, once again, was stunned. She had seen the hyperbole about millennialism on the web, but had written it off as more bluster from the radical fringe. "But—"

A man, about Christy's age, in a white shirt and a solid red tie knocked on the door. He looked upset. He gestured apologetically to Christy, then said, "Excuse me, Bill, there's something on CNN. I think you'll want to see this."

"Bad?" General Collins asked.

"Real bad," the man said.

General Collins leapt to his feet and motioned for Christy to follow. They jogged down the hallway to a large conference room. The room was crowded, but silent. A path opened for the General so that he could have a clear view of the television.

LAROSA SMITH AND ANOTHER GROUP surrounded a television in a conference room about a half mile away in the White House. President Hank Norton sat at the head of the conference table. Tony Fabrizio, LaRosa and Royce Monahan, the Secretary of Defense, were to his right; Clint Glenn, the Chairman of the Joint Chiefs of Staff, and Conrad Tucker, the President's Chief of Staff, were to his left. Diane Beezer, the Press Secretary, was speaking quietly on the telephone, behind General Glenn, with her back to the group.

CNN was presenting a live report. The reporter was a young man, his clean cut blonde hair waving in the wind. There was a sense of urgency in his tone. "Behind me you can see a large gray building, about eight stories high, which is the Womack Army Medical Center, where I understand the fourteen wounded troops have been taken. We cannot confirm the severity of the injuries, although we have an unconfirmed report that all fourteen soldiers are dead, killed by a rain of bullets from the shooter's automatic weapon. This is Andrew Bradley, reporting from Fort Bragg in Fayetteville, North Carolina. Back to you, Frank."

CNN cut back to the news anchor, Frank Simpson. "Thank you, Andrew, for that report," Simpson said, then looked into the camera poignantly. "Once again for those of you just joining us, we have an unofficial report that a white soldier opened fire on a table full of African-American soldiers in the mess hall at Fort Bragg in North Carolina during breakfast this morning in what appears to be yet another racially motivated attack in the military. Fourteen soldiers have been reportedly injured in the shooting; unconfirmed reports indicate that they may all be dead. Hold on—we're going back to Andrew Bradley outside Fort Bragg."

"Thank you, Frank. I have with me John Daniel, a corporal in the 82nd Airborne Division at Fort Bragg. I understand from John—"

The camera panned to a young soldier dressed in military fatigues. The black bristles on his shaved head hinted at a widow's peak. He had deep set eyes and a pronounced chin.

"That's John Daniel's son," Royce Monahan said, with a thick Boston accent. The Defense Secretary's round, wire-rimmed glasses gave him a professorial appearance, a look that he had cultivated in his teaching days at Harvard. It was at Harvard that Monahan and Hank Norton began their friendship thirty years before.

"The Speaker of the House?" Fabrizio asked, his bushy eyebrows furrowed upwards in surprise.

"Quiet. I want to hear this," President Norton said. Norton ran an informal ship, but it was clear that he was the captain. At 61, he still maintained a youthful and vigorous appearance—a few stray white hairs in his chestnut hair were his only concessions to the aging process. A long scar on his left cheek, a souvenir from the jungles of Vietnam, enhanced his tough guy image.

"Everybody's gonna say that ol' Jimmy's crazy, but he knew what he was doing," the young soldier said to the reporter excitedly. "Ol' Jimmy's not crazy, he's a hero. Those black boys were saying that they were gonna frag some white ass, but they ain't gonna frag anybody now." Daniel was fidgeting, obviously agitated. The reporter put his hand on his shoulder, trying to calm him.

"Now, John, I served in the military and know what you're saying, but can you tell the people at home what you mean when you say that these soldiers threatened to frag other soldiers?" the reporter asked.

Daniel nodded his head vigorously, still fidgeting. "They were threatening us with friendly fire," he said. "So now we've gotta watch the enemy and our backs. No way I'm gonna fight alongside those boys now. Well, hell, there ain't no way anybody's gonna fight alongside *those* boys, anymore."

"So, John, you heard these African-American soldiers threaten that they were going to fire at white American soldiers in a combat situation?"

"No. I didn't hear it myself. Jimmy said that some of the guys overheard a bunch of 'em talkin' in the showers or somethin'."

Simpson interrupted. "Andrew, can you ask Mr. Daniel if he can tell us the full name of the shooter and if he can relate how the shooter was apprehended?"

The reporter repeated the questions. "His name is James Waldren. That's W-A-L-D-R-E-N. A true American hero," Daniel said.

"How was he apprehended?" the reporter asked.

Daniel looked grim. "The MPs shot and killed him. Right in the heart."

The station cut back to the anchor desk. "An incredible story developing this morning, folks," Simpson chirped. "A race war erupting in the military—"

"Shut that damn thing off," the President commanded. Diane Beezer, a petite brunette in her mid-thirties with a pageboy hair-do, scurried to turn off the television. The President looked at Secretary Monahan angrily. "How the fuck did this happen, Royce?"

"Do you mean the shooting or the press leak?" the Defense Secretary asked.

"Both, dammit," President Norton said. "This is the United States Army. Where's the discipline? How can we rely upon these men to defend our country?"

LaRosa saw Monahan glance at General Glenn. The General took the cue. "Mr. President, if I might answer the question," he said. Clint Glenn was an imposing figure. He was a tall, broad man, groomed for military service from an early age. His silver hair was neatly trimmed, his taut face clean shaven. "This is an isolated incident. There are over 1.5 million men and women serving in the Armed Forces, over 100,000 at Fort Bragg alone, and there are bound to be conflicts. The rank and file are not Boy Scouts. We have some violent men. It's remarkable that we have so few incidents."

Monahan joined in. "Fourteen men were killed," he said. "Obviously, this is a regrettable incident, but the Army is a risky busi-

ness. We lose troops every week. Training accidents. Equipment failures. Armed skirmishes throughout the world. The most troubling
thing about this whole episode is that we weren't able to control the
press. General, do we know how the information was leaked?"

"The Commanding General at Fort Bragg will report to me at
noon," General Glenn replied. "I'll have all the details then. I intend to
find out how that fool corporal was allowed to speak to that reporter,
as well."

"General, there have been dozens of racial incidents in the Armed
Forces over the past two years," Tony Fabrizio said. "The corporal said
that the African-American soldiers had threatened to shoot at other
American soldiers. Are we getting to the point where relations are so
bad that soldier can't trust soldier?"

The General's expression was grim. "You've gotten right to the heart
of it, Mr. Vice President. The truth is that I don't know, and that's a
very bad thing. An army can't function without trust. I'm meeting with
the Joint Chiefs this afternoon. I know that it would be an unprecedented step, but I want to speak with them about a contingency plan
for segregating our forces by race. This is a matter of national security."

The President slammed his fist into the table. "Dammit, Clint,
we're in the middle of a race relations crisis in this country!" Norton
shouted. "We can't go threatening to segregate the military. National
security or not, I don't even know if I can legally order that. God, look
what happened to the publisher of the *New York Herald Times* a few
weeks ago. He wrote that ridiculous editorial against school integration
and he ends up dead a week later. What's going to happen if we try to
segregate the military? We might have a mutiny on our hands."

There was a brief silence. LaRosa cleared her throat. "May I speak?"
she asked.

"Sure. What's your take on this, Rosie?" the President asked.

LaRosa felt all eyes turn to her. "The only evidence that this incident was triggered by a threat made by African-American soldiers is the
television interview with an obviously racist white soldier," she said.
"And he based his accusation on third- or fourth-hand accounts of a
conversation in a shower. I think we need to discover the truth before
we start making policy decisions of this magnitude."

"That's a fair point," the President said. "General, I want you down
at Fort Bragg this afternoon, and I want a *full* report first thing tomor-

row morning. Talk to the other Chiefs and the top brass from each of the Armed Forces. I need to know if we still have a reliable Army. I want to hear what the officers on the ground think about race relations on their bases. Tony, will you and Rosie work with the Justice Department to see if I have the constitutional authority to order the segregation of our military forces in a national emergency?"

"Of course," Fabrizio said.

"Mr. President?" It was Diane Beezer, the press secretary. "We'll need to make an official statement to the press."

"Royce, work with Diane on a statement," the President ordered. "Keep it fuzzy. Do your best to minimize the damage that was done by that idiot on TV. And Connie, get John Daniel over here before I have someone frag his Republican ass."

THIRTY-FIVE

BEN'S BUS ARRIVED at the Greyhound station in Washington on time at six o'clock, Tuesday morning. He preferred the train, but a one-way bus ticket was thirty dollars cheaper, and he was still hoarding cash. He had hoped that today might be his last day as a fugitive, but after Saturday's fiasco in Central Park he had learned to lower his expectations.

At least Fritz Fox was alive and was expected to recover. Ben assumed this was the Knights' intention. He had been relieved to learn that he was dealing with humane maniacs. He held out some hope for Debby's survival.

Ben walked outside the dingy, red brick bus terminal. The sun would not rise for over an hour. He thought that the city would still be asleep; he was surprised to hear a distant cacophony of car horns. Washington's morning traffic problem was apparently even worse than New York's.

Ben yawned and stretched his limbs. He was exhausted. On Friday night he had slept in the comfort of Adams Thompson's apartment, but had been too restless to doze more than a few hours. After the brutal attack on Fritz Fox on Saturday, he had spent the next three days dodging in and out of the shadows of New York City—the Public Library, the YMCA, dark bars and the Salvation Army shelter at night. Sleep had not come easy in a strange bed with dozens of stranger bedfellows. The four hours of sleep on the bus had been the best he had since Thursday night.

The computers Ben had seen at the Public Library had been a godsend. The IBM ThinkPad that he had coveted had proven, to this point, useless because he had nowhere to connect the modem. The computers at the library did not have the CyberLine program loaded, but they had provided access to the Web. Ben had opened a new e-mail account on one of the hundreds of web sites that now offered free e-mail.

He had sent an e-mail message to LaRosa Smith on Saturday and had been thrilled to get her reply on Monday, when the library re-opened. Her reply had been brief: "Lafayette Square at ten o'clock on Tuesday." It had not been the warm response he had hoped for in his best case scenario, but it was not the cold shoulder that he arguably deserved. He trusted that she would not betray him even if she still held a grudge from their law school days. He had no other options.

Lafayette Square was across Pennsylvania Avenue from the White House, two miles from the bus station—about a forty minute walk. Ben was still hatless, figuring that his baldness was an asset in a world where recognition could mean death. Still, his head was cold.

Ben walked west along K Street, the most direct route to the White House. The neighborhood near the bus station was seedy and the environs got progressively worse, as parking lots and warehouses gave way to collision shops and dilapidated low income housing projects. Automobile traffic along K Street was light, but the sound of car horns remained constant off to his left, in the direction of Pennsylvania Avenue.

Ben walked amidst the projects, greeted by an occasional icy stare from an unforgiving black face. His nerve endings jangled, but he fought the urge to turn towards the perceived safety of Pennsylvania Avenue. He wondered whether his fear was rooted in racism or the unknown or the animosity he saw in the eyes of strangers he passed. He did not consider himself a racist, but, here, he found himself very aware of race.

Before he could decide the issue, he reached Mt. Vernon Square and the refuge of the high rise office towers along New York Avenue. Ten minutes later he was at 15th Street, just north of the White House compound.

The White House was under siege. Hundreds of cars and buses clogged the surrounding streets, horns blasting, not moving. Thousands of people, mostly African-Americans—shouting, whistling, chanting—enveloped the White House compound, which included the Treasury Building along 15th Street, the Old Executive Office

Building along 17th Street and the White House in between. The crowd at the rear of the White House lined the black, cast-iron fence that encircled the compound and spilled across Pennsylvania Avenue, which was blocked off from automobile traffic, into Lafayette Square.

The atmosphere was frenzied. Men in yellow rain jackets, the acronym "NOMAAD" printed in large block letters on their backs, trotted through the crowd, exhorting them to make their presence felt. The noise was thunderous. Many carried hand-made picket signs with frightening messages: "Death Match 2000," "Bash White Trash!" "End the Slaughter," "Remember Bloody Monday," "Have You Fragged Someone Today?" "Wake Up Hank!" and countless others.

Ben tried to push his way through the mob in Lafayette Square. It was not even seven o'clock, but he was concerned. The Square was packed shoulder-to-shoulder. Rosie would never be able to find him if the mob did not break up by ten.

Ben walked around the periphery of the rally. A sea of humanity had completely encircled the White House compound, filled the Ellipse and the lawn surrounding the Washington Monument and was spreading to The Mall, the three-mile national park that ran from the Capitol Building to the Lincoln Memorial with the Washington Monument in the middle.

Pennsylvania Avenue had become a parking lot. Buses continued to flow into the area and were starting to fill Constitution and Independence Avenues on either side of The Mall.

It was obvious that something big was happening, but Ben was in the dark. He had not read a newspaper since Sunday, his world view reduced to his own dire circumstances. He walked down Constitution Avenue, towards the Capitol and against the flow of people hustling purposefully towards the White House. Ben was curious about the reason for the hostile rally, but his overtures were met by angry glares.

He tried to stop a heavy set young black woman in front of the National Museum of American History, a windowless white marble building. "What's going on here?" he asked.

He saw hatred in her eyes. "Fuck you, Skinhead!" she answered, pushing Ben back a step.

There was a break in the steady flow of foot traffic; the woman's shout alerted others to Ben's presence. He was suddenly surrounded. He walked backwards, slowly, in a tight circle, trapped. A rush of adrenaline left him dizzy, the details of a hundred angry faces and voices blended into an anonymous ring of hate. People shouted at him, but he could not hear the words.

A large man emerged from the ring. He was wearing a Washington Redskins football jersey with the number "66" over a sweatshirt. "What are you doing here, Skinhead?" he asked menacingly.

"I'm not a Skinhead," Ben said, raising his open palms to demonstrate his peaceful intentions. "I've been on a bus all night, and I don't even know what's going on here."

Number 66 scowled. The crowd growing around them wanted a fight. He pushed Ben. "Bullshit! You're not so tough without your posse now, are you?" he said.

"Posse? I'm a Jewish kid from New York here to see the Smithsonian!" Ben said, exaggerating his New York accent. "I don't want any trouble."

Number 66 looked confused. The mob taunted him. The big man approached. Ben stepped back. Number 66 pushed Ben hard in the chest, knocking him off balance, then kicked him in the backside, with enough force to topple him over. "Outta my way, Jew boy!" Number 66 shouted, then pushed his way through the ring.

A collective laugh went up from the crowd. Ben stayed down, his hands covering his head. The ring broke up. A few people kicked him as they passed, then they were gone.

Ben sat on the sidewalk in front of the National Museum of American History, still breathless. A wiry young boy, about fourteen or fifteen, approached him.

"Are you okay, mister?" the boy asked. He had a kind face.

Ben shook his head slowly from side to side. "I thought that I was going to die," he said.

"I saw the whole thing," the boy said. "This crowd is stoked. They want some white blood on the ground today."

Ben started to push himself up; the boy offered him his hand. Ben dusted himself off. "Thanks. Nothing broken," he said. He walked over to a shallow amphitheater overlooking a disabled fountain in front of the museum and sat down on the granite steps. The boy followed. "So what *is* going on here?" Ben asked. "I really did get off a bus this morning."

"Some crazy white Army dude killed fourteen brothers yesterday," the boy said.

Ben's jaw dropped. "How? Where?" he asked.

"Fort Bragg. North Carolina. They were eating breakfast and 'bam,' he shot them. His own regiment."

"Geez. Did they catch him? Did he say why he did it?" Ben asked.

"They shot that motherfucker dead," the boy said. "He ain't saying anything. Some guy on TV said that the brothers had threatened to frag the white boys, but he's full of BS. Ain't no brothers *that* stupid."

"You're probably right," Ben said. "So what's the rally for?"

"The NOMAADs think the Klan is looking for a war. We're here to show them that if they want to fight, we're ready to fight back. Men, women and children."

"Who are the NOMAADs?" Ben asked. "I saw the name on those yellow jackets for the first time today."

"The National Organization for Mutual African-American Defense. It's like the NAACP with some firepower," the boy said with pride.

Ben's eyebrows shifted up. "Really. Are they armed today?" he asked.

"Naw. This is just for show. But we're ready." The boy stood. "My name is Stanton. Stanton P. Allgood. Remember that name. Some day I'm going to be famous," he said, smiling, but with eyes as serious as the Grim Reaper.

Ben saluted him. "I don't doubt that for a minute. I'm Ben," Ben said, hesitating. "Ben Pierce."

"I know who you are," Stanton said. "I saw your picture in the *Post* on Sunday. You shaved your head, but I recognized you after you said that you were a Jew from New York."

Ben tensed and glanced down the street, scoping out his escape route. Then he stared into Stanton's eyes. They were sympathetic, not threatening. "We were talking about you at Sunday brunch. You didn't do it, did you?" Stanton asked.

Ben shook his head. "No. I'm being set up."

"You have an honest face," Stanton said. "That's why that big guy didn't pummel you. He only kicked you because he had to save face in front of his friends."

"You're a perceptive guy, Stanton. How old are you?"

"Fifteen. My dad's like that, too. He's a doctor."

Ben smirked. "Maybe he could sew me up and put me back together."

"Naw. He's a research doctor," Stanton said. "At least he used to be. He's the director of the National Cancer Institute now. He says he's just a paper pusher."

Ben's eyebrows shifted up, again, his interest piqued. "The National Cancer Institute—isn't that part of the National Institutes of Health?" he asked.

"Yep. We live close to the NIH campus in Bethesda."

"Does your father work with Calhoun Stewart?" Ben asked.

"Dr. Stewart's his boss. I don't think dad likes him very much. Do you know him?"

Ben shook his head. "Only in my nightmares," he said. Stanton looked at him quizzically. Ben shrugged, stood up, then said, "Never mind. I've got a lot of problems right now, and he's just a small part of them." Ben extended his hand. "Stanton, it's been a pleasure talking with you. Thanks for the friendly ear. I don't feel like I have too many friends right now."

Stanton looked like he wanted to say something, but decided against it. He just waved farewell. Ben started towards the street. "Ben, hang on," Stanton called out. Ben turned. "Do you have a place to stay tonight?"

"I'm hoping to meet a friend later this morning," Ben said. "I haven't planned past that."

"My mom and dad say that we should help people in need. I think they would help you."

Ben shook his head. "Adults aren't like that," he said. "They don't want to get involved with people. When they say they want to help, it usually means they want to throw money at a problem so that they can feel good about themselves. Honest face or not, your folks aren't going to let a fugitive stay in their home." He almost said something else, then stopped himself.

Stanton finished the thought for him. "Especially, a white one," he said. "That's what you were thinking, right?"

Ben was embarrassed by Stanton's directness. He shrugged.

"My dad's not like that," Stanton said. "He was active in the civil rights movement in the Sixties. He's a doer, and he's teaching us to be doers, too."

"He's taught you well," Ben said. "I'm sure he's proud. But I don't know who I can trust anymore. Thanks for the offer, but I think it's better for me to stay flexible. I'll probably just sleep in Union Station or a shelter tonight."

Stanton shrugged. "Have it your way. We're in the phone book if you change your mind. My father's name is Raymond Allgood."

Ben watched Stanton jog down Constitution Avenue towards the White House, then he hobbled slowly in the other direction, towards the Capitol. He wanted to get as far from this crowd as possible. He would return to Lafayette Square at ten, but he already knew in his heart that Quixote had larger windmills to tilt.

LAROSA SMITH WAS HUDDLED in a meeting with Tony Fabrizio, Dan Raskin, the Attorney General, and John McArthur, a senior lawyer in the Civil Rights Division of the Department of Justice. They were in Fabrizio's office preparing for a scheduled nine o'clock briefing with the President.

"You need to keep in mind that the Constitution was written over two hundred years ago," Raskin said, his thick Midwestern twang still evident after twenty years in Washington.

Raskin, a tall, lanky man, just shy of fifty years old, with black hair, dark deep set eyes and thick eyebrows, was leading the discussion. McArthur, a younger, shorter man, nearly bald, with impish blue eyes, appeared content with this arrangement.

"The drafters could not predict every situation that might arise," Raskin continued. "We've done a very quick review of a morass of judicial decisions that are all over the board. We—"

"Dan, we're all lawyers here," Fabrizio interrupted. "We know these are complicated issues. But the President needs legal advice *now*. Tell us what you know and what you don't know. We're looking at a national security emergency, and we may have to make a decision without perfect knowledge."

"Fair enough," Raskin said. "John's been up all night researching the issues. There are three constitutional rights and powers that are in conflict. The president's power as commander-in-chief of the armed forces; Congress' power to make rules for the government and regulation of the armed forces; and the right of the troops to the equal protection of the laws under the Due Process clause of the Fifth Amendment."

"Dan, this sounds a lot like the gay rights issues we faced a few years ago," Fabrizio said. "Our solution then was the 'Don't Ask, Don't Tell' rule."

"The issues are almost exactly the same, except that the courts are more suspicious of racially discriminatory actions than almost any other type of government action," Raskin said. "The courts have upheld the constitutionality of the 'Don't Ask, Don't Tell' rule because it's *rationally related* to achieving a *legitimate* government purpose—the need of the military to preserve unit cohesion. The courts would apply a higher standard to a racially discriminatory practice—we would have to prove that the rule is *necessary* to achieve a *compelling* government objective."

"Do you think that we could satisfy that standard in this case?" Fabrizio asked.

Raskin rolled his tongue inside his cheek. "Yes. Yes, I do," he said. "The courts give great deference to the Executive and Legislative Branches in military matters. John, tell them about the cases you found."

McArthur blinked, as if jolted from a catnap. He shifted himself upright in his seat. "The courts have cited unit cohesion as the single most important factor in a military unit's ability to succeed on the battlefield," he said. "Given the state of race relations in the Army right now, we think there's a strong chance that a court would uphold the President's decision to segregate the Armed Forces."

LaRosa shook her head in disbelief. "So the President would not be doing anything clearly illegal if he chose to segregate troops based on national security concerns?" she asked.

"That's our opinion," Raskin said. "That decision would be more controversial than the gay rights decision because of the sheer numbers and the current state of race relations, but the legal issues are the same. There would be a legal challenge, but it would go all the way to the Supreme Court to be decided."

"And racial tensions would hopefully cool down on the military bases in the meantime," Fabrizio observed.

Raskin joined LaRosa and Fabrizio for the President's briefing; McArthur excused himself. The conference room in the West Wing of the White House was empty when they arrived. Conrad Tucker, the President's Chief of Staff, strode in a few minutes later. Tucker was a short, arrogant man in his mid-thirties with a stylized haircut and an ever-present five o'clock shadow. LaRosa could not stand him.

"We're waiting on Royce and Clint," Tucker said. "Their helicopter just left the Pentagon."

"That's fine," Fabrizio said. "Can you have someone bring in some coffee?"

LaRosa suppressed a smile. Fabrizio despised Tucker, too. She guessed that most of the staff was still stuck in the traffic disaster that had paralyzed the downtown area. Sure enough, Tucker returned five minutes later with a pot of coffee, four cups and a contemptuous expression on his face.

General Glenn and Defense Secretary Monahan entered the room on his heels. "Well, well, they've finally got the Boy Wonder doing some productive work, heh Connie?" Monahan said with a smirk. "Can you rustle up a couple more cups, please?"

The rest of the high-powered group enjoyed a laugh at Tucker's expense. LaRosa almost felt sorry for him, as he stomped out of the room. The incident was forgotten when President Norton stormed in. His expression was grim. He looked haggard.

Everybody sat—Tucker, Monahan and Glenn to the President's left, Fabrizio, LaRosa and Raskin to his right. "Royce? Clint? What's the situation on the ground?" Norton asked gruffly.

Monahan deferred to the General. "Mr. President, the situation at Fort Bragg itself is bleak," General Glenn said. "Racial tension is high. The Commanding General has ordered all troops confined to barracks except for meals and daily drills. There have been fist fights, but no serious injuries. Unfortunately, my conclusion is that the XVIII Airborne Corps situated at Fort Bragg is not combat ready. Trust has completely disintegrated."

The President shook his head and expelled a long, slow breath. "Dammit. This is my worst fucking nightmare," he said. "I've been up thinking about this all night. There is *no* acceptable solution to this problem. How bad is it elsewhere?"

"Racial tension is high everywhere, but not to the point of jeopardizing national security," General Glenn said. "The top priority today on every base is damage control. We're organizing open discussions led by trained counselors at the fighting group level. Let the boys get everything out on the table and hash it out like men. I think we can contain this problem to Fort Bragg."

"Well, that's good news," the President said sincerely. "Have you determined the facts surrounding the incident at Fort Bragg?"

"We've taken statements from witnesses," General Glenn said. "Unfortunately, the witnesses that we really need to hear from are all dead. Private Waldren, the shooter, was killed by the MPs. Several white soldiers claim to have heard second- or third-hand reports that certain black soldiers were heard joking in the shower about 'fragging some white boys.' All of the black soldiers who were identified were among the fourteen men killed in the incident. We have not found one soldier, black or white, who will step forward and admit to witnessing the incident in the showers personally. The bottom line, Mr. President, is that we will never know whether the incident actually occurred or was fabricated by racist antagonizers."

"Your recommendation, General?" President Norton asked.

The General stared into the President's eyes. His voice was unwavering. "We need to segregate the troops at Fort Bragg by race immediately," he said. "The XVIII Airborne Corps is critical to our combat readiness."

LaRosa cringed. She noticed similar reactions by the others around the table. At least the recommendation was limited to Fort Bragg. A national policy of a segregated military would have been cataclysmic. Still, she thought the General might be over-reacting.

"Dan, can I legally order the segregation of Fort Bragg?" the President asked.

"Mr. President, the order would probably be challenged in court, but we could make a very strong case. If it's a matter of national security, my advice is to go for it," Raskin said. "By the time the Supreme Court settles the issue, the crisis should be defused."

The President filled his cheeks with air, then blew it out as he searched around the table for a way out of the worst crisis of his presidency. "Rosie, you've looked like you wanted to say something for some time now," he said. "What's on your mind?"

LaRosa hesitated, collecting her thoughts. "I held my tongue because I was hoping that somebody else would make my point," she said. She glanced sideways at Fabrizio, then directed her gaze at the President. "I want to be a good advisor, but I don't want to be thought of as a good *black* advisor. I'm not the voice of Black America."

"Rosie, you know better than that," President Norton said. "If you bring some insight into African-Americans with you, God knows we can use it, but you've got one of the great young minds in this Administration and your advice is always valued. Now spit it out." He smiled.

"Okay," she said, then swallowed hard. "Any form of forced segregation, although evenly applied to all races, will be seen as a slap in the face to African-Americans. It's a step backwards in what has already been a long, slow march towards equality. Even if you take extraordinary measures to make the arrangements equal, something that was never done under the old separate but equal doctrine, African-Americans will be infuriated. That mob outside will seem like a backyard barbecue compared to what you'll see if the government appears to be sanctioning a return to the separate but equal doctrine."

The President frowned. "I think we all understand that there'll be a negative backlash," he said. "But we have a threat to our national security here. I don't like it. I don't feel like I have any good alternatives to choose from, but that's what makes my job so tough. I'm the one who has to make those difficult choices."

"I don't think Rosie is downplaying the difficulty of the decision," Fabrizio said. "She's just warning that the reaction from the black militant groups may be a greater threat to national security than we're thinking. Right, Rosie?"

"Yes. Have you looked at that mob out there?" she asked. "That rally was organized in less than a day by the NOMAADs. This is an armed group. Today they're showing you their strength. Another day they may come to fight."

The President's eyebrows raised. "Dan, does the FBI have a briefing paper on the military strength of this organization?"

"I'd have to check with Gerry Kate on that, Mr. President," Raskin said.

"Do it," the President ordered. "Let's assume for the moment that the two national security threats are equal. What other options do I have?"

General Glenn clenched his teeth. "Mr. President, we need to make an example of Fort Bragg," General Glenn said. "We need to demonstrate to the troops stationed across the country that we're dealing with this situation seriously. If we take no action after fourteen black soldiers are killed in a racial incident, don't we risk inciting the black groups, anyway? What in God's name are *they* even asking for out there today?"

The President looked around the table. Each of his advisors shrugged in turn as the President's gaze shifted from one to the next. Finally, LaRosa spoke.

"I'm not speaking for the mob, and I have no inside information here," she said warily. "But I think they're just sending out a warning today. They're saying that they will not stand for terrorist attacks against African-American targets. They're looking for a strong reaction from the White House, for evidence that serious steps will be taken to prevent racially-motivated attacks without punishing the victims."

"You sound like you have a suggestion," the President said hopefully.

"I think you need to get on national TV tonight and pacify the nation," LaRosa said. "You need to assure the people that this is an isolated incident by a lunatic acting alone. Tell them about the counseling program instituted by General Glenn, that ensuring the combat readiness of our troops is our top priority this week. Give everybody a few days to cool down. Issue a gentle warning that the temporary segregation of Fort Bragg is being considered as a last resort if the situation cannot be brought under control, but only if absolutely required to return the troops to combat readiness."

General Glenn was not pleased. "We can't go telling the world that our troops are not combat ready!" he said, his arms flailing up into the air.

"We can tweak the words, General Glenn," LaRosa said. "The idea is to soothe, let things calm themselves rather than dumping fuel on the fire."

The General scowled, but President Norton raised his palm in his direction. He looked around the table. "What does everybody else think?" the President asked.

"I think Rosie's point is a good one," Dan Raskin said. "Nobody's thinking rationally now. Any dramatic action you take will inflame one group or the other. It's like the old legal tactic—when in doubt, get a continuance."

Fabrizio and Tucker agreed. Royce Monahan, the Defense Secretary, appeared to be on the fence, perhaps torn between his loyalty to General Glenn and not wanting to be on the losing side of a vote that was probably already decided. "It's worth a try," he said finally. He turned towards General Glenn. "Fort Bragg is locked up tight for now, Clint, and there doesn't appear to be any imminent threat of a combat situation."

The General glared at him, but remained silent. "Connie, ask Diane Beezer to reserve a half hour of network time tonight," the President said. "Tony, do you mind if I borrow Rosie for a few hours to work on my speech?"

Fabrizio grinned. "Just as long as I get her back by tomorrow, Hank."

The President turned to General Glenn. "Clint, would you like to work with Rosie on the national security angle?"

"I'll review it before you sign off on it. Fax it over to the Pentagon, Miss Smith," the General said gruffly. "I've got an army to run today." He got up from his chair and stalked out of the room, his back ramrod straight, his ears flaming red.

BEN HAD CIRCULATED through the crowd in Lafayette Square for three hours before giving up hope of meeting with LaRosa. He was disappointed, more in his bad luck than in her. He knew the insanity of a law firm in the middle of a crisis and imagined that the situation in the White House today had been far worse. If what Stanton Allgood told him this morning was true, the nation was careening towards a civil war, desperately in need of a strong leader at the helm. There did not appear to be any easy answers.

Ben wandered about the Mall during the afternoon, then gravitated to Union Station as dusk approached. It was not the sleazy train depot that he expected. He entered through a cavernous, domed area, with an information counter in the center and a gigantic electronic train schedule suspended from the ceiling. There were only a few benches in the room, and small signs warned against loitering. The station was crowded, mostly with businessman and other well-dressed urbanites.

Ben wandered to his left, discovering a plush shopping mall and an enormous food court one floor below. Finally, after searching for twenty minutes, he found the passenger waiting rooms. He looked for a place to lie down.

It was only seven o'clock, but Ben could barely keep his eyes open. The seating was designed to discourage vagrants from setting up camp. He found a relatively private stretch of bench near Gate A, three attached seats without armrests, and removed his backpack. The steel frames dug into his sore body.

Ben recalled Stanton Allgood's generous but naive offer. The notion of calling crossed his mind, but there were a dozen reasons to reject it. He could not trust anyone. There was probably a reward for his capture. The FBI had spread the word that he was a dangerous man, a drug dealer. The man who turned him in would be a hero, his name in all

the newspapers. The good doctor, while no doubt a man of fine character to have raised a boy like Stanton, would not care if an FBI death
squad snuffed out the life of a fugitive drug dealer. A *white* drug dealer.

Still, the idea was not without appeal. A warm bed. A shower. A
home-cooked meal. Intelligent human contact. *The possibility of an ally.*
That was the thought that nagged at Ben all day. It might take days to
schedule another meeting with LaRosa. He needed an Internet connection to send her a message and check for her response periodically.
Even if he got lucky and found a way to send and receive e-mail,
LaRosa might be preoccupied for days with the Fort Bragg situation.

Dr. Allgood's connection to Calhoun Stewart intrigued Ben.
Stanton implied that there might be bad blood between them. Without
access to Debby or LaRosa or even Woody, he bore his secret alone. He
needed a sounding board. Someone to tell him that he was doing the
right thing and that it would all work out in the end. Dr. Allgood
might be a friendly ear, someone he could trust. He drifted off to sleep,
weighing the pros and cons of calling the Allgoods.

"Wake up, son!" Ben heard a muffled voice and felt a powerful hand
on his shoulder. He bolted to a wakeful state, expecting to see a police
officer's gun trained on him.

"Calm down, boy. I'm a friend." The voice came from a large
African-American man. He appeared to be in his mid- to late-forties
and was wearing a long, black pea coat. There was something reassuring about the man's face and manner.

Ben squinted as his eyes adjusted to light. "Who are you?" Ben
asked.

"I'm Ray Allgood. My son, Stanton, told me I might find you here.
If you can look me in the eye and tell me you're innocent, I'm prepared
to offer you sanctuary."

THIRTY-SIX

R AY ALLGOOD'S MAROON BUICK pulled into the driveway at 441 Asbury Lane, his Bethesda home, just before ten o'clock. Stanton rushed out of the large, brick house at the sound of the car door slamming shut.

"Hi, Ben!" he said. Ben saluted him. "Dad, the President was just on TV talking about the Fort Bragg murders and the rally today!"

"Is he going to start a war?" Dr. Allgood asked with genuine concern. His expression alarmed Ben.

"I don't think so!" Stanton said. "Mom's thrilled. She thought for sure he was going to do something stupid."

"Okay, son, that's great. Let's get Ben inside and settled, and then you can catch me up. Is your sister home?" Dr. Allgood asked.

"No, she's got a sleepover tonight," Stanton said.

Dr. Allgood turned to Ben. "Two of my girls are off at college. Too busy to even come home for the holidays. Diana, my youngest, is something of a gossip, but luckily she's out tonight. You should be safe here."

"Thanks," Ben said, following Dr. Allgood and Stanton up the front walk. The prospect of accepting the Allgoods' help had both frightened and intrigued Ben. He desperately needed an ally, but his margin for error was zero. If his instinct about the Allgoods' motivations was wrong, he was a dead man. He came to an abrupt halt.

"Why are you helping me, Dr. Allgood?" he asked.

Dr. Allgood stopped and sent Stanton ahead, into the house. "A couple of reasons. But for now, let's just say I've been where you are now and somebody helped me," Dr. Allgood said, putting a large hand on Ben's shoulder. "I'll tell you about it when you're rested. Let's just get you a hot shower and a meal."

They walked up the steps and entered the front door. Dr. Allgood located his wife, Claire, and introduced her to Ben. Claire Allgood had long, flowing black hair and a round face highlighted by wide, half-moon eyes. She forced a smile and shook his hand nervously.

Ben assumed her anxiety stemmed from having a suspected violent drug dealer in the house, but wondered if her reaction would be any different if he was a clean cut white guy courting young Diana. Was he imputing his race consciousness to her? Was *he* anxious because he was in a black home or because the Allgoods were strangers or because he was exposing himself to risk of capture?

Ben thought that he would feel the same way sleeping in a white stranger's home under the best of circumstances. There was something about Dr. Allgood that inspired trust. Ben was certain, almost, that Ray would not turn him over to the authorities.

Claire Allgood led Ben to the guest room upstairs, which had a private bathroom, and gave him clean towels. Ben thanked her profusely, and she smiled warmly as she excused herself. Ben's tension eased with this brief glimpse at her soul. These were good people.

Ben took a long time in the shower. He found fresh clothes on the bed, a black sweatshirt and gray fleece pants, with a plastic bag and a note to put his dirty clothes in it. The sweats were a little small, but it was refreshing to be wearing something clean. He found the Allgoods sitting at the kitchen table downstairs. A sandwich sat on a plate in front of an empty place at the table.

"That's for you," Claire said, pointing at the sandwich. "It's roast beef. And give me *that bag*. I don't know whether to wash those things for you or just burn them."

Ben laughed. "So he does smile," Ray said. "We were beginning to wonder."

"I haven't had much to smile about lately," Ben said, forcing a crooked grin. "But right now you people seem like a godsend." He munched on the sandwich hungrily.

"So what brings you to Washington?" Ray asked. "If the FBI is chasing you, this probably isn't the safest spot for you."

Ben waited to finish chewing a bite. "I need to speak to somebody in the White House," he said. "I was trying to meet a law school classmate of mine in Lafayette Square today, but we either missed each other in the crowd or she got tied up in the middle of the Fort Bragg crisis."

Ray looked interested. Claire walked back in just before Ben finished his sentence. "You're tied up in the middle of that mess, too?" she asked.

"No, mom, he was just saying he couldn't hook up with his friend today because *she's* involved," Stanton explained. "She works in the White House."

"Really, now. What does she do?" Claire asked.

"She works with the Vice President," Ben said.

"Why do you need to speak with someone in the White House?" Ray asked.

"It's a long story," Ben said warily. "And a dangerous story. Powerful people want me dead. If I involve you, you might be in danger, too."

Ray and Claire exchanged a meaningful glance. Ray spoke. "We were talking about you the other day at brunch. There were things in the newspaper story that didn't make sense. Harvard law degree. Bright future at a wealthy law firm. No history of drugs or violence. That didn't sound like the profile of someone who would get involved with dealing drugs and try to kill his mentor. Claire and I thought it sounded like a subterfuge. Are you involved in something else that the FBI doesn't want to talk about? Espionage, maybe?"

Ben was taken aback. The Allgoods were all leaning forward, waiting for his answer. "No!" Ben said, louder than he had intended. "I walked into a conspiracy. More like pushed into it, but that's another long story."

Ben paused, a momentary hesitation while he decided whether to plunge into the story, but it had dramatic effect nonetheless. The Allgoods were wide-eyed.

"I'm hesitating again because someone you know may be involved in the conspiracy," Ben said. "Stanton told me that you know Dr. Calhoun Stewart."

"Of course," Ray said. "I report to him. He's the director of the NIH. Let's just say that there's no love lost between Cal Stewart and I. Bringing him down would be just one more reason to help you."

That was enough for Ben. "Do you remember the murder of Adams Thompson just after Thanksgiving?" Ben asked.

The Allgoods were skeptical at first as Ben told his remarkable tale, but as the night wore on and all the evidence unfolded, they too became convinced that the Jinx was real.

"So there you have it," Ben said. "Some very powerful people appear to be on the verge of toppling the United States government."

"This is incredible," Claire said. "There has to be some way to stop them."

"That's why I need to get inside the White House," Ben said. "The FBI and the police are off limits. If I write a letter, it gets thrown on a pile with all the other conspiracy theories. They've destroyed my credibility, so I can't go to the press."

Ray studied the copy of the Poem that Ben brought down from the guest room. "Something really troubles me about all this," he said.

"Gee, no shit, dad," Stanton said.

"That's not what I mean," Ray said. "I keep wondering about Cal Stewart's role in this plot. The others' roles are more obvious."

"We're all getting tired," Claire said. It was nearly three o'clock in the morning. "Why don't we get some sleep and put our heads together again in a few hours to see if we can't figure out how we can best help Ben."

"That sounds about right to me," Ray said. "Ben looks like he's about to fall off his chair."

Ben smiled. "It has been a few days since I've had a good night's sleep."

They all walked up the stairs to the bedrooms together. Before they parted, Ben turned to the Allgoods. "I can't thank you enough for your help. I was lost."

"And now you're found," Claire said. "And Grace will lead you home. You're safe here. The Lord brought you to us, and he's watching over you."

"We won't speak a word of this to anyone," Ray added. He looked at Stanton. "Right, Stanton."

"I'm cool," Stanton said.

Ben gave him a playful punch in the shoulder. "You better be," Ben said.

The Allgoods chuckled, and appeared to be feeling pretty good about themselves. Ben collapsed on to the bed in the guest room, still dressed in the borrowed sweat clothes. He was asleep before his head hit the pillow.

For the second time that evening, Ben was awakened by Ray Allgood's large hand shaking his shoulder. Ben emerged from his slumber with some difficulty, but without alarm. "Ben, we need to talk," Dr. Allgood said. "Come with me to my study downstairs."

Dr. Allgood shut the door to the study and took his seat behind an oak desk with brass and leather accessories. Ben dropped wearily into a chair opposite him.

Dr. Allgood fumbled for words, unable to look Ben in the eyes. He looked frightened. "That thought I couldn't grab before...about Cal Stewart...I knew what it was, I just can't tell anyone about it, but I think it may be important," Dr. Allgood said. "One of the reasons I came looking for you was that Stanton told me that Stewart might be involved in your troubles."

Ben was not sure how to handle the situation. "Do you want to tell me about it?" he asked.

"I'm torn," Dr. Allgood said. His eyes met Ben's for the first time. "You're a good man. I can tell. I've trusted you enough to take you into my home, but I haven't even trusted Claire with this secret."

"Let's talk a little and see where it goes," Ben said. "You told me earlier that you were once in a similar situation to me and somebody helped you."

"I was a little younger than you," Dr. Allgood said. "I was active in the civil rights movement in Atlanta in the Sixties. Martin Luther King. When I started out, Martin was like a god to me. We were college kids. We would have followed him anywhere. But the hatred and violence that we saw every day got to me. The bombings. Those little girls that died. Some of us could not control our rage. Martin stood above it all like Gandhi. But civil disobedience was not good enough for us. We broke away and joined a radical fringe group."

"Did you attack white targets?" Ben asked.

"No, we were more interested in organizing an armed defense against white hate, much like the NOMAADs are doing today," Dr. Allgood said. "We went from high school to high school across the South and recruited young blacks to join us. The Klan got wind of our activities, and a few of their boys tried to intimidate us. They weren't ready for us to fight back. We bruised them up pretty good." He smiled at the memory.

"We were working a few towns away the next day when a mob armed with clubs came looking for us," Dr. Allgood continued. "They cornered us in a community church. I will never forget the sight of that little pastor holding off an angry mob with a shotgun and the grace of God. A white pastor. He put himself at risk to protect me and my colleagues from our persecutors."

"Well, I'm sorry that you were ever put in that situation, but I'm glad for the perspective it's given you," Ben said. "It was a relief to share my story with a sympathetic ear tonight." He paused, then changed the subject. "Are you involved with the NOMAADs?"

"Not directly," Dr. Allgood said. His voice became stronger. "But if the white hate groups start a war, I'll be one of the first to sign up to fight. I'm happy to leave the planning to the younger men who still have the passion to devote their lives to such matters. I've encouraged Stanton to get involved."

"Do you think a race war is a real possibility?" Ben asked.

Dr. Allgood did not hesitate. "Yes, I do. More so after tonight than before."

Ben was confused. "I thought Stanton said that the President's speech helped to defuse the Fort Bragg situation?"

"The President walked through that minefield about as well as any man could," Dr. Allgood said. Ben saw him swallow hard. "My concerns deepened while I was listening to your story tonight. Two things that didn't mean much to me before have taken on a far greater significance."

Dr. Allgood paused, again. Ben let the silence encourage him to confide his concerns rather than force the issue. "The first thing was an interview on TV with a soldier at Fort Bragg," Ray said. "A white soldier. He accused the dead black soldiers of inciting the shooter to action when they threatened to 'frag' white soldiers in the heat of combat. The accuser was John Daniel, Jr."

Ben's jaw dropped. "The Speaker's son," he said.

"It upset me, and no doubt all African-Americans, that this racist soldier could not support his accusation with any evidence," Ray said. "I think The Speaker's son may have incited another soldier to murder those African-American soldiers."

"My god, it's their Final Vengeance!" Ben said.

"They're trying to start a second civil war," Dr. Allgood said grimly. "A race war."

Ben was shaken. "This keeps getting bigger and bigger," he said. "They failed this time, but who knows what they'll do next."

Dr. Allgood cast his eyes downward. "I think I know," he said. "This is humiliating. My personal ethics and morals mean everything to me, and I've compromised them both."

Ben leaned forward and spoke reassuringly. "Dr. Allgood, I owe you. Anything you say goes no further unless you tell me it's okay."

Dr. Allgood breathed in a gulp of stale heated indoor air for strength, then put his life in Ben's young hands. "Cal Stewart came to me about three weeks ago," Dr. Allgood said. "It's all so clear now, but then I had no idea what he was doing. He asked me to approve a grant to Calhoun College. They didn't follow the application procedures, which would've taken several months. The research project itself seemed innocuous, except that they were trying to circumvent the regulations against experimentation on prisoners. That's where he tricked me, dammit."

"What do you mean?" Ben asked.

"He made me focus on the prisoner issue. I got all bent out of shape about breaking the rules. After he convinced me that I *had* to approve the grant, he was suddenly concerned about the racial implications of Calhoun College, a predominantly white school, experimenting on African-American prisoners. He told me to limit the experiment to white prisoners. It sounded like a reasonable request."

Ben tried to tug on his mustache, only to realize it was no longer there. He stroked his upper lip instead. "I'm almost afraid to ask," he said. "But how did Stewart convince you to approve the application?"

Dr. Allgood put his head in his hands. "He had pictures. The only time I ever cheated on Claire. I love her. I love my kids. There was no way I could hurt them like that. No way I could risk losing them."

Ben shook his head. "Unbelievable. The devious bastards got an African-American bureaucrat to authorize illegal research on white prisoners," Ben said. "Then one day an anonymous source leaks it to the *New York Herald Times* or the *Washington Post*—"

Dr. Allgood finished the sentence for him. "And I've triggered the Second Civil War."

THIRTY-SEVEN

L AFAYETTE SQUARE was once again peaceful on Wednesday morning. LaRosa Smith strolled along the red brick walkways, her mood exuberant. The President had delivered her speech word for word, and the pundits had unanimously proclaimed Norton's perform-ance a success. "A political tour de force." "President Norton pulls a rabbit out of his hat."

Part of that success had been attributable to the President's strong, soothing presence, but most of it had been her words, her cool think-ing under pressure. Even the African-American groups had seen the logic of the President's conciliatory, understated reaction. There would be no riots this week. It was for moments like this that she loved poli-tics. Small acts with grand consequences.

She sat down on a park bench near a statue of Andrew Jackson on horseback. Despite her personal triumph, she felt badly about leaving Ben Kravner in the lurch. After the fiasco on Tuesday had settled down, she had sent Ben an e-mail offering to meet him in Lafayette Square at ten o'clock this morning. She glanced at her watch. It was ten now, and the only other people in the Square were a dozen homeless men and women and a handful of tourists.

Ben had not responded to the e-mail, and there was no sign of him. She was concerned. Sancho Panza. Grand quests. She and Ben had shared a running joke about tilting at windmills, pursuing the impossible dream. She had just beaten the windmill; Ben was fight-ing for his life. He had abandoned her three and a half years ago—so why did she feel so guilty that her life was peaking when his had hit bottom?

* * *

"ARE YOU FEELING A LITTLE FEY this morning, Miss Barnett?" The voice of The Spy pierced through the darkness like an invisible knife. Debby sighed. The morning had started off so well. After not eating at all on Monday and sparingly on Tuesday, the agents had brought her a hearty breakfast this morning. They had even let her use the bathroom upstairs.

She hated The Can. Of all the indignities she had been subjected to—imprisoned in a dark basement, stripped to her underwear, shackled to a pole, beaten by Gerry Kate—The Can was the worst. She had to call down an agent, and it was always a male agent, whenever she had to relieve herself. Her most private moments. She cringed at the thought. Now she wondered if they had raised her spirits only so she would have further to fall.

"I don't know what that means," Debby said warily.

"It's an old Scottish word," The Spy said. "It's the feeling of one who is doomed."

Debby felt the anger flash through her body. Her jaw tightened, her backbone straightened. She wondered if The Spy could sense her reaction in the darkness. She barely suppressed a snarl. "I am a survivor," she said bitterly. "I will not give up hope until you snuff out my last breath."

"Very good, Miss Barnett." The Spy clapped his hands, five times, slowly. "Wonderful performance. Bravo. Much better than your father's on the day he died."

"My father died in a car accident! You can't rile me with your lies." She was not nearly as convinced as she tried to sound. The police had found no evidence of foul play. But this man was evil. He was capable of killing—and enjoying it.

"Very well, Miss Barnett. Your courage is admirable. If you don't want to hear how your father died like a sniveling coward, I can respect that."

Debby had felt little fondness for her father while he was alive. Andy Colleen had not been a model father, showing little interest even for a non-custodial parent. For the first time, she realized the enormous pressure that he had been under. She wondered why they had killed him. It had to be true. Or was The Spy just trying to confuse her? "Why did you kill him?" she demanded.

"Now, now, Miss Barnett. I'm not in the mood to talk about your father, anymore. Let's talk about you. I do hope you're ready to tell me the truth today." She heard him walking towards her, then felt his cold hand grab her face. "I would hate to put another mark on your pretty little face."

She tried to pull away, without success. "Let go of me," she growled through clenched teeth.

The Spy released his grip. "Very well, Miss Barnett. You control your destiny. Now tell me how you came into possession of the Poem. The truth!"

Debby startled at the ferocity of The Spy's words. She had never seen his face but could almost envision his wolf-like features in the darkness, sharp teeth, glowering eyes, a menacing smile that masked the heart of a predator. She could feel him prowling around her, circling, waiting to pounce on her first mistake.

"Miss Barnett, you've had two days to think of a better story," he said. "But remember who you are dealing with. I can smell a lie. Maybe I'll toy with you and let you trap yourself like on Monday, maybe not. The truth, Miss Barnett. The truth!"

Debby knew he was right. But she also knew that if she gave him everything he wanted, she would be of no use to him. His reaction would be violent—but better than the alternative. She began to whimper. "I told you the truth. I received the Poem in the mail from my father."

"And were there any instructions?" The Spy asked. He was standing behind her.

"No," Debby muttered helplessly. She braced herself. The stiffness of her body did not lessen the impact. The Spy's closed fist smashed into her face with bone-crunching force as he shouted: "Strike two, Miss Barnett!"

Debby shrieked from the crushing pain. She felt her nose break and the harsh metallic taste of blood in her mouth. Then her head bounced off the steel pole to which she was shackled and everything went black.

BEN FOUND CLAIRE ALLGOOD ALONE, washing dishes, when he plodded into the Allgoods' kitchen at ten-fifty-five.

"Good morning, Ben," she said cheerily.

Ben was still groggy. He mumbled a greeting.

"Ray went in to the office and Stanton went to a friend's house," she said. "We reminded him not to say *anything* about you."

Ben felt better after breakfast. He needed to regroup, plan his strategy. He was safe at the Allgoods' home, but the Knights were striking with a fury. Their first attempt to thrust the nation into civil war had failed, but it was only a matter of time before they struck again. His life, Debby's life, were meaningless compared to the bloody destruction that would be wrought by a race war.

Ben became aware of the sad yearning that lingered just beyond his consciousness. He had become so accustomed to its presence that he only thought about it when something reminded him of Debby. He felt guilty that he did not think of her more often. He missed her terribly and knew that her chances of survival diminished each day it took to bring the Knights to justice.

Dr. Allgood had said the night before that the grant to Calhoun College would not be finalized for another week. It would take another week or two after that, maybe more, before the experiment could become operational. They would need to work with the prison warden, select the participants and the control group, and obtain consents from the subjects.

If the Knights leaked the details of the experiment before it was seriously underway, it would not be a credible reason to trigger a war. *Would it?* The Knights' original intent had almost certainly been to trigger the war after JJ Alexander became president, over a year later. The hastily conceived and ill-fated attempt to start the war at Fort Bragg was strong evidence that the Knights had been forced to accelerate their plans without adequate preparation.

Still, the reaction to the experiment was largely in their control. Ben was certain that the Knights had ties to the white supremacy groups. But he wondered how effective those groups would be in launching a full-scale war. He always thought of the Klan and the other groups as vocal but ineffective. They were run by psychos. The religious right. Egomaniacs.

But Ben was hesitant to underestimate The Royal Order of the Millennium Knight. They had power, money and an evil passion. Somehow the descendants of the seven brothers and two sisters of Jimmy MacDougall had taken an impossible, vengeful dream and transformed it into nightmarish reality over the course of 160 years. Fueled by hate and passion, they had killed seven presidents. They had risen from obscurity to positions of power over seven generations. No, he would be a fool to think that The Royal Order was doomed to fail based on their own incompetence.

Ben needed the Internet. He wanted to try to reach LaRosa one more time, but he could not rely on her alone. There was no time for another foul up. It was time to start gathering supporting evidence on his own. If The Royal Order of the Millennium Knight was responsible for the deaths of seven presidents, the ancestors of the present day Knights would be connected to those presidents or their assassins. They might be lurking on the periphery, but he was going to find them.

Claire directed Ben to their second telephone line, in Ray's study. Ben placed Adams Thompson's laptop, the sleek, black IBM ThinkPad, on the desk and sat in Dr. Allgood's upholstered chair. He signed on to CyberLine using Thompson's cyber-name and password. He by-passed the RealTime rooms, his usual haunts, in favor of a direct connection to the World Wide Web. He checked the free e-mail account that he had established to communicate with LaRosa. There was a message from Quixote from the night before.

Ben, sorry about today. I'm sure you figured out the problem.
I'll try again at 10am Wednesday in Lafayette Square. Rosie

Ben cursed his luck. It was almost noon. He sent LaRosa another message requesting that she meet him at noon on Thursday. He thought about sending Woody a note, but it was too risky. The FBI had by now confiscated Ben's home computer. If they had reviewed his e-mail, they knew about Woody and would probably be monitoring his telephone line for incoming communications. He frowned, hoping that no harm had come to his friend.

Ben returned to the World Wide Web. He was about to undertake a monumental task. It was like researching a complex legal issue. He needed a point of entry into the materials, something related to the topic that would point him to additional sources. He revisited the web site with presidential biographies that he had reviewed a few weeks earlier. The site offered a brief account of each president's life, some highlights of his Administration's accomplishments and a sentence, sometimes two, about his death.

Ben collected the names of the known presidential assassins and cabinet members who had served the dead presidents. Then he used the web search engines to find information on each known contact. He wrote down the names of every person that was connected to the first group of contacts. After three hours of research, he had not found a single person with a name matching the surnames of the Knights.

Ben slammed his fist on Dr. Allgood's desk. He did not have time to collect volumes of information from obscure sources. Frustration was a feeling he often had when he was doing legal research. An eager associate at a law firm could run up a substantial bill following up dozens of blind leads. He recalled an incident in his first month at Kramer, Fox and smirked. A partner had asked him to research what seemed like an obscure point of corporate securities law. He had reviewed hundreds of cases and prepared a thirty-page memorandum. He had spent 75 hours on the issue, which had cost the client over ten thousand dollars, only to find out that most of the research had already been accumulated in a law review article. Kramer, Fox had billed the client, anyway. Nobody noticed.

Then an idea struck him. Woody had heard of the 20-Year Jinx in high school. Other people must have known about it, too. Maybe somebody else had been intrigued enough to do the research. It was a lark.

Ben entered the word "jinx" into the web search engine. It returned 4,766 hits. The hits were sorted by relevance, so Ben was prepared to scan the first few dozen. The first several items were about a musical group named JINX. Hi-Jinx, a fictional super-heroine inspired another. A few sports articles. One site called "The Jinx" set Ben's heart aflutter, but it was only about a newsletter written by a very lonely man who collected odd bits of trivia.

Ben tried another search: "20 Year Jinx." He thought that this would produce a narrower range of web sites, but the search produced almost eight million hits. The first three hits were irrelevant—a car racing site, a sports story, another sports story. Then his heart almost stopped. The fourth hit was entitled: "The President is Dead."

Ben perused the short summary. It was a link to an article written five years earlier about the 20-Year Jinx, which was described as a phenomenon that manifests itself when, about once every twenty years, the president of the country dies in office.

Ben clicked on the link. His excitement grew as he started to read the first paragraph: "You will learn more about the 20-Year Jinx in this publication than anyone has known to date." The article went on to list the presidents who died in office and described, in detail, how they died.

But then the story went downhill fast. The author was deranged. Ben read the entire essay, which devolved into rantings about how strange men visited the author during the night since he was a child and planted ideas in his head. He claimed to have been an unwitting participant in the Kennedy assassination through telepathic communication. Ben's heart sank.

Then he noticed a detail that had initially escaped his eye. The last line of the article read: "If you have any other interpretation I would be happy to listen." The line was footnoted. The footnote said: "<u>E.g.</u>, see the writings of Prof. Maxwell Caldwell."

Ben entered a web search for "Maxwell Caldwell." The search produced almost ninety thousand hits—capturing any site that used the words "Maxwell" or "Caldwell," but hopefully prioritizing any site that used both. The very first one was an entry for West Plymouth State College.

The web site for the college was only a mouse-click away. It was a small state college in the Berkshire mountains of western Massachusetts. A list of faculty members included one Maxwell Caldwell, a tenured professor of history. Ben tried to find additional information about Professor Caldwell on the college's web site, without success.

Ben looked at his watch. Half past four. It was nearing the end of the academic day. He found Claire preparing dinner in the kitchen. "Would you mind if I made a long distance call or two?" Ben asked meekly.

"Do you think that's a good idea?" she asked. "You said that the FBI would probably be monitoring calls to your friends and relatives."

"I'm just following up a lead I found on the Net," he said. "No risk to me or you."

Claire told Ben to make all the calls he needed. He called West Plymouth State College and asked for Professor Caldwell. The operator connected him.

"Hello," a gravelly male voice answered.

"I'm trying to reach Professor Maxwell Caldwell," Ben said.

"This is he," the voice said. "Who am I speaking with?"

Ben hesitated. "My name is Nathan Pierce," he said. "I'm doing some research on something called the 20-Year Jinx, and I came across your name."

"I haven't written about that for years," Professor Caldwell said, his voice laden with suspicion. "That project destroyed my reputation. People called me a crackpot. My advice is to find another topic for your paper. There's nothing there."

Ben wondered if the Professor was merely suffering from the disenchantment of a failed project. Could the Knights have gotten to him? "What was your research about?" Ben asked.

"I tried to find an explanation for the deaths of seven presidents elected every twentieth year from 1840 through 1960. The pattern seemed too significant to be coincidental. I collected data to support a conspiracy theory. Reams of data. But there's nothing. I did not find one connection between any two deaths."

"Why did you stop researching?" Ben asked cautiously.

"I became a laughingstock," Professor Caldwell said sadly. "The fate of so many conspiracy theorists. My colleagues didn't think it was serious research. I was denied tenure at an Ivy League university the name of which I swore shall never again cross my lips and have toiled in relative anonymity for the past twenty-five years."

"Nobody ever threatened you?"

"Blast it! If only they had," the Professor said. "Then I would have known I was on to something."

Ben could not contain the excitement in his voice. "Professor, you *were* on to something. I've stumbled upon a conspiracy that would explain the 20-Year Jinx, and you may have the evidence to help me prove it!"

THIRTY-EIGHT

BEN WAS BLEARY-EYED. It was only four o'clock on Thursday afternoon, but he had been driving for nearly ten hours. He had wanted to leave for West Plymouth immediately after speaking with Professor Caldwell on the telephone, but Claire Allgood had convinced him that he needed at least one more decent night's sleep before he attempted a long trip. Ben smiled. Something about Claire reminded him of his mother. Everybody's mother.

The Claire-induced pause had given Ben time to reflect and plan rather than act impulsively. Caution was critical when a solitary error in judgment could doom him. He had sent an e-mail message to LaRosa canceling their meeting that morning and asking her to send him her schedule for the next few days.

Ray and Claire had been eager to participate in Ben's cloak and dagger adventure vicariously through their car. They had insisted that he borrow Claire's white Ford Taurus. The trip had been uneventful, but it took longer than it normally might have because Ben had chosen a circuitous inland route, via Interstate 81, to avoid the heavily traveled northeast corridor on Interstate 95. The pilgrimage had seemed even longer because Ben anticipated the holy grail at its end.

West Plymouth State College was nestled in the northwest corner of Massachusetts in the town of West Plymouth. The last hour of Ben's trip had been spent on narrow mountain roads that weaved dangerously along the steep precipices of the Berkshire Mountains. Some of the vistas had been stunning, but Ben eyed the darkening sky warily.

Professor Caldwell sprang from his chair when Ben knocked on his open office door. "You must be Mr. Pierce," he said excitedly, emerging from behind his cluttered desk. He shook Ben's hand vigorously. "I expected you earlier. I was afraid you weren't going to come."

The gravelly voice, laced with just a hint of a New England accent, was the same one Ben had heard on the telephone, but the Professor was not as Ben had envisioned. He had expected an older man with stooped shoulders, thinning white hair, chiseled New England features and professorial dress. Instead, he found before him a vibrant, muscular man of about fifty-five with thick brown hair, cut short in a military style, and a penchant for short sleeve dress shirts.

"It's a pleasure to meet you, Professor Caldwell," Ben said, smiling. "I may be more eager to hear your story than you are to tell it."

Professor Caldwell looked at Ben oddly. "You look very familiar," he said. "Were you a student here?"

"No," Ben said tentatively. He had hoped to avoid giving the Professor too many details, but he now realized that was not going to be possible. There were so many emotions in the Professor's eyes— excitement, curiosity, suspicion, fear. Like a child about to embark on his first ride on the *big* rollercoaster. This man had lived in exile from serious academia for twenty-five years, and now he was on the verge of redemption. He wanted to know everything. He deserved to know everything. "Can we close the door?" Ben asked.

The Professor shut the door, then sized Ben up, none too discreetly, top to bottom. Ben was wearing the second hand clothes from the Salvation Army thrift shop, now fresh after a rigorous cleaning by Claire Allgood, but ragged nonetheless. The Professor's eyes lingered on Ben's shaved scalp. His expression changed to serious.

"You're not one of those lunatics are you?" the Professor asked warily. "A few years ago some fool came in here and got me all excited again over nothing. He sounded serious at first, then started talking about extraterrestrials and psychic phenomena. Blast it! I can't take the highs and the lows like that." He tapped his chest twice with his fist. "Bad ticker."

"I'm deadly serious and as sane as they come," Ben reassured him. "This is a real live conspiracy. It involves some of the most powerful men in the country."

The Professor still looked skeptical. "And how did you come to be aware of this powerful conspiracy?" he asked.

Ben paused, inviting himself to sit in an unpainted oak chair facing the Professor's metal desk. The Professor followed his lead, walking back behind the desk and clearing space on the cluttered desktop to obtain an unobstructed view of Ben's face before sitting.

Ben realized that his threshold for trust had lowered dramatically in a world where every human contact was fraught with risk. He had no choice. He needed Max Caldwell even more than Max Caldwell needed him. As had become habit, Ben instantly calculated alternate escape routes in the event the conversation took an unexpected turn.

"I'm a trusts and estates lawyer in New York City. Do you remember the Adams Thompson murder just after Thanksgiving?"

And so Ben launched into his second retelling of his incredible tale in as many days. Professor Caldwell was spellbound. The truth was more fantastic than any theory he had dared to construct in all his years of research. The Professor was skeptical at first, just as Woody and the Allgoods had been, but his doubt melted away more quickly than the others, perhaps because of his burning desire for redemption.

When Ben was done telling the story and all of the Professor's questions had been answered, Max Caldwell pulled out a file from a drawer in his desk. The red binder was six inches thick. He dropped it on the desktop, producing a dramatic thud. "Eight dead presidents," he said. "Seven years of work. I haven't looked at this file in fifteen, maybe twenty years."

The Professor fondled the file preciously, hesitant to initiate the review of its contents, perhaps savoring the moment before years of ignominy were vindicated, perhaps fearing that the moment would be lost, his dream dashed once again. Ben leaned forward like a starving man watching steak sizzle on a grill. "I'm almost afraid to look," the Professor said with genuine apprehension.

Ben grinned his crooked grin. "I have a good feeling about this, Max," he said. They had become familiar during the course of the afternoon, now going into the early evening, perhaps even friends. "A real good feeling."

The Professor ran his hand through his bristly hair, then smiled. "Perhaps you're right, young Ben, perhaps you're right. Let's dive in."

The Professor removed several piles of paper from his desktop, then withdrew eight smaller manila folders from the red binder. He spread them out across the surface of the desk in a fanfold pattern. "Pick a card, any card," he quipped.

The folders held a remarkable collection of data about each of the eight presidents who died in office, including Zachary Taylor, whose death fell outside the scope of the twenty-year pattern that had first intrigued Max Caldwell when he was a graduate student in history at the still undisclosed Ivy League institution that spurned him. The Professor had charted each president's family members, friends, business associates, cabinet appointees, political enemies, doctors, lawyers, household staff and any other acquaintances or contacts that he could find. Then he had collected information about each of those contacts, including hometowns, schools and colleges attended, family members and any other persons that might have exerted influence. A similar collection of data had been assembled for each known assassin.

The precise circumstances of each president's death were set out in far more detail than Ben had seen. It was difficult to believe that one man had assembled all of this information without the benefit of the Internet. The total amount of data was mindboggling and, to the untrained eye, completely unconnected.

But when Professor Caldwell and Ben scrutinized the records for links to the suspected Knights, the work was quick. A man named Alistair Glenn was a cook in the White House during the short Administration of William Henry Harrison. Harrison was reported to have died of pneumonia, but poisoning now sounded like a reasonable alternative. They did not have the resources to determine if Alistair Glenn was the ancestor of Clint Glenn, The General, but the emerging pattern suggested that this was merely a formality that could be confirmed by President Norton's analysts.

None of the Knights' surnames appeared in the Zachary Taylor folder. The diaries of John Wilkes Booth, Abraham Lincoln's assassin, indicated that Booth had been a spy with the Confederate army and had aspirations of abducting or assassinating President Lincoln as early as the summer of 1864. One of Booth's Confederate army friends had been Stephen Andrew, a captain in a regiment of Carolina militiamen, and probably an ancestor of Ty Andrew, The Senator.

James Garfield had been killed by Charles J. Guiteau. Guiteau had a long history of unstable behavior. He had been an itinerant failure who had sought careers in law, theology and politics. He purportedly had shot Garfield after several months of unsuccessfully lobbying for various high level government positions, including the ambassadorship to Vienna, a position he had been unqualified to hold.

Barnaby Daniel, a State Department staff member, had lived in the same boarding house as Guiteau and had stated "despairingly" to investigators that perhaps he had encouraged Guiteau's delusional behavior. Guiteau had pleaded insanity to the assassination, claiming that he was "God's man on earth" and that the assassination was "divine inspiration." The defense had failed, and Guiteau had been hung.

President McKinley had been shot by Leon Czolgosz at the Pan-American Exhibition in Buffalo, New York. Czolgosz was an anarchist. None of his radical colleagues had appeared to be connected to the ancestors of the Knights. However, one of the Secret Service agents guarding McKinley was Bryan Kate. Interestingly, Czolgosz had admitted that he had acted alone in the killing, although there had been confirmed reports that the Secret Service agent, Kate, had been distracted by another man in the crowd just before McKinley was shot by Czolgosz. That man was never identified. Bryan Kate was present at Czolgosz's execution.

Warren G. Harding was thought to have died of either a heart attack or a stroke. His wife had not permitted an autopsy. President Harding was rumored to have had a number of sexual affairs, and there had been speculation at the time of his death that his wife had poisoned him. This was never proven. However, Mrs. Harding's personal physician had been Dr. Theodore Stewart.

A brain hemorrhage purportedly had felled Franklin Delano Roosevelt, and no potential links to any of the Knights could be found to support a contradictory theory. Ben and the Professor found this hole in their theory disheartening, but the balance of the data so overwhelmingly supported the conspiracy that they dismissed it. It was not so difficult to imagine that one or two links in a chain 160 years old would be broken.

Professor Caldwell had not researched Ronald Reagan's Administration, but President Reagan had also survived two terms, despite having been shot early in his first term. It was possible that a connection would be found between the Knights and John Hinckley, Jr., Reagan's assailant, but, still, a second attempt had never been made. The conspiracy was not infallible.

The pattern resumed in the Kennedy file. Kennedy had been shot by Lee Harvey Oswald. Caldwell's folder was filled with information gathered in support of the numerous conspiracy theories that had emerged after the assassination of JFK, which had in fact been his original inspiration. Caldwell's own research showed that Oswald had been employed by a Dallas businessman, George Alexander, for a period before the assassination, suggesting that perhaps the Mafia, Fidel Castro and the military-industrial complex had indeed been innocent of any involvement.

Ben's stomach rumbled ferociously by the time they finished reviewing the files. It was nearly ten o'clock. He had not eaten since early afternoon. The Professor was elated. He did not seem to notice that they had worked through dinner.

"This calls for a cigar," the Professor said, reaching into a humidor on the shelf beside his desk. He slid the cigar back and forth under his nose, a look of pure joy locked on his face. "My only vice," he said, winking. "Do you smoke?"

"No, thanks," Ben said. Ben was an ardent non-smoker. But this was a day to make allowances for small peeves. "But don't let me stop you."

The Professor took a long drag on the cigar. The small office quickly filled with foul, blue smoke. "This is incredible!" he said. "All that time I was right. So many of my colleagues looked down their noses at me. Blast it! I can't wait to see their faces now."

The Professor's exuberance concerned Ben. There was still a long way to go before this conspiracy was broken. Ben had purposely neglected to tell Professor Caldwell about his discussion with Ray Allgood and the frightful conclusion that the Knights were pushing the nation to the brink of civil war. Caldwell was content knowing that the presidential deaths were linked. But if he carelessly bragged about his new found success to the wrong person, the Knights might become alarmed and set their end game in motion immediately. *Dammit, too many people know about the plot already!*

"Max, I know you're excited about all this, but we still need to keep it quiet," Ben said. "The FBI is after me, and they'll be after you, too, if this gets out."

"Well, blast it, we've got to tell somebody! We've got to expose these bastards!" Caldwell said.

"I'm on top of it," Ben said. "I have a contact in the White House. But I need you to stay quiet until the President deals with this as he thinks best. These are powerful, vengeful men. They may do something crazy if they think they're cornered."

The Professor took another long drag on his cigar. He looked thoughtful. "Well, then I'm going with you to Washington. This is my baby, too. Let's go right now!"

Ben's mind darted. He did not like this idea at all. His luck had held out with him working alone and calling the shots. He liked Max Caldwell, but he had an ego—an ego that might get in the way of Ben's instincts. Ben glanced at his watch. The Knights would be meeting in the Millennium Nights room in less than two hours. "There's something I need to do tonight," Ben said. "I have to make an Internet connection by midnight."

"Fine, fine," the Professor said. "We'll go first thing tomorrow. You can stay with me and my wife tonight."

The Professor was not going to let Ben out of his sight. His adrenaline seemed to be pumping, maybe for the first time in twenty years. He wanted to be the Hero. Ben relented. "Fair enough," he said.

The Professor's wife was already asleep when they arrived at the Caldwells' home, not five minutes from the college. It was a quaint, two-bedroom house with yellow shingles and a white picket fence encircling the perimeter of the yard. The front door opened into the living room. The Professor hung their coats on a coat stand in the corner behind the door.

The room was sparsely furnished, the hardwood floors making it seem even more so. A soft, blue and white plaid couch was to be Ben's bed for the evening. Matching brass lamps stood guard over the couch, perched on two pine end tables, one of which shared the space with a telephone. The Professor told Ben to use the telephone line for his Internet connection.

The Professor retired for the evening after a brief meal of ham sandwiches and potato chips, and Ben immediately hooked up the laptop in the living room. Once again he resisted the temptation to e-mail his friends and family. He found an e-mail from Quixote waiting for him.

> *Ben, this is my schedule for the next few days. Things seemed*
> *to have calmed down. You can call me at my direct extension*
> *in the Old Executive Office Building at (202) 555-7679.*
> *Thursday: In and out of office (meetings)*
> *Friday: Meeting 9-12; free 12-6; New Year's Eve Party @*
> *Kennedy Center*
> *Saturday/Sunday: Family visits (e-mail me)*
> *Monday: No scheduled meetings*
> *Rosie*

Ben made a mental note of her schedule, then opened the CyberLine program using the cyber-name "The General," the last symbol being the number one rather than the letter "l." It was almost midnight. He entered the RealTime area and found the Millennium Nights room.

It was still empty. His heart began to race. He desperately wanted to enter the room. He had the password. He needed to know their plans. Dammit, he *needed* to know! They had already tried to trigger a rebellion once. Was the Calhoun College research project their only other planned event? Did he have a week to stop them? A month? A year? Ben hated uncertainty. If he knew the probabilities of the relevant events, he could make an informed decision. Now he was guessing.

The Doctor was the first to enter the room. Ben's doubts returned. What if they detected him? Did The General have a distinctive cyber style that Ben would not be able to mimic? Did he participate actively in the discussions or was he passive? The Heir Apparent entered the room. Then The Senator. The Caretaker. The Speaker. The Spy. Only The General was missing.

He had to make a decision. What was the downside risk? They would change to a new room or a new mode of communication. Any hope of the authorities trapping them in the room would be lost. But they could not locate Ben based on a RealTime chat communication. They could only track the cyber-name "The General" to Adams Thompson's account and find that the account was logged on from a remote location. What was the upside? He might learn a key fact or the status of the Calhoun College research project or another planned incident that he had not yet uncovered.

There was no choice. He had enough evidence now to prove the Knights were conspiring to commit treason. Even if they adopted a new, secure means of communication, they could not escape their fate. The real risk was that Ben or the White House might be too slow to act—many people would die if the Knights incited the race-based militias to war. He had already lost two valuable minutes. He mouse-clicked on the Millennium Nights room. A pop-up window requested the password. He typed "TipTy2000."

Moderator: "The Genera1" has entered the room.

The Heir Apparent: General! You're early today.

The Genera1:   So it seems.

The Heir Apparent: Fine. Let's get started. We've had a busy week. Who wants to start? General? Spy?

The Spy: No communications from BFK since escape last Friday. Continuing to monitor close contacts. DB remains in Maryland safe house. Holding back info. Will crack next session.

The Senator: Have you harmed her?

The Spy: A little battered and bruised. She knows last chance is coming. Let her think about it a few days. I may do some skiing after Super Conference.

The Senator: And if she tells you what you want to hear?

The Spy: She'll stay alive at least until story confirmed. We'll play by ear after that.

The Heir Apparent: General, why don't you brief us on the Fort Bragg affair?

The Caretaker: Before The General does that, I think that we should take a moment to recognize The Speaker's son for the outstanding job that he did in provoking the incident.

The Doctor: And for his performance on national TV.

The Heir Apparent: Hear, hear. You'll slap young John on the back for us, won't you now, Speaker!

The Speaker: Thank you, gentleman...Indeed I will. I'm mighty proud of that boy.

Moderator: "The General" has entered the room.

Moderator: "The General" has left the room.

Ben's heart was in his throat. He had known that his exit would not be invisible, but he had hoped to leave the room before The General entered. But he was hypnotized by the discussion as, breathless, he watched his theory confirmed beyond doubt. Perhaps the momentary overlap, when there were two Generals in the room, would be attributed to computer error.

The Heir Apparent: What was that?

The Senator: It looked like a computer blip.

The Spy: Have you ever seen a computer blip like that in all the years we've been meeting here? That was an intruder.

The Senator: But the program won't allow two people with the same name. I tested it once to make sure.

The Spy: Look carefully at the two names. Last letter slightly different. Number "1" vs. letter "l." BFK has made his first, and last, mistake.

The General: What's going on?

The Spy: Imposter entered room with cyber-name almost identical to yours. It must be BFK.

The General: Was any information compromised?

The Heir Apparent: He probably knows that we were behind the Fort Bragg situation.

The Spy: I've got an agent with 24-hr CyberLine contact. We'll know the point of presence where BFK connected within the hour.

Moderator: "The Spy" has left the room.

The Senator: That boy concerns me. The longer he's out there, the better the chances that he finds a sympathetic ear.

The Heir Apparent: Hell, he's just desperate. He has nowhere to turn. He can't look to the authorities for help. Fritz Fox will be in the hospital for a couple of weeks. He doesn't have enough credibility to go to the press. What's he going to do, write a letter to the President?

They get a dozen letters from these nuts every week. Relax. Let's stay on alert, but we can't let this paralyze us. The Spy will take care of Kravner shortly.

The Senator: I certainly hope so. I'm not sure that we can mobilize quickly enough if our hand is forced in the next few weeks.

The Heir Apparent: General, why don't you brief us on the Fort Bragg situation and then we can work through our contingency plans.

The General: The situation at Fort Bragg has cooled down considerably. I tried to escalate the tension by recommending segregation of the troops at Fort Bragg, but the President chose to accept other advice. If we view the incident as a first volley in a long war, it was successful. The reaction of the men indicates that the racial divisiveness runs deep.

The Heir Apparent: And the reaction by the NOMAADs suggests that they can be provoked.

The Senator: But is it a war we are certain we can win? The rally at the White House was an impressive display of force.

The General: We'll need to gauge the success of the Super Conference this weekend. If we can unify the white supremacy groups, we may be able to assemble an army of over 100,000 men. That's a powerful force. Keep in mind that the U.S. Army only has about 500,000 men.

The Speaker: Do you have an estimate of the NOMAADs' manpower?

The General: We think that they've trained about 50,000 men.

The Speaker: There must have been more than that at

the rally alone. And they assembled on only one day's notice.

The General: There were a lot of women and children in that crowd. A lot of old men, too. You need young men to fight a war.

The Heir Apparent: General, how quickly after the Super Conference could we mobilize an army?

The General: That depends upon our initial objectives. It would take a few days for me to work up a battle plan. We need to organize the troops. A limited fighting force could prob- ably be assembled and trained in two to three weeks if properly motivated—a few months to train the entire army. I've been laying the groundwork for participation by U.S. military personnel, but I was working under the assumptions that we had anoth- er year and that we would control the presidency. We should not count on that support right away.

Moderator: "The Spy" has entered the room.

The Heir Apparent: I don't want to commit to an immediate attack when we address the Super Conference, but we do need to organize a quick strike as a contingency plan. If Kravner is not apprehended, we need to be prepared to strike at the first hint that we've been compromised. What targets would we attack if it were only possible to prepare for a limited engagement?

The General: NOMAAD HQ in Washington. If we take out their leadership, they'll be demoral- ized. A single strike to one of their training compounds might cause the rest of their troops to desert.

The Caretaker: Would it be possible to organize an attack by January 17?

The General:	Possible, but not recommended. Why?
The Caretaker:	Martin Luther King Day. There will probably be large rallies. The black leadership will be concentrated. And the emotional impact could work for us two ways—motivating our troops and demoralizing theirs.
The Doctor:	Would the Experiment be far enough along to provide an effective trigger for the hostilities by mid-January? Allgood has signed the paperwork, but The Caretaker won't even have the check until early next week.
The Caretaker:	I've already spoken to the warden at the state prison. He's a good old boy, and he's prepared to work with us. We can start interviewing candidates next week and start a test group the week after if we push it.
The Heir Apparent:	Push it. Hopefully, we won't need to pull the trigger, but we need to have the gun cocked. I don't want to die in a blaze of glory. If we start this war, I want to win it. We can't do that without the public's sympathies, if not their support, and we can't gain their sympathies without a plan.
The General:	I'll start preparing something that we can present at the Super Conference.
The Spy:	We won't need them. BFK logged on to CyberLine this PM using Pub's account. Accessed network from Pittsfield, MA. Albany, NY field office working with MA, NY and VT state police to set roadblocks tomorrow AM. BFK has made a fatal mistake.

THIRTY-NINE

BEN AND PROFESSOR CALDWELL were mired in a traffic jam on Wednesday morning, and they had not even left West Plymouth. A light snow was falling. "Is there usually so much traffic this early?" Ben asked.

"We get a lot of skiers during the Christmas break. But that jam up is northbound on Route 7, heading into Vermont," the Professor said pointing ahead to a gridlocked intersection. "Usually, traffic gets tied up southbound, but not until later in the morning. There's probably a wreck."

"Well, lucky for us," Ben said, as he steered the Allgoods' white Taurus through the intersection into the southbound lane on Route 7. A thin film of snow covered the road. Ben gripped the steering wheel tightly. A small line of cars formed behind them. The Professor was in a jolly mood, pointing out Mount Greylock, the highest point in Massachusetts, then one ski resort or historical site after another. Ben turned on the radio. The Professor did not take the hint, tuning the radio to a local Pittsfield station as he continued to chirp away merrily.

"—is calling for snow, snow and more snow!" the radio announcer said cheerfully. He was even more annoying than the Professor. "We're expecting another six inches today, which will leave us with a soft powder base of 22 inches. Terrific news if you're hitting the slopes, not so good if you're stuck commuting to work! Let's hope those overworked, under-appreciated boys in the Transportation Department can get those roads cleared for tonight's New Year's Eve festivities! And if you're leaving the Pittsfield area this morning, leave a little extra drive time— we've just gotten a report that the state police are stopping traffic all across the area to check for snow tires. If you don't have 'em on by now, you're looking at a fifty dollar fine!"

"That must have been the reason for the traffic jam up in West Plymouth," the Professor said. "The Vermont border is just a mile north of that intersection."

"Geez, you'd think the Massachusetts state police would be checking cars coming into the state, not going out," Ben said, his voice trembling ever so slightly. Even a routine traffic stop carried life threatening risk. He did not have false identification. He was driving a stranger's car. And one other doubt nagged at him. "Max, do you know anything about the Internet?" Ben asked.

"A bit. I tinker around some with my computer," the Professor said.

"Last night I logged on to CyberLine on someone else's account. I entered a chat room using a new cyber-name. I was pretty sure nobody could trace my location, but now I'm starting to get a little paranoid."

"No, you're right," the Professor said. "At least not to the precise telephone line. But CyberLine would have a record of the point of presence that you accessed, which would be Pittsfield unless you dialed long distance." The Professor chuckled. "You don't think this snow tire check is just for you, do you?"

Ben's silence was his answer. He was troubled. He no longer believed in coincidence. Entering the Millennium Nights room had been a mistake.

"Nonsense, boy, you are being paranoid," the Professor said. "It's just a snow tire check. One, two, three and we're on our way."

Ben pulled off the road. Several cars passed, many of the drivers going out of their way to register their disgust with Ben's pace over the past several miles. Ben looked directly into the Professor's eyes. "I would think you of all people would be suspicious of coincidences, Max. Don't you think it's unusual that they're checking tires on New Year's Eve? And on the way out of the state? Even if it is just a tire check, they might recognize me. I'm on the FBI's Ten Most Wanted list. Hell, even if they don't recognize me with the shaved head and all, we're toast if they ask for identification. I don't have a fake ID."

"Well, they're not looking for me," the Professor said. "Let me drive."

Ben clenched his teeth. The Professor seemed blinded by the perceived proximity of the glory that had long eluded him. "I don't think you understand the risk here, Max. Gerry Kate—the FBI—wants me dead. They don't know about you yet. You're putting yourself in the

line of fire. Let's go back to your house, I'll drop you off, and then I'll
try to figure something out."

"Like what?" the Professor asked with a sneer. "Do you think they're
going to go away if they don't catch you today? Blast it! These are smart,
powerful men. They have resources. Don't you think they're going to question why you were in Pittsfield, Massachusetts? If you found me, what
makes you think they're not going to find me, too? We're both *already* in
danger, and time is not on our side. We're in this together, my friend."

Ben peered out the window at the slow-moving traffic. The
Professor was probably right—and was determined to go out in a blaze
of glory even if he was wrong. "So you think we should chance it now?"
Ben asked.

"We've got a couple of options," the Professor replied. "We can try
to walk around their dragnet, if that's what it is. Bennington, Vermont
is twenty miles north of West Plymouth with the Green Mountains in
between. If we stay off Route 7, which is the only road to Bennington,
we wouldn't make it until late tonight. I could rent a car there. The
other choice would be to drive through the mountains into New York.
They can't cover every route out of the area. They've probably blocked
Route 7 at both ends, all the nearby entrances to the Turnpike, and
Route 20, the main road from Pittsfield to Albany."

The Professor pointed to an intersection about one hundred yards
ahead. "That road off to the right loops around Jiminy Peak and then
on into New York," he said. "It ends in Albany, too, but it's a lot narrower and more dangerous than Route 20. If I were a betting man, I'd
lay odds that they aren't watching that one on a snowy day."

The idea of trudging through snow covered mountains for an entire
day was not appealing to Ben's pioneer spirit. The odds were in their
favor. "What do *you* want to do?" Ben asked.

"I'll drive," the Professor said. "Relax and enjoy the scenery."

The Professor guided the Taurus skillfully along the windy mountain road, through the snow covered pines. The road ascended the
mountain along a steep path. Rickety wooden guard rails, long in dis-
repair, were soon all that separated them from precipitous drops into
the valley below. They passed the entrance to a deserted picnic area on
the left as they neared the summit of Jiminy Peak.

A sign warned of a dangerous curve. Ben gasped. The summit was
capped by a gigantic, exposed granite block. The roadway ahead was

blasted out of the rock—a granite wall bounded the path on the left, a granite cliff dropped off to the right, plunging two hundred feet to the pine forest on the slope below. The Professor negotiated the hairpin turn cautiously, slowing to a crawl. "They call this Dead Man's Curve," the Professor said.

Ben snickered. "Sounds like a line from a 'B' movie."

"They've had some crashes on this corner that would make a stunt director drool," the Professor said.

The descent was easier. After the roadway cornered the granite block, it descended gradually along a straight path for several hundred yards, then resumed its winding ways as it crept towards the valley. They passed through the quaint town of Pine Springs, which sat at the confluence of three mountain roads two miles before the New York border.

Ben saw the roadblock through the falling snow first. A single unmarked car, a black sedan, blocked the westbound lane. A makeshift removable gate allowed traffic in both directions to pass through the eastbound lane. The trooper had chosen his location carefully—there was no room for a car to pass on either side of the roadblock. The Professor slowed the car almost to a stop.

"What do you want to do?" he asked.

Ben's heart raced. "He's seen us," Ben said. "We're cornered. If we turn around, he'll radio ahead for backup and they'll trap us on Jiminy Peak."

"We can ram through that barrier," the Professor said.

"The cops will track us," Ben said. "Our only hope is that they don't recognize me. If he asks to see my ID, back this thing up as fast as you can and turn it around. We'll have to take our chances on Jiminy Peak."

The Professor pulled the car up to the roadblock. He rolled the window down. "Good morning, officer," he said. "I heard on the radio you're checking snow tires. We should be okay."

The trooper was dressed for the part. Black leather jacket. Fur lined cap. Dark sunglasses. Grim face. He bent down and leaned into the open window. He looked carefully at Ben. Ben froze when he saw the trooper's badge. FBI. Albany Field Office. "Identification please," the agent said gruffly.

The Professor handed over his driver's license calmly. Ben's mind was spinning. The agent had not recognized him. Maybe he would let them pass. The agent glanced at the Professor's license and returned it. "You, too, buddy," he said to Ben.

Ben's heart was in his throat. His eyes wide, he looked at the Professor and cocked his head in a gesture that he thought was clear. The Professor hesitated. "My friend doesn't have his wallet with him," he said.

"I was not speaking to you, Mr.—" The Professor's name had not registered.

"Maxwell," the Professor offered.

The agent scowled. "What's *your* name, son?" the agent asked.

The Professor interrupted before Ben could answer or stop him. "Nathan Pierce," he said.

Ben could not see the agent's eyes through the sunglasses, but there was a momentary hesitation, maybe a facial twitch, that set off Ben's internal alarm. "Hit the gas! He's FBI!" Ben shouted.

The agent made a move for his gun. The Professor slammed his foot on the gas pedal. The wheels spun in the new snow for a split second, then found turf. The Taurus rocketed backwards. The trooper crouched into shooting position and fired three rounds in rapid succession.

Two bullets glanced off the car's body; one shattered the front wind-shield. The Professor and Ben screamed, shielding their heads from the flying glass, an icy blast of wind whipping in through the small open-ing in the center of the windshield. The Professor slammed on the brakes. The car spun.

When the car settled, Ben and the Professor looked at each other dizzily. Neither of them was hit. Ben's side of the car was now facing westbound. The agent was about fifty yards down the road, seemingly torn between running to the Taurus with guns blasting or dashing back to his own vehicle to give chase. "Hit it, Max!"

"Which way!"

"Back up the mountain! I've got an idea," Ben said. We've got to get a lead on him."

The Professor hit the gas pedal. The agent ran back to his car. The chase was on.

The road was treacherous. The agent was content to follow at a safe distance, no doubt secure in the knowledge that his buddies were wait-ing on the other side. Then the Taurus began the ascent up the long approach to Dead Man's Curve. "Take it a little faster up the straight-away, Max."

"What's on your mind?" the Professor asked.

"We've got to take out the agent and head back down this side."

The Professor rolled his eyes. "And how do you propose to do that without a gun?" he asked.

"We've got to sideswipe him," Ben said. "The airbag won't protect him from a side impact. We'll turn the car around and time the impact just as he's turning the corner on Dead Man's Curve."

The Professor frowned. "We might all go flying over that cliff if we hit him too hard."

"Nobody's going over the cliff," Ben said. "We need his car. Thirty miles per hour should be enough to rattle his head against the window without sending the car through the guard rail."

The Professor still looked skeptical. "It's our only chance," Ben said. "There's going to be an army of cops waiting for us on the other side, and they'll find an excuse to shoot."

The Professor picked up the pace. The agent lagged behind. Ben looked back as the Taurus entered the turn. "We've got about two minutes," he said. "Let me out here; turn the car around in that picnic area, and I'll signal when you should start."

"Wait a minute!" the Professor shouted. "Blast it! I'm not going over that cliff by myself!"

"We don't have time for this!" Ben yelled back. "Get out. I'll drive."

The Professor got out of the car, and Ben slid over to the driver's side. He fastened his seatbelt, then rolled down the window. "He's going about fifteen miles per hour. I'll go from zero to thirty, trying for an average speed of fifteen miles per hour. Signal me when he's about the same distance from the corner as I am," Ben said. The Professor, wide-eyed, mumbled his understanding.

Ben turned the car quickly and waited, about thirty yards from the corner. The Professor had positioned himself on the ground and was peeking around the corner. He gave Ben the signal almost immediately.

Ben swallowed hard. Thirty miles per hour might not be enough to push another car over, but the Taurus would sail through the wooden guard rail if the timing was even a little off. At least his death would be spectacular. The final scene from the movie *Thelma and Louise*, when the two co-stars drove their car into the Grand Canyon to avoid capture, flashed into his mind, and the image froze there.

Ben pushed the gas pedal to the floor. The Professor was running
back towards him to avoid the collision. The Taurus accelerated. Ben's
heart pounded. Two seconds passed, twenty yards to go. The cold wind
whistled through the bullethole in the windshield. Ten yards. There
was nothing but snow and sky in front of him. Ben let go of the steering wheel and let loose a primal scream, his foot firmly on the gas
pedal, waiting for the sound of splintering wood and the horrifying,
weightless feeling of a man plummeting earthwards from the sky.

The sound was thunderous. Metal on metal. Ben jerked forward
from the impact, then back as the airbag exploded into his body. He hit
the brakes hard. The Taurus and the black sedan skidded across the
roadway towards the guard rail. Ben heard the awful sound of splintering wood, then it stopped and there was only the sound of the wind.

The nose of the Taurus was imbedded in the door of the agent's car,
a Plymouth. The Plymouth was resting on the guard rail. The left front
corner had broken through, and one wheel hung perilously over the
cliff. The Professor chugged up to Ben's window breathlessly. "Are you
okay?" he asked.

"A little shaken up, no real damage," Ben said. "How's our friend?"

The silence was encouraging. The Professor peeked through the
window of the Plymouth's back door. "He's not moving," he said.

Ben joined the Professor. His head and knees ached. He was wob-
bly. "We've got to move quickly," Ben said. "Listen to the radio. If they
ask him for an update, tell them that all is well. I'll move the Taurus
back past the picnic area and block the road."

Ben moved the car, then rejoined the Professor. The radio had been
silent. Ben checked the agent's pulse. He was alive. Ben and the
Professor dragged him through the passenger side of the Plymouth,
then carried him to the Taurus. They handcuffed him to the door.

Ben stood by the side of the cliff holding the agent's gun. He had to
decide quickly. If he kept it, the FBI would be justified in shooting
first, asking questions later. If he left the gun behind, he was defense-
less. Ben slid the weapon into his jacket pocket. There was no sense
deluding himself. The FBI had shot at him twice. He was in a fight for
his life.

The Professor, who was about twenty pounds heavier than Ben,
entered the passenger side of the Plymouth gingerly, wary of the front
wheel teetering over the ledge on the other side. Ben was even more

cautious entering the driver's side. Their fears proved for naught, though, as the three wheels on firm ground proved sufficient for the task.

"What's your twenty, Agent Simmons?" the radio crackled. Ben and the Professor looked at each other.

Ben picked up the transmitter. He put his hand over his mouth to muffle his voice. "Suspects are approaching the summit of Jiminy Peak and proceeding cautiously," Ben said.

"Roger that," the voice answered.

Ben and the Professor descended back down the western slope of Jiminy Peak in the Plymouth, with Ben at the wheel. Five minutes later, Ben picked up the transmitter, again. "Simmons here," he said.

"Go ahead, Simmons."

Ben tried to add urgency to his voice. "Suspects have evacuated the vehicle and are proceeding on foot down the eastern slope of Jiminy Peak! I am following on foot. We need all hands covering the base of the eastern slope of Jiminy Peak. All hands!"

"Roger that, Simmons. We'll handle it."

Within seconds, they heard the bulletin broadcast over the radio. The roadblocks were lifted. Forty-five minutes later Ben and the Professor heard a second bulletin broadcasted to all hands. Shortly thereafter they abandoned the unmarked car near Troy, New York, just north of Albany.

Ben called Ray Allgood at his office in Bethesda, warning him to report the Taurus stolen and to take any precautions for his family he deemed appropriate. A taxi took Ben and the Professor to Albany, where the Professor rented a brown Toyota Corolla. He signed the rental agreement as "M. Caldwell." The rental went undetected by the FBI, which was searching for car rentals or airplane or train ticket purchases by anyone with the name of Kravner, Pierce or Maxwell.

FORTY

THE PRESIDENT'S NEW YEAR'S EVE GALA at the Kennedy Center was still in full swing at one o'clock in the morning. The President and the First Lady had left the party after the President's midnight toast, but most of the five hundred invited guests remained, drinking and dancing the night away to the Big Band sound of the Lyle Bradshaw Quintet.

The entire Rooftop Level of the Kennedy Center had been converted to an elegant party hall. There was dancing on the long, narrow parquet floors of the South Foyer, an exquisite buffet dinner was served in the North Foyer, and the rich and famous mingled over drinks in the red-carpeted atrium between them. A giant Douglas fir decorated with holiday ornaments reached nearly to the top of the twenty-foot ceiling in the atrium. Small cocktail tables lined each room.

Ray Allgood, decked out in black tie and tails, sat glumly, alone, at a cocktail table in the corner of the North Foyer overlooking the Potomac River. He was nursing a bourbon, straight up, while Claire mingled with the Washington elite in the atrium. She had been disappointed that Ray was not in a dancing mood.

Ray had been honored to receive the invitation to the Gala. It had crossed his mind that he was invited more to fill a quota for distinguished African-Americans in government service than for his personal accomplishments, but Claire had been excited and he had been proud. His mood had gone deep south earlier in the day.

The call from Ben Kravner had alarmed him. Now the Knights had surely connected him to Ben. The pressure upon them would build as they sensed that another leak had sprung in the dyke. Would they keep trying to plug the leaks, kidnapping or murdering all those that stepped in their way, or would they let the floodwaters break through, unleashing the Second Civil War before the appointed time?

Ray took another sip of his drink. He was not like Ben. He had a family. He could not hide. Could he fight back? He had no significant contacts in the Washington establishment. He was a doctor, damn it. For the first time he wished he had played the Washington game, attended more cocktail parties, politicked to improve his position. Like Cal Stewart had done.

He felt trapped, helpless. He made a decision. He would tell Claire everything the next morning. Together they would decide what to do with their lives with everything on the table. It would be agonizing, but there was no other way.

Ray took his glass in hand and roamed among the shoulder-to-shoulder crowd, first in the North Foyer, then the atrium, looking for Claire. He saw her along the perimeter of the atrium talking animatedly with a slender young African-American woman. The woman was pretty enough to be a model or an actress. He quelled the impure thought that so naturally flashed into his mind. *Never again.*

Ray observed from afar as a steward in a white tuxedo handed a note to the young lady speaking with Claire. The woman looked surprised, then excused herself, slinking away gracefully, like a cat.

Then Ray's eyes met Claire's from across the room. She smiled. She was beautiful, too. After all these years of marriage, he was still in love with her. The notes of a familiar tune floated into the atrium from the South Foyer. For one more night his life would be normal. He set his glass down on a table. A beautiful lady who still loved him needed to dance.

LAROSA SMITH WAS SURPRISED to receive a message on New Year's Eve. Tony Fabrizio was still at the party with his wife. Who else would be summoning her at this hour? She opened the unsealed envelope. "*Sancho needs to speak with you urgently.*"

It was Ben. Her heart raced. She asked the steward if there was someone waiting for her downstairs, then apologized to Claire Allgood when told that a man was expecting her reply.

The steward escorted LaRosa to the elevator in the South Foyer, which descended to the Hall of Nations on the first floor. He led her to a makeshift security desk in the Grand Foyer, a cavernous hallway with ornate glass chandeliers swooping down from a sixty-five foot ceiling.

She was surprised to find an older man, probably in his mid-fifties, waiting for her. He was a large, muscular man with sharp, angular features and a military-style buzz cut. She recalled Ben's warning that the FBI was involved in his conspiracy. Was Buzz Cut an agent looking to tie up a loose end? The man forced a smile. *Something's not right, girl.* LaRosa turned to flee.

"Miss Smith, wait!" Buzz Cut shouted, putting a hand on her shoulder. A brawny younger man in a tuxedo stepped between LaRosa and Buzz Cut from behind the security desk.

"Back off, sir," the Tuxedo said, patting the bulge of a weapon under his coat. "Secret Service. Is everything okay, Miss Smith?"

LaRosa looked into Buzz Cut's eyes. "I'm a friend of Sancho's," he said. "We have information that we need to get to the President. Please. I need you to come with me."

He looked sincere. And surely there were many more discreet opportunities for the FBI to abduct her than at the President's Gala.

"Give me a minute," she said to the agent. "I was expecting somebody else." The Secret Service agent backed away. LaRosa led Buzz Cut out of earshot. "Where's Ben? And who are you?" she asked.

"Professor Maxwell Caldwell, at your service," Buzz Cut said, bowing and making a sweeping gesture with his arm. He was trying hard to be suave, but succeeded only in appearing goofy. There was something stiff and unpolished about him, like a London street urchin playing Lords and Ladies. "Young Ben is close by," he continued. "He asked me not to disclose the location before I was sure that you were cooperative."

"How do I know you're not FBI?" LaRosa asked.

A thoughtful look crossed the Professor's face. "I guess I'm flattered that you think I might be, but other than the fact that I don't think I look like an FBI agent, I don't know." He shrugged, then raised his arms over his head. "Blast it, frisk me and check for a gun or a badge if you're worried."

LaRosa laughed. "You'd like that wouldn't you?" she said.

The Professor smiled. "You saw right through me, honey. C'mon. Ben's at the Lincoln Memorial."

A chill breeze whipped off the Potomac, as LaRosa and the Professor hiked the short distance along the river from the Kennedy Center to the Lincoln Memorial. Ben stepped out from behind one of the twelve colossal columns at the top of the monument when LaRosa and the Professor were halfway up the forty-one marble steps.

LaRosa hardly recognized him. Only a thin layer of stubble remained of his long, silky black hair. The mustache on which he subconsciously tugged was no more. He looked pale and haggard.

Ben climbed down the steps to greet them. "Hi, Rosie," he said awkwardly. His hands were in his jacket pockets. The left corner of his mouth curled up into a crooked grin. "It's been a long time."

LaRosa swallowed hard. It was the same old Ben. Few words. Awkward. Heart on his sleeve. It was not the heart of a felon.

"Let's get some coffee at my office," LaRosa said. "I need to sober up and hear your story."

FORTY-ONE

RAY ALLGOOD STARED at the ceiling. Claire lay in bed next to him under the covers, purring quietly, her naked body spooned into his. It was New Year's Day, and the new year had brought new ideas. They had not taken a family vacation in a long time. Stanton and Diana could afford to miss a couple of weeks of school. A European vacation would be educational, after all. There was no need to alarm Claire and the kids. *No need to throw away a lifetime.* Yes, a vacation was a better alternative than a confession. He would make the arrangements on Monday.

THE BAHAMAS. BERMUDA. WAIKIKI. Christy Kirk shivered. The sun's warming rays had lifted above the horizon almost two hours ago, but no amount of mind control could convince her semi-frozen body that Langtry, Colorado, in the foothills of the Rocky Mountains, was a tropical paradise. Not after a three-hour stakeout amidst the snow drifts on New Year's Day.

It had not been as difficult to learn the location of the Super Conference as Christy had imagined. Over the past month, she had expanded her network, finding that by and large white supremacists, particularly the rank and file, were not particularly bright. By dropping hints that she was in the know, she had accumulated bits and pieces of information from several contacts. The low level members generally had not known details, but most had been eager to share what they did know, off the record, to impress her with their status.

By the time she had spoken with Gar Henderson, the Exalted Cyclops for the Klan in Yadkin County, North Carolina, she had enough information to convince him that she knew all about the Super Conference, then she had leaned on him for the details after he confirmed it. He had reluctantly told all, swearing her to secrecy, after she threatened to inform some of the more temperamental leaders of his indiscretion.

Christy raised her binoculars. Gray smoke rose from the chimney of the main lodge, a gigantic log cabin in the center of the forty-acre Aryan Kingdom compound. The trees had been cleared for several hundred yards around the ten-foot barbed wire fence that surrounded the facility. She did not see any guards patrolling the perimeter. Two armed sentries stood watch at the main gate. A handful of burly men exercised lightly in the yard.

Christy had positioned herself near the base of the tree line on the ridge facing the rear of the camp. She had a clear view of most of the buildings inside. Six log bunkhouses surrounded the main lodge—two on the north side, two on the south side and two in the rear, directly in front of Christy. The northern half of the compound, to Christy's left, was a training ground—an obstacle course, a shooting range and some sort of pit. The only structure was a long, narrow blockhouse, which Christy guessed contained munitions.

The choice of the Aryan Kingdom's compound for the Super Conference was ominous. The group was led by Samuel Diggs, one of the fiercest and most vocal believers in the tenets of Christian Identity. Diggs was among those who expected the new millennium to bring about a race war that would introduce the "era of perfection," when all non-Aryan people would be eliminated or expelled.

The incident at Fort Bragg had made Christy wonder how far these lunatics were willing to go to help fulfill that prophecy. Were there links between the Armed Forces and the white supremacy movement as Tom Hardy had implied? Were they preparing to draw the NOMAADs into a bloody battle of the races?

Christy hoped that the answers might lie in the Super Conference—a "leaders only" meeting of the most powerful white supremacy groups and anti-government militia. Over two hundred vicious, hateful men gathered in one place. If these groups unified, they would massacre the fledgling NOMAADs. If they had the backing of the United States military, well, Christy shuddered at the possibilities. Either way, it was the news story of the century, a story that Christy knew she was becoming a part of, a story that could propel her into the spotlight—as a reporter *and* as a national heroine.

Adams Thompson's words on the day she had pleaded for this assignment echoed in her mind. "Good newspapermen report the news, they don't make it." Unfortunately, that helpful tidbit was in conflict with Christy Kirk's third rule of journalism—dare to write the great story.

Shortly before nine o'clock, the activity in the compound increased. Dozens of figures began filing from the bunkhouses to the main lodge. The yard had emptied by five after nine. Christy waited five more minutes to make sure there were no stragglers. She scanned the grounds one final time with the binoculars. The sentries at the main gate were the only people visible.

Christy did not hesitate. Somewhere deep inside of her a neon warning light flashed, but she chose to see only visions of fame and glory. *No great story was without risk.* That's what she had told Roger Martin. She emerged from behind the pines, backpack slung over one shoulder, and bounded down the ridge in full winter regalia—green ski jacket, navy blue nylon pants and enough layers below them to clothe a family of four—her heart in her throat the entire way.

The barbed wire fence was penetrated quickly with a pair of cheap hardware store wire cutters. Christy shuffled through the snow, her shoulders bent low, using one of the empty bunkhouses for cover. She peered around the corner. The main lodge was only twenty yards away. There were several windows on the rear wall. The side wall was windowless, but there was no way to circle completely around without being exposed to the windows for at least two or three seconds.

She took a deep breath of the frigid, pine-scented air, then made a dash for the side wall. She caught her breath, then prowled cautiously around the corner, hunched over below window level, stopping under the first window. She peeked inside. It was the kitchen. She crept over to the next window. The room was packed with men.

Christy fumbled through her knapsack, then removed a small black box, a sophisticated electronic listening device that she had purchased two days earlier from one of dozens of web sites catering to the amateur spy. The electro-acoustic receiver was packaged by the manufacturer as a device for the diagnosis of plumbing leaks because of its ability to pick up tiny vibrations such as those made by dripping water, but most sales were for the purpose of illegal surveillance. Christy had tested it against her neighbor's apartment door, and it amplified voices with exceptional clarity. Two output jacks allowed her to listen and record at the same time.

Christy moved quickly now. She attached the small ceramic receiver to the lower corner of the window with medical tape, then slipped on the headset. A man's resounding, unaccented voice was clearly audible. He spoke in a measured cadence, like a preacher from a pulpit.

"—in common. We have each tended our own flock over the years, strong men destined to lead, but we are guided by a singular vision— God's vision. The Book of Revelations tells us that He is the Beginning and the Ending of all things and foretells the warning signs that the End is coming. Many men of God have seen the warning signs as the twentieth century winds down and have predicted that the dawn of the new millennium will mark the beginning of the End. My friends, they were right. The time of the Apocalypse is now."

CAL STEWART ROLLED HIS EYES. He looked at Buddy Frederick to his left. Buddy mouthed the words, "What a fucking idiot."

But he was their fucking idiot. Samuel Diggs was a charismatic and powerful man. Not only would his flock follow him unquestioningly into holy war, but he was respected by most of the other white supremacist leaders, as well. Stewart found this odd, because Diggs was not the stereotypical, macho white supremacist bully. He was somewhat meek in appearance—only average in height and build, wire-rimmed glasses, neatly trimmed hair and goatee—but he exuded intelligence and confidence. He almost made this bullshit seem credible.

Stewart looked around the room. Many were already nodding in agreement. *Whatever it took.*

The main lodge was the central meeting place for the members of the Aryan Kingdom. As one entered the room through the main door, there was a rudimentary kitchen to the far right, a stage with a lectern to the far left. In the center, which was most of the expansive meeting hall, there were ten rows of institutional fiberglass tables with attached benches.

Samuel Diggs stood at the lectern on stage. The room was packed solid, every man intently focused on the speaker.

"The preservation of our race is demanded and directed by God," Diggs continued indignantly, pounding the lectern. He used his hands constantly when he spoke, to dramatic effect. "*We* are the descendants of the twelve tribes of Israel. The descendants of Cain, the Jews, are the children of Satan, and they have intermarried with the Africans to pro- duce a Godless subhuman species of mud people. These mongrels have crept among us and are destroying the social fabric of America. Forced integration, under the control of Jew lawyers and government officials, is destroying our schools, our neighborhoods, our cities and ultimately our nation. High illegitimate birthrates among blacks and other non- Aryan peoples will one day make them the majority and give them political control of our country—just as they now control major cities."

Stewart knew the alliance with the white supremacists was necessary to assure the success of their plan, but it made him uneasy nonetheless. His own rage had been inherited from his father and was rooted in a wrong that had been committed against his ancestor. These men believed—truly believed—that their hate was ordained by God, and their zeal for bloodshed exceeded that of all the Knights, with the pos- sible exception of The Spy.

Gerry Kate had not been able to attend the Super Conference. He was preoccupied with the manhunt for that pesky lawyer. But Stewart had met the others for the first time, and he was relieved to find that JJ Alexander was of a similar mind. He believed that a brief civil war would be necessary to gain power and enact the sweeping legal changes necessary to put blacks in their rightful place, but Alexander would not support the widespread murder of innocent men, women and children.

"The Book of Revelations tells us that those who patiently obey God despite their persecution will be protected in the time of Great Tribulation and Temptation, and the conquerors will be made pillars in the temple of God and citizens of the new Jerusalem, a city of heaven on earth," Diggs continued.

"We are the conquerors!" he exclaimed, his fist pounding the air violently. "We have prepared our followers for the Great Tribulation by providing them with military training, building fortifications, stockpil- ing weapons and supplies, and educating ourselves of our responsibili- ty as rulers of the everlasting Aryan Kingdom, waiting only for the sig- nal from God that the Apocalypse is upon us."

Stewart surveyed the room with concern. He wondered if The Heir Apparent had the power to stop this leviathan they were about to unleash.

"That day of reckoning is near," Diggs said. "The new millennium will bring the long-awaited battle between the children of darkness and the children of light, the Aryan Race, the true Israel of the bible. *We will be the hand of God! We must—*"

"Samuel!" A tall man said, rising to his feet in the center of the great room. He was the only man in the room wearing a sport jacket. Stewart recognized him as Bryn Cook, the Grand Dragon of the American Association for the Advancement of White Persons, a relatively sophisticated splinter group of the Ku Klux Klan and one of the largest groups represented. Stewart leaned forward expectantly.

"I think I speak for most of us in this room when I say that you're preaching to the choir," Cook said. "We're all prepared to become martyrs to reserve our place in the Kingdom of God. But who are you to declare yourself the leader of this rebellion? It's God's fight and God will pick his own leaders and God will let us know when the time has come to fight the good fight."

There was a general murmur of agreement throughout the room. Stewart and Frederick glanced at each other apprehensively. All previous efforts to unite the white supremacy groups had failed because of leadership disputes. This was the moment of truth.

"This is not my Conference," Diggs said. "God *has* spoken. There are four men among us who have been sent to lead us into battle." He paused for effect. "My friends, we are in the presence of the Four Horsemen of the Apocalypse."

AT FIRST THERE WAS SILENCE, then an unsettling buzz of excitement. These men did not strike Christy as the type to buzz excitedly. Temptation got the better of her judgment. She leaned her back against the wall, beside the window, and rose only enough to raise her eyes above the sill. She peered inside, shielding her eyes to lessen the glare off the glass, as an eerie scene unfolded.

STEWART AND FREDERICK SMILED at the wide-eyed reaction of the soon-to-be Generals of the Unified Forces of the Aryan Knights of the Millennium. Four men strode dramatically out of the wings to center stage, forming a semi-circle around Samuel Diggs at the lectern. They were clad in velvet robes with gilded linings, their faces concealed by pointed hoods, all in the colors of the Four Horsemen of the Apocalypse as described in the New Testament—from left to right, white, red, black and pale.

Diggs addressed the awestruck audience. "These are men of power. Their identities will shock you. Under direct instructions from God they have infiltrated the highest reaches of government, and they are prepared to lead the Aryan people in the holy war. But, as you can understand, they are reluctant to reveal themselves to non-Believers before the appointed time. If there are any among us who are not pre- pared to be guided by the hand of God in the Holy War, then renounce your place in the Kingdom of God now!"

Diggs surveyed the room, a much-practiced look of fury etched into his features. Cal Stewart's eyes followed Diggs's gaze. The men were spellbound. Then Stewart saw something in the rear window. He nudged Frederick. They rose and walked towards the front door of the lodge. Stewart felt the angry stares. Nobody else rose to leave.

"Only two cowards who refuse to fight God's fight?" Diggs asked, scanning the room imperiously once more. "Then my Aryan brothers, I give you the Royal Commanders of the Unified Forces of the Aryan Knights of the Millennium."

CHRISTY WAS ENTRANCED. The scene unfolding before her was more incredible than any scenario she had imagined.

Diggs stepped down off the stage and claimed an empty chair in the first row. The man in the white robe lifted his hood. It was John Daniel, the Speaker of the House of Representatives. A palpable excite- ment filled the room, mixed with a collective sigh of relief that Samuel Diggs had not tricked them into anointing him their leader.

Then the red hood was lifted, revealing Ty Andrew, the Majority Leader in the Senate. The suspense was starting to build. The black hood came off. The Conference roared its approval when Clint Glenn, the Chairman of the Joint Chiefs of Staff, the man who oversaw the entire United States military force, was exposed. They now began to see the enormity of the opportunity that had been delivered to them.

Christy was stunned. Colonel Hardy could not have had any idea how deep the white supremacy movement had penetrated the military. Then she gasped. The Super Conference erupted into pandemonium. The pale hood had been peeled off to reveal JJ Alexander's weather- beaten face.

All of the men in the lodge simultaneously leaped to their feet, applauding, howling like wolves and stomping their feet. Their dream, viewed as evil but unachievable by mainstream Americans, was about to become reality. These men, unified in purpose but long separated by ego, became one, a singular malevolent force that was at the same time electrifying and frightening.

Christy shuddered. For the first time her fear overcame her zeal to write the story. These were the *leaders* of the white supremacy movement, and they had been so easily moved to follow. What hope was there that their followers would see the irrationality of the slaughter they were planning?

Her fear intensified as the possible permutations fell into place in her mind's eye. The story was even bigger than a racial holocaust. JJ Alexander was a shoo-in to be the next vice president of the United States. One bullet from an Aryan assassin's rifle and he would be president. And General Glenn controlled the United States military. *They were planning a coup.* The entire nation was at risk.

Christy yanked off her headset and stuffed it and the black box into her knapsack. She removed the micro-cassette from her recorder, slipped it under her nylon pants into the back pocket of her jeans and inserted a fresh one into the recorder. As she was lifting her knapsack, she saw a small-framed man turn the far corner of the lodge.

Cal Stewart stared directly at her. Christy's eyes widened; her stomach rose into her throat. Stewart's sinister smile paralyzed her for a split second, then she darted in the opposite direction, still looking over her shoulder, straight into the waiting arms of Buddy Frederick.

JJ ALEXANDER ALLOWED THE MEN'S PASSION, *his* men's passion, to build into a frenzy. They would need that enthusiasm to rouse their followers to action. Soon. Very soon. Things were not going as planned. Ben Kravner had slipped through their net yet again. And now it seemed that he had somehow, incredibly, come into contact with Ray Allgood, the man who was to take the fall for igniting the Second Civil War. Or the Holy War. Whatever they wanted to call it, it had to start soon.

Finally, Alexander approached the lectern. He raised his arms to signal the boisterous mob to quiet. "The dawn of a new era of perfection is upon us. God has called upon you to prepare for this moment, and you have individually met the challenge. You have sought out the true believers and prepared them for the coming holy war. You have trained them, armed them and reinforced their spirit. Your forces, fighting in isolation, could hinder the forces of Satan, but you would ultimately be defeated. This Goliath will not fall by the slingshot. But if we stand united, as the Unified Forces of the Aryan Knights of the Millennium, *we* become the Goliath to Satan's David. *We* wield the power to cleanse our land of Satan's followers."

The Heir Apparent turned and pointed to The General behind him. "Under the leadership of General Glenn, it is imperative that the Unified Forces assemble and begin to train immediately. The Apocalypse is closer than you think. In his great wisdom and with an almighty sense of irony, God has commanded us to commence the Holy War on Monday, January 17, 2000—the day the birth of Satan's mongrel child, Martin Luther King, is commemorated. We will meet with each of you, the Generals of the Unified Forces, this weekend to discuss our strategic battle plans, the strength of your forces, their tactical role in the Holy War and—"

Alexander was interrupted by a commotion at the main entrance. His audience's attention was diverted when Cal Stewart and Buddy Frederick burst through the door, holding back a struggling Christy Kirk.

CHRISTY WAS KICKING Stewart and Frederick and unleashing an onslaught of vile invective that would have made any of the Generals or their legion proud and their mothers blush. Most of them seemed to find the scene amusing. "Well, well, what do we have here?" Alexander asked.

"We saw her outside the window," Cal Stewart said. He held up her tape recorder. "It looks like she was taping the Conference."

One of the Generals rose to his feet in the center of the room. It was Franklin Verdant. "That bitch is a reporter for the *New York Herald Times*. She interviewed me a few weeks ago," Verdant boomed. "Her name is Christy Kirk."

"Well, Miss Kirk, do you have anything to say for yourself?" Alexander asked. "As you know, this is private property and this is a very private meeting."

Christy glared at him scornfully. "Fuck you," she said and spat in his direction. Her heart raced, but she was determined to present a brave front. Her eyes darted from face to face, searching for options, but finding only bloodlust in the souls of the men that controlled her destiny. Diggs and Alexander had incited them into a fervor. A chill ran down her spine.

"What shall we do with her, gentlemen?" Alexander asked expectantly.

Several suggestions were shouted, most of which laid claim to either Christy's virtue or her life. Dizziness overcame her. The shouts began to blend together. She felt the two men gripping her arms firmly, but the rest of the room faded into the distance as her mind transported her to another time, another place—a defense to the sinking realization that this episode was not going to end well.

Alexander stepped down off the stage and spoke quietly with Samuel Diggs, then returned to the lectern. "Gentlemen," he said into the microphone. The shouting continued. "Gentlemen!" The mob settled. Alexander continued forcefully, his voice resonating throughout the room. "Mr. Diggs has proposed that we let Miss Kirk spend a night in the brig. Her fate will be decided tomorrow."

TONY FABRIZIO, wearing a baggy Notre Dame sweatshirt and blue jeans, paced beside the mahogany conference table that dominated the center of his palatial office. Ben could already tell that he was not going to be as easy to win over as LaRosa had been. He still had the mind of a prosecutor, and he was skeptical about the evidence that had been presented to him. It was his life on the line, yet Fabrizio remained tough and fair-minded.

Ben, LaRosa and Max Caldwell were huddled at one end of the massive table. LaRosa had warned that Fabrizio might be difficult, and it was agreed that she would lead the discussion. The Vice President stopped pacing and faced them.

"It would make an interesting novel," he said. "But I'm not sure I buy it in a court of law. There are too many leaps of faith that strain credibility."

"We admit the evidence is mostly circumstantial," LaRosa said. "But you can get a conviction on circumstantial evidence if there's no *reasonable* doubt."

"But I have doubts myself," Fabrizio said. "For example, I have my doubts about the evidentiary value of the Poem."

The evidentiary value of the Poem. The words cut through Ben like the sound of fingernails scratching on a chalkboard. He had not told LaRosa about the sealed envelope. He had agreed with Debby that he would unseal the envelope again and burn it this time. But the sealed envelope was still in Kramer, Fox's vault. Had Fabrizio somehow guessed his ethical breach?

"The defense will argue that it's fiction, written either by Adams Thompson for his own amusement or by Ben or Debby as a creative alibi for their crimes," Fabrizio said.

Ben relaxed. No, his secret was safe. He could discreetly dispose of the sealed envelope and the trust document when he recovered the Poem from the vault.

"Ben said that the Poem was written on old, tattered paper," LaRosa said. "Can't forensic experts prove that it was written in the mid-1800s?"

"That's true," Fabrizio said. "Okay, let's assume that the Poem wasn't written recently. How do we prove it's not fiction?"

"Well, that's the essence of the case," LaRosa said. "It's the 20-Year Jinx. The presidents have died in office every twenty years, just as ordained by the Poem."

"But the Poem is vague," Fabrizio said. "It speaks of acts of vengeance, never of a specific crime."

"History has revealed the nature of the crime," LaRosa argued. "That's not too big a leap for a jury to make. The MacDougalls blamed William Henry Harrison for their brother's execution. They vowed payback against the presidency. Tit for tat."

"Even if a jury buys the Jinx thing, we still can't prove that the modern day Knights agreed to commit a crime," Fabrizio said. "We can't charge them for offenses perpetrated by their ancestors."

Ben was amazed at the sharpness of Fabrizio's mind. He was forcing them to cast aside intuition and make the case more rigorously than they had done before. But LaRosa was holding her own. She was every bit as brilliant as he remembered from law school.

"But the pattern of assassinations by their family in accordance with the Poem is evidence of an agreement by the present generation to continue the pattern," LaRosa said confidently. "Especially when their actions provide corroboration."

"Okay, let's try another tack," Fabrizio said. "Let's assume that there is in fact a conspiracy to assassinate the next president. There's no direct link between the Poem and the group of men you claim are acting in concert. How do you connect your suspects to this family that supposedly disappeared 160 years ago?"

"Perhaps the data that I've collected will be of some service," Professor Caldwell said. "We can associate one member of each Knight's family to one dead president."

"That's an unusual coincidence, Professor, but none of them pulled the trigger," Fabrizio said. "It also doesn't tie them back to the MacDougalls."

"But the coincidences are mounting," LaRosa said. "All of the suspected Knights are linked together by a naming convention derived from the names of the first nine presidents and vice presidents and the MacDougall siblings, once again tying the Knights to the MacDougalls and to presidents. I'm willing to bet that, with the help of the CIA, we'll be able to show that the MacDougall family disappeared around 1840 and that the ancestry of each of our suspects can be traced back to that time and no further."

Ben pumped his arm under the table. *Way to go, Rosie. You've got him.*

"I'm still not convinced," Fabrizio said.

Damn! Enough is enough, Ben thought. He reminded himself that this was the Vice President of the United States talking, and he held his tongue in check.

"Before we call in the hounds, we need to make sure we can articulate a winning case against the suspects. You've made a credible argument for the conspiracy against the first seven presidents, but The Assassin is dead. How can we prove that the remaining Knights still intend to carry out the assassination? Just because their parents gave them the names doesn't mean they're prepared to do the crime."

Ben silently fumed. *The Jinx was real!* He had eavesdropped on the Knights in the Millennium Nights room. Vice President or not, Fabrizio was missing the big picture. The country was in jeopardy, and he was dwelling on niggling details. Fritz Fox's wary voice echoed in Ben's mind. *Patience, young Ben. Patience.*

LaRosa opened her mouth to address Fabrizio's point, but Ben interrupted before she could begin.

"For crissakes, I saw them talking about me and Debby in the Millennium Nights room," Ben heard himself say. He could tell from Fabrizio's obvious astonishment that his tone was sharp. A mental image of Fritz Fox slapping his hand against his bald crown popped into Ben's mind. *Oy vey. Too late.*

Ben plowed ahead. "Whether or not we can prove the case in a court of law, we *know* that these guys are out to kill you and launch a race war and their actions support that intent!" Ben said, then began ticking off the Knights' actions on his fingers. "Thompson's inflammatory editorials, General Glenn's proposal to segregate the military, John Daniel's son showing up in the middle of the Fort Bragg incident, Dean Frederick telling me the story of the MacDougalls, Gerry Kate fabricating charges against me and launching a nationwide manhunt, JJ Alexander setting himself up as the next vice president, Ty Andrew giving you a sly push in that direction, and Cal Stewart setting up Ray Allgood to trigger the Second Civil War. We can't sit by and let this happen because we can't work out a few technicalities!"

Silence. LaRosa bit her lip. Fabrizio maintained his composure. His eyes locked with Ben's. "I believe you, son," he said. "And I admire your passion. But these are powerful men we're up against, and they'll hire the best lawyers. We can't risk embarrassing the President by accusing them of treason with a half-baked case."

"But we know in our hearts that the conspiracy is real," LaRosa said. "With the CIA's help, we can build a case that's plausible enough to avoid a public relations nightmare. At least we'll stop these nuts from taking over the country—and killing you."

Fabrizio began to pace alongside the table, again. Ben was sure the Vice President would come around. Once he got past the technicalities, the evidence was overwhelming. *Technicalities—like the sealed envelope.* Ben wondered once again whether he should disclose his ethical slip. But he had been over this before with Debby. She was right. He could not pass the buck. It was his duty to destroy the envelope in Kramer, Fox's vault and the first envelope that was still in his desk at home. *Oh God.*

Clong! In that moment, terror struck. He had left the original envelope with the broken seal in his apartment. It was in the hands of the FBI now—the hands of the Knights. The defense could prove that he had opened the sealed envelope, and the Poem would be inadmissible in court. *There's got to be a way out of this. Think!*

"Okay, you've convinced me," Fabrizio said. "The facts are too undeveloped to bring to the President yet, but let's see what the CIA can find."

LaRosa frowned. "The CIA is prohibited from collecting information on Americans by executive order," she said. "You need to talk to Hank immediately if you want to override that order."

"What about another executive agency, like the Secret Service?" Fabrizio asked.

"The FBI has exclusive jurisdiction over the collection of information on Americans unless special procedures are agreed with the head of the agency and the Attorney General," LaRosa said. "If we're trying to keep the FBI out of the loop, you probably don't want to involve Dan Raskin. The Attorney General is Gerry Kate's boss," she said for the benefit of Ben and the Professor. "He'd be interacting with Kate on a daily basis, and he might inadvertently tip Kate off."

"I'll talk to the President this morning and get Frank Garcia over at CIA into the loop," Fabrizio said. "One last point. The announcement of this conspiracy to the public will be mind-blowing. These are men at the highest level of government guiding the nation into a race war. I've accepted their leader as my running mate. We need to have a reaction prepared. It has to be big, and it has to be bold."

LaRosa bobbed her head vigorously in agreement. "If we're going to drop a bomb like that, we'd better be ready to defuse it," she said. "The President's State of the Union address is scheduled for Tuesday, the 18th. That would give us just over two weeks to build our case and prepare a response."

Ben frowned. "Are we giving the Knights too much time?" he asked. "They may already have contrived the Fort Bragg incident because of me. Now they know I've been in contact with Ray Allgood. They may feel pressure to act quickly."

"They'll have to leak the story about the racially biased experimentation or some other triggering event before they launch an attack," Fabrizio said. "The CIA will need at least a week for their investigation, anyway. Rosie, I know you've got a lot on your plate, but can you think about what Hank should say in the State of the Union address?"

"You got it, Chief," she said.

"Well, I think that wraps this meeting up," Fabrizio said. "The Rose Bowl beckons."

Ben tensed. The Poem was inadmissible. He could not lead the Vice President of the United States on a wild goose chase. *Think!*

"Professor Caldwell, it's been a pleasure," Fabrizio said. "You've done a great service to your country, and I'm sure we'll speak again. We'll arrange protection for you and your wife."

"Thank you very much, Mr. Vice President," the Professor said. "The pleasure has been all mine."

Then the Vice President turned to Ben. Ben's heart pounded. They needed another, untainted copy of the Poem. But without Thompson's copy, they would not have probable cause to search the residences of the other Knights.

"Ben, I believe your story, but you're a fugitive from the FBI," Fabrizio said. "I'm placing you under house arrest. We'll set you up with a cot in one of the empty offices down the hall and post a Secret Service agent outside."

Ben's mind spun desperately. "I understand," he said. *Think!* Debby's copy of the Poem was no doubt in the hands of the FBI, too, and it was just a photocopy, anyway. The Assassin probably had the original. *The Assassin.*

Fabrizio started to rise, his large hands gripping the edge of the table. "Any questions? Final thoughts?"

Now or never. "I've got one," Ben said. He felt his voice tremble. Fabrizio shifted his weight back into the chair, then looked at his watch.

"The Poem was in a sealed envelope when I found it in Thompson's safe deposit box," Ben said. "I later discovered that the envelope was the object of a trust agreement and shouldn't have been opened. I resealed the original copy of the Poem, but I left the envelope with the broken seal in my apartment. I'm afraid the FBI has it now."

Fabrizio's jaw dropped. "Then your copy of the Poem is inadmissible in court," he said incredulously. "Your case depends on it."

Ben glanced over at LaRosa. She looked away, her lips pressed together tightly. "I've got an idea, though," Ben said. "Debby Barnett's photocopy of the Poem is probably in the FBI's hands, too, but her brother must have the original. If we can find The Assassin, we've got an admissible copy of the Poem."

FORTY-TWO

THEY CALLED IT HOUSE ARREST, but to Ben it was sanctuary. For the first time in nine days he awakened confident that he
would live to wake another day. He rested on the fold-up cot that had
been imported into the office adjacent to LaRosa's, staring up at the
elaborate stenciled pattern on the ceiling.

Ben's mind turned to Debby. He had ceased to obsess over her, and
that made him feel guilty. Viewed from a distance, he could not
remember how much of the relationship had been the product of her
manipulation and how much had been real emotional sharing. He
would fight for her, as a friend, but he questioned the love that had
once seemed so real.

Ben stuck his head outside the office door. A man in the uniform of
the Secret Service was seated on a chair in the hallway.

"Mornin'," Ben mumbled.

"Good morning. I'm Chuck Carlisle, your host for the day," the
man said cheerfully. Agent Carlisle was balding, about forty years old,
but appeared to be in near-perfect physical condition. He tossed Ben a
white towel that had been draped over the back of his chair.

Ben's eyes were drawn to the service revolver holstered on Agent
Carlisle's waist. "No need to toss in the towel," Ben cracked. "I'm
unarmed."

Carlisle grinned. "Let's get you cleaned up," he said. "Rosie told me
she'd bring you some clean clothes this morning."

LaRosa was puttering in her office when Ben and Agent Carlisle
returned from the washroom. Ben knocked on the door. He tried to
hide his apprehension behind a mask of good cheer. "Mornin', Rosie,"
he said. "Sorry about that bomb I dropped on you yesterday."

LaRosa smiled awkwardly. Ben saw no anger in her eyes, just sadness. "I left a bag of clothes on your cot," she said. Ben was still wearing the second hand clothes from the Salvation Army thrift shop. They reeked of body odor. "Why don't you change and then we can talk."

Ben returned shortly, clad in a dark green polo shirt and blue jeans. "Perfect fit," Ben said. "Thanks, Rosie."

LaRosa motioned for him to close the door, which he did, then he claimed a chair opposite her desk. She still seemed uneasy. Ben knew that this was about more than the sealed envelope. It was about a moment forever burned in their souls. Ben remembered the exact date—May 25, 1996. The Saturday night before LaRosa's law school graduation. The moment he had peered into her eyes and seen love.

Ben stole a glance at her eyes now. They were moist. He had lived with his own pain and guilt for months after that day, emotions that had softened with time but still panged whenever he saw the name of Quixote on his CyberLine PenPal list.

"I can't tell you how many times I almost called you," Ben said, breaking the uncomfortable silence. "I was so embarrassed about standing you up in front of your family at graduation. But it was hard to pick up the telephone, and days turned into weeks and weeks into months. You know how it is. It just gets tougher and tougher."

Ben saw LaRosa fighting within herself for the courage to speak her mind. No one was better at articulating complex legal and social issues, but she had always struggled with sharing her emotions. It was difficult for him, too, but people seemed to *know* how he felt. Somehow he telegraphed his emotions in a way that was both a blessing and a curse.

"I loved you," she said finally, her voice quivering. "I thought you loved me, too. I would have slept with you that night if you kissed me."

"I know," Ben said, squirming. "I wanted to. Something held me back."

"I've wanted to know what that something was for three and a half years," Rosie said. She had a pained, almost mournful expression. "I believe you're innocent, and I'll help you no matter what you say. But I need to know why you didn't kiss me that night. Why didn't you show up at my graduation? Why—"

"Why did I shut the closest friend I have ever had out of my life?" Ben interrupted.

"Yeah. Just, why?"

Ben paused to collect his thoughts. He owed her an honest answer. "I struggled with that question for a long time," he said. "I was afraid."

"Because you were falling in love for the first time? Afraid that the age difference was too great? Afraid of telling me you didn't feel the same way I did?" LaRosa asked, searching his eyes for truth.

"Those would be easy cop-outs," Ben said. "I was falling in love for the first time, but I was ready for it. I thought about the age difference, but eight years isn't all that much."

LaRosa closed her eyes. Ben saw her swallow hard. "Was it because I'm black?"

It was obvious that this was the answer she feared most, a demon that had haunted her for so many years. Their friendship had been relaxed, caring and sincere. There had been none of the edginess that characterized many of Ben's other relationships with people of color. The constant wariness in their eyes, their manner, always on alert for a hidden agenda, as if friendship could not be motive enough for a white man to talk with a black man. He gazed directly into her green eyes. They still made his heart melt.

"It's more complicated than that, but if you need to hear a short answer, it's yes," Ben said. "But please don't lodge the short answer in your mind and shut out the rest of what I have to say."

Two tears streamed down her face, one on each cheek. She nodded for him to go on; she was listening, but did not have the capacity to speak *and* hold back the floodgates.

"I was afraid of how everybody else in my life would react," Ben continued. "I had no doubts about you. I've never felt a more intimate bond with anybody, and I doubt that I ever will. But I thought about my parents and my grandparents—future employers, maybe—but mostly family. They've always been so proud of my accomplishments, and they've been dying for me to hook up with a nice Jewish girl so that we could make them perfect little grandbabies. I could picture their horror when I brought you home. It seems silly saying those thoughts out loud—they are so inconsistent with what I think I believe. But the feelings were real, and I was too embarrassed to face you."

"Nobody was talking about marriage," Rosie said sadly. "It was a kiss. We would have made love. After that, who knows. Maybe it would have ended painfully, maybe not. But when you abandoned me, that hurt me badly."

"Rosie, I was so ashamed of what I did—I still am—but I have the gift, and the curse, of being able to see the future," Ben said. "Not like one of those wacky clairvoyants. I can play events out in my mind. I see almost every alternative possible in my mind's eye, and I'm amazingly good at assessing the probability of each alternative occurring. If I kissed you that night, we would have been together for life. We were soulmates."

LaRosa wiped her eyes. "Would that have been so bad?" she asked tearfully, tacitly agreeing with the conclusion.

Ben did not hesitate. "No. It wouldn't have been bad at all," he said sincerely. "I haven't made many decisions in my life that I regret, but I wish I could do May 25, 1996 over again. I've met many more women since then, been close with a few, but nothing compares with what we had. There was an honesty to our relationship that was unique—I don't know if I can ever be that open with another person again."

"I know I can't be," LaRosa said. "I've dated some since then, but I haven't been in love. I just can't trust, anymore. My work is my passion."

"Still tilting at windmills?" he asked, smiling as he took the cue to change the subject.

She smiled back, obviously relieved to move on. "I've still got big dreams," she said.

"My fondest memories of law school are the heated debates about social issues that we all had in the cafeteria," Ben said. "Everybody had an opinion. We cared."

"We thought we could take on the world," LaRosa agreed.

"But you're the only one doing it," Ben said. "Most of us sold out to the big law firms. I'm not even two years out of law school, and I haven't had a conversation about a meaningful social issue in months. Lunchtime chatter at Kramer, Fox is about business, women or sports. The impossible dream is making partner, not making the world a better place. I haven't done Don Quixote proud."

LaRosa laughed. "Quixote isn't only about grand dreams—he's about following your dreams whatever they are and trying again and again after each failure. You haven't lived the life of Quixote unless you've tried and failed, over and over again."

"Have you had any failures?" Ben asked.

"Just in love."

"Ouch. There I go, leading with my chin, again," Ben said.

"What about you?" LaRosa asked. "How are things going at the firm?"

Ben grinned the crooked grin. "Assuming you mean before I was chased through the halls by the FBI and then accused of dealing drugs and trying to kill the senior partner, terrific."

She laughed. "Fair point. As Ricky Ricardo used to say, 'You've got some 'splaining to do, Lucy,'" she said in her best Cuban accent.

"Still hooked on old TV re-runs, I see," Ben said.

"I watch from time to time, but Tony keeps me pretty busy."

"What exactly do you do for him?" Ben asked.

"I'm his Chief of Staff," she said. "I juggle his calendar, run interference on the Hill, act as his liaison with the President's staff, and run his campaign. But mostly I'm his political sounding board. We talk about all the important issues. He's a great guy. He reminds me of you in many ways."

Ben's eyebrows shifted upwards. "How so?"

"He has an honesty that comes from his core," she said, then paused. "I thought I'd be mad at you, but I'm not. You gave me the answer that I feared the most a little while ago, but it was from your heart. It didn't hurt as badly as I thought it would."

"I'm not a racist," Ben said. "Am I?"

"No."

Ben was not content to drop it. His consciousness of race had amplified over the past week—as a wanderer through the low-income housing projects near the bus station in Washington, encircled by an angry black mob at the NOMAAD rally, as a guest in the Allgood home, and as an observer of an incredible racist conspiracy. "What makes someone a racist?" he asked.

"Pardon the pun, but I don't think the answer is black and white," LaRosa said. "The dictionary would define it as someone who thinks that a person's character and ability are determined by race. But most people think that race or ethnicity have something to do with character, and they're probably right. We all pick up our values based on the culture in which we're raised, and there are cultural differences between the races and other ethnic groups. A true racist thinks the differences are biological and can't be changed."

"A fine distinction," Ben said.

"And maybe not one that's relevant," LaRosa said. "It doesn't matter whether those that hate or discriminate or tolerate discrimination think that African-Americans are biologically flawed or just culturally different. What matters is that they think it's acceptable to treat African-Americans differently."

"But everybody has their own prejudices," Ben said. "Some people don't like Italians or Jews or Hispanics because of their cultural traits. A lot of people get married to someone from the same ethnic or racial group because of their similar backgrounds and character traits. Is that wrong?"

"I don't think so," LaRosa said. "But where do you draw the line? Is it okay to limit your choice of marital partner solely to one cultural group? How about your friends, your neighbors, your business partners or your customers?"

"Somewhere in there I know you've crossed a legal line," Ben said.

"But what's *right*?" LaRosa asked.

"Like you said, it's not black and white," Ben said. "It's probably not *right* to exclude any racial or ethnic group entirely from any of those classes."

"Including marriage partners?" LaRosa asked.

"Including marriage partners. But that doesn't mean that a person is wrong to take membership in a racial or ethnic group, or traits unique to a group, into consideration in making important life decisions," Ben said. "For me, being married to an African-American woman would carry a lot of consequences irrelevant to my relationship with the woman, like my family's reaction."

"So you're not a racist, but your family is, so it's okay to discriminate against African-Americans?" LaRosa asked.

Ben blushed. "You make it sound so stupid, but that's a fact of life," he said.

"Racism is a fact of life in this country. But it's a fact that we need to change," LaRosa said.

"So how would you change the world, Quixote?"

"We need to change people's mindset," she said. "We need to raise a generation that doesn't even think about skin color."

"Dream on."

"You know I will," LaRosa said.

Ben smiled. His feet rested on LaRosa's desk. "This reminds me of law school," he said. "I haven't thought this hard about something that's truly important in a long time."

"Well, I've got a proposition for you," LaRosa said. "More like a challenge."

"Uh-oh."

"You heard Tony yesterday. If we prove this conspiracy of yours, there's going to be a huge backlash," she said. "Tony and the President want me to spearhead the development of a program to counter it, and I hear you have some time on your hands."

"I'm flattered," Ben said sincerely. "I'll do whatever I can to help."

"For now, just think," LaRosa said. "We've got a once in a lifetime opportunity to change things, really change things. It's like law school—what would you do to solve the race problem if you didn't have to worry about politics?"

"Only this is real," Ben said.

"This is real."

CHRISTY HEARD THEM before she saw them. Her delicate frame was tied, tightly, to a post in the northeast corner of the barbed wire fence surrounding the Aryan Kingdom compound. She sobbed quietly, her spirit broken. The bone-chilling chorus of a mob overcome with bloodlust resonated over the small, snow-covered hill that separated her from her fate.

She was cold. The icy wind cut through her white wool sweater, blue jeans and thermal underwear. Stewart and Frederick had removed her ski jacket and nylon pants, her hat and her gloves.

Christy had not been to church for several months, but she began to pray. No one outside the Aryan Kingdom compound knew her whereabouts. There would be no last minute cavalry charge. No choppers swooping in, guns blazing. She prayed for her soul, not her life. She prayed for America.

The mob piled over the crest of the hill. Each man carried a firearm at his side—rifles, semi-automatic machine guns, pistols. JJ Alexander shouted, "Halt!" when the men were about one hundred feet from Christy. He instructed them to spread out across an imaginary line forming the third side of a triangle with the northern and eastern ends of the fence.

"Miss Kirk! You have been sentenced to die by firing squad for crimes against the Unified Forces of the Aryan Knights of the Millennium. Do you have any last words?" Alexander shouted.

Christy suppressed her sobs. She closed her eyes to collect herself, then reemerged, her head held high, her jaw thrust forward, resolute. "Go fuck yourself, you Nazi pig!" she screamed.

Alexander faced the men. "Gentlemen, it's time to prove your allegiance to the Unified Forces," he said in a loud, commanding voice. "Every man aims for the heart. No man can claim innocence."

Christy cringed as two hundred weapons were raised.

"Ready!" Alexander shouted impassively.

She could not decide whether she wanted to scream or vomit. *Where was the fucking cavalry, anyway?* Christy tried to look as many men in the eye as she could. Most appeared unmoved. Gar Henderson turned away. Franklin Verdant glared back at her with the contempt he wore like a Satanic mask.

"Aim!" Two hundred pairs of eyes lined up behind two hundred gun sights.

A strange calm came over Christy. Her body relaxed. Her mind stopped racing. The moment was suspended in time and space; it seemed to last forever. She squared her shoulders and thrust out her chest; she stared straight ahead, unblinking, daring death to take her with the unwavering irreverence with which she lived.

"Fire!"

SOLITARY CONFINEMENT can do strange things to a person's mind. Debby Barnett had spent most of the past nine days handcuffed to a pole in the dark, dank basement of the Maryland safe house. Almost a full week had passed since her last encounter with The Spy. Her face was still tender from The Spy's two sucker punches; she was sure her nose was broken. Her body was stiff. She had only been allowed to walk briefly each day at meal time. But the effects of sensory deprivation on her mind had been the most dramatic. She was losing it.

Debby slept as much as possible—she had lost track of night and day. When she was awake, she did not know how to pass the time. She was at the same time desperate for human company and afraid of it. She was anxious and paranoid, fearful that every creak in the floorboards signaled the approach of The Spy.

The Spy was on her mind now. She rocked gently in place, trying to connect her thoughts. It was hard to retain focus. Strike Three was next. She remembered that. If she did not tell him the truth, she would die. Would that be so bad? Death was inevitable, anyway; why prolong the agony? She wondered if she had just spoken her thoughts out loud. Did that make a difference? If a tree falls in the woods and nobody hears it, does it make a sound? What was the truth? How much of the past several months was real and how much was a dream? So many questions, no answers.

The walls were moving, again. In and out. The Spy was controlling it. He was determined to make her crazy. The sliver of light under the door was a tease. Brighter, then dimmer, brighter, then dimmer. She needed the sun. Was today Sunday? The Spy was going to pay for his mind games. She could play dead, then kick him in the head. She giggled at the rhyme, then repeated it out loud several times. What rhymes with cutting off his balls?

A loud noise, like a thunderclap, startled Debby. Panic consumed her. Were the walls falling now? The door opened. She covered her eyes to shield them from the blinding light. She heard footsteps. She rocked with her head buried in her arms, petrified.

"Good evening, Miss Barnett," The Spy said softly. *Why is he shouting?* "How are you this evening?" The Spy left the door open this time. The only light was a low wattage bulb hanging in the staircase.

Debby began to sob. "I want to go home. I want this nightmare to be over," she said. Her mouth and tongue were stiff. She spoke in a labored manner, similar to a deaf person's speech, the words slurred.

"Now, now, Miss Barnett, it's only natural to be a little disoriented in your situation," The Spy said gently. "I'm not such a bad guy. I might have been a little ill-tempered the other day because I was under a lot of pressure."

He paused, then said: "I'll make you a deal. Let's speak the truth tonight, and tomorrow maybe we can arrange a walk outside for an hour or two. Maybe even a picnic lunch. Would you like that?"

Debby wiped her eyes. "You won't hurt me if I tell you everything?"

The Spy chuckled. "Of course, not, Miss Barnett. You're a lovely woman. What kind of man do you think I am?"

She started sobbing, again. "But how do I know?" she wailed. "How do I know for sure that you won't hurt me, again? I know you're going to kill me if I talk and you're going to kill me if I don't. Just kill me, already, dammit! Get it over with—please."

The Spy squatted down in front of her. He wiped her tears with his handkerchief, then rubbed her face gently with the back of his fingers. "Miss Barnett, you have to trust me. I'm a man of my word. I will not hurt you if you tell me the truth."

She was becoming accustomed to the bright light. The Spy's face was not as menacing as she had imagined. He had a pleasant smile. At least there was hope if she submitted. "What do you want to know?" she asked.

"Tell me how you learned about The Poem," The Spy said.

"I found it in my brother's apartment."

A look of surprise crossed The Spy's face. "Your brother? I wasn't aware that you had a brother."

"I wasn't, either," Debby said. "I found a letter from him in my father's place. He's my illegitimate half brother—he's older than I am."

"Hmmm. I see. What's his name?"

There was no longer any reason to hesitate. "Van Buren Andrew Stone," Debby said. "He's The Assassin."

FORTY-THREE

A S THE WEEK WORE ON, Ben and LaRosa had wandered in and out of the other's office regularly to discuss issues, take their meals and shoot the breeze. The stiffness that had characterized their first meetings had eased. Ben had found himself full of energy despite his recent ordeal. LaRosa had also seemed perkier as the two old friends rekindled a flame long extinguished.

By the time Wednesday morning rolled around, they were ready to create law. Ben was seated in one of LaRosa's guest chairs, legs crossed, a yellow legal pad in his lap. His face was clean-shaven; a thin layer of matted black hair already covered his scalp. It was like old times. She was the teacher; he was the student.

Ben had been advocating an approach that focused on the plight of the underclass generally. He argued that legislation should focus on remedying crime, drugs, the lack of educational opportunities and the feelings of hopelessness that make it difficult for African-Americans to escape the cycle of poverty. LaRosa once again accused him of taking too academic a view of what was essentially an emotional issue.

"Discrimination is not just a poverty issue," LaRosa said, her feet resting on the desk a la Tony Fabrizio. She spoke dispassionately, as if lecturing, distancing herself from a subject that was all too near.

"Being African-American means suffering a thousand slights and subtle insults every week," she continued. "It means always wondering if you're being treated fairly and knowing that most of the time you're not. Middle class blacks live with feelings of oppression and rage that whites can't begin to understand. That emotional burden is easy to discount, but it's an enormous quality of life issue for African-Americans. Think about how you'd feel if one of your co-workers, who you *know* is no better than you, was earning twenty thousand dollars more than you. Multiply that feeling by ten times a day, 365 times per year. Then scratch your head and see if you can figure out why African-Americans suffer from high rates of heart disease."

"Is it that bad for you?" Ben asked.

LaRosa paused. "No," she said. "There are occasional slights, and I let them bother me more than I care to admit, but for the most part I've been lucky. But when I go out to a restaurant, I find myself wondering why I've been seated near the kitchen when there's an open table by the window. Or if I'm shopping in the mall, I feel the clerk watching me closely when I take something to the dressing room. They're small slights, but they add up."

"Well, any initiative we come up with to deal with racial discrimination wouldn't be limited to the underclass," Ben said. "My point is that we need to understand the causes of discrimination and poverty to develop solutions to those problems."

"Gee, that's a tough one. Let's try two hundred years of slavery and oppression followed by thirty of polite indifference," LaRosa said sarcastically.

"That's a little harsh."

"Is it really? Which do you take offense to, the slavery, the oppression or the indifference?" she asked.

"I don't take offense," Ben said. "But I do think such broad terms are more appropriate for the pulpit than for meaningful debate. I agree that historical, government-sanctioned discrimination is a significant cause of the problems of African-Americans today. But it's a problem that the federal government has been addressing for the past forty years. Why aren't African-Americans uplifting themselves from the underclass at a faster rate? Why are these problems so resistant to solution if the causes are purely historical?"

"Because it's not purely historical. We still live in a segregated society," LaRosa said. "Even when we live or work or go to school side by side, there's almost always an intangible distance between us that transcends space. There's an artificiality, a polite indifference, an invisible wall in most black/white relationships."

"But that's not promoted by the government," Ben said. "It's like we were talking about the other day. You can't legislate love or friendship or collegiality. Individual people need to break down those walls one at a time."

"So what the world needs now is love, sweet love?" LaRosa cracked. Ben flashed his crooked grin. "Love and a house in the suburbs."

"Cute. So now we're back to throwing money at the problem. What do you think would happen if we started building low-income housing in the suburbs?" LaRosa asked.

"Probably white flight to new suburbs," Ben replied. "But you can't legislate emotions. You can't force people to stay with people they don't want to be with. Any program that Tony adopts needs to provide opportunity to African-Americans and address people's feelings about integration."

"That's easy to say from the ivory tower, but it's so much harder to implement," LaRosa said. She hesitated, as if wavering whether to speak her mind. "Integration was the goal of the civil rights movement in the Sixties, but I think the black leadership went about it the wrong way after Dr. King was killed. Integration might have been easier to achieve if the black leadership had pursued it without the giant chip on their shoulder. Most of the leaders that stepped forward after Dr. King died were militants more interested in racial posturing and personal power than in working together with whites to find a common solution."

"I think you're right," Ben said. "But most whites are afraid to say it because they fear being branded as racists. It's become a taboo. The tensions are so high that we can't talk honestly with each other."

"Be the voice of White America," LaRosa said. "What would you say if you could speak without fear?"

"I'm not sure I'm comfortable with that," Ben said warily.

"I'm not comfortable being the voice of Black America, either," LaRosa said. "But somehow I feel that I've become just that in this Administration. Like you said, it starts with individuals. If two old friends can't talk honestly about it, we can't expect the American people to do it."

"Nothing held back?" Ben asked.

She smiled. "Everything on the table. No secrets, no lies."

Ben collected his thoughts. Two young lawyers with a combined five years of real world legal experience discussing, maybe deciding, policies that would affect 250 million people's daily lives. He felt as if it was at the same time overwhelming and the fulfillment of his destiny. He was making a difference in people's lives.

"While it's not fair to stereotype an entire race, I think that most white people perceive African-Americans as resisting assimilation," Ben began cautiously. "All immigrant groups since the mid-1800s faced discrimination, but they gradually melded into a single, mainstream culture. All ethnic groups maintain some elements of their culture—religious practices, weddings, music, slang terms—but they adopt many of the common elements of society—the way we dress, speak, choose friends, respect strangers and obey laws. Most whites see young black kids speaking Ebonics, dressing in rap attire, walking the walk, playing boom boxes loud in public, not respecting other people's space and adopting a menacing attitude. Why shouldn't mainstream America flee from that?"

"Is that how you think?" LaRosa asked.

It was all out on the table. LaRosa's face did not betray her emotions; Ben wondered what she thought of him now. But he knew she was right. If they were going to peer into the minds of all Americans, they had to lay bare their own perceptions.

"You know, I didn't think that way until I started working in New York," he said. "When we were in law school it was easy to take lofty positions because I hadn't seen the real world. I hadn't ridden the subway at nine o'clock at night with a band of black teenage gangsta rappers roaming from car to car. I didn't have a co-worker who was murdered in Greenwich Village by a black teenager for the fifteen bucks in his wallet. You're forced to stereotype for your personal safety even though it goes against everything you want to believe. When I deal with another lawyer in a business suit, I don't see his color. Same with the guys who run the local grocery or the dry cleaners. But, yeah, if I'm out on the street and I see a black kid dressed in baggy pants walking the walk, I'm conscious of his race, and I have a strong desire to avoid him."

LaRosa snorted, shaking her head. "Honestly, I'd avoid him, too," she said.

Ben laughed nervously. "I'm not saying I don't understand the alienation," he said. "Thumbing your nose at your persecutors is not an unreasonable response. But it's not a response that bridges gaps."

"Alienation is the right word," LaRosa said. She shifted forward in her chair. "African-Americans aren't going to reach out to join a society that's spurned them; the government, mainstream America, needs to bring them back into the fold."

"But how do you reach out to forty million people on a personal basis?" Ben asked.

LaRosa rubbed the bristles on the back of her neck while she thought. "I think we need a national dialogue on race," she said. "A real dialogue, with real people, not a half dozen bullshit town hall meetings with the president."

"But what makes you think people will speak their minds?" Ben asked. "It's hard for me to open up to you. Many people, maybe most people, will be inhibited from saying what they really mean. The Internet is the only place where I feel that I can really speak my mind."

LaRosa paused, deep in thought. "Then why not create the dialogue on the Net?" she asked.

"Well, the poor, the people we want to reach most, aren't going to be on-line," Ben said.

"Maybe not, but like I said before, discrimination isn't a poverty issue. If we can engage the leaders of the community in a meaningful discussion, we can understand people's expectations," LaRosa said. "If whites expect African-Americans to assimilate, and African-American leaders agree to encourage that as long as white community leaders encourage acceptance and nondiscrimination, we have a meeting of the minds."

"Anonymity cuts two ways," Ben said. "Open Internet chats would be vulnerable to intrusion by racist agitators."

"We could use trained moderators to screen out antagonizers," LaRosa said. "The moderators could also take the discussion in constructive directions where the conversation seems to be breaking down from lack of initiative."

"I guess we need to start somewhere," Ben said.

"It'll take time to break down people's prejudices, white and black, but it won't ever happen unless we try," she said.

"But I still think the race dialogue needs to be coupled with programs that target the problems of the underclass," Ben said. "We need to attract better teachers to inner city schools and make an honest effort at eliminating drugs and violence from inner city neighborhoods. We've got to give these kids hope that they can lift themselves out of poverty if they work hard."

LaRosa raised her eyebrows. "Any program that attempts to do all that on a national scale will be expensive," she said. "It's political suicide."

"Fabrizio said he wanted a revolution," Ben said with intensity. "Revolutions don't come cheap."

FORTY-FOUR

THE ROYAL ORDER OF THE MILLENNIUM KNIGHT met on-line for the first time in the new year in the wee hours of Friday morning. They were now meeting in a private room with the innocuous name "Buddy's Bar & Grill." The Knights were all present at exactly one o'clock.

The Heir Apparent2: Gentlemen, our forefathers dictated our mission—claim the presidency by force and vanquish the Negro race as the Final Vengeance for the murder of Jimmy MacDougall. We expected one more year to complete our objectives, but now we face the challenge of preparing for battle in less than two weeks. I want a brief update of your activities and your vision of our strategy. Spy, you're up first.

The Spy2: BFK has disappeared. Middle-aged white male traveling with BFK when eluded dragnet identified self as Mr. Maxwell, but not verified. Driving Ray Allgood's car.

The Doctor2: Do we know how Kravner made contact with Allgood?

The Spy2: No. Don't know how much Allgood knows, either.

The Speaker2: Does he have White House connections?

The Doctor2:	I don't think so. He's a research doctor. He was invited to the President's New Year's Eve party this year, but only because I was asked to provide a list of high ranking minority administrators at NIH.
The Spy2:	Agents report Allgood was a stiff all night at party. Easy target, but no immediate threat. In Europe with family, probably running from us. Agent following him and reporting to me 2x/day. Scheduled return: Sat 1/14.
The Senator2:	I think it's critical that we keep him alive at least until he takes the fall for the Experiment. We'll have no chance of winning public support if we launch an attack without provocation.
The Doctor2:	Our attack would appear justified as a response to the disclosure of the Experiment whether Allgood's dead or alive. It's too dangerous to keep him alive.
The Speaker2:	People will see a pattern. Think about the reaction by the press to Fort Bragg. White man accuses black men of inciting racial violence, but the black men were conveniently killed before the accusations could be confirmed or denied. The press may be more receptive to conspiracy theories if that happens again so soon after the first incident. That reporter who showed up at the Super Conference was only the first of many.
The Doctor2:	Perhaps Allgood's home would make an appropriate target on King Day.
The Heir Apparent2:	Something personal, Doctor?
The Caretaker2:	I'm with The Doctor—Allgood is an arro-

gant SOB who needs to be taken to the
whipping post.

The Speaker2: Once the press reports that Allgood
authorized the Experiment, he's a natu-
ral target of the white supremacy movement. As long as we wait until after the
leak, his death shouldn't arouse suspicions.

The Heir Apparent2: General, do you see any logistical problems?

The General2: Not if we work the timing right. We
should leak the story late on Saturday to
make the papers on Sunday, 1/16, then
stage the attacks on Monday.

The Heir Apparent2: Good. Spy, any other intelligence to
report?

The Spy2: DB confessed Sat PM. Assassin had
bastard son. DB thinks he's taken on
role of Assassin. She thought he had
identified Pub and trying to contact us.
Knowing their father, I'm more concerned that brother is out to exact
revenge against us—may have already
murdered Pub.

The Heir Apparent2: Does he know our identities?

The Spy2: DB never contacted him, so she doesn't
know. But our IDs evident if King Day
attack successful.

The Heir Apparent2: We still must decide how much information about the Unified Forces will be dis-
closed after the attacks. It may be possible to conceal our identities until after
The Assassin is eliminated.

The Spy2: Assassin shouldn't be a factor. We need
military protection if/when we announce
participation, anyway. Assassin will be

least of our concerns. Recommendation: proceed as planned.

The Heir Apparent2: That's a reasonable point. Doctor, Caretaker, what's the status of the Experiment?

The Doctor2: The Caretaker should have received a check on Tuesday.

The Caretaker2: The Experiment is underway.

The Heir Apparent2: Excellent. General, your battle plans?

The General2: We're trying to do an awful lot in short time, but I think we can plan a successful limited engagement on King Day. The most difficult tactical issues arise in planning the next steps. I want a plan in place for at least the next month and a clear view of the end game before our first strike. Like you said earlier, we haven't even decided if we're going to disclose our involvement right away. That's a critical tactical issue.

The Heir Apparent2: What targets have you selected for the first strike?

The General2: We want maximum damage with minimum troops. The NOMAADs have scheduled a candlelight vigil at the Washington Monument at 6:01 p.m. on King Day—marking the time of King's death on the day they celebrate his birth. Snipers will be positioned to take out the NOMAAD leadership at exactly 6:01 p.m. At the same time, a bomb will explode in NOMAAD HQ and an assault team will attack a NOMAAD training facility to be designated. We'll arrange for a bomb to be placed in Allgood's home, as well.

The Heir Apparent2: Will the troops be prepared in time?

The General2:	There are 22 organizations, with a total of 1,500 troops, that are at or close to combat readiness. I'm looking for a NOMAAD target that's convenient to one of our facilities. We don't have the resources to drop storm troopers from the sky. We've got to march right up to the front door, blow it in and take them out. Nothing fancy.
The Heir Apparent2:	Let's address the big picture tactical issues. I think we need to assume that somehow our involvement with the Unified Forces will be disclosed. We've already revealed ourselves to the white supremacy leadership. They've been sworn to secrecy, but there are bound to be leaks. Hell, that Kirk woman found out about the Super Conference; another snoop will discover we're behind the Unified Forces. Do we add more value remaining in our present positions as long as possible or demonstrating to the American public that men of power and influence stand behind the Unified Forces?
The Senator2:	Bear in mind that we'll be arrested if we remain in our present positions and we're exposed.
The Spy2:	And, in due time, executed.
The Heir Apparent2:	If we reveal ourselves, we become outlaws. I'd lose the vice-presidential nomination. We could only claim the presidency by force—a military coup. General, what's our position with the military leadership?
The General:	Unclear. There are white supremacists at all levels, but they've never been forced to choose between white power and the U.S. government. As political

outsiders we might gain the support of a
few military bases, but we'd face overwhelming opposition. We need to stake
a legitimate claim to the presidency if we
want to control the Armed Forces.
There'd still be active resistance—
minorities make up about 20% of the
enlisted troops—but we'd have the law
on our side.

The Heir Apparent2: Catch-22. We need to control the Army
to stage a successful coup, but the Army
won't support us unless we have a legitimate claim to power. We don't have a
year to wait for the election!

The General2: No catch. If the offices of the president
and the vice president are both vacant,
The Speaker is next in line.

The Heir Apparent2: Intriguing. You're absolutely right.
Speaker, are you prepared to lead the
nation into civil war?

The Speaker2: Whatever it takes.

The Heir Apparent2: Then the plan is complete. It's one year
early, but the Final Vengeance is within
our grasp. Hell, it's ironic, but we'll claim
the presidency exactly as our ancestors
envisioned after all—by the handiwork
of our own assassin.

FORTY-FIVE

THE NEWS FROM THE CIA on Friday afternoon was not good. "We can't find The Assassin," Frank Garcia said. "Without Stone's copy of the Poem, we can't show a direct link between the suspected members of The Royal Order of the Millennium Knight and the presidential assassinations."

Ben, LaRosa and Tony Fabrizio listened glumly as Garcia, the CIA Director, and his analyst, Mitch Adler, reported their findings.

"You agree that Ben's copy of the Poem would be inadmissible?" Fabrizio asked.

"Yes," Garcia replied. "But other evidence is falling into place. If we can locate The Assassin, we can make a credible case. Not airtight, but credible. Mitch, run through our conclusions."

Adler looked more like a lawyer than a spy, Ben thought. He was in his late twenties, wore designer eyeglasses and sported a slight paunch. His thick, black hair was slicked straight back. He articulated the CIA's findings in a relaxed manner, leaning forward, rarely breaking eye contact with the Vice President.

The CIA had found evidence supporting the naming convention. A clandestine search of Calhoun College revealed only pictures of old English horsemen and ducks where Ben had described the portraits of the brothers and sisters MacDougall; however, the original deed to the Calhoun College property was located in public records. It included a quitclaim deed signed by each of the siblings.

There had been no electronic evidence of the Millennium Nights room on CyberLine. However, accounts linked to the Knights' cyber-names had been issued to false identities, paid for with canceled credit cards billed to canceled post office boxes. The Knights had covered their tracks well, but the coincidences were mounting.

Professor Caldwell's research had also been validated. The CIA had confirmed that ancestors of each of the Knights were connected to either one dead president or his assassin in some peripheral capacity. They had even found a link to the death of Franklin Roosevelt that the Professor had overlooked. No trace of any ancestor could be found before 1840, and no trace of the MacDougalls could be found after that year. Jimmy MacDougall's gravesite had been located on the Calhoun College grounds, and he had indeed died in 1840. The cause of death could not be determined.

Still, without the Poem, there was no direct link between the presidential assassinations and the naming convention. The naming convention itself was odd, but it was not evidence of a crime. Even if the Knights' ancestors could be linked to the presidential assassinations, there was insufficient evidence of a conspiracy by the present day Knights.

The last line of analysis pursued by the CIA had been an evaluation of the suspects' recent activities. Adams Thompson's editorials had been inflammatory, but not criminal. General Glenn's recommendation to segregate the military, while extreme, had not risen to the level of misfeasance, and was supported by court decisions upholding the military's "Don't Ask, Don't Tell" policy relating to homosexual conduct.

JJ Alexander's suggestion that the parties be unified for the 2000 election had been founded on a platform of racial unity, hardly evidence of a conspiracy to incite a race war. It was also difficult to argue that Cal Stewart's demand that Ray Allgood limit Calhoun College's experiment to white prisoners had been racially inflammatory because Stewart's stated purpose had been to *avoid* a backlash from African-American groups.

The presence of John Daniel's son at the epicenter of the Fort Bragg incident had been suspicious, but The Speaker himself had not been implicated, and any role his son had played in the event could not be proven. Gerry Kate appeared to have led a vendetta against Ben Kravner, but the evidence, which Ben alleged was planted, did support the charges, and ultimately it would be Ben's word against the FBI.

"The bottom line is that without the Poem we don't think we can win this case in court," Adler concluded. "Even with the Poem, it's not a slam dunk."

Fabrizio chewed on his lower lip, processing the new information, then asked: "But you agree it's likely that these men are participating in a conspiracy to assassinate the next president and launch a race war?"

Garcia nodded his head gravely. "Absolutely," he said. "And if this Royal Order controls the FBI, they could easily be assembling the firepower to do it. The FBI has an enormous black operations budget that the Director controls."

"The FBI also has exclusive jurisdiction over the white supremacy and paramilitary groups," Adler said. "So if the FBI's involved in the conspiracy, nobody's minding the store. Any illegal activities are probably going unmonitored."

"That's a frightening thought," LaRosa said.

"So what do I do?" Fabrizio asked helplessly. "What do I advise Hank to do?"

Ben stroked the bristly beginnings of a new mustache. An idea was forming. But it was a longshot, and he hated to be thought the fool. He turned the idea over and over in his mind while the CIA Director offered his advice.

"If we find The Assassin and obtain his copy of the Poem, we have probable cause," Garcia said. "We can make the arrests and search the Knights' homes and offices. It could be a public relations disaster if we can't prove their guilt, but the stakes are too high to ignore the evidence."

"And if you can't locate The Assassin?" Fabrizio asked.

"It's a tougher call. The President could look pretty damn foolish," Garcia said. "But you *do* have Ben's copy of the Poem—it's just not admissible in court. Maybe you can wriggle out of the public relations mess. Ben should expect to be disbarred after the Knights' lawyers get through with him."

Ben rolled his eyes. *Wonderful.* The recital of his name seemed like a cue. "Can I bounce an idea off the group?" Ben asked.

Fabrizio tossed up his arms. "Why not? It seems like we're running out of them," he said.

"JJ Alexander volunteered to run as your vice president soon after Adams Thompson's murder. Why would he do that?" Ben asked, looking from face to face as he spoke, then answered his own question before anyone else could interrupt.

"The Knights must have learned that Stone had assumed the role of The Assassin, and Alexander feared assassination after his election as president," he said. "Now, as vice president, he expects to become president after The Assassin kills you, Mr. Vice President. Why not turn the tables back on him? If you nominate *him* as the presidential candidate, he becomes the target."

Everybody's reaction was the same. They cringed. Garcia was the first to speak. "What if they've already located The Assassin?" he asked. "If Gerry Kate has your friend, Debby Barnett, then he knows Stone's name by now. Maybe we can't find him because the FBI already has him in custody."

"The risks are too big, Tony," LaRosa said, shaking her head vigorously. "If you confront JJ, and he knows that The Assassin has been taken out of play, you've handed them the keys to the White House. If he is worried about The Assassin, confronting him might incite the Knights to attack immediately and do whatever damage they can before they're brought to justice. They'd be facing the death penalty for treason, anyway."

"What else can we do?" Fabrizio asked. "Doing nothing carries big risks, too."

"Maybe we could offer JJ a plea bargain in exchange for his confession," Garcia suggested. "Ben's right. JJ's dramatic change of plans suggests that he was worried about The Assassin. We could guarantee no death penalty."

"But what if we guess wrong?" LaRosa asked, her brow furrowed. "We don't know their strength. If General Glenn is involved, they may have military backing."

"Shitfuck!" Fabrizio said. "We need more intelligence. We need to know how much time we have before they plan to strike. How can we make informed decisions without information?"

All eyes turned to Garcia. "If they have broad-based support, it's in the military and the radical fringe," Garcia said. "Any intelligence gathering would be under the jurisdiction of military intelligence and the FBI—and we know who controls those functions."

"What can you get for us on short notice?" Fabrizio asked.

"This kind of operation can't be thrown together," Garcia said. "The CIA does not have any domestic intelligence gathering function. We'll need operatives undercover in the white supremacy movement and the military. We can insert a limited number of agents at low levels, but that won't yield the intelligence that you need, when you need it."

"Tony, I'd err on the side of caution here," LaRosa said. "The State of the Union Address would be an ideal time to reveal the conspiracy and the remedial programs we're thinking about, but it's not carved on tablets from God. Rather than incite the Knights to war, let the CIA do some groundwork. If the Knights are unprovoked, there's still another year before their plan kicks in."

"But they're already on alert," Garcia said. "The Fort Bragg incident may have been a botched attempt to start the war. They may be setting the stage for a second attempt with that Calhoun College research project. We need to stop them before emotions run high and people die."

Fabrizio paced by the fireplace. The others stared at the ground. Finally, the Vice President spoke. "I've got to clear it with the President, but I'm willing to try Ben's idea," he said, still pacing. There was fire in his eyes. "I want JJ's confession. I'm not convinced that the Poem is sufficient to send these traitors to the gas chamber even if it is admissible evidence, and, dammit, I want them dead. But we need to control The Assassin; if the Knights have located Stone—even if they *might* be in contact with him—I can't risk handing JJ the presidency."

Fabrizio glared at Garcia and Adler. "We've got ten days before the State of the Union address," he said. "*You've* got to find The Assassin first. Otherwise we wait and take our chances on war."

Ben could feel the tension in the room. Nobody appeared confident that The Assassin would be found. As long as he and Dr. Allgood roamed free, Ben knew that the Knights would be under pressure to act. The passion of the MacDougall clan could not be doubted. The nation was at the brink of civil war, and the United States government was powerless to stop it.

Ben's heart pounded. He was responsible. He had opened the sealed envelope. He had somehow alerted the Knights that their secret had been discovered. He was the reason that the Knights were accelerating their plans. Ben began to sweat. He knew what he had to do.

"If I surrender to the FBI, that should buy you some time," he blurted out. "I'm the reason the Knights are feeling a sense of urgency."

A concerned look crossed LaRosa's face. Ben saw something in her eyes that he had seen only once before, on the night before her law school graduation. He turned away, swallowing hard. LaRosa remained silent.

Fabrizio reflected on Ben's proposal. "That's a courageous offer," he said. "But once you leave the White House compound, we can't guarantee your safety. My paternal instinct tells me to forbid it, but we're staring into the barrel of a loaded gun. This is the gravest national crisis we've faced this century."

"If I surrender to the police and somebody tips the press, it'll be hard for the FBI to murder me," Ben said. "I'll offer to plead guilty to the drug charges and keep quiet if Gerry Kate offers the same deal to Debby Barnett."

Fabrizio glanced around the table. "Any better ideas?" he asked. LaRosa's eyes were cast down. Garcia and Adler shook their heads. Fabrizio turned back to Ben. "Son, your country thanks you," he said. "Relax this weekend. We'll arrange for safe passage to the D.C. police on Monday morning."

Ben stroked his nascent mustache nervously. *What have I done.*

FORTY-SIX

BEN SMILED TENSELY. "I guess this is it," he said. It was four o'clock on Monday morning. Ben sat in the passenger seat of LaRosa's red Pontiac, dressed once again in the thrift shop clothes that he had purchased in New York. The car was parked on Indiana Avenue, near Capitol Hill, three blocks from the D.C. police headquarters.

LaRosa fought back tears. She seemed to have difficulty finding the words she wanted to say. Ben knew how she felt. Although they were both still guarded in matters of the heart, the old feelings had returned. They were soulmates.

"You don't have to do this, you know," she said, searching his eyes for the courage to reveal her heart.

"I know," Ben said grimly. "But a lot of people might die if I don't surrender. I couldn't live with that on my conscience. I'll be okay as long as you make that call to the *Washington Post* in twenty minutes. If my surrender is public, the FBI can't murder me."

"I don't think you want to spend a lot of time in the D.C. jail—you'll probably run into a few of those gangsta rappers you're so afraid of," LaRosa said.

Ben forced a crooked grin. He was so tense it hurt. "I'll get by," he said softly. He puffed up his chest in mock bravado. "What's that famous quote from Nathan Hale? 'My only regret is that I have but one life to give for my country.'"

"Get real."

"Okay, I'm scared half to death, maybe a little more," Ben said. "Just don't forget about me rotting in jail after you and Tony ride out on the white horse and save the day."

Ben saw LaRosa swallow hard. She smiled awkwardly and looked directly into his eyes. A tear ran down her cheek. "I won't ever forget you," she said in a hoarse whisper.

Sadness filled Ben's heart. He might never see her again. He leaned towards her, hesitantly, their lips magnetically drawn together. Their first kiss was a tender kiss.

"I love you, Rosie," he said. "I always have."

Then he exited the car and jogged down Indiana, not looking back, tears filling his eyes.

Moments later, his eyes dried but puffy, Ben passed through a metal detector and entered the gray marble lobby of the D.C. Metropolitan Police Department Headquarters. A uniformed police woman directed him to the Desk Lieutenant's office on the third floor.

Business was slow at four in the morning. Light poured from a solitary doorway about halfway down the empty third floor hallway. Ben's footsteps echoed in the dimly lit corridor as he walked hesitantly towards the light.

Ben wavered momentarily, then entered the room. He strode up to a long marble countertop. The desk lieutenant, a big-boned black man with short salt and pepper hair, was reading a newspaper at a beat up wooden desk behind the counter.

Ben waited patiently. Finally, after thirty seconds had passed, Ben cleared his throat. No reaction. Three calendar pages tacked to a bulletin board behind the lieutenant's desk hinted at the pace of progress in this office—they were for October, November and December, 1999.

"Excuse me," Ben said softly.

The lieutenant shot Ben a derisive glance. "Have a seat," the lieutenant said, motioning toward a fold-up chair against the wall next to the door.

With a thin layer of black stubble on his head and dressed in ratty attire, Ben figured that he was not impressive enough to warrant priority over the newspaper.

"But, sir—"

The lieutenant glared at him. "Have a seat," he said sternly.

Ben took two steps toward the chair then doubled back to the counter. The lieutenant looked up from his newspaper, visibly agitated. Before the lieutenant could find the surly words to match the sneer on his face, Ben silenced him. In a loud, clear voice that reverberated

throughout the near-empty third floor, Ben said: "My name is
Benjamin Franklin Kravner. I'm on the FBI's 'Most Wanted' list. I'm
surrendering to the Washington D.C. Metro Police to avoid being
murdered by the FBI."

The lieutenant's jaw dropped. "If you don't want me," Ben said softly, in his best imitation of W.C. Fields, "All things considered, I'd rather
be in Philadelphia."

The desk lieutenant was not amused.

FORTY-SEVEN

JJ ALEXANDER SAT PENSIVELY at the head of the massive conference table in the windowless MacDougall Room at Calhoun College. The others, Ty Andrew and John Daniel to his left and Gerry Kate, Buddy Frederick and Cal Stewart to his right, were talking in hushed tones about nothing that mattered to him. The urn that had become Adams Thompson's final resting place stood neglected on the cabinet behind Alexander's chair.

Alexander's eyes were fixed on a print of a duck in flight, but his thoughts were far away. A single bell chimed ominously in his mind, giving way to the mournful strains of the bagpipes and an image of himself taking the oath of office on the Capitol steps, clad in the traditional tartan of Clan MacDougall.

He had lived his whole life chasing the dream that his father instilled in him, a dream that had been passed down proudly, fervently, over seven generations. Jefferson John Alexander, the descendent of Alexander MacDougall, the oldest of the nine siblings of Jimmy MacDougall, was to rise to the presidency of the United States and oversee the vanquishment of the Negro race in America, dramatically achieving the Final Vengeance of Clan MacDougall.

Victory had appeared within reach two months ago. Then a series of fluke events beginning with the death of Adams Thompson had nearly dashed his dreams, first jeopardizing The Royal Order itself, then presenting a solution that deprived him of the glorious moment that filled his fantasies. Now, with the capture of the young lawyer, Ben Kravner, his hopes were rejuvenated.

Alexander's ruminations were interrupted when Clint Glenn burst into the room, dressed in full military uniform, the array of war decorations tacked to his left breast gleaming like a multi-colored children's toy. General Glenn took his place beside John Daniel on the left side of the table. It was ten past four on Thursday afternoon. The General offered no apologies.

Alexander sat upright, rolled his chair to the table, and called the first live meeting of The Royal Order of the Millennium Knight to order. His blue eyes regained their characteristic intensity as he surveyed the faces of his cousins.

"Gentlemen, we have critical decisions to make this afternoon," the leathery-faced leader of the Knights said. "With Kravner in custody and under our control, we're under less pressure to go on offense this Monday. I think we should take the time to work out an aggressive strategic battle plan, properly train our forces and lay the groundwork for participation by the military in our effort after I become vice president next year."

Clint Glenn leaned forward. "JJ, I disagree with you on that," he said. The others turned towards The General. He was an imposing figure even to JJ Alexander. He barked his words in short, staccato bursts, punctuated with sharp gestures with his hands. "We know Kravner spoke to Allgood. Maybe others. We're combat ready. The troops are fired up. I say we make our move now."

"I've got to side with Clint on this one," Ty Andrew drawled, his eyes darting from face to face. He was wearing a gray three-piece suit that barely contained his girth. "I admit that I was hesitant to start the bloodshed, but once we stoked up those good ol' boys at the Super Conference, we passed the point of no return. The longer we wait, the greater the risk that someone spills the beans, whether its Kravner, Allgood or some dumbass country boy all excited to shoot up some nigras."

Gerry Kate concurred. "Kravner is no longer a threat," he said. "He understands that if he tries to communicate his knowledge to anybody, Miss Barnett will be killed. That said, I agree with Ty. I'm more worried about our friends than our enemies."

Alexander searched for an ally. Buddy Frederick and Cal Stewart were leaning forward, nodding their heads in quiet agreement with the others. John Daniel's chair was tilted back. He stroked his pronounced chin. His deep set brown eyes betrayed no emotion. "What about you, John?" Alexander asked. "You're unusually reserved today."

Daniel shifted forward. Alexander knew that words did not come easily to The Speaker. He built his reputation in the House of Representatives as a backslapping, deal-making operator, not as an orator. He spoke slowly, selecting his words with care so as not to offend.

"JJ, I know that your role in our plan is important to you. It's important to all of us," Daniel said. "It was dictated by our ancestors. So I'm in the awkward position of leapfrogging over you into the presidency if we go with Clint's plan. You're our leader. You'll be right beside me if we go that route. But I defer to your judgment."

Alexander mulled over Daniel's words. He could not state his true motivation. It would seem petty and vain. *Hell, it was petty and vain.* Each of them had sacrificed normal lives to return honor to the MacDougall name. This was not about one man's quest for glory. It was about family honor. It was about revenge.

"Tradition is important, but I'm hesitant more out of caution than for the sake of tradition or self-fulfillment," Alexander said. "Clint, tell us about your battle plan for King Day. If time will improve our chances of victory, I don't want to rush into a fight just because we can smell blood."

The General described in bone-chilling detail the tentative battle plans for the Unified Forces on King Day. General Glenn would set up a command center at the Aryan Alliance compound in western North Carolina, about twenty miles southeast of Asheville. Over 1,500 troops would be transferred there from other training facilities on Friday and Saturday.

The Experiment would be leaked to the press on Friday. Cal Stewart would make an anonymous telephone call to the *Washington Post* in the afternoon, disclosing some of the details of the illegal research on prisoners being conducted by Calhoun College. Buddy Frederick would be given as a contact. Frederick would confirm that the Experiment was being conducted on prisoners, but that it had been approved by the National Institutes of Health. He would give the reporter Cal Stewart's office and home telephone numbers.

Stewart would confirm that the research was illegal if in fact it was being conducted as described by the reporter, but he would ask that the story be delayed until he could check with Ray Allgood. Stewart would let it slip that Allgood was black. He would promise to fax the reporter a copy of the paperwork on Saturday night. The reporter would see the handwritten restriction limiting the Experiment to white subjects initialed by Ray Allgood and would realize that he had a hot story. It would be too late for the Sunday edition, so the story would break on Monday morning.

During the early morning hours on Monday, a tactical team would surreptitiously place fire bombs at NOMAAD headquarters in Washington and in the home of Dr. Raymond Allgood. The bombs would be set to explode at precisely one minute past six o'clock on Monday night.

Cal Stewart and Buddy Frederick would remain in their offices on Monday morning to respond to press inquiries about the Experiment. They would cast blame for the incident on Ray Allgood, expressing outrage at the apparent racially motivated restriction of the illegal experimentation to white prisoners. They would travel to the North Carolina command center in the afternoon.

JJ Alexander would participate in a scheduled King Day luncheon with Tony Fabrizio at the White House on Monday afternoon. He was to book a flight to Asheville and arrive at the command center before six o'clock.

General William Collins was to speak at the NOMAADs' candle-light vigil at the Washington Monument on Monday. The rally was set to begin at 6:01 p.m., and a sniper would be prepared to assassinate General Collins as soon as he stepped to the microphone.

Gerry Kate, together with Franklin Verdant, the Chairman of the Aryan Alliance, would lead an assault on Camp Tubman, the NOMAADs' training facility in South Carolina. Camp Tubman was only fifty miles from the Aryan Alliance compound. A convoy of troop carriers and light artillery would leave the command center at four o'clock, Monday afternoon. Over one thousand troops would assemble behind the cover of the ridge separating the NOMAAD encampment from Cowpens National Battlefield, and then storm "right through the front door" at 6:01 p.m., as General Glenn succinctly put it.

The NOMAAD trainees were expected to be dining or watching General Collins's speech on television at that hour. Heavy resistance was not anticipated. It would be a massacre. The assault team would retreat to the command center to defend against any military reprisals, although none were expected.

A special tactical squad comprised of five former U.S. Army commandos, now active participants in the white supremacy movement,

would be poised to assassinate President Norton and Vice President
Fabrizio at precisely 6:01 p.m. Conveniently, the two were scheduled to
meet all evening, with their staffs, to prepare for the State of the Union
Address on Tuesday. Four commandos would slip into the White House
compound in disguise. The fifth man would be equipped with an arsenal of the latest military firepower, compliments of the federal government, that would be more than sufficient to blow up the White House
and half the city if the raiding party failed to kill Norton and Fabrizio.

"Which half?" John Daniel had asked with a wink. The Speaker
would be the only Knight left behind in Washington. He would be
sworn in as the President of the United States some time early Monday
evening as the next in the line of succession after Vice President
Fabrizio.

At seven o'clock Monday night, Eastern Standard Time, telephone
calls would be made to various news agencies claiming credit for the
attacks in the name of the Unified Forces of the Aryan Knights of the
Millennium as retribution for crimes against white people. The calls
would be placed by members from pay phones in different cities across the
country. The leadership of the Unified Forces would not be identified.

President Daniel would address his grieving countrymen on national television later that night. He would assure the nation that bringing
the Unified Forces to justice would be the FBI's top priority. In fact,
Gerry Kate would control the pace of the investigation to allow Clint
Glenn to build support within the military. The white supremacy movement already had strong roots in the Armed Forces, among the leadership as well as the rank and file. Glenn would test the willingness of the
top brass to defend the President's constitutionally suspect agenda.

"If the military supports us, then damn the Constitution and anything else in our way!" General Glenn concluded. "Let the Second
Civil War begin."

It was clear to Alexander that The General's plan was frighteningly
workable. There was no reason to delay. But he had realized at the
Super Conference, and perhaps even before that, that his cousins did
not have a uniform vision of their end game. He now viewed it as his
role to bring them all together today.

"Clint, I think you're getting a little ahead of yourself," Alexander
said. "We haven't reached agreement on the scope of this war yet. Hell,
if we can avoid bloodshed entirely, that's all the better."

"Bullshit!" All eyes turned towards Gerry Kate. Fury filled The Spy's eyes. "Our ancestors commanded us to drive every goddam nigger out of this country. Our mission is not complete until cold steel has run through that last black heart."

CyberLine had provided a convenient medium for the Knights to meet regularly and in secret over the past five years, but it had deprived them of the ability to gauge the depth of the others' passion, their sincerity—their sanity. Alexander had never met Gerry Kate before. Still, it did not shock him that Kate was now proving to be the most militant of the Knights. He was appalled nonetheless at his unflinching resolve to murder an entire race.

General Glenn responded first. Alexander held his breath.

"Gerry, JJ's right," Glenn said.

Thank God. Alexander released his breath slowly. He saw Cal Stewart and Buddy Frederick react similarly.

"If blacks accept our agenda peacefully, then there's no reason to extend the war beyond the King Day attacks," Glenn continued. "But if the NOMAADs want to fight, and I'm certain they will, then we'll be ready. But we're soldiers, not terrorists. We will not kill old men, women and children."

Kate's ears were bright red. His eyes darted from face to face. "Then what are we trying to achieve here?" he asked incredulously. "I thought we were in agreement. Do you think they're going to raise a white flag and say, 'Okay, we're vanquished, let's start a new game?' This is no game! We—"

"I guess I've had a different vision," Alexander interrupted. "And I think the others will agree. I know Cal does. Blacks are inferior by nature. If we remove all affirmative action programs and prohibitions against discrimination, they'll vanquish themselves. The—"

"Dammit, that's not what our ancestors were thinking," Kate said. "For God's sake, most of them were already slaves in 1840!"

Ty Andrew cleared his throat. "You need to get a grip on reality, son," The Senator said in his deep, Southern drawl. "There's got to be some serious mental illness in our family tree to keep this conspiracy alive for so many years. But, by God, somehow we've done it, and we're on the verge of bringing honor and power to the MacDougall name like no other family has known in history. There are a lot of people in this country who would agree that men need to rise or fall on their own merits. There are few who would support us if we announce ourselves as demonic killers. We are William Wallace and Robert Bruce; we are not Adolf Hitler and Josef Stalin."

Alexander stifled a smile as he noticed The Spy rolling his eyeballs. "Eloquently put, Senator," Alexander said. "The President's role will be to remove all racial bias from the law. People will be free to act as they see fit. Whether they take race into account or not will be a personal choice. If Congress does not support these presidential decrees, the military will step in to enforce them. John? Clint? Do you agree?"

The Speaker and The General nodded their assent.

Gerry Kate stood and glared at his cousins. "You are all deluding yourselves if you think your plan will avoid a bloody race war," he said bitterly. "Once you put the match to the kerosene, you can't tell it to stop burning."

The Spy stalked out of the room.

After the meeting was adjourned, Buddy Frederick poured six glasses of scotch from the cask that had been brought to America 170 years earlier by the patriarch of Clan MacDougall. The Royal Order of the Millennium Knight drank a toast to their first American ancestors and to the imminent achievement of their Final Vengeance.

"May God Bless Jimmy MacDougall and each of his descendants and may his Persecutors suffer eternal Damnation," Alexander said. Each of the other Knights responded, "Aye," as had been their ritual in the Millennium Nights room these past five years.

As they parted company, a bell chimed ominously in JJ Alexander's mind. The hellish dream of his nine drunken ancestors was about to become reality.

FORTY-EIGHT

THE DELIVERY BOY WAS LATE with the morning edition of the *Washington Post,* but Ray Allgood was too restless to wait. The National Cancer Institute was officially closed for the King Day holiday, as were all federal agencies, but Ray had been in Europe for two weeks, and he was eager to clean out his inbox. Diana and Stanton were still asleep. He left a note reminding them to spend the day catching up on the schoolwork they missed while away in Europe.

It was five past six o'clock on Monday morning when Ray left the house. The sun had not yet risen. Ray climbed into his maroon Buick and frowned at the vacant spot where Claire's Taurus was ordinarily parked. The car had sustained considerable damage in the crash on Jiminy Peak. Ray had reported it stolen, as Ben Kravner had suggested, and the police had not questioned him before the family left for Europe. His oldest daughter, Samantha, had arranged for the car to be repaired and driven back to Bethesda.

The Taurus was in fine working order when they had returned on Saturday, but Claire had fled to her mother's home in Virginia in it on Sunday.

On the last night of their eight-city tour, in Paris, Ray had confessed his infidelity and unwitting involvement in The Royal Order's scheme to Claire. She had been devastated. She had trusted him so deeply that the possibility of his breach had never entered her consciousness. Her sky had fallen.

For the first time in twenty years, he had cried. Not for himself, but for the pain he had caused her. He had sworn that not even an impure thought would cross his mind from that day hence. He had sworn that he would sign a pact with the devil to protect his family from The

Royal Order of the Millennium Knight. And he had sworn to love her forever.

Ray backed out onto Asbury Lane. It was out of his hands now. He had said all the right things in Paris and was genuinely contrite. He had faith that twenty years of loving marriage would count for something in the end. For now, his focus had to be on his other problem. He needed to confront Cal Stewart, the devil himself, about the Calhoun College grant. Ray Allgood was smart enough to know that his life was still in danger. He wished he was smart enough to figure a way out.

THE *WASHINGTON POST* LAY FACE UP on President Norton's desk. The banner headline screamed: "Black Cancer Chief Experiments on White Prisoners!"

Hank Norton was livid. "Who the fuck is Ray Allgood and why is he ruining my life!" the President shouted, his arms flailing about in no particular direction. He was pacing behind his desk in the Oval Office. Tony Fabrizio, LaRosa Smith, Conrad Tucker, the President's Chief of Staff, and Helen Briggs, the Secretary of Health and Human Services, were on the receiving end of his invective.

Fabrizio shot LaRosa a worried glance. LaRosa took the cue—let Helen Briggs do the talking. Tony had not briefed the President about Ray Allgood's involvement in the conspiracy.

Briggs was a smooth one. At forty-five, she was young to hold a Cabinet post, but her family was well-connected and were heavy contributors to Hank Norton's campaign fund. She was nicely dressed in a gray business suit, but her usually tidy hair-do was askew, revealing the hurry with which she must have left her home after reading the story in the *Post.*

"Dr. Allgood is the director of the National Cancer Institute and a profoundly ethical man," Briggs said. "I haven't had the opportunity to speak with him or Dr. Stewart, the NIH director, but I'm sure there's some misunderstanding here. Both experimentation on prisoners and the use of race as a criteria for selecting participants in a research project would be clearly illegal, and I'm confident that Dr. Allgood would not be involved in such activities."

The President was not satisfied. "Dammit, Helen!" he snapped. Briggs recoiled from the sharpness of his tone, a look of fear crossing her face. "Three weeks ago it was Fort Bragg and the fucking NOMAADs tied up traffic out there for an entire day," the President continued, gesturing outside towards Pennsylvania Avenue. "Now I'm going to have the fucking KKK in my backyard! Somebody has got to get out there and give our federal employees some sensitivity training!"

"Well, I sure hope it's not you," Fabrizio quipped, his broad grin designed to break the tension in the room as it had in so many tense rooms before. "Relax, Hank. We'll get this under control. Let Helen talk to her people before the press finds them. The federal offices are closed today, so maybe that'll buy us a little time."

Norton slumped into his chair, but he did not smile. His shoulders were rigid, his brow wrinkled. "I'm sorry, Helen," he said. "I don't want history to remember me as the man who presided over a race war. My State of the Union Address is tomorrow night. The last thing I need is the Klan or some other group of rabble-rousers protesting on Capitol Hill in front of the TV cameras."

LaRosa glanced at Fabrizio. He had told the President over the weekend that he did not think the investigation of the conspiracy was far enough along to arrest the Knights before the State of the Union Address. The President's current draft of the speech included vague promises to address the existing state of racial tension, but did not raise the issue to the level of a national priority. LaRosa was working on an alternative draft. Hank Norton was upset now; she shuddered as she imagined his reaction when Fabrizio told him the true impact of the *Post* story.

The President excused the group. Helen Briggs made a quick exit, but the Vice President lingered. Tucker remained seated. LaRosa closed the doors after Secretary Briggs was out of earshot.

"Hank, this situation is more serious than you think," Fabrizio said.

CLINT GLENN LEANED on the window frame of his command center, a log cabin that had been constructed for him the week before. He had traded the dark green dress uniform of the United States Army for a slate gray one reminiscent of the uniforms worn by the Army of the Confederacy in America's first civil war. He stared at the map of Camp Tubman that occupied most of the opposite wall, then peered out the window. It was noon, lunchtime at the Aryan Alliance compound, but the main yard was bustling with activity.

Twenty-five troop carriers, recently painted slate gray, were lined up in five rows of five. Mechanics hovered over the trucks' open hoods, tweaking their engines into perfect tune.

Even the roar of the engines could not drown out the boisterous yells of five hundred troops simulating the attack on Camp Tubman on the training fields one last time. A constant stream of loud pops, like thousands of firecrackers ignited at once on the Fourth of July, emanated from the firing range, as another battalion of five hundred troops prepared for the defense of the command center in the event of a retaliatory strike. Still another battalion, the other half of the Camp Tubman strike force, was in the mess tent.

General Glenn, framed in the window of the command center, nodded confidently. This was a fighting force of which he could be proud—tough, disciplined, pure white.

JJ ALEXANDER STOOD AT THE LECTERN, silent, smiling, waiting for the applause to subside. LaRosa Smith looked on from a large, round table with eleven African-American religious leaders of little renown. The big honchos, Douglas Malone, the chairman of the NAACP, General William Collins, the NOMAAD chieftain, John Tubbs, the director of the Southern Christian Leadership Conference, and a number of others were seated on the dais with Vice President Fabrizio and Alexander. A total of 140 men and women, most of them notable African-Americans, some of them members of the press, filled the White House's State Dining Room to capacity.

LaRosa surveyed the room. The mood was somber. Everybody wanted to know how Fabrizio and Alexander, mainstream America, were going to react to this morning's story in the *Washington Post*. The expectation of a collective slap on the wrist for the transgression of their brother, Ray Allgood, hung over the room like a dark cloud.

LaRosa wondered whether Alexander would take an inflammatory or conciliatory approach.

"Tony Fabrizio and I have spoken of our dream for America many times over this past month," Alexander began. "We dream of an America that is free of racial strife."

LaRosa snorted softly. *Yeah, a lily white America.* Alexander was thumbing his nose at his audience, and they did not even know it. She had not noticed the dual meanings in his speech when Tony Fabrizio announced him as his vice-presidential pick. How could he keep a straight face?

"Realizing that dream starts with individuals," Alexander continued. "It starts with fathers and sons, mothers and daughters, blacks and whites. But the dream stops if we attribute the acts of individuals to an entire class of people. It stops if African-Americans cannot forgive all whites for the depraved act of one white soldier at Fort Bragg. It stops if white Americans blame all African-Americans for the misguided act of Dr. Raymond Allgood."

With those words of conciliation, the dark cloud dissipated. LaRosa was puzzled by JJ's approach, but she joined the crowd, rising to her feet and half-heartedly applauding the hypocritical words of The Heir Apparent.

Alexander basked in the warmth of the ovation, then plunged forward as his audience cooled. He continued with more of the same rhetoric for five minutes, before deferring to the Vice President.

Alexander stepped back from the lectern, as the now enraptured crowd stood once again. LaRosa felt the electricity running through this group of sophisticated leaders, and she realized what JJ Alexander had done. He gave them a taste of the dream, lifting their hope ever higher, so that they would have farther to fall.

LaRosa closed her eyes and crossed her fingers as Fabrizio launched into his remarks.

"I've worked with JJ Alexander in the Senate for the past seven years," Fabrizio said. "I've known him as a worthy adversary, a man of both principle and passion. But it's only in the past month that I've truly known him as a man and as a friend. I've come to know that the state of race relations in America is more than a political issue for JJ, it's a deeply-rooted passion that he has carried since his youth, indeed one that has been passed down from generation to generation by the Alexander clan."

LaRosa watched Alexander's reaction carefully. His head was cocked towards the Vice President, accepting the accolades gracefully, smiling stiffly. The color drained from his face at the mention of previous generations of the Alexander clan. She smiled as she imagined the thoughts running through his mind.

"I'm going to let you all in on a secret," Fabrizio continued. His expression changed from earnest to sad. LaRosa marveled at how he did that. "JJ Alexander has cancer."

A low rumble of gasps and exclamations of shock and dismay rolled across the room. Alexander's shade quickly morphed from pale to crimson. LaRosa was amused. He had to suspect that Fabrizio was toying with him, but he could not be sure. Fabrizio held up his right hand for silence.

"Wait, wait, please," Fabrizio said. "JJ's cancer is in remission, and there is no imminent danger to him. But it was he who came to me just over a month ago and suggested that we combine our campaigns. You see, JJ Alexander wanted to leave a legacy for his grandchildren that would never be forgotten. He was willing to give up part of his dream to assure that his goal of an America free of racial strife was realized in his lifetime."

Fabrizio's strong voice resounded through the stillness of the room. LaRosa watched Alexander. His head was bowed; confusion no doubt reigned within. "Ladies and gentlemen," Fabrizio said, pausing dramatically. "It is with great pleasure and admiration that I yield to the Senator from Texas, who I hope will be the next President of the United States of America."

RAY ALLGOOD FILED the last of his incoming mail. He almost enjoyed being in the office on weekends and holidays. His time was spent so much more productively when there were no telephones and meetings, the bane of the administrator's existence. His inbox had been daunting, but only a few items had required urgent attention. He looked at his watch. It was almost one o'clock. Even those items could wait until tomorrow.

Almost on cue, the telephone rang. Ray scowled at it. He was tempted to let it ring. But it might be Claire or the kids.

"Allgood," he answered gruffly.

"Dr. Allgood, this is Roger Martin of the *New York Herald Times*. Would you like to comment on this morning's article in the *Washington Post?*"

"What article?" Ray asked warily.

"The one about your authorization of illegal experimentation on white prisoners in Georgia," the reporter said. "Haven't you seen it yet?"

"No." Ray's mind raced. The shit was hitting the fan. He wondered if Claire had seen the story. If The Royal Order leaked it, they were preparing to launch the race war. But why? Ben Kravner was safely in custody. *They couldn't be worried about me.* Ray thought that he had sent the right message by fleeing to Europe for two weeks. Leave me and my family alone, and I'll leave you alone. Maybe they were simply fanning the flames.

"Ah, here, it says you could not be reached for comment," the reporter said.

"I have an unlisted telephone number," Ray said automatically. His mind was elsewhere. *I'm about to start the Second Civil War.* The reporter asked another question. Ray did not hear it. He hung up the telephone. It started to ring again a few seconds later. He let it ring. Ray was dazed. He needed to go somewhere and think. Anywhere.

TONY FABRIZIO AND JJ ALEXANDER sat in the Oval Office waiting for the President, making small talk, but Alexander's mind was churning. Fabrizio was up to no good; he smelled a trap. His flight to Asheville left in two and a half hours, at four o'clock. The presidency, the vice-presidency, nothing mattered now except getting on that plane. He rubbed his left leg against his right ankle. The .22 caliber Smith & Wesson revolver was like life insurance; he had hoped never to use it.

With a gleam in his eye, Hank Norton strode into the Oval Office. Alexander and Fabrizio rose to greet him. The President shook hands with Alexander vigorously and slapped him on the back.

"Congratulations, JJ! I tried to talk Tony out of his decision, but he couldn't be swayed," he said, winking.

"It's a great honor, Mr. President," Alexander said, maintaining his composure. They all sat. Alexander saw Norton and Fabrizio exchange glances.

"We know everything, JJ," the President said calmly.

"You know *what?*" Alexander asked. He tried to maintain a blank look. His heart pounded. It did not matter if they knew; all that mattered was getting on that plane.

"About the conspiracy," Fabrizio said.

"I don't know what you're talking about," Alexander said. *Remain calm.* He looked at his watch. "Gentlemen, I've got to catch a plane." He stood to go.

"Sit down, JJ," Norton commanded sternly.

Alexander walked towards the door. "This meeting is over," he said.

"There are two Secret Service agents outside," Norton said. "It would be better if you didn't make a scene."

Alexander stopped and turned towards them. "You're making a big mistake," he said, his blue eyes glowering. The muscles around his jaw tightened as he clenched his teeth.

"We know where The Assassin is," Fabrizio said, watching Alexander for a reaction. "We know that he's safe and you won't be able to stop him."

Alexander snorted, unmoved. "Who is The Assassin?" he asked, shaking his head, his face scrunched into his best look of disbelief. His mind churned. *They think I'm afraid of The Assassin.* The Assassin had become almost irrelevant. The election was now anticlimactic. By November, the nation would be mired in civil war. By tonight, Norton and Fabrizio would be dead, and John Daniel would be at the helm. *I can bluff my way out of this.*

Fabrizio's thick, dark eyebrows shifted downwards under the weight of his furrowed brow. His eyes flashed. "Van Buren Andrew Stone. The man who you thought was going to assassinate me and make you president," the Vice President said angrily. "We know all about The Royal Order of the Millennium Knight, the assassinations of seven presidents and your plans for a race war. Shitfuck, we know that your dad was responsible for the murder of JFK."

"Tony, this is absolutely insane!" Alexander exclaimed. "Conspiracies, Assassins, Knights—this sounds like some kind of children's game!"

"It's no game," President Norton said. "We know you're behind the Fort Bragg incident and the illegal medical research story in this morning's *Post.*"

"We also believe that you have something bigger in mind," Fabrizio added. "And you're not going to leave this room until you confess."

Suddenly Alexander felt light-headed. "I want to call my lawyer immediately," he demanded.

"We can't let you do that, JJ," the President said. "Lives are at stake. We're not worried about the admissibility of your confession in court. We're going to stop you and your cohorts from starting a race war that nobody can win."

Alexander paced across the Oval Office. The imprisonment was illegal, but in about four hours nobody would care. *Everybody in the West Wing is going to die at 6:01 p.m.* It was the final irony. He had joined forces with Tony Fabrizio to avoid the risk of death by The Assassin's bullet. Now that ploy had backfired. He was trapped.

Alexander ran his hand through his thinning, silver-streaked blonde hair. If he surrendered, he faced treason charges and the death penalty. The White House was guarded like a fortress. He felt the weight of the puny handgun on his ankle. There was only one way out.

Alexander's gaze shifted to his adversaries, first to Norton seated behind his desk, arms folded tightly in front of him, then to Fabrizio. Alexander pulled the chair that he had vacated a safe distance away from the Vice President, then sat. He crossed his right leg over his left, then yanked the pistol from its holster above his right ankle.

"Don't move!" Alexander said, training the gun on Fabrizio. Alexander stood. Fabrizio's mouth hung open. Norton's jaw was clenched tight; he looked at the intercom. Alexander swung the silver Smith & Wesson towards the President. "Back away from the desk, Hank," he said.

"JJ, this is crazy," Fabrizio said calmly. "Put down the gun. There are two Secret Service agents right outside the door."

"You don't have to die here, JJ," the President said. "It's over. Put down the gun."

"It's not over," Alexander said. "We're going to walk out of here like old friends. You're going to smile at the Secret Service agents and tell them we're going for a stroll in the Rose Garden."

Norton shook his head. "I'm not going to do that," he said. "The fate of the nation is at stake. You can shoot me or Tony with that pea-shooter if you want, but you're not leaving this room a free man."

"And you'd better pray those agents shoot to kill," Fabrizio said angrily. "Because if people die today, you'll wish you were dead after I get through with you."

Alexander felt beads of perspiration dripping down his forehead. His heart pounded. Breathing was difficult. He loosened his tie. His balance felt shaky. There was no way out. No, there was one way.

Alexander backed away two steps from the desk, then swung the gun towards himself, inserting the short barrel into his mouth.

Fabrizio rose from his seat slowly, his palms raised. Alexander backed away another step. "It doesn't have to end like this, JJ," Fabrizio said.

Alexander slid the gun out of his mouth. "You've left me no choice," he said. His hands trembled.

"There are always choices," Fabrizio said. "You don't have to die today."

Alexander took another step back; Fabrizio followed, his palms still in front of him. Four feet separated them. Alexander fought the demons in his mind. He faced death in every direction. His finger tightened on the trigger. He closed his eyes. It was time to die for The Royal Order of the Millennium Knight.

"JJ, don't do it," Fabrizio said. "You can't let a race war be your legacy. Your grandchildren weren't born to hate. They'll never understand what you've done here."

Alexander's finger relaxed on the trigger. Guilt and sorrow overcame him as he thought about his grandchildren.

"We can offer you a plea bargain," Fabrizio said. "If you help us, we won't ask for the death penalty. You'll see your grandchildren grow up. They'll live in a better place."

Alexander continued his slow, steady retreat. The gun weighed less than a pound, but his arm was suddenly heavy. He could not betray his cousins. He was their leader. They trusted him. *They all have children and grandchildren, too.*

"I'll deal," Alexander said. "But only if the deal applies to the others, too."

Fabrizio glanced at the President. Norton nodded his assent. "Done," Fabrizio said. "We'll seek life imprisonment for treason and any conspiracy for crimes as yet not committed."

"There was a murder, too," Alexander said.

"Who?" Fabrizio asked.

"A woman reporter," Alexander said. "Christy Kirk. *Herald Times.*"

Alexander watched the Vice President struggle to control his emotions. "Okay," Fabrizio said finally. "No death penalty for the murder of Christy Kirk."

"And minimum security prison," Alexander said. "We won't last a day in Leavenworth."

Fabrizio wrinkled his brow. "I can't do that, JJ," he said. "You're a politician. Think about the public reaction."

"You don't have much time," he said. "The Apocalypse begins at 6:01 p.m. tonight."

Fabrizio and Norton both looked at their watches. One-fifty. "It's a deal," the President said grimly. "But that's it. Give Tony the gun."

Alexander lowered the revolver and offered it to Fabrizio. Fabrizio took it, then unleashed a punch, a right cross, that struck Alexander on the left side of his face with a loud slap, knocking him to the floor. Alexander saw stars, he felt a bruise rising on his cheekbone, and he heard Fabrizio, who was standing directly over him, say: "Fuckshit, that was for JFK."

* * *

LAROSA SMITH LEANED AGAINST THE WALL of the Oval
Office, listening in disbelief.

"Dammit, Bill, martyring yourself is not going to solve the race
problem," Norton said. General Collins, the NOMAAD leader, was
seated across the desk from the President in the Oval Office. Tony
Fabrizio was pacing beside him. "We can avoid this war. We're calling
in the D.C. police to deal with the bomb in your headquarters building, but *you've* got to call off the rally tonight, and *you've* got to evacuate Camp Tubman."

"Do *you* back down from terrorists threats?" Collins asked indignantly.

"We do not negotiate with terrorists," the President said. "But we
do protect ourselves from them. We'd live in a different world if Dr.
King had this opportunity."

Collins reflected on the President's words. "You're right. There's no
reason for me to make myself a human target for a coward hiding
behind a sniper's scope. I'm willing to cancel the candlelight vigil
tonight," he said. "But I'm not evacuating Camp Tubman. If they want
to fight us toe to toe, bring 'em on."

"How many men do you have at Camp Tubman?" Fabrizio asked.

"About five hundred," Collins said.

"They'll be coming at you with one thousand men plus artillery,"
Norton said.

LaRosa felt the frustration boiling over. "Killing five hundred good
African-American men will not resolve anything," she said. "And neither will a full scale race war. We need to work our way into mainstream America by softening people's attitudes towards African-
Americans, not make them more afraid of us."

Collins ignored LaRosa. "We'll take whatever support you offer," he
said, looking first at the President, then at Fabrizio. "But if you can't
stop them, there will be bloodshed. We may lose the first battle, but we
will *not* lose the war." Collins leaned forward, his hands on his thighs,
poised to exit. "Is there anything else that I can do for you?"

Fabrizio and LaRosa slumped into the chairs across from the
President after General Collins departed. "So much for the easy way
out," President Norton said glumly. "Rosie, get Royce Monahan in
here with the Commander-in-Chief of the U.S. Atlantic Command
and a map. We've got to find a military base that can get some firepower to Camp Tubman by six o'clock."

LaRosa and Fabrizio looked at their watches in tandem. It was two-thirty. "Can we trust them?" LaRosa asked.

"CINC USACOM, Admiral Jordan, is Jewish. I think we can take our chances with him," the President said. "I've known Royce for thirty years, and I hope to God I can trust him. With three and a half hours to go, prayer is our only other option."

ROYCE MONAHAN RUSHED into the Oval Office at three-thirty. He was breathing hard. A uniformed naval officer accompanied him. Admiral Jordan, CINC USACOM, was a tall, distinguished man with a full head of white hair. He appeared unruffled, despite having sped to the White House by helicopter from his headquarters in Norfolk, Virginia.

"Royce, Admiral, we've got a crisis," President Norton said. "We don't have time to fill you in on the details, but we need enough firepower to repel an attack by one thousand troops, with artillery support, on a target in South Carolina—and we need it in place by six o'clock."

Monahan gaped in disbelief. "Tonight?" he asked, his eyes wide.

"Yep," Norton said.

"Clint Glenn should be here," Monahan said.

"He and the rest of the Joint Chiefs are out of play—don't ask why," the President said, his intense brown eyes signaling the finality of the order.

Monahan turned to Admiral Jordan. "Pete, what do we have available?"

"Where in South Carolina is the target?" Admiral Jordan asked, his tone neutral, his demeanor calm. CINC USACOM exercised combat control over eighty percent of the U.S.-based armed forces and was responsible for the integration of combat ready units of the Army, Navy, Air Force and Marines to meet any challenge.

"It's Camp Tubman, a training facility for the NOMAADs," LaRosa said. "It's north of Spartanburg and Greenville, near the North Carolina border."

"The Hell's Angels, Company D, out of Fort Bragg is in-country. I can get a squadron of Apache attack helicopters over there in an hour," Admiral Jordan said confidently.

Norton, Fabrizio and LaRosa all grimaced simultaneously. Monahan looked at the Admiral. He shrugged. "What's wrong?" Monahan asked. "We've resolved the race issues on the base."

"Fort Bragg is not an option," the President said. "What are our alternatives?"

LaRosa saw Admiral Jordan blow out a short breath, his first sign of concern. "Limited, given the time we have," he said. He unfolded a map and spread it across the President's desk. "Fort Campbell has our largest stock of Apaches, but it's in western Kentucky, about 330 miles from Spartanburg. An Apache has a range of about four hundred miles, but it's top speed is 168 miles per hour. It'll take almost two hours—a little close for comfort unless we get the birds in the air right now."

"Do we need Apaches?" Fabrizio asked. "We must have an Air Force base closer than Kentucky. What about Shaw Air Force Base in South Carolina or Robins in Georgia?"

Admiral Jordan shook his head. "The Apache's night-time capabilities are superior to any other helicopter. That aside, the Air Force doesn't maintain an arsenal of attack helicopters—they have mostly transports," he said. "I've got one Marine Expeditionary Unit deployed at Camp Lejeune in North Carolina. They have four Super Cobras and four Hueys, but the Hueys don't have the range to make it 250 miles to the target. Four Cobras won't be enough to stop a thousand motivated soldiers with artillery support, especially at night. If Fort Bragg is out of play, Fort Campbell is your best option."

"Get the commanding officer at Campbell on the horn," the President ordered. "Let's see how fast we can get those choppers in the air."

Each of them instinctively checked the time. It was three-forty-five.

FIFTEEN HUNDRED GRAY-UNIFORMED TROOPS lined the training grounds of the Aryan Alliance compound in perfect military formation—three battalions, each battalion lined up twenty across and twenty-five deep.

Franklin Verdant stood at attention in front of White Battalion. General Glenn ambled past the front line, inspecting the troops, then offered Verdant a firm salute, complimenting him on the readiness of his men. Black Battalion, headed by Gerry Kate, received a similar review. Finally, Red Battalion, the troops that were to defend the command center under the leadership of Buddy Frederick and Cal Stewart, were granted The General's seal of approval.

General Glenn climbed a makeshift podium to address the troops. He glowered dramatically at the men, then offered his final instructions. He spoke without the benefit of a microphone, but his words were, as always, clear and concise: "Blast those fucking niggers to hell!" he yelled, his taut face contorted into a frightening battle mask, his right fist thrusting high into the air as he spoke.

The General's words were met with a rousing cheer. Moments later, at precisely four o'clock, the troop carriers rolled from the Aryan Alliance compound, in single file, a long, gray snake winding its way through the foothills of the Blue Ridge Mountains towards the South Carolina border.

B COMPANY, 1ST BRIGADE, 101st Airborne Division was involved in a spirited basketball game in the Fort Campbell gymnasium when a wide-eyed private raced in with a message. Colonel Jeffrey Woods, the Commanding Officer of B Company, thought the orders were a bizarre joke. Ten minutes to get twenty birds in the air, two hours to fly 330 miles at top speed, instructions for attack on a *domestic* target to be delivered in the air. *It had to be a joke.* But no one would ever be able to say that the Screaming Eagles could not get the job done. Better to be a fool in the clouds, than caught with his pants down on the ground.

Colonel Woods barked out commands. Half the soldiers of B Company sprinted for their flight gear, the other half raced to prime the birds. At exactly 4:05 p.m. Eastern Standard Time, twenty green Boeing AH-64D Apache attack helicopters climbed vertically into the air, each fully loaded with two M230 30mm automatic cannons and eight Hellfire missiles.

A voice crackled over the two-way radio instructing the pilots to set their flight coordinates. Their destination was Cowpens National Battlefield in South Carolina, USA. *A goddam national park.* Colonel Woods shook his head and smiled. They would not let the Apaches fly too far from home before they called them back and had their laugh at B Company's expense. He started to nod his head vigorously when the radio crackled, again. *Here it comes.*

"This is not a drill," the voice said. Colonel Woods's smile disappeared; his eyes widened. "Estimated time of attack: 6:02 p.m. Eastern Standard Time. Combat instructions to follow. Over."

Colonel Woods was not a man who had lived his life in fear. He had fought in Panama and Iraq. He had flown death-defying missions in the mountains of Bosnia. But he could not squelch the chill that ran through his body. The United States was at war with itself. The Second Civil War was about to begin.

FORTY-NINE

FOUR HUNDRED AND FORTY MEN, the NOMAAD fighting force, sat crammed into the cafeteria at Camp Tubman. Colonel Hardy stood in their midst, relaxed, strolling and talking as if he was lecturing a class in Military History at West Point.

"Few people know this," Hardy said, "But the Battle of Cowpens, fought on the other side of that giant ridge out there, was one of the critical battles in the Revolutionary War." He had not yet told them about the imminent attack.

"An outnumbered, out-trained, out-supplied band of colonial misfits, kicked the living shit out of the British," the Colonel continued. "Does anybody know how they did it?"

Hardy surveyed the crowd of young, black men. No volunteers. "They did it with superior tactics," he said. "And they did it with heart, a courage born from their conviction that they were fighting for their basic human right to freedom."

Hardy paced silently among his rapt audience as he framed his words carefully in his mind. "General Collins has informed me that Camp Tubman will be attacked by an army of white supremacists in less than two hours," he said. "We have time to evacuate the camp. But I can teach you tactics that will allow us to defeat a force that will outnumber us better than two to one. What I can't teach you is heart. Men, the choice is yours. Do we run and hide from oppression or do we stand and fight for our freedom?"

"WHAT'S UP, JJ?" Fabrizio said, making no effort to conceal his disgust for his former running mate.

Alexander was handcuffed to a ladderback chair in a conference room adjacent to the Oval Office. His hair was in disarray. A purple welt was evident on his left cheek.

"I neglected to tell you something important in the confusion after you sucker-punched me," Alexander said, smirking. "I wouldn't want to jeopardize my plea bargain."

Fabrizio grabbed Alexander by the collar; his teeth were clenched. "Making that plea bargain with you was one of the toughest things I've ever had to do," Fabrizio said, his eyes ablaze. "I'm praying for you to give me a reason to break it."

"Sorry, Tony, not this time," Alexander said. "There's a bomb in Ray Allgood's house. There might not be time to get the bomb squad in there, but you should be able to get everybody out by six o'clock."

Fabrizio looked at his watch. It was five o'clock. "You son of a bitch," he said, pacing across the room, gnashing his teeth. Then he stopped and faced Alexander. "We were ready to give up the West Wing of the White House to your commandos, but I think I just came up with a better idea."

STANTON ALLGOOD SAT AT THE DESK in his bedroom, his head bopping to the rhythm of Will Smith's latest rap album while he struggled with two weeks' worth of algebra homework. He had the house to himself. Diana was studying at a friend's house. Just the same, his parents complained about the loud music so often that he wore headphones out of habit. He did not hear the telephone ringing.

THE PRESIDENT, the Vice President, and Conrad Tucker huddled around the massive conference table in the center of Fabrizio's office on the second floor of the Old Executive Office Building. They were reviewing LaRosa Smith's draft of the State of the Union Address, which was scheduled to be delivered the next night.

LaRosa was alone in the informal sitting area to their left. She slammed the telephone down. "Nobody's picking up at Allgood's house or at his office," she said.

"Try the Bethesda police," Tucker suggested.

"I did," she said. "Twice. They keep putting me on hold. It's five-twenty. I feel like I've got to do something."

"Maybe the whole family is at the candlelight vigil out there," Tucker said, pointing out the window towards the Washington Monument.

LaRosa walked over to the window. The sun had set, and twilight was creeping over the city. The Monument was lit up against the darkening sky. Thousands of people were waiting on the lawn surrounding the monument and had spilled over on to the Ellipse.

"I'm driving out to Bethesda," she said. "I'll keep trying to reach Allgood on my cell phone. Traffic should be light because of the holiday."

THE NOMAAD PARTISANS looked up into the sky. They heard the helicopters before they could see them. Then two green Bell UH-1H Iroquois "Hueys" appeared over the top of the Department of Commerce Building across 15th Street and swooped low over the crowd by the Washington Monument. The racket was deafening. The people held their hands over their ears, shaking their heads at each other. Was General Collins making a dramatic entrance?

The mystery was soon over. An announcement was broadcast over a loudspeaker from one of the helicopters. "This is the United States Air Force. Tonight's rally has been canceled due to a bomb threat. Please leave the area in an orderly fashion. There is no need to panic."

The announcement was repeated three times. Then the Hueys left in the same direction from which they came. The crowd dispersed in what could only be described as a scene of controlled chaos. It was five-forty-five.

COLONEL TOM HARDY PEERED OUT from behind the chimney of his perch atop the centermost building in Camp Tubman, one of dozens of simple, white shingle barracks. He pointed his binoculars to the west. One hundred and forty seven men, all clad in gray cotton sweatsuits, dodged among the hickories and oaks that lined the western border of the property leased to the NOMAADs. The sun had just fallen below the massive ridge that loomed over the compound; the gray twilight failed to provide adequate cover. The envelopment maneuver could only succeed if it was a complete surprise to the enemy forces massing on the other side of the ridge.

Then Hardy glanced to the east. Another equal force of NOMAAD volunteers was scurrying along the eastern rim of the compound. A third group waited anxiously behind the cover of the buildings within the camp. This group, led by Colonel Hardy himself, would take the brunt of the Unified Forces' attack.

Hardy raised his binoculars and scanned the top of the ridge a half mile away. There was no movement. He was counting on the over-eagerness of the inexperienced Unified Forces' troops for the success of his trap. The double envelopment maneuver required patience, an overconfident enemy and balls of steel. The Unified Forces would come charging down the ridge, through the open pasture, into the valley. The NOMAAD units on the flanks had to resist the urge to attack until the enemy was past them. The NOMAAD troops hiding behind the barracks would repel the charging forces with a buzz saw of gunfire, then the units on both flanks would encircle the enemy.

The Battle of Cowpens, Hardy's inspiration, was one of the few examples in history of a successful double envelopment. General Morgan, the leader of the Colonial forces, trapped the British by feinting a retreat, drawing the British troops between two American units on their flanks. The retreating forces then turned and fired upon the British, and the two units on their flanks surrounded them.

The maneuver worked in Revolutionary times; Hardy was less confident that it would be successful in a modern battle. Automatic weapons would allow the Unified Forces' to cut down NOMAAD troops on all sides, especially with their numeric advantage. The Unified Forces' artillery also carried far more explosive force than the British cannons. The Colonials had only lost twelve men; the NOMAADs would lose many more.

Hardy scanned the perimeter of the compound. Both NOMAAD units were in place. There was still no sign of the Unified Forces at the top of the ridge. And no sign of the Screaming Eagles.

Once the battle began, the attack helicopters would be useless. Attack helicopters were primarily deployed to destroy armored and mechanized targets. They could be employed to support light infantry on the ground in a low-intensity conflict, but it was critical that the helicopter pilots be able to identify both the enemy and friendly positions. The NOMAADs were equipped with high intensity flashlights to reveal their location, but the disadvantage of the double envelopment maneuver was that once the troops were fully engaged, it would be impossible for the Apache gunners to distinguish between the enemy and the NOMAADs.

Hardy looked at his watch. Five-fifty-one. In ten minutes it would be dark enough to provide adequate cover for the double envelopment. It looked as if they were going to need it.

***

LAROSA'S HEART was in her throat. She looked at her watch. Five-fifty-one. She was not going to make it. Traffic was jammed up on Wisconsin Avenue, near Tenley Circle. She dialed the Allgoods' home telephone number. No answer. She prayed that they were out and not simply avoiding telephone calls from the press. She had a bad feeling. Five-fifty-two.

She dialed Ray Allgood's number at the National Cancer Institute. "Allgood," a man's voice answered.

"Ray!"

"Yes," Dr. Allgood said warily.

"This is LaRosa Smith, Vice President Fabrizio's Chief of Staff. Is there anybody in your house now?"

CHUCK CARLISLE, the Secret Service agent who had guarded Ben Kravner, was stationed inside the lobby near the Visitors' Entrance to the Old Executive Office Building. A bead of sweat formed on his balding scalp. Another man in the uniform of the Secret Service had walked in off the street. He was at least fifteen years younger than Carlisle, and he was military trim.

The younger agent nodded at Carlisle. Carlisle returned the gesture, resisting the urge to yank out his gun. The White House would be blown apart if the commandos did not check in at the appointed time. The imposter passed through the security checkpoint, and entered the Old Executive Office Building.

Thirty seconds later, at five-fifty-five, Carlisle spoke softly into his two-way radio: "Alien Three is in the House."

RAY ALLGOOD RAN A RED LIGHT on the corner of Wisconsin and Elsemere Avenues. His heart pounded. The neon numerals on the Buick's dashboard clock told a frightening story. Five-fifty-nine.

The Buick's tires squealed as it cornered the right turn on to Bellevue Drive. Ray blasted the horn as he sped through his neighborhood. Six o'clock.

Ray barely touched the brake pedal as he made the sharp left on to Asbury Lane. The Buick careened into the driveway ten seconds later. Ray burst out the door and sprinted up the front walkway, shouting, "Stanton! Diana! Get out of the house!"

He leaped on to the front stoop, hurdling three steps. His hands shook as he fumbled for the front door key. He shouted for his children, again.

The force of the explosion knocked Ray off the front stoop. Glass shattered. He saw flames rip through his home as he tumbled backwards, shouting, "My babies!" amidst the deafening roar. Claire's image flashed in his mind. His arms hit the ground first, then his back. Pain seared through his body, then his head flung back against the concrete walkway, and everything went black.

A LONG SLATE GRAY LINE of troops stood poised to charge the last three hundred yards to the crest of the ridge that separated them from Camp Tubman. Restless fingers massaged the triggers of their automatic rifles. Many had waited their whole lives for this moment, Gerry Kate among them.

But The Spy remained calm. He walked among the troops, his rifle slung over his shoulder and a toothpick dangling from his mouth, urging them to hold the line.

He was confident that the battle would be over quickly. A handful of men guarded the road near the top of the ridge, ready to intercept anyone trying to leave the camp. Another group waited a mile away just inside the unmarked entrance to Camp Tubman, prepared to snare any intruders who might jeopardize the attack.

Kate looked at his watch. Six o'clock. He wandered over to Franklin Verdant, dried leaves and pine needles crackling under his weight. Verdant rested against a twisted hickory tree near the edge of the pastureland.

"Any last words of inspiration for the troops," Kate asked.

Verdant had his game face on. His wrinkled brow threatened to drive his dark, bushy eyebrows into the lower reaches of his face. "Tell them: 'No survivors,'" Verdant said fiercely.

Kate walked purposefully up the side of the ridge, about fifty feet. He turned back to face the men. "Ten hut!" he shouted. The troops on both sides of the road snapped to attention. "Victory is ours to take, my friends. It will be the first of many. Strike fear into their black hearts! Take no survivors!"

Kate turned sideways as if to throw a football, thrust his right arm forward, and hollered: "Charge!"

One thousand men unleashed a fearsome rebel yell, bursting forward up the hill, three deep, forming a battle line almost a quarter mile wide. Gerry Kate strode up the ridge, behind the lines, Franklin Verdant in tow. The Spy proudly watched the troops tumble over the crest. The Unified Forces would be on top of the surprised NOMAADs within four minutes. Victory would be sweet.

The roar of the howling troops muffled as they hurtled down the leeward side of the ridge towards the NOMAAD encampment. Kate and Verdant jogged towards the peak to view the slaughter. When they were not ten yards from the summit, the volume of the Unified Forces' howls began to increase, again. Kate and Verdant shared a quizzical look, then, suddenly, the herd of wide-eyed troops stampeded over the ridge. Kate and Verdant were knocked to the ground, stunned.

Kate rose quickly. "Get back here and fight, you cowards!" he screamed at the retreating gray line.

Then the sound of metal whooshing through air, made him whirl. The Spy gawked in silent astonishment. Twenty Apache attack helicopters rose vertically above the crest of the ridge, not fifty yards away. They bobbed in the twilight like giant green bumblebees, their Hellfire missiles aimed at The Spy like 160 turbo-charged stingers.

One of the Apaches unleashed a dozen rounds of cannon-fire at the ground directly in front of Kate. Dirt sprayed all about him, jolting him from his momentary paralysis. He dropped his weapon and raised his arms over his head, his mouth still hanging open in utter disbelief.

JJ ALEXANDER HEARD A DOOR BANG OPEN down the hall. He rolled his eyes, then exhaled deeply. The same sound followed, again, some seconds later, this time closer. He rolled his eyes, again. A third door banged against a third wall as it was forced open.

Then, suddenly, the door to the conference room where he was imprisoned swung open with a loud crash. Two uniformed Secret Service agents plowed in, guns drawn, one stooped, the other from up high. They lowered their guns when they saw Alexander cuffed to the chair atop the conference table in the center of the room.

"Where's the President?" one of them asked angrily.

Alexander rolled his eyes. "You idiots, don't you recognize me?" Alexander said, too weary to lash out at them with the viciousness he felt in his heart. "It's a trap. They let you in here."

Two more men wearing the uniform of the Secret Service entered the room. "The West Wing is empty," one of them said.

"Call your man with the rocket launcher and tell him to abort," Alexander ordered. "What's your drop dead time?"

"Six-ten," another commando said. He seemed to be the leader. "We still have eight minutes to get out and switch targets."

Alexander closed his eyes. *Fools.* "They know you're in here," he said. "The building is surrounded. If your man outside launches the rocket, he's only going to kill us. The instant you radio him, to abort or switch targets, the Secret Service will triangulate on the signals and take him out. Call in the abort code. It's him or us. Either way, it's over."

JOHN DANIEL ADMIRED his widow's peak in the mirror in the bedroom of his Georgetown apartment. He thought the dash of gray around his ears made him look presidential. He practiced his look of horror, raising his right hand to his temple, then brushing it down along the side of his face, then finally sweeping it over his gasping mouth. *"10.0!" "10.0!" "10.0!" "9.0 from the Russian judge."*

He heard the opening strains of the theme for the Seven O'clock News. "John! The news is on," his wife, Sharon, called from the den.

The Speaker practiced his look once more, this time mouthing the words, "My God. How could this happen?" Then he winked at himself, and rushed to the living room to catch the day's top stories.

The news anchor led off with the cancellation of the NOMAADs' candlelight vigil at the Washington Monument due to a bomb threat. The television cameras had captured the Hueys dramatically circling the Monument and dispersing the crowd.

Daniel panicked. Had an overeager Secret Service agent spied the snipers before they could take out their targets? There was no report of the presidential assassination. But that only meant that the West Wing of the White House, his new home, had not been destroyed. The story would not break until he was notified, so that some semblance of order could be restored before the public had time to panic.

The door buzzer sounded. Sharon jumped up from her perch on the couch to answer it.

"Wait, I'll get it, honey," Daniel said abruptly. He sprang towards the intercom, gently sliding his wife out of his way.

"Yes," Daniel said into the intercom.

"This is the Secret Service, sir," a man's voice replied. "May we come up?"

Daniel breathed a sigh of relief. The deed had been done. "What do you want?" Daniel asked, trying to inject an edge of wariness into his voice.

"We need to speak with you privately, sir," the voice said. "It's urgent."

Daniel pressed the entry buzzer. There was a knock on the door two minutes later. Daniel dug his fingernails into the meat of his forearm to steel himself. *My God. How could this happen?* He opened the door.

Two uniformed Secret Service agents stood in the doorway. Their guns were pointed at his heart. "Johnson Martin Daniel, you're under arrest for the crime of treason against the United States of America," one of them said.

Even the Russian judge would have given Daniel a perfect ten for the look of horror that crossed his face.

FIFTY

BEN SAT WIDE-EYED in the first row of the gallery that ringed the House Chamber on Tuesday night. The buzz of excitement on the floor of the House of Representatives was more electric than was typical for the President's State of the Union Address. It was always an Event—it was easier to get a ticket to the Super Bowl than to the President's annual speech to a joint session of Congress. But, tonight, the crowd seemed to sense that they were about to witness something extraordinary.

Perhaps they were primed to expect the unexpected after Tony Fabrizio's surprise announcement that catapulted JJ Alexander into the role of presidential heir apparent. Or maybe they had spotted the clues.

Fabrizio, as the President of the Senate, sat alone atop the three-tier rostrum that rose majestically above the House Chamber, a large American flag draped on the wall behind him, flanked on either side by giant portraits of George Washington and Lafayette. The position next to Fabrizio, ordinarily occupied by the Speaker of the House, was vacant. JJ Alexander and Ty Andrew, the Senate majority leader, were also mysteriously absent.

The spectators rose to their feet as the Sergeant-at-Arms announced the entrance of the Supreme Court Justices. Whether it was the crowd's energy, his newly won freedom, his impending fifteen minutes of fame, love or some combustible combination of all of them, Ben felt more alive than ever before. He turned to his left and squeezed Debby's hand, as the nine black-robed Justices strode down the center aisle.

Debby smiled weakly. Her elegant black evening dress hung slackly over her gaunt figure. Her make-up barely hid the black and blue marks on her face. An FBI agent, a true blue All-American one, sat to her left, ready to escort her back to a minimum security prison after the night's festivities. She was being held for the murder of Adams Thompson, Jr., despite her protestations of innocence. The evidence against her appeared overwhelming, but Ben was determined to fight for her freedom. He now had powerful friends who might help him, but, until then, the FBI insisted upon holding her in custody.

After the Justices took their places on the House floor, in the front row of one of the six wedge-shaped seating sections, the Ambassador Corps entered. Ben turned to his right and squeezed LaRosa's hand. She smiled radiantly. This was her night—her man, Tony Fabrizio, was about to shine. But in Ben's eyes, she was the shining star. Intelligent, warm-hearted and stunningly beautiful, LaRosa Smith had once again captivated him. For now, he was too happy to be confused. There would be time to sort out the women in his life.

Maxwell Caldwell sat to LaRosa's right. The Professor looked uncomfortable in black tie, but it was his night, too. After twenty-five years of ignominy, his reputation, a scholar's most valuable possession, was about to be restored.

Next to the Professor sat a young man who had learned to always trust his instincts, even if it was simply a craving for a cheeseburger. Stanton Allgood was in attendance in his father's stead thanks to an impromptu visit to the local burger joint half an hour before the blast that destroyed the Allgood home. Ray Allgood was in stable condition at The Bethesda Naval Hospital with a concussion and a broken arm.

After the President's Cabinet entered the House Chamber, the Sergeant-at-Arms said in a loud, clear voice: "Mr. Vice President, the President of the United States!"

Hank Norton strode confidently down the center aisle, smiling and shaking hands with friend and foe alike. In this one moment each year, a façade of nonpartisanship was erected. The Republicans were prepared to knock it down an hour later, on national television, when one of their leaders rebutted the President's rosy view of the State of the Union. But, tonight, the Republicans were unaware that the advance copy of the President's speech was a red herring.

Finally, President Norton advanced to the lectern on the middle tier of the Speaker's rostrum, directly below Tony Fabrizio. He grasped the sides of the lectern firmly. His expression was serious. "Mr. Vice President, Members of Congress, honored guests, my fellow

Americans: I have come before you to report the State of the Union for the last time."

The crowd erupted in spontaneous applause. Rather than basking in the ovation for the benefit of the television cameras as he had done seven times before, Norton raised his hand for silence.

"For the last seven years I have had the privilege and the joy to report that the Union has been doing just fine, as we have witnessed unprecedented economic expansion fueled by remarkable technological change," he continued. Then his expression turned grave. "But today I have the unenviable task of reporting that the State of the Union has never been worse, a task made easier only because we think we see a way out of the darkness."

A few murmurs and gasps could be heard in the gallery, but for the most part the audience, including the Congressmen and members of the Norton Administration, sat in stunned silence. This was not the speech they had seen.

"As difficult as it is to believe, we are the victims of a conspiracy that has been perpetuated against all Americans by a single depraved family over the course of 160 years. These madmen have assassinated seven United States presidents, infiltrated the highest reaches of the federal government and taken the nation to the brink of its second civil war."

A low rumble of whispers rolled through the chamber. "But there's a bright side to this dark tale, as well," the President continued. "Because it's also a story about our future, about how a handful of young Americans unearthed this dark conspiracy and risked their lives to bring it to light."

Ben sat tall in his chair. He thought about his parents watching at home, knowing that their son had been responsible for saving the nation. *Yeah, by illegally opening Thompson's sealed envelope.* He had to keep reminding himself not to let his head swell.

Ben surveyed the audience as the President launched into a detailed retelling of the tale of the MacDougall family vendetta. Seven generations, seven dead presidents, with their eye always on their hideous Final Vengeance at the turn of the millennium. Expressions of shock, amazement and horror were frozen on every face, political neophyte and veteran alike.

"They came within a whisker of achieving their goal," President Norton said. Ben felt LaRosa squeeze his hand. His moment had arrived. "A courageous young man, Benjamin Franklin Kravner, brought the conspiracy to our attention two weeks ago," the President said. Adrenaline roared through Ben's veins. The President gestured in his direction. "Ben, please stand up and show America our future."

Ben stood stiffly and gave a weak wave of the hand. The audience applauded loudly. Ben bowed his head humbly in acknowledgement, his face flushed. He sat down quickly.

The President raised his voice to speak through the ovation. "Sitting on Ben's left is Miss Deborah Barnett and two seats to his right is Professor Maxwell Caldwell, both of whom played substantial roles in bringing these traitors to justice," he said.

Debby sheepishly rose halfway, then sat immediately. The Professor stood proudly, accepting the acclaim as humbly as he could under the circumstances. He sat reluctantly when the applause began to fade.

"As it became clear to The Royal Order that their conspiracy was crumbling, they accelerated their plans to incite America into civil war—the Final Vengeance for their ancestor's death," Norton said. "The incident at Fort Bragg was their work, as was the undertaking and disclosure of the racially targeted medical research reported in the press yesterday. We have withheld an announcement for national security reasons, but yesterday evening the United States Army and the Secret Service thwarted military strikes by an armed white militia against the United States government and certain African-American targets. We were this close to civil war." He held his thumb and forefinger a fraction of an inch apart.

"You will notice that a number of prominent government officials are absent tonight," Norton said, then proceeded to identify the seven members of The Royal Order of the Millennium Knight to the crowd's astonishment. "These men have all been taken into custody by the Justice Department and will be tried and convicted for high treason against the United States of America."

The audience rose and applauded. Norton raised his hand for silence. "But punishing these traitors is not enough," he said. "No punishment can bring back the seven great Americans who died without fulfilling their legacies as President of the United States. No punishment will right the ten thousand wrongs committed against African-Americans in the name of The Royal Order of the Millennium Knight. No punishment can heal the psychic wounds inflicted in the bitter race war waged over the past century and a half."

Norton paused for effect. "One month ago JJ Alexander eloquently, and we now know deceptively, launched his vice-presidential candidacy by recalling the slumbering dream of Martin Luther King,"
Norton said. "We need to awaken the Dream. Racism will never be
banished from our society if we wait passively for a generation to be
born devoid of racist thoughts. Like the vengeful conspiracy perpetuated by the descendants of Jimmy MacDougall, racism is passed down
from generation to generation, one father to one son. It can be done
passionately, by preaching the politics of hate, or tacitly, by observing
skin color as a trait worthy of importance. Racism will only end when
parents, black and white, find the intellectual strength to quiet their
racist impulses or strong-minded children overcome the urge to submit
to their parents' bigotry."

Ben blushed as he recognized the source of the President's words.
He looked over at LaRosa; she avoided his gaze.

"Ladies and gentlemen, the State of the Union is a state of mind.
Tonight, the Union is in turmoil, a nation torn asunder by radical
forces. Tomorrow, if we dream a common dream, we can become of
one mind, one nation, where all men and women are truly created—
and treated—equal."

Everyone in the gallery rose to their feet and cheered the President's
words. Ben squeezed LaRosa's hand. It was a magnificent speech. She
smiled at him and mouthed the words: "It's not over yet." Norton
remained poised at the lectern, waiting for the crowd to quiet. Then he
went on.

"But we realize today, more than ever, that equal treatment is not
enough. America's great economic expansion in the nineteenth and
twentieth centuries took place on an unequal playing field. African-
Americans did not have the opportunity to participate in most of that
economic expansion because of discrimination that was tacitly, if not
expressly, sanctioned by the United States government—as a result of
the influence of The Royal Order of the Millennium Knight and otherwise. Our frontiers are closed. Our vast resources have been largely
allocated. Our efforts to share opportunities among all Americans ring
hollow now that most of the prime opportunities are out of the reach
of those that were left behind."

Ben's chest swelled with pride; his eyes misted. *Revolutions don't
come cheap.* He had convinced LaRosa to recommend the politically

risky programs that would be necessary to truly solve the problems of the underclass. He had made a difference in people's lives.

"I will work with Tony Fabrizio and the next Administration to assure that we ring in the next millennium with a true Second American Revolution, not a Second Civil War. Tony and his staff have been working on specific proposals, and I'll leave it to him to present them for the consideration of the Congress and the American people. God bless you and good night."

The members of Congress, the President's cabinet, the Justices of the Supreme Court, the Ambassador Corps and the entire gallery simultaneously rose to their feet and erupted in a thunderous ovation. Norton hurried from the rostrum, humbly acknowledging their approval, as he made his way up the center aisle towards the exit, shaking hands as he went.

Ben closed his eyes, absently applauding the President, saying a silent prayer of thanks to a God in whom he did not believe. *It's over.*

FIFTY-ONE

THE NATION WAS SPELLBOUND by the stunning revelations made in President Norton's State of the Union address on Tuesday night. But by Wednesday morning, LaRosa Smith was already absorbed by the mundane tasks of managing Tony Fabrizio's life, present and future.

Fabrizio reclined in his chair, arms folded behind his head, shoeless feet resting on his desk inches away from a half-eaten Danish. LaRosa leaned forward in one of the guest chairs, absent-mindedly drumming her fingers on the desk, waiting impatiently as ever for Fabrizio to capture the thought that eluded him.

Finally, he spoke. "Revolutionary change, not evolutionary change," he said. "I need to show the American people that the words I say are more than rhetoric. We need to restore their faith in the government. Shitfuck. We need to restore their faith in me—I came within a whisker of leading them into holocaust. Picking Tom Stevenson as my VP won't cut it."

"You once told me that you were thinking about putting a black man on your ticket," LaRosa said, her tone and expression suggesting some combination of wariness and hope. "Are you still considering that option?"

"Nope," he said. LaRosa was disappointed. The American people were not blaming him for the crisis. Fabrizio was a shoo-in no matter who he selected as his running mate. It was a perfect time to break new ground. Then she brightened. "A woman?" she asked.

"It's a possibility," he said. "You just had a birthday, didn't you, Rosie?" he asked.

She wrinkled her nose. "Yeah, thanks for reminding me," she said suspiciously, wondering what sparked the dramatic shift in the topic of conversation. "Thirty-five, if you're wondering—and I weigh 116 pounds if you need to know that, too."

Fabrizio chuckled. "Always a straight shooter. It's one of the things I like best about you," he said.

She glanced skywards. "Can we get back on topic, Chief? You've got me on the edge of my seat wondering who your 'revolutionary' candidate might be."

Fabrizio removed his feet from the desk, leaned forward in his chair, and placed his interlocked hands firmly on the desk. His eyes twinkled as they looked directly into hers. He seemed to enjoy teasing her.

"I want you," he said, smiling. "You satisfy the age requirement—I don't think there's any restriction on height or weight."

She was stunned. Was he kidding? She did not know whether to laugh or risk playing the fool. Finally, words came. "That's not funny if you're kidding, and it's insane if you're not," she said flatly, waiting for Fabrizio to break out laughing at her expense.

"Well, it's no joke and we can argue about my sanity some other time," he said. "I saw you in action in pressure situations over the last few weeks. You impressed me with the way you handled General Glenn during the Fort Bragg crisis. You expressed your opinion articulately, unfazed by the artillery lined up against you, and cautiously built consensus. You helped Hank make the hardest decision of his presidency. The speech that you wrote for him, on short notice, was brilliant. *You* averted a disaster. You saved lives. You showed real leadership."

"But I've never been elected to any position in my life. I'm an advisor," LaRosa pleaded.

"The country doesn't need another politician in a position of power right now," Fabrizio said. "We need real leaders with a real vision."

"The vision thing is back," she wisecracked.

"It's one thing to toss out political slogans, it's another thing to be a true visionary," Fabrizio said. "You're a remarkably perceptive young woman. You can sense public opinion. You know in your heart what's right and what's wrong. And you have the intellect to blend public opinion and your moral conscience to build a solution that seems reasonable to almost everybody."

The Vice President was on a roll, and, for once, LaRosa was content to let him run with it. "I enjoyed watching you and Ben play off each other," he continued. "You've developed the foundation for a plan that will revolutionize this country. I want you to help me implement that plan, and eight years from now I want you to run it. If you accept my offer, you *will* be the first woman and the first African-American to be President of the United States."

LaRosa could feel the pride gushing up inside her as Fabrizio spoke. She had difficulty suppressing a smile. When Fabrizio finished, she gave in to temptation and grinned a crooked grin straight out of Ben Kravner's repertoire.

"You're making my head swell," she said, wondering at the same time why she was thinking of Ben Kravner during the most important moment of her life. "I don't know what to say."

Fabrizio smiled. "You should be proud," he said. "And you should say 'yes.'"

Before LaRosa could say, "Let me think about it," the intercom buzzed. It was Dan Raskin, the Attorney General. The Assassin had surrendered to the FBI.

RASKIN USHERED FABRIZIO and LaRosa into a small, dark room at FBI headquarters. A man was sitting calmly at a scarred wooden table on the other side of a two-way mirror. He was sitting with his right side facing the mirror, but he turned towards them as they entered, as if he could sense their presence behind the glass.

LaRosa glanced at Fabrizio. His eyes were locked on to the eyes of The Assassin, the man whose mission in life had been to bring about Fabrizio's death.

He did not look like a killer to LaRosa, but then again neither did the other members of The Royal Order of the Millennium Knight. He was a tall, well-built young man with sandy hair and a weather-beaten face. He was wearing a light blue cotton shirt, blue jeans and work boots. A suede jacket was slung over the back of his chair; a cowboy hat rested on the table. An FBI agent entered the room, introduced himself as Agent Cashman, and Marlboro broke eye contact with the mirror.

Agent Cashman sat in the chair opposite Marlboro. Cashman was about forty years old, large-framed, but not fat. His light brown hair was thinning. "Please state your name," he said.

"Van Buren Andrew Stone."

"Mr. Stone, we've been searching for you for over two weeks—what led you to turn yourself in?" Cashman's manner was relaxed, not intimidating.

"I read in today's newspaper that you're holding my sister for the murder of Adams Thompson. She didn't do it."

"Did you kill Adams Thompson?"

"No." Stone was not going to make this easy. It was obvious to LaRosa, and no doubt everybody else watching, that he was holding back information. His body was tight. He was afraid of something or someone.

Cashman seemed to see it, too. He maintained his relaxed style, moving away from questions that could be answered with a simple yes or no response. "Then why have you been hiding from the authorities?"

"I didn't even know you were looking for me," Stone said. "I was hiding from the men you arrested on Monday—The Royal Order of the Millennium Knight."

"Are you the member of that group known as The Assassin?"

"No, sir. My father was assigned that role, but he renounced it before his death."

"Your sister claims that she found evidence in your apartment that you had assumed the role of The Assassin and that you were tracking Adams Thompson in order to make contact with the other members of the group," Cashman said.

"Sir, my father renounced his role, and he was killed because of it. I was tracking Adams Thompson so that I could find the men that murdered my father."

LaRosa's eyebrows perked up. The conspirators would all get life sentences for conspiracy to commit treason and the murder of Christy Kirk under the agreement negotiated by JJ Alexander. The death penalty would not even be considered. The agreement did not cover other crimes. She hoped Cashman would follow that line of questioning.

"Do you have any evidence that your father was murdered?" Cashman asked.

"He spoke to me a week before the crash. He intended to withdraw from the group. He planned to hunt the other members of the group and stop them. He thought that the others suspected him, and he feared for his life."

"Did the group members explicitly threaten his life?"

"Not explicitly," Stone admitted. "When he tried to withdraw from the group, they strongly suggested that he reconsider. The threats were veiled, but he knew what they were saying. He agreed to remain in the group, but he had already decided to run."

LaRosa's heart sank. She looked at Raskin. He grimly shook his head. There was no hard evidence of foul play in the crash that killed The Assassin. Veiled threats by anonymous members of an Internet chat room reported second-hand by the victim's son over a year after the incident would not even be admissible in court.

Cashman pursued the line of questioning. "Did your father have personal contact with any of the members of the group?"

"No," Stone said, tentatively. "Well, yes. The Spy initially contacted him. They met, but on a no-names basis. The Spy was disguised."

"What was the nature of The Spy's contact with your father?

"It was 1995. The Spy told my father that the other members of the group were meeting regularly on the Internet, and they wanted my father to join them."

"Why was your father treated differently than the other members?"

"Our ancestors planned it that way. The Assassin's role at the turn of the millennium was predefined. I assume you've seen the Poem?" Stone asked.

Cashman nodded affirmatively. "There was no need for The Assassin to participate in the Final Vengeance," Stone continued. "That part of the scheme was left flexible, presumably because the MacDougalls knew there could be big changes in the way people lived 160 years later. Keeping The Assassin out of the loop prevented him from interfering with the larger plan."

"How did the other members of the group get together?" Cashman asked.

"When our ancestors parted in 1840, each one took with him or her two sealed envelopes, except for my ancestor, Colleen MacDougall, who was only given one. The first package was to be opened in 1930 by the youngest Knight in each family older than eighteen years of age. It contained instructions providing the first and middle names to be given the Knight's next born son and that son's first born son. My grandfather opened the envelope and named my father Van Buren Andrew, as instructed, and my father gave me the same name. The second package was to be opened by the oldest Knight in each family in 1995. That envelope contained the Key—the code for finding the other Knights. My father did not have that package, and he did not participate with the other Knights until they contacted him."

"Why was The Assassin given the first package?" Agent Cashman asked.

"It must have been a failsafe," Stone said. "If the larger group needed to revise the plan, as it turned out they did, there was the hope that they could identify The Assassin."

"Was your father a willing participant after he was contacted?" Agent Cashman asked.

"No."

"Then why did he name you in accordance with the naming convention?"

Stone thought deeply, chewing on his lower lip. "Did your father ever feel passionately about anything?" he asked.

Cashman shrugged. "Geez, I don't know," he said, glancing sheepishly at the mirror. Then he snorted. "Baseball. Pop loved the Sox. He took me to Fenway Park when I was nine years old and Yaz hit a slam to win a game against the Yankees. Pop went wild. I never saw him like that before."

"And do you still enjoy baseball?" Stone asked.

Cashman smiled. "Still a diehard Sox fan. I've lived in D.C. for almost twenty years, but I still read the box scores every morning."

"My grandfather was passionate about The Royal Order of the Millennium Knight," Stone said. "He instilled that passion in my father when he was young, never telling him the details, but filling his head with stories of our family's grand deeds and preparing him for a special role at the turn of the millennium. It was an exciting game for a little boy who idolized his father."

"So why did he renounce his role when he was contacted by The Spy?"

"Two things," Stone said. "The Vietnam War and me. He fought alongside men of color. He saw fathers and sons die. He questioned all that he had been taught to believe. He named me in accordance with the naming convention out of respect for his father, but he had already begun to question whether he would inspire me to hate and kill. I lived in Los Angeles with my mother; he returned to San Francisco to his wife. When they divorced a few years later, he spent more time with me in Los Angeles, but he never spoke of The Royal Order until he snapped."

"That was right before he was killed?" Cashman asked.

"Yes, sir," Stone said. "He told me the entire story and gave me a photocopy of the Poem and a list of the nicknames of the other members. He told me that he was going to find their true identities and kill them all. He asked me to think about completing his mission if he failed. I wrote him a few days later to say that I would, but he was murdered before we spoke again."

Cashman paced across the room. "Let me ask this question one more time, Mr. Stone. We're prepared to reduce the charges against you to manslaughter if you confess. Did you kill Adams Thompson?"

"No. I identified him as The Publisher because of the tone of his editorials. I was following him, hoping that he would lead me to the others. I was prepared to use force if my surveillance continued to be unproductive."

"Were you following Thompson the night he was killed?"

"Yes. But I didn't kill him and my sister didn't, either," Stone pleaded. He squirmed. His eyes were wide with fear. LaRosa's heart began to beat faster. *He knows.*

"Did you see who murdered him?" Cashman asked.

"I saw the killer's face," Stone said. He turned to look directly into the mirror, again, his piercing blue eyes locked on to a presence he seemed to feel but could not see. "But I want somebody else in this room before I say any more. Somebody I know I can trust."

Stone stood when the Vice President entered the room. "Will I do?" Fabrizio asked. Stone shook his hand and grinned. "I saw the killer's face again in the newspaper this morning. It was Agent Cashman's boss—Gerry Kate."

Fabrizio winked in the direction of the mirror. LaRosa smiled. *Bingo.*

FIFTY-TWO

THE CEMETERY WAS ON TOP OF A GRASSY HILL in a small clearing in the northwest corner of the old MacDougall plantation, now the grounds of Calhoun College. This section of the campus, rarely visited by Calhoun students, was a half mile from the nearest building and remained heavily forested with birch and pines. A row of dogwoods encircled the clearing.

In early March, when the delicate white flowers of the dogwoods were in bloom, the scene was stunningly beautiful and serene. But it had rained that morning, the second day of February, and the grim shadow of the barren trees did nothing to shake the mid-winter gloom. A solitary beam of sunlight emerged from the turbulent sea of dark purple clouds to make an attempt, focusing like a beacon on the grassy hill, momentarily producing an eerie, almost biblical, effect, then vanishing into the churning sky.

Ben and Debby entered the clearing from a lightly worn path in the woods. It was cold and dank, a wet forty degrees, and it seemed even colder clad in the garb of the Scottish Highlands—white peasant shirts and plaid kilts with the traditional tartan of Clan MacDougall. A green backpack was slung over Debby's shoulder.

The sunlight glistened on the dewy grass and wildflowers that surrounded the makeshift wooden markers on the graves of Debby's great-great-great-great-great grandparents and their eldest son, Jimmy. Debby knelt on the wet ground, set her backpack down and pulled out a bottle of fine Scotch whiskey, three glasses and the urn that contained the ashes of her natural father, Van Buren Andrew Colleen.

"He'll be here in a few minutes, I'm sure," Debby said. "Punctuality is not a family trait."

"Me arse is cold, lass," Ben said, trying on a new Scottish accent. "I hope he's taken the high road."

Debby giggled. Ben smiled, then surveyed the landscape. Her smile could not mask her sadness. Her bruises had almost healed, but the mental scars would last a lifetime. He could only imagine the anguish she had endured awaiting a certain death in the dark solitude of the Maryland safe house.

He had been there when she had been rescued on the night of the King Day attacks, only a short while after his own release from prison. It was an emotional moment. She had screamed with fright as a half dozen men thundered down the steps to the basement, only believing that her rescue was real when Ben had come to her and hugged her weak, battered, body, whispering in her ear that everything was going to be all right.

They had both run an emotional gauntlet over the past two months, but Ben felt guilty that somehow he had emerged from their adventure a champion while Debby seemed destined to remain a forgotten footnote in history. At least she had fared better than poor Christy Kirk, the reporter whose shredded body had been discovered the week before in a gorge near the paramilitary compound of the Aryan Kingdom.

The Knights could not be sentenced to death for the murder of Christy Kirk, or for the conspiracy to commit treason, under the plea bargain negotiated by JJ Alexander, but Christy's death had not been in vain. The micro-cassette found in the back pocket of her jeans would be admissible to show the brutality and evil intent of the Knights, virtually assuring that all of them would receive capital punishment as co-conspirators with Gerry Kate in the murder of Adams Thompson. They would be remembered as the most contemptible traitors in American history.

Ben, on the other hand, had charmed the nation. The attention had been unrelenting for the past two weeks, but Ben's unassuming manner had made him a media darling. He could not satisfy everybody, though. His crooked grin had graced the stages of Letterman, Oprah and Larry King Live, while he had spurned Leno, Springer and Geraldo.

Ben had been careful to remind each interviewer of the forgotten heroes—Debby Barnett, Christy Kirk, Ray Allgood, Woody Taylor and

Max Caldwell—but they had usually smiled blankly, barely listening to his words, then asked again how he had evaded the FBI dragnet on Jiminy Peak.

No matter how many times he had to tell the story, though, he had always left out certain parts. He had kept his promise to Ray Allgood, although Ray had confided to him that he told Claire about his affair while they were in Europe. Ben also had neglected to tell about his second trip to Atlanta when he had seduced Kimberly Frederick in the MacDougall Room, not knowing that she was The Caretaker's daughter. It was a memory he would always cherish, privately. He had met with her briefly before he came to the cemetery, and they had agreed to remain friends.

Ben's professional life was also on the upswing. Fritz Fox was recovering nicely, and he had all but assured Ben that he would make partner at Kramer, Fox in record time. It was an unheard of endorsement, and two months ago Ben would have been ecstatic.

Now, he was thinking of leaving the default career path. He had too many grand ideas to waste his life managing other people's estates or orchestrating corporate mega-mergers. He had windmills to tilt, and his new friends in high places were determined to give him that opportunity.

Tony Fabrizio had told him to name the job he wanted in the Justice Department or any other federal agency. That prospect was intriguing. His discussions with LaRosa had awakened a passion that had lain dormant since law school. He would have the opportunity to make a difference in people's lives. In the Civil Rights Division of the Justice Department, he could help Fabrizio and LaRosa usher in the Second American Revolution.

LaRosa. She seemed to be always on his mind nowadays. She had been announced as Tony Fabrizio's running mate, and the public outpouring of support from all segments of society was heart-warming. The people were ready for a revolution. She was looking for a chief-of-staff who she could trust.

The job was Ben's most exciting professional option, but it created so many issues. For one, he did not have her political instincts. He enjoyed being her sounding board on substantive issues, but he knew nothing of the workings of government and might become more of a burden than help.

Then there was a small matter of the heart. He had fallen in love with her all over again—or maybe he only now realized that it was she who he had loved all along. They were soulmates. His family's acceptance was still an issue. But he would no longer quell his passions to satisfy their prejudices, whether real or imagined. If she could trust him again, he would love her without inhibition. It was a role inconsistent with chief-of-staff.

A faint sound from the woods shook Ben from his daydream. As it drew closer, the familiar, somber melody of "Amazing Grace" wafted through the forest much as it had on a fateful day 160 years before.

Nine children of James and Anne MacDougall solemnly encamped around the graves of their parents and brother. Alone. Angry. Grieving. Intoxicated. A deadly blend of alcohol, emotions and fiery Scottish blood. Alexander. Frederick. Kate. Thompson. Glenn. Andrew. Daniel. Stewart. Colleen. The architects of a conspiracy that had almost toppled a nation.

Ben, still fixated with the inner workings of people's minds, wondered how the MacDougalls had come to that fateful moment of insight when personal fury was transformed into a vendetta for the ages. It had been the isolation and secrecy, the singularity of purpose, the strength of the bond between father and son, and the passion with which it had been imparted that had permitted this insane notion to be perpetuated.

It would have been easy for young people with fire in their hearts to plan ritualistic family meetings where a single moment of sanity by any one of their progeny could have doused the spark of hate residing in each of their souls. But they had not, and seven presidents had been jinxed because of it.

A tall man, about thirty years old, emerged from the woods, bagpipes pressed to his lips. Van Buren Andrew Stone bore little resemblance to the Marlboro Man, shedding one uniform for another, denim and leather in favor of the tartan of Clan MacDougall.

Tears welled up in Debby's eyes, as she rose and scattered their father's ashes over the graves of their ancestors while the mournful tones wailed through the morning stillness. Then Ben followed suit, spreading the ashes of Adams Thompson, Jr., which he had reclaimed from Kimberly Frederick earlier that morning.

Ben poured three glasses of Scotch. Stone set down his pipes and raised his glass. "To The Assassin," he said. "May his soul forever rest with the knowledge that by his death tens of thousands of lives, black and white, were spared and our nation was forever changed for the better."

"Aye," said Debby, as they gulped their drinks. Her eyes locked with Ben's once more. Ben could see that she was still in love with him. If he dropped to his knee, right there in his plaid dress, she would consent to marry him.

He sighed. Two months earlier that would have been his dream come true; but they had traveled a different road—and that had made all the difference.

ABOUT THE AUTHOR

Larry Kahn is an attorney specializing in the taxation of domestic and international mergers and acquisitions. He resides in Atlanta, Georgia with his wife, Ellie, and two children, Matthew and Michael. Mr. Kahn graduated first in his class from the State University of New York at Albany in 1982 with a B.A. in Economics. He developed a keen interest in race relations while attending Yale Law School, where he received his J.D. degree in 1985. Mr. Kahn was employed by a large New York City law firm before joining BellSouth Corporation in 1993. His passions include family, politics, tennis and Murphey Candler Little League baseball. The Jinx is his first novel.